CCGUCUGAAGTPGCCAAUAUAUGUGAAGGUCACAUCAAGAGTCCGU
GTPGCCAAUAUAUGUGAAGGUCACAUCAAGAGTCCGUCUGAAGTF
JAUAUGUGAAGGUCACAUCAAGAGTCCGUCUGAAGTPGCCAAUAL
AAGGUCACAUCAAGAGTCCGUCUGAAGTPGCCAAUAUAUGUGAAG
AUCAAGAGTCCGUCUGAAGTPGCCAAUAUAUGUGAAGGUCACAUC
TCCGUCUGAAGTPGCCAAUAUAUGUGAAGGUCACAUCAAGAGTCC
AAGTPGCCAAUAUAUGUGAAGGUCACAUCAAGAGTCCGU
GTPGCCAAUAUAUGUGAAGGUCACAUCAAGAGTCCGUCUGAAGTF
JAUAUGUGAAGGUCACAUCAAGAGTCCGUCUGAAGTPGCCAAUAL
AAGGUCACAUCAAGAGTCCGUCUGAAGTPGCCAAUAUAUGUGAAC
AUCAAGAGTCCGUCUGAAGTPGCCAAUAUAUGUGAAGGUCACAUC
AAGTPGUCCAAUAUUPUGUCAAUAUUPAUCAAAGTPGAGGUGAAGTP
JAUAUGUGAAGGUCACAUCAAGAGTCCGUCUGAAGTPGCCAAUAUAU
GGUCACAUCAAGAGTCCGUCUGAAGTPGCCAAUAUAUGUGAAGGL
CAAGAGTUCAAGAGTC **THE GEMINI MAN** UAUAUGUGAAGGUCACAUC
TCCGUCUGAAGTPGCCAAUAUAUGUGAAGGUCACAUCAAGAGTCC
AAGTPGCCAAUAUAUGUGAAGGUCACAUCAAGAGTCCGUCUGAAGTF
UAUAUGUGAAGGUCACAUCAAGAGTCCGUCUGAAGTPGCCAAUAUAL
GGUCACAUCAAGAGTCCGUCUGAAGTPGCCAAUAUAUGUGAAGGL
CAAGAGTCCGUCUGAAGTPGCCAAUAUAUGUGAAGGUCACAUC
TCCGUCUGAAGTPGCCAAUAUAUGUGAAGGUCACAUCAAGAGTCC
AUCAAGAGTCCGUAAGTPGCCAAUAUAUGUGAAGGUCACAUCAAGAC
JCUGAAGTPGCCAAUAUAUGUGAAGGUCACAUCAAGAGTCCGU
GTPGCCAAUAUAUGUGAAGGUCACAUCAAGAGTCCGUCUGAAGTF
UAUAUGUGAAGGUCACAUCAAGAGTCCGUCUGAAGTPGCCAAUAUAL
GGUCACAUCAAGAGTCCGUCUGAAGTPGCCAAUAUAUGUGAAGGL
JCAAGAGTCCGUCUGAAGTPGCCAAUAUAUGUGAAGGUCACAUC
GTCCGUCUGAAGTPGCCAAUAUAUGUGAAGGUCACAUCAAGAGTCC
GAAGTPGCCAAUAUAUGUGAAGGUCACAUCAAGAGTCCGUCUGAAGTI

THE
GEMINI
MAN

HIS TIME IS NOW

RICHARD STEINBERG

doubleday

new york   london   toronto   sydney   auckland

-M-3|98 23.00

PUBLISHED BY DOUBLEDAY
a division of Bantam Doubleday Dell Publishing Group, Inc.
1540 Broadway, New York, New York 10036

DOUBLEDAY and the portrayal of an anchor with a dolphin are
trademarks of Doubleday, a division of Bantam Doubleday Dell
Publishing Group, Inc.

All of the characters in this book are fictitious, and any resemblance to
actual persons, living or dead, is purely coincidental.

BOOK DESIGN BY JUDITH STAGNITTO ABBATE

Library of Congress Cataloging-in-Publication Data

Steinberg, Richard, 1958–
      The gemini man: a novel / Richard Steinberg. — 1st ed.
         p.   cm.
      ISBN 0-385-49051-8
      I. Title.
   PS3569.T37549A89   1998
   813′.54—DC21   97-24623
                                                                    CIP

To my harshest critic, my most fervent supporter, the only one who has always been there no matter what . . . Gloria Usiskin Steinberg; this book, and all my works, are most gratefully and most joyously dedicated.

CCGUCUGAAGTPGCCAAUAUAUGUGAAGGUCACAUCAAGAGTCCGU
GTPGCCAAUAUAUGUGAAGGUCACAUCAAGAGTCCGUCUGAAGTP
UAUAUGUGAAGGUCACAUCAAGAGTCCGUCUGAAGTPGCCAAUAU
GAAGGUCACAUCAAGAGTCCGUCUGAAGTPGCCAAUAUAUGUGAAG
AUCAAGAGTCCGUCUGAAGTPGCCAAUAUAUGUGAAGGUCACAUC
TCCGUCUGAAGTPGCCAAUAUAUGUGAAGGUCACAUCAAGAGTCC
AAGTPGCCAAUAUAUGUGAAGGUCACAUCAAGAGTCCGU
GTPGCCAAUAUAUGUGAAGGUCACAUCAAGAGTCCGUCUGAAGTP
UAUAUGUGAAGGUCACAUCAAGAGTCCGUCUGAAGTPGCCAAUAU
GAAGGUCACAUCAAGAGTCCGUCUGAAGTPGCCAAUAUAUGUGAAG
AUCAAGAGTCCGUCUGAAGTPGCCAAUAUAUGUGAAGGUCACAU
AAGTPGUCCAAUAUUPUGUCAAUAUUPAUCAAAGTPGAGGUGAAGTP
UAUAUGUGAAGGUCACAUCAAGAGTCCGUCUGAAGTPGCCAAUAUAU
GGUCACAUCAAGAGTCCGUCUGAAGTPGCCAAUAUAUGUGAAGGU
CAAGAGTUCAAGAGTC **THE GEMINI MAN** UAUAUGUGAAGGUCACAUC
TCCGUCUGAAGTPGCCAAUAUAUGUGAAGGUCACAUCAAGAGTCC
AAGTPGCCAAUAUAUGUGAAGGUCACAUCAAGAGTCCGUCUGAAGTP
UAUAUGUGAAGGUCACAUCAAGAGTCCGUCUGAAGTPGCCAAUAUAU
GGUCACAUCAAGAGTCCGUCUGAAGTPGCCAAUAUAUGUGAAGGU
CAAGAGTCCGUCUGAAGTPGCCAAUAUAUGUGAAGGUCACAUC
TCCGUCUGAAGTPGCCAAUAUAUGUGAAGGUCACAUCAAGAGTCC
AUCAAGAGTCCGUAAGTPGCCAAUAUAUGUGAAGGUCACAUCAAGA
UCUGAAGTPGCCAAUAUAUGUGAAGGUCACAUCAAGAGTCCGU
AGTPGCCAAUAUAUGUGAAGGUCACAUCAAGAGTCCGUCUGAAGTP
UAUAUGUGAAGGUCACAUCAAGAGTCCGUCUGAAGTPGCCAAUAUAU
GGUCACAUCAAGAGTCCGUCUGAAGTPGCCAAUAUAUGUGAAGGU
CAAGAGTCCGUCUGAAGTPGCCAAUAUAUGUGAAGGUCACAUC
TCCGUCUGAAGTPGCCAAUAUAUGUGAAGGUCACAUCAAGAGTCC
AAGTPGCCAAUAUAUGUGAAGGUCACAUCAAGAGTCCGUCUGAAGT

CCGUCUGAAGTPGCCAAUAUAUGUGAAGGUCACAUCAAGAGTCCGU

PART ONE

Prisons

The rainbow never made it to Piatigorsk.

Three colors only were in evidence: the white of the snow, the gray of the sky, the black of the souls and the hearts.

No trees or plant life of any kind broke through the crust of the moonscape. No birds with their bright plumage ever appeared in the sky or came to rest on the power lines, the only break in the desolate scene. In fact, the only life of any kind that had ever been seen here was the gray shadows that passed for humanity.

The only sounds: the wind, the muffled sob, the anguished scream, the snap of a breaking arm, leg, skull, or frozen power line.

This impotent, infertile, icy piece of forgotten ground had a name, a dot (the smallest) on some maps, and little else.

Its four buildings, the only for over one hundred miles in any direction, were run-down, haphazardly patched, just waiting for the right wind from the perfect angle to blow them away into the complete oblivion they so well deserved.

But somehow, each year, Piatigorsk remained, a monument to the lunacy of its creators.

The helicopter completed its third orbit of the site before its radio crackled to life.

"C-H. C-H. This is D-B. Go ahead, please." The voice was hoarse and slurred.

The pilot keyed his microphone. "D-B. D-B. This is C-H. Request permission to land."

"C-H. C-H. This is D-B. State your purpose."

"D-B. D-B. This is C-H. I have aboard Major Valerii Vitenka, personal representative of General Medverov. The major carries priority papers from Internal Security, Moscow Central."

A long silence of crackling static.

"C-H. C-H. This is D-B. You are clear to land. You will be met."

The pilot put down the microphone and turned to the passenger sitting behind him.

"We've been cleared. When we hit the ground, keep your head down, your faceplate on, and move quickly away from us. The ice chunks the blades will kick up are like bullets. Get inside as quick as you can!"

Vitenka zipped up his parka. "Aren't you going to shut down?"

The pilot shook his head. "Not here! Engine will freeze up and we'll be stuck until spring. We'll be back for you sometime tomorrow, if we're lucky."

Vitenka nodded, pulled his sable-lined hood over his head, and gave a thumbs-up sign.

The helicopter banked sharply, coming down at a steep angle. It pulled up at the last moment, thudding to a stop on the frozen ground. A crewman slid the door open and Vitenka jumped out.

It seemed like being in the center of an insane blizzard. Snow and ice flew crazily in all directions, forming a solid white wall, obscuring everything within sight. Vitenka felt painful, heavy thumps against his body as he was pelted by the ice.

He took a few careful steps forward, desperately trying to pierce the flying whiteness and debris. Looking for the promised reception or guide, he took another step, then was knocked to the ground as something heavy struck the back of his head.

He lay there for a full minute as he tried to regain his breath. To somehow get back to his feet. Suddenly, he felt a tug at his arms. He resisted at first, instinctively, but then gave in to it. Two minutes later, the storm, kicked up by the rotor blades of the cargo helicopter, abated.

Slowly, Vitenka raised his head.

Three men stood around him. One stood on either side, holding onto his arms. The third stood a little bit in front of him, looking down at him. All three had their faces obscured by heavy furred parka hoods.

The men on either side slowly helped him to his feet. The man in front gestured ahead and to the right. Vitenka fell into step behind him. Five minutes later, they walked through an open, heavy steel door and into the nearest building. The door was quickly closed and secured behind them.

The four of them stood in a dark confined antechamber. Vitenka could barely see the others, but he felt them move and could almost make out the furry shapes around him.

After a minute that seemed like ten, an inner door opened, flooding the chamber with light. The men moved through. Parkas were peeled off and carefully hung on nearby racks. The two men who had dragged him in—he could now see that they were a corporal and a private— saluted and left down a dimly lit corridor. The third man, a line sergeant well over fifty, looked Vitenka over slowly.

"You can hang that *thing*"—he spit out the word with contempt— "over there."

Vitenka took off his expensive winter snowsuit, trying to ignore the tone in the man's voice, then turned back to him.

"I am Major Vitenka," he began. "I carry priority . . ."

"Whatever," the sergeant said in a disinterested voice. "This way." He headed off to his right.

Vitenka paused, then followed. So far, nothing was as he had anticipated. And for a precise man like Vitenka, nothing could be more disconcerting.

The dark corridor was lit by dully flickering, orangy, bare lightbulbs hanging more than fifteen meters apart. The result was dim islands of light directly under each bulb, separated by pools of twilight. Vitenka could sense, more than see, doors every few feet along one side of the corridor, but no light escaped from them.

Finally, they came to the end of the corridor and a door marked "Director, Custodial Affairs." The sergeant knocked loudly twice, then opened the door.

Vitenka had to blink to protect his eyes from the assault of bright light that cascaded from the room. Squinting, he walked through.

"Major Vitenka," a short hard man with an incongruously warm smile said, as he came out from behind his desk. "Welcome to Detention Barracks 6210."

Vitenka opened his eyes fully, taking in the bright office and little man at its center. He snapped to attention.

"Major Valerii Vitenka, sir! I carry priority papers from Internal Security, Moscow Central."

The man casually returned the salute.

"Colonel Igor Ruinov, at your service, Major." He gestured at an overstuffed leather chair in front of the desk. "Please." He returned behind the desk, sitting casually in his large, heavily padded swivel rocker. "You are hell and gone from Moscow Central, Major. What can I do for you?"

Vitenka tried to sit at attention in the comfortable lounger, but its soft padding made it very difficult. "Sir! I bring you the personal compliments of Lieutenant General Medverov."

Ruinov shrugged. "A long way to come for that, Major." He casually dropped his hands to his lap.

"The general has instructed me to inform you that your work at this facility has not been without notice. He wishes me to express to you his deep satisfaction and gratitude for a job well done."

Ruinov was a smiling cipher. "Gratifying."

Vitenka was put off by the man's seeming indifference.

"I assure you, sir, the general is most taken with your record of achievement." He paused. "And if I might add, personally, I took the liberty of reviewing the dossier on this facility before I left. Your accomplishments in maintaining order here are extraordinary, by any standards. You should be very pleased."

Ruinov studied the man across from him carefully. His insignia showed him to be a military academy graduate with more than six but less than eight years of service. His ribbons were predominately for conduct and efficiency, none for combat. His hair was precisely three centimeters above his collar, six above his ears. Service-manual perfect. His uniform, new and freshly pressed, had been tailored to give him a perfect fit.

In short, he was everything Ruinov hated. Rich, pampered, educated, inexperienced.

"Major, have you ever been to a 62 series detention barracks before?"

"No, sir. But I am directly responsible for overseeing their weekly productivity reports and thereby have an intimate knowledge of them."

Ruinov nodded in a tired way. "Let me explain to you some of the realities of a 62 barracks which may have escaped your notice." He gestured at the map on the wall behind him. "We are 161 kilometers from the nearest settlement—161 kilometers of ice storms, gale-force winds, and a summer temperature that never rises above minus nine degrees Celsius."

He paused, pulling a cigar from a desk drawer. He offered it to Vitenka, who shook his head.

"We maintain order, Major," he said as he lit up, "because in this quaint piece of Hell there is no alternative if the prisoners wish to survive." He exhaled a deep blue cloud of smoke. "They understand this, as does the staff. To create disorder, in these conditions, is an act of suicide."

A silence settled between them.

"Uh, sir," Vitenka began after a minute. "I carry priority papers from . . ."

"Internal Security, Moscow Central." Ruinov smiled. "I feared you had forgotten all about them."

Vitenka handed them across the desk.

Ruinov broke the seal. "Let's see what Moscow Central's priorities are these days." He flipped through the first two pages. "Fairly routine." He looked up at Vitenka. "It says you have the full confidence of Medverov and that pack."

Vitenka pulled himself to an even straighter attention in the soft chair.

"A two-edged endorsement," Ruinov said as he continued reading. He stopped midway through the third page. "What are these Neftegorsk Accords?"

"Sir, they were signed by President Yeltsin and the American president, Clinton, I believe in late 1995."

"I don't recall hearing anything about it." He paused. "Of course up here, news travels very slowly. Only recently, we discovered that man had walked on the moon." He returned to his reading. "What is the meat of the thing?"

"In exchange for American loan guarantees for the purchase of

American durable goods, the Russian Republic promises to repatriate all American citizens being held in Republic prisons in three phases."

Ruinov rolled the cigar in his mouth as he continued reading. "And they are?"

"First, all status offenders. Illegal immigrants, hooligans, and the like. Second, nonpolitical statute offenders such as robbers, rapists, drug dealers."

"Good riddance."

Vitenka nodded. "It *will* remove a tremendous burden from our penal systems."

Ruinov turned a page. Suddenly, he froze. Flipping back and forth between two pages, he read and reread several paragraphs.

"Specials?" His voice was low and stunned.

"It was felt," Vitenka said flatly, ignoring Ruinov's tone, "that it would be appropriate to include special political prisoners in the third phase. They cost the most to maintain and serve little purpose in this new world order."

"In this new world order of yours, espionage is not to be punished?" Ruinov looked shocked.

"On the contrary," Vitenka said easily. "It has been determined that espionage will be punished by a term of imprisonment not to exceed five years. We will turn over *only* those individuals whom we have held for longer than that period."

Ruinov returned to his reading. "I don't know how many of those we . . ." He stopped as he turned to the last page. "My God!"

Vitenka leaned forward in response to the exclamation. "Colonel?"

Ruinov was turning white, his breath becoming labored. In this cold office, sweat broke out on his forehead. He looked, for all intents and purposes, like a man having a heart attack.

"Colonel?"

Ruinov slowly looked up at Vitenka. "You cannot be serious! There has been a typographical error, transposing of the numbers, something!" He paused, then continued breathlessly. "You *cannot* be serious!"

Vitenka, a puzzled expression on his face, reached out and took the papers from the colonel. Trying not to stare at the obviously frightened man, he compared the last page to the information he read off his personal memo book.

"You will transfer to my custody prisoner 90-1368, classification

Sigma-Theta-Alpha. Currently in the sixth year of a life sentence." He stopped, then looked up. "It is all in order, sir."

Ruinov slowly shook his head. "It is *not* in order."

"Sir?"

"This man," Ruinov began in a hushed tone, "1368. You actually intend to release him?"

"He falls within the terms of the accords." Vitenka had never had orders questioned before and wasn't sure how to deal with it now.

"No."

"Excuse me, sir?"

Ruinov stood up with more speed than Vitenka would have thought him capable. He pounded his fist on the desk.

"You heard me, Major. I will not take the responsibility for unleashing that . . ." His voice trailed off as he struggled for the word. Finally, in exasperation, he repeated himself. "I will not accept that responsibility."

"My apologies, sir," Vitenka began slowly, "but your orders and your duties are explicitly clear."

Ruinov nodded. "I quite agree with you, Major. My orders *and* my duties are clear. Unfortunately, they are also in conflict."

"Sir, I don't understand." Vitenka's expression mirrored his emotions. Pure turmoil.

"Let me make myself clearer to you, then." He took the papers from the confused major. "Before I execute these orders, I am going to damn well confirm them with General Medverov! Then, and only then, will I carry them out." He paused, his anger displayed through his savage chewing of his cigar.

"1368 will be released *only* on the express authorization of Medverov and after my strongest objections have been noted and certified for the record." He chewed through the cigar, pulled it from his mouth, and threw it against the wall. "Do you understand me, Major?"

Vitenka didn't. Not even a little bit. But the colonel had the rank and there was no going anywhere until tomorrow afternoon anyway.

"Sir! Yes, sir!" he said as he snapped to attention.

Ruinov pressed a button on his desk. A moment later, the line sergeant returned. "Yeah?" he said.

Ruinov walked over to him. "Get me General Medverov on the shortwave, Alexi."

"It could be difficult, sir. Sunspot activity . . ."

"I don't give a shit! Get it done, Line Sergeant Dnebronski!"

Dnebronski came to attention for the first time. "Sir!"

Vitenka held up a restraining hand before the sergeant could leave. He turned to Ruinov.

"Colonel, while you confirm the orders, might I see the prisoner?" He used what he hoped was his most charming voice.

Ruinov took several deep breaths. "Dnebronski, see that the major is escorted to Barracks 3."

Dnebronski and Ruinov exchanged significant glances.

"Do it, Alexi." Ruinov's voice sounded worn-out, exhausted.

Dnebronski shrugged. "Sir." He started out of the office.

Vitenka came to attention and saluted. Ruinov looked him over for long moments before returning the salute. Vitenka pivoted and started out of the room.

"Major Vitenka?"

Vitenka turned back to the colonel.

"The Americans have a saying. Be careful what you wish for, because you *might actually* get it." Ruinov turned his back as the major left the office.

Dnebronski was waiting for the major when he came, slowly, out of the colonel's office.

"This way, sir," he said casually. He headed off down the dim corridor.

Vitenka fell into step alongside. "Tell me something, Sergeant."

"Yeah?"

"In confidence, is the colonel a well man?"

Dnebronski chuckled. "Until you came." Almost as an afterthought, he added "sir." They continued on for two minutes in silence.

"By the way," the sergeant finally asked, "which prisoner am I taking you to?"

"90-1368 Sigma . . ."

Dnebronski suddenly stopped. "You have got to be kidding!"

Vitenka had reached the end of his patience. This attitude coming from an officer who outranked him was one thing, but this refusal to accommodate his priority orders by an underling was just too much.

"You will come to attention, Line Sergeant!" Vitenka's voice was crisp and authoritative.

Dnebronski stood there, staring at Vitenka as if he'd lost his mind.

"I ordered you to attention, soldier! If you do not want to face disciplinary actions, you will . . ." He stopped as he heard the distinct snapping sound of a Makarov semiautomatic pistol being cocked. He looked down to see the barrel of the casually held pistol pointing at his groin.

"Major," Dnebronski began slowly, "you aren't in Moscow now. Here on the dark side of the moon, we have our own way of doing things. And the smart man learns how to adapt to it."

Vitenka stood stock-still. He had heard of cases of claustrophobic insanity in the 62 Barracks before. The cold, the isolation, the pressure of dealing with the Republic's most dangerous criminals.

"What do you want, Line Sergeant?" he said softly.

Dnebronski shook his head as if he were dealing with an idiot child.

"Major, I've been ordered to take you to Barracks 3. I'll do that. But if you want me to take you to 1368, you'd better give me a reason with more teeth than 'orders.' "

The pressure of the barrel of the gun against Vitenka's pelvis convinced him to do things the sergeant's way.

"I have orders," he said slowly, "to take custody of 1368 and deliver him to the Americans."

"Bullshit!"

Vitenka slowly reached into his pocket and pulled out his priority papers. He handed them to Dnebronski.

"The last page, Sergeant."

Dnebronski quickly scanned down the page. As he read, a smile spread across his face.

"Thank the saints," he muttered under his breath. He lowered the hammer on the gun and holstered it. He clapped Vitenka on the back. "Major, you are about to make some men very happy." He started down the corridor, followed, a moment later, by a very confused Vitenka.

Dnebronski threw open a door at the end. "Sacha, Mikhail, Janos, come with me and bring your weapons."

The three men looked up at him from their card game.

"Why?" one of them asked.

"We're going to pay a call on 1368."

The men's faces turned from disinterest to fear.

Dnebronski shrugged. "It might be to say good-bye to the bastard."

Reluctantly, they stood up, pulled on their jackets, grabbed their Kalashnikovs, and trooped into the corridor. Halfway out, one of them stopped, turned around, went back in, returning with three extra clips of ammunition.

Vitenka watched the reluctance, the barely suppressed fear, and shook his head. He followed the men down another dark corridor.

"Sergeant," he said quietly once he'd caught up with him, "what in hell is going on here? The colonel acts as if it is an act of treason to release this man and you all act as if this is Second Christmas."

Dnebronski raised his eyebrows as he directed Vitenka down a flight of stairs. "We cross from building to building underground. It's simpler and a hell of a lot warmer."

At the bottom of the stairs, they started through a bone-chillingly cold tunnel, reinforced on the sides and ceiling with wooden planks.

"You're taking him," Dnebronski said once they were well into the tunnel. "What did they tell you?"

Vitenka stumbled, braced himself against the wall, then continued on. The soldiers ignored him.

"He is an American intelligence agent who was captured by Internal Security forces six and a half years ago. He received a life sentence, and was sent here."

As they stepped out of the tunnel, the men paused to warm themselves around a space heater at the foot of another flight of stairs.

"Typical," Dnebronski said. He took off his gloves and warmed his hands. "Major," he said without looking up, "1368 is not an intelligence agent." He looked deeply into Vitenka's eyes. "He is the fucking Devil." He put on his gloves and started up the stairs. Vitenka followed close behind.

"When he was first brought here," Dnebronski said as they climbed, "he was under heavy sedation. Our orders were most simple. He was to be held under maximum security under close detention. We could restrain him, punish him, but under no circumstances could we kill him.

"When he regained consciousness, he attacked and killed the nurse corporal who was attending him. He also seriously injured three guards before he was restrained."

He pointed to his left. They were on the third floor now. Steel doors lined both sides of a well-lit corridor.

"Since that time," Dnebronski continued, "he has killed two more guards, crippled two others, and escaped twice."

"Escaped?"

Dnebronski nodded. "The first time, we found him passed out on the ice after four days and nights of subzero freeze. Don't ask me how he survived. I don't ask the Devil how he does his tricks."

Vitenka saw two soldiers standing sentry duty in front of a steel door at the end of the corridor.

"And the second time?" he asked.

For the first time, Dnebronski seemed shaken.

"Somehow, he crossed the snow plain and made it to the settlement of Kurtsk." He paused as if reliving a painful memory. "He caused the death of a civilian family of four and two members of local militia forces before we finally caught him up."

They stopped ten feet from the guarded door.

Vitenka looked shocked. "He was never tried for the murders?"

Dnebronski took a deep breath. "1368 is classified Sigma-Theta-Alpha. Politically sensitive. If the colonel had his way, he would've driven a stake through the man's heart years ago. But Moscow's orders, we couldn't touch him. Just restrain him as best we could and hope he died of natural causes."

The men fanned out against the far wall, pointing their rifles at the closed and bolted door. Dnebronski signaled for the sentries to join them. The weapons were cocked and held tightly against their shoulders.

Dnebronski put his hand on the door's heavy bolt.

"This is 1368."

Vitenka held up his hand. "The man is sedated, no?"

Dnebronski shook his head. "We don't have enough for the psycho cases, so we have to ration it." He hesitated. "Besides, he's pretty much built up a tolerance to the stuff we got." He pounded on the door with the butt of his pistol. "Prisoner 90-1368! You will rise, move to the far wall, and kneel against it! You will cross your legs at the ankles with your hands on your head in plain view! If you are not in this position when the door is opened, you will be fired on!"

Vitenka pointed at the viewing hatch. "Aren't you going to check?" The men's fear seemed to be contagious.

"No. I know of a guard who lost his eye that way." He pounded on the door three times. "The door is opening in ten seconds!"

Beads of sweat stood out at the old sergeant's temples as he slowly drew back the bolt. With a last look at Vitenka, he pulled the heavy door. He immediately jumped back, gun cocked and pointed through the door.

Vitenka waited a moment, until he saw the barest nod from Dnebronski. He slowly stepped toward the door.

Standing between all those ready-to-fire rifles and this apparently murderous monster reminded him of an old African saying he had picked up while stationed in Angola.

When two elephants fight, it is the grass that gets trampled.

He peeked around the corner.

The man was in the demanded position, on his knees, hands on head, ankles crossed.

Trying to ignore the taste of sweat on his lips, Vitenka stepped forward.

"Prisoner 90-1368, I am Major Vitenka of the Russian Republic's Internal Security apparatus," he said in letter-perfect but accented English. "I wish to speak with you."

Silence from the man in the baggy prisoner's uniform.

"Can you hear me? I wish to speak with you." When no answer was forthcoming, he tried again. "It is to your advantage to speak with me."

"Yeah, right," came the monotoned reply.

Vitenka felt the fear behind him, all those nervous men with twitching fingers on the triggers.

"Prisoner 90-1368, arrangements have been made for your release and return to America." He paused, waiting for a response that never came. "To accomplish this, I must speak with you and obtain confirmation of your identity."

"Come on in," the man said without moving, still facing the wall. There were no emotions, no intonation at all to that chillingly flat voice.

Torn between his growing fear of the prisoner and his natural desire to not be perceived as a coward, Vitenka took a step forward.

"Major!" Dnebronski's voice was an urgent whisper. "If you step inside, I cannot guarantee your safety!"

Vitenka looked from Dnebronski to the prisoner. "Prisoner 90-1368, I am here to arrange your release. Do you understand that?" His throat felt dry and he had a suddenly insatiable need for chilled vodka. "I assure you that this is no trick. I mean you no ill will."

"Then," the man said as he slowly turned his head and looked back over his shoulder, "you have nothing to fear in coming in." He turned back to the wall.

Long moments passed. Vitenka bit his lips, seemed to hesitate, then walked into the cell.

"Keep out of the doorway, Major!" Dnebronski called from the corridor.

The cell was six feet by seven feet, barely enough room for the prison cot that lined one wall of the room. A covered bucket that served as sink in the morning, toilet for the rest of the day, stood in the corner. The walls were decaying cement, reinforced with steel bars in a crisscross pattern. A cage within a tomb.

Vitenka kept his gaze fixed on the man on the floor. "What is your name, Prisoner 90-1368?"

"90-1368" was the atonal reply.

"If you do not cooperate, your release will be jeopardized."

"I'm not big on cooperation," the man said calmly. "But . . ."

"Yes?"

"I might be more communicative if I was allowed to stand." He paused. "I think much better on my feet."

Vitenka steeled himself for the worst.

"Very well."

"Major!"

"Line Sergeant! You will not fire as long as the prisoner obeys orders. Do you understand?"

Dnebronski nodded. Some fools could not be saved from themselves, no matter how hard you tried.

Vitenka turned back to the prisoner. "Your movements will remain slow and quite deliberate at all times. Do you understand?"

"My movements are always deliberate, Major." He slowly uncrossed his ankles, lowered his hands, braced himself on the floor, and stood up.

He was just under six feet tall, thin, under 160 pounds. His chestnut-brown hair was streaked with gray and thick. His face was drawn, skin pale, but his eyes burned with an inner fire that shook Vitenka to his core.

And they seemed to see everything.

Hoping his nervousness didn't show too much, Vitenka smiled at the prisoner.

"The Russian Republic has seen fit to exercise its mercy upon you. You are to be released."

The man stared, unblinking, at Vitenka. "I'm touched."

"Don't you understand? We are releasing you. You can go home."

"And all I have to do is?" The man's expression was completely blank, as if he didn't have a care about anything in the world. Including life.

"Nothing, I assure you. Merely answer a few simple questions."

The man shrugged, causing the soldiers to jump back.

"Line Sergeant!" Vitenka shouted.

"Sir!"

"I want no accidents! Do you understand me?"

"Sir!" Dnebronski motioned for his men to stand easy. They didn't, but they did stand easier.

Vitenka turned back to the man. "My apologies, sir. Now for my questions."

"You know, the last man who asked me questions left dishearted."

Vitenka was pulling his memo book from his pocket. "You mean disheart*ened,* sir?"

"As you like."

Vitenka looked up into that blank face and burning eyes so suddenly that he dropped his memo book. Before he could react, the man bent down and picked it up. He held it out to the unnerved officer.

Slowly, holding his breath with every movement, Vitenka reached forward, taking the book from the man. He quickly opened it, preferring to concentrate on the notes within than to look at the cheerless smile that played at the corners of the man's mouth.

"What is your name, sir?"

"Brian Newman."

"And your middle name?"

"David."

Vitenka put check marks next to each of the items as he got his answers.

"Date and place of birth?"

"July 23rd, 1956. Los Angeles, California."

"Your mother's maiden name?"

"Greenhaitz."

Vitenka looked down the column of identifying information. He had no desire to prolong this any longer than absolutely necessary.

"Sir, what position did you play on your high school football team?"

"Fullback and middle linebacker. Why? You recruiting for Patrice Lumumba University?"

Vitenka closed the book and pocketed it. "I am satisfied." He looked up at Newman. "Would you like me to explain the procedures we will be following for the release?"

Newman shook his head. "Not especially. It'll either happen or it won't." He turned to his left, looking out the door at the nervous guards. "I assume they told you about me."

Vitenka wasn't sure how to answer that. As it turned out, he didn't have to.

"They've developed quite a legend around me, you know?" He kept his eyes locked on the guards while he talked to Vitenka. "They tell you the one about my daring escape to Kurtsk?" He laughed lightly. "About how I terrorized the townsfolk?"

"They said," Vitenka began slowly and quietly, "that you killed a family and some militiamen."

Newman turned back to him. "Really?" He slowly shook his head. "It gets better every time. Do tell me, what's my total body count up to now?"

"They said nine people."

For the first time, an expression crossed the empty face. It was a mixture of amusement and sadness.

"Nine." He said it flatly, as if he were trying to fathom the figure. "That's amazing."

Unconsciously, Vitenka took a step toward him. "Are you saying it is not true?"

Newman looked up at him. "Am I?" He turned and walked over to the bed. "If we're traveling tomorrow, I should get my rest." He paused. "It will be tomorrow, won't it?"

"Barring the unforeseen, yes." He turned and stepped toward the door. "I will return in the morning to discuss the details." He stepped out of the cell.

Dnebronski quickly holstered his gun, stepping forward to close the door.

"Line Sergeant Dnebronski?"

Dnebronski stopped as the cold voice floated out to him from the cell. He turned to look inside.

Newman was smiling warmly at him. But there was no warmth in his voice.

"You shouldn't tell stories out of school. Don't you know what happens to bad little boys who make things up?"

Shaking, Dnebronski slammed the door shut and quickly threw the bolt.

The next morning, Vitenka was summoned to Ruinov's office immediately after breakfast.

"So," the colonel began without preliminaries, "what did you think of 1368?"

Vitenka thought many things. About how men isolated from civilization must find a scapegoat to blame their conditions on. About how easy it is for the simplest event to be blown up into the most horrific. About how naive and superstitious most Russian soldiers still were.

He said, "He seems to have held up well."

Ruinov stroked his beard. "Then you still intend to release him?"

"Yes."

Ruinov paused before responding.

"It seems," he finally said, "that General Medverov agrees with you. I just got off the radio with him."

"And?"

Ruinov held up his hands in a gesture of futility. "He refuses to see. There was nothing I could do but lodge my objections." The man looked as if he were in pain.

"Colonel Ruinov, if it would not be presumptuous, may I ask you a personal question?"

Ruinov nodded.

"Sir," Vitenka began, "if you consider this man such a threat, if you think he is that dangerous . . ."

"I do not think it, Major. I know it."

"Then, sir, with respect, why object to his leaving? Why not just let the Americans deal with him?"

Ruinov stood up and started pacing in the tiny office.

"When I was a boy, I lived in a small village on the Don. One day, when I was out hunting with my older brother, we came across a dog that was foaming at the mouth. It didn't see us, just crossed the road and wandered into a field. My brother said we should go after it. Kill it before it hurt someone. But I wanted to continue our hunt. I said it was someone else's dog, it was their responsibility. We continued our hunt. The next day, I heard that the dog attacked and killed a young child."

He stopped, turning to face the younger officer.

"For over six years, I have sat behind this desk and watched 1368. The analogy to the rabid dog is, in my opinion, tame. He is a cold, calculating killer. Here, we have him under at least some control. To let him loose on an unsuspecting public is something I can not willingly do."

Vitenka stood up. "But surely, sir, your analogy is flawed. If Newman is a killer, then he killed in patriotic duty! To carry out his missions, then in attempts to escape. There is no reason to believe that he represents any threat to his own countrymen. All of that assuming that he *is, in fact,* a killer."

"You have doubts?"

"I have, well, questions."

Ruinov stepped back behind the desk. "I do not." He pulled some papers from his desk and quickly signed them. "Fortunately, it is not up to us to make this decision." He handed the papers to Vitenka. "I only pray that you're right. I'll order him prepared."

Several hours later, Vitenka watched while a detachment of prisoners swept the helipad clear of snow, ice, and debris. Twenty minutes later, Ruinov joined him.

"They just called. They're bringing him down now."

"Good," Vitenka said. "The helicopter is due any minute now."

The sound of metal on metal caused them to turn, looking behind them.

Newman, surrounded by five guards, stood in the doorway to the main building.

A thick leather belt ran around the waist of his parka. Connected to it were five chains. One each ran to shackles around his ankles and wrists. The fifth to a heavy leather collar around his neck, forcing him to walk in a hunched position. In addition, handcuffs held his wrists and legs close together.

It would be so easy, Ruinov thought as he looked at the demon that plagued his dreams. *So easy.*

He thought about reaching out as the prisoner shuffled by. The gentlest touch would topple him over in the ankle-deep snow. In the pile, with all the restrictive shackles . . . A broken neck could be made out to be an understandably unfortunate accident. A thing easily explained to Moscow, to the Americans.

And to Ruinov's God.

Newman stopped less than a foot past the silent colonel. He turned, looked at the short, combat-hardened former commando, then he smiled.

"You'll never get a better chance, Igor," Newman said with just a hint of a smile.

Ruinov stared into those burning, challenging, mocking eyes, then he slowly lowered his hand to his sidearm. The butt of the powerful automatic slid effortlessly into his palm.

At that moment, the helicopter flashed overhead. Five minutes later, it was idling its engines on the ground.

Newman sighed, then shook his head and chuckled at some private joke.

Ruinov watched as three armed soldiers climbed down and helped Vitenka and the guards load Newman into the back of the chopper. After checking that Newman was secured, Vitenka returned to the colonel.

Ruinov was yelling into the ear of a junior officer who had just come running up. He turned when Vitenka approached.

"Good-bye, sir. On behalf of General Medverov, I want to thank you for your cooperation."

Ruinov was white-faced. "Dnebronski is dead," he said sadly.

"What?"

"They just found his body at the foot of a flight of stairs."

Vitenka's head was spinning.

"He slipped! The stairs were icy! I myself almost . . ."

Ruinov was ignoring him, staring instead at Newman in the helicopter. "Take the bastard," he mumbled. "Take him far away." He turned to start back to the building. "Before he turns my command into an abattoir."

Vitenka watched the old man go, then slowly turned to the helicopter.

Newman, half leaning out the door, shrugged and raised his eyebrows.

The cold that swept through the young officer from Moscow had nothing to do with the gathering storm.

The soft "round midnight" jazz filled the night air.

Its special rhythms, subtle arrangements, were piped through invisible speakers into the living room, where the guests mingled; out to the backyard, where couples danced and dined off the lush buffet; finally to the pool area, where the people settled into comfortable patio furniture, talking in low tones among the tiki torches, as they contemplated the glowing Japanese lanterns that floated in the water.

In the distance, colored lights hung in the nearest trees of the nearby woods, luring the more romantic pairs to rural, loving walks; or breathless couplings beneath a canopy of breathtaking stars peeking through newly greened branches.

Despite it all, the romance, the music, the soothing ambiance, Patricia Nellwyn was unhappy. And, although she would never admit it, particularly to herself, she felt awkward and uncomfortable as the one unattached woman under sixty at the affair.

She hated coming to these things alone.

She hadn't planned to. Didn't want to. But attendance was mandatory, and a late afternoon call from her intended date had forced the issue.

In fact, many issues.

And she hated confronting her own issues.

At thirty-seven, she was capable of looking back on the first half of her life with a certain satisfaction. She'd set her professional goals high, achieving almost all of them faster than she had ever dreamed possible.

The first woman to finish in the top 2 percent of her class in a previously all-male university. First in her class at the Peter Bent Brigham Medical School at Harvard University. A board-certified, practicing psychiatrist before her thirtieth birthday.

In the last seven years, she'd had two major papers on personality disorders published in prestigious medical journals. The work had been hailed as "preliminary to a breakthrough," high praise from a medical community that still basically viewed women doctors as glorified nurses.

Professionally, life had been good, culminating with her appointment to the staff of the Volker Institute, one of the top facilities of its kind in the world.

Personally, though, her life had been significantly less promising.

She was driven, often working twenty-hour days, forgetting that a world, or a lover, existed outside her research. She'd never been any good at the social graces that seemed to come so effortlessly to other women. Didn't know how to flirt, never took the time to learn. She had no patience for the games of courtship, the compromises, the sacrifices it took to begin or maintain a relationship.

Her loves, and they seemed to come less and less frequently, were one-way affairs which ended, inevitably, with angry whispers in the dark and a slamming door.

Which brought her back to the party around her.

Attendance at the quarterly staff cocktail party, thrown by the chief of staff at his home, *was* required. It was a time for office politicking, networking, and good old-fashioned sucking up. Husbands and wives jointly worked the room, single junior staff members (no one could even think about becoming senior staff if they were unmarried) would display their "significant others" in the best possible light. *Always* the perfect person to complement themselves and reflect favorably on the Institute's image of itself and its staff.

Patricia had spent days preparing, planning with her typical obsessiveness. The perfect dress (conservatively flattering), the perfect conversation pieces (she'd made a quick but thorough study of the likes and dislikes of all the important senior people), and, most important, the perfect escort.

Although their relationship had been severely fraying for weeks, she'd begged her current lover, a naval attaché, to accompany her.

This was going to be her big move—until his call that afternoon.

Now, still tasting the bitterness and anger that she'd poured on the man when he'd canceled, she stood off to the side and watched.

To hell with them all! she'd thought. The conservative, acceptable dress had been scrapped in a fit of fury. In its place, a deep red sequined dress, with a low scoop neck and high slit, clung to her.

She knew that they'd talk. Hell, she'd already pretended not to hear the whispers of "why would a beautiful girl like that come alone?" But they'd say that anyway. Might as well give them something real to talk about.

She'd nodded politely at the pejorative glances of the senior staffers, then inwardly rejoiced at their other, more covert, lustful glances.

She smiled sweetly at the worried wives, who clung to their husbands if they happened by to say hello.

She nursed her single drink of the evening—*some* conventions had to be adhered to if she was going to flout the others—and watched the clock move as if it were stuck in molasses.

This was Plan B. Make the best of a bad situation. Put in an appearance, albeit a dramatic one, thank the chief of staff and his wife for "a simply marvelous time," then a quick exit to the all-night Munich club scene.

Hopefully, a few hours of anonymous debauchery with a nameless body, an escape from her usual, mundane routine, would restore her energy, mood, and outlook on the world.

"Well, well," a man's deep voice said from behind her. "If it isn't Clinical Patty, all decked out in grown-up clothes."

She angrily whirled around, then laughed as she recognized the source of the voice.

"Took a bath, washed my hair, and everything," she said with a growing grin.

The man nodded approvingly. "Helpful hint, though. The slit and the neckline aren't supposed to meet."

"You don't approve?"

He smiled. "I'm a scientist. I remain open to new ideas."

They both laughed as she threw her arms around him.

"I didn't know you were back yet, Jack," Patricia said as she finished her drink and grabbed two more from a passing waiter.

Dr. Jack Clemente, sixty-seven years old, 150 pounds spread sparingly across his six-foot-four frame, chief of behavioral research at the Institute, took the drink handed him.

"We flew in late this afternoon."

"How's Jenny?"

He smiled. "Fine." He pointed across the patio at a short, heavyset woman lasciviously attacking the buffet. "She sent me over to keep you company while she feeds."

Patricia laughed bitterly as she put her arm around him. "How'd you know?"

"I am a trained observer," he said in an intentionally pompous voice. "I see things that mere mortals cannot!" He paused. "Clinical Patty is dressed like a girl. Not just a girl, but a highly noticeable girl. She chooses a design, color, even a place to stand to create maximum effect, knowing that none of these grim-faced bastards *likes* maximum effect from anybody! Let alone its female drones."

He paused as a coughing fit came over him. He held a handkerchief over his mouth, then, when it had passed, continued in a noticeably weaker voice.

"Conclusion: Clinical Patty is off the leash, on the prowl. This leaves us with one final question." His voice grew low and sympathetic. "Your choice or not?"

"Not."

"I warned you about diplomats."

She leaned up, kissing him on the cheek. "I just keep picking pale substitutes for you, until the day you agree to run off with me."

"What about Jenny?"

"Just leave me the credit cards and the bankbooks, darling," Jenny said as she came up to them. "The rest she can have."

The two women embraced warmly.

"How was Washington?"

Jenny shrugged. "I wouldn't know. I spent *my* time in Georgetown and Virginia malls."

Patricia looked at Jack, who was wiping a dribble of blood from the corner of his mouth. She pretended not to notice.

"I thought you two were on vacation?"

"So did I," Jenny said with the slightest touch of bitterness.

Jack polished his glasses on the lapel of his jacket. "Something came up."

Jack Clemente never used few words when many would do, and he never just answered a question. There was always a biting retort or bitter sarcasm. "Something came up" was so atypical that it immediately set off Patricia's alarm bells.

She looked at him for a long moment, then turned to Jenny.

"Okay," she said slowly. "What happened?"

"We're there three hours," Jenny said readily, "just unpacking, when Jack gets a call from someone in the Pentagon. Some damned assistant to the assistant to the associate deputy secretary. Next thing I know, I'm a mall rat." She gave her husband a dirty look. "Jack, he spends every day locked up in some kind of stupid meetings."

Now Patricia was *really* intrigued.

"So, old pal," she said, nudging him, "what gives?"

Jack smiled slightly, gave his wife an annoyed look, then turned back to the young woman.

"You know how it goes, Patty. The U.S. government gives us over half the Institute's grants-in-aid. Somebody over there gets a harebrained idea, they call the Institute and the Institute calls me." He paused. "It's a bitch being indispensable."

"How would you know?" his wife chimed in as she covertly handed him a clean handkerchief.

Patricia noticed, but said nothing. It was an open secret that Jack had cancer, but he had yet to announce it officially, and his colleagues respected his privacy.

Besides, at the moment Patricia was far more concerned with the tone in his voice. It reeked of importance, of new challenges, of something very special, and she needed something special in her life right now. If it couldn't be a relationship, it might as well be work.

Jack pretended not to notice the intense stare he was getting from Patricia. He looked out at the partygoers, sipped his drink, finally gave in and turned back to her.

"I assume that's not uncontrollable lust in your eyes?" He paused. "All right. But just between us, right?"

"Of course."

"I mean it's the Chinese water torture for you if you ever . . ."

"Give!"

He stepped closer to her, looking around as he did.

"There's something special coming up." His voice dropped low and conspiratorial. "Nobody wants to talk about it openly, but it's getting the Defense Department's highest priority. Virtually unlimited funding. Not to mention the tightest security. They're dumping it in our laps and demanding miracles overnight."

He looked down at his younger colleague. Her eyes were wide open, she was absolutely still, hanging on his every word.

After a full minute of silence, Patricia pressed him. "Come on! What's it all about?" she said in an excited whisper.

Jack looked embarrassed. "I've really said more than I should have."

"What field?" she pressed.

"Well . . . I never could turn down a beautiful woman."

"You never had the opportunity," his wife said between forkfuls.

He gave her a dirty look.

"You remember the Eisenrich study on the effects of prolonged stress on type A3 personalities?"

She nodded eagerly. "Aberrant behavior reflexes. Decompensation lability syndrome. Phased atavistic tendencies. That kind of stuff."

Jack nodded. "The project concentrates in those areas." He stopped, as if he'd said too much. "Generally in those areas, you understand."

"Geez," she whispered. "ABR, DLS, phased atavism." Her voice seemed far away. "How many of the conditions manifested in how many subjects? Five? Ten? Fifteen?"

"All in one."

She stared off into the trees as the exciting prospect washed over her.

"One," she said dreamily. "All in one." She quickly turned back to her boss. "That's *my* field, Jack! You know that! You've got to let me in on this! What's it all about? How do I get inside?"

Jack held up his hand. "It's not my call. Staffing decisions will be made by the chief, in consultation with the DoD project manager."

Patricia's mind was racing. She didn't notice as a young couple, both of whom were on staff, came walking by.

"Mrs. Clemente," the husband said. "Jack. Great dress, Patty."

Patricia suddenly looked down at herself. She let out a quiet yelp.

"The chief decides? Shit!" She paused, shaking her head. "Tonight, of all nights, I had to give my libido a day pass!" She looked up at Jack. "What can I do?"

Jack laughed. "Wearing that rig, all I can suggest is that you sleep with him," he said jokingly.

Jenny shook her head. "I'm afraid she isn't his type," she said, "or his proclivity."

Patricia's eyes darted everywhere as she tried to think of something.

"I've got to be part of this . . . got to . . ." Her voice trailed off as she suddenly looked up at Jack. "Project manager."

"What?" he said between sips of his drink.

"You said it's the chief's decision in consultation with the DoD project manager. Who's that? How do I get to him?"

Jack looked around the yard, finally spotting the person he was looking for. He nodded toward him. "By walking seven meters in that direction."

Patricia spun around, scanning everyone within twenty-five feet of them. "Which one?"

"That rather self-important-looking gentleman by the buffet."

"Navy suit, red power tie," Jenny added casually. "He flew back with us."

Without taking her eyes off the man, Patricia reached over and took the older woman's plate. "Jenny, you look starved," she said distractedly, without turning away. "Let me get you some more." She started across the yard.

Jenny watched her go. "I didn't much like doing that, Jack."

He shrugged. "Orders are orders."

She looked up at him. "Is all this game playing really necessary?"

Jack looked over at Patricia as she approached the man by the buffet. "He seems to think so."

Patricia quickly gathered her thoughts as she approached the food-laden table, and carefully studied the man in the blue suit.

In his fifties, he was tall, six foot five, maybe taller. Powerfully built, his shoulders bulged the seams of his off-the-rack suit jacket. A deeply tanned, heavily lined face, with dark circles under otherwise clear eyes. His posture was ramrod-straight, weight evenly distributed, wearing midrange black leather shoes with laces, polished to within an inch of their life.

In an instant, she realized he was line military, not a civilian DoD employee.

And he was sniffing at the plate the waiter had just handed him.

She smiled as she casually walked up to him. "There's a door prize for the person who can come closest to identifying the main entree."

He looked over at her briefly, then back to his plate. "I don't have a clue," he said in a confused voice. "And I'm afraid to ask."

She cursed herself for forgetting to ask Jack the man's name.

"Dr. Madel's specialty is fifteenth-century German cuisine. It can get a bit bizarre." She slowly played at putting some salad on her plate.

"Who's Dr. Madel?" he asked as he put his plate down.

"Head of the greenhouse."

"You mean he's the gardener?" He turned to her with a quizzical expression.

She laughed what she desperately hoped was an alluring laugh. "No. That's just what we call it. It's actually the Center for Vegetative and Catatonic Subjects. They put him in charge of the refreshments this year."

"They have burgers back in fifteenth-century Germany?" He paused. "My name's Alex Beck, by the way."

"Patricia Nellwyn."

Damn! she thought. *I should've said "Patty."*

They shook hands. She felt the hard callus along the edge of his right hand.

"I don't recall seeing you around here before," she said simply.

"I just arrived today." He looked out at the party. "In fact, other than Dr. Tabbart and Dr. Clemente, you're the only person here I've met. Are you connected with the Institute?"

Finally, an opening she could use.

"I work in the Behavioral Research Center with Jack Clemente," she said eagerly.

He seemed suddenly interested. "Really?"

"For the last four years."

Beck gestured at a nearby table. They walked over and sat down.

"I may be doing some work with some of your people," he said as he stopped a waiter. He handed Patricia a glass of champagne and took a beer for himself. "That's why I'm here."

"Well, if behavioral research is what you're looking for, we're the best in the business." She kicked herself in the ankle for sounding like a P.R. flack. "That is, we have some of the best minds in the business."

Beck smiled at her obvious discomfort. "Are you one of them?"

She tried to remember how to sound demure. "I like to think so," she said in a semimodest tone.

"Oh come on," he prompted, "you can do better than that."

To hell with demure. "If I wasn't," she said in a firm voice, "I wouldn't be here."

He took a long drink of his beer, then looked at her with the most piercing stare she'd ever seen from a nonpsychotic.

At least he didn't *seem* psychotic.

"What do you know about unlearning instinctive behavior?"

Something about the stare bothered her, so she decided to back off a little bit, until she had a better handle on the man.

"That's an odd question for a garden party."

The stare was unrelenting.

"You said you were one of the best. Prove it." A regretful look passed over his face. "I'm sorry. I get carried away sometimes." He took another swig of his beer. "It's a tough question to ask a nurse."

All game playing, hesitancies, and ambitions were instantly brushed away.

"Doctor," she said in a low, angry voice.

"Excuse me?"

"M.D., Ph.D., and almost a decade of clinical experience with some of the toughest psychopathologies you or anyone else could ever come up with." She was angry at Beck, at the naval attaché, at the misogynistic medical establishment, at men in general.

"It is so damned condescending," she said as she leaned forward, "for you, for anyone, to just blithely assume that any woman working in a medical establishment is a nurse. I don't look at you and automatically assume that you dig ditches for a living!"

To her surprise, Beck was smiling. "I stand properly chastened."

His smile embarrassed her.

"I'm sorry," she said quietly. "You just pushed one of my buttons at the wrong time." She paused. "What was your question?"

"Unlearning instinctive behavior. Is it possible?"

"Sure. Pavlov extended out to the nth degree. Anybody can be conditioned to do anything."

"What about survival behaviors?"

"Why not? Same principle. Maybe harder to do, but the idea's the same."

The smile disappeared from Beck's face. "How?"

Patricia had pulled herself back together. Now she recognized a chance to impress the man.

"Two ways. One, behavior modification using positive and negative stimulus. Like touching a lit lightbulb. Survival instinct and experience prevent us from doing that, right?"

"Right."

"So, you give the subject an even more unpleasant experience than being burned by the bulb, every time he refuses to touch it. Then give an overwhelmingly pleasant experience when he does. After a while, if the positive reinforcement is strong enough, he'll go around looking for bulbs to touch, just to get the reward."

"And be left with charred hands."

She shrugged. "An unfortunate by-product."

Beck seemed deep in thought.

"What's the other way?"

"Chemically induced, posthypnotic suggestion. Plant an idea deep enough in a subject's subconscious, and they'll happily put a shotgun in their mouth and pull the trigger. Just because they've become convinced that it'll clear up their sore throat."

"The problem with both your suggestions, Doctor"—he stressed the word—"is that either way, you're left with an essentially deformed, vulnerable individual."

Something in his tone struck her as odd.

"In what sense?" She had completely forgotten the reason for her conversation with him.

Beck looked off into the woods and when he spoke, his voice seemed far away.

"Take a garden snail . . ."

"A snail?"

"As an example. A snail can detect salt from over a hundred meters away. The equivalent of miles to you and me. When he detects it, he immediately begins to alter his course to avoid it, because instinctively he understands that if any portion of him comes in contact with any amount of salt it will, in effect, dissolve him."

Patricia leaned back and considered. "What's your point?" Although she knew, and was considering it already.

Beck kept looking at the woods. "Remove his survival instinct, and he will eventually crawl out into that salt and dissolve, painfully, away."

"In theory, then," Patricia said as if she was talking to herself, "you would have to condition or teach the snail to continue to avoid the salt while removing the other parts of his survival behaviors."

"Could it be done?"

"With a snail? Sure." A long pause. "I think."

Beck turned to her. "Let me add to the problem."

"Okay." She was shocked. A tear hung unnoticed in the corner of his eye.

"Ninety-five percent of survival behaviors are avoidance, right?"

"Right."

"But what if you had a subject, a subject where ninety-five percent of the survival behaviors were aggressive, or attacking? Could you remove those behaviors and leave the individual intact? No worse off than you or me when it came to dealing with survival issues?" His voice had taken on a pleading tone.

"The experts would say no."

"So I've been told," Beck said quietly, looking down into his beer.

"But," she said as she considered the problem, "it might depend on whether the behaviors were natural or had been learned."

"Dr. Tabbart, your chief of staff, disagrees."

She laughed, more loudly than she'd intended. "I'm not surprised."

Beck looked up at her. "And Dr. Clemente thinks it would be a long shot at best."

She thought carefully before responding. "Jack's a good man. A brilliant clinician."

"But . . ."

"No disrespect intended, but breaking new ground isn't his strong suit."

Beck was smiling again. "And it *is* yours?"

Tact was thrown out the window and Clinical Patty emerged full-blown.

"Look, I don't know any of the details of your project, but I know one thing. You need me on it."

Beck finished his beer. "And what project would that be?"

"Jack Clemente's one of the best. I love him like a father. But what you need is someone who isn't afraid of taking chances. Someone open to new ideas and unconventional thinking."

"Really?" He sounded . . . amused. He stood to leave. "It was a pleasure talking to you, Dr. Nellwyn." He started off into the house.

"Listen," Patricia said as she rushed to catch up with him, "you screw around using conventional therapies with a full-blown DLS with phased atavism, you're going to end up with one of two things!"

Beck stopped and turned to face her. "And they are?"

She looked him right in the eye. "A dead man or another plant for Dr. Madel's nursery."

For over a minute, Beck just looked down into the young woman's eyes. Finally, a shadow seemed to pass over his face as he started to turn away.

"I assure you, Doctor, the latter will *never* happen." He turned and walked away.

Patricia just stood there, looking at the spot Beck had been standing on, her mind awash with replay after replay of their conversation. She didn't notice when Jack came up behind her.

"So? How'd it go?"

She looked up into his gaunt face. "Maybe I can get work as a hooker," she said in a deeply depressed, quiet voice.

Jack put his arm around her. "That bad?"

"Worse."

He took a deep breath. "Well, at least you have the dress for it."

The next morning, her mood having plummeted still further, seething with anger directed against herself, she wandered down an Institute corridor toward the main elevator banks. She was distracted as she tried to continue her analysis of her conversation with Beck.

It *was* an interesting challenge.

All the current thinking on rehabilitating violent tendencies held to a single theme. Remove those tendencies, use therapy, medication, conditioning, or surgery, and you have succeeded. No matter the subject's capability to cope with the world thereafter.

She'd seen the results of those treatments. Those washed-out, colorless, emotionally neutered individuals were, in Patricia's mind at least, worse off than when they had manifested their violence.

But society was deemed better or at least safer for their change.

She stepped into the empty elevator, pushing the button for her office on the third floor.

"Hold, please!"

She reached out, pushing the Door Open button as the source of the call, a young resident, came running up.

"Guten Morgen, Dr. Nellwyn."

She glanced at the young man, desperately trying to remember his name.

"Hi." She returned to her thoughts.

"You are presenting today? Yes?"

She snapped back out of her thoughts. She hated people who insisted on small talk.

"What? No," she snapped.

The young man seemed genuinely surprised.

"Really?" He paused. His English wasn't very good and he struggled for the words. "This *morgen,* Dr. Tabbart leads third-year rounds. I thought I heard him mention something about you are being there."

Patricia looked over at him in surprise as the elevator doors opened. She hurried out.

After the party, she'd skipped the clubs, preferring instead to head home and drown her troubles in Kahlua. She'd awakened that morning, still in her dress, thirty minutes after her alarm had rung. It was possible that in the anger, frustration, and liquor, she'd forgotten. She kept her head down as she headed for the safety of her office.

"Dr. Nellwyn!"

She stopped as a nurse came over to her.

"Hi," Patricia said quickly. "I'm just going to pop into my office, right? Be right with you."

The nurse put a restraining hand on her shoulder. "You don't have time. The chief's been paging you for the last twenty minutes."

"Shit!"

"It's okay. I called and said you were dealing with an emergency."

Patricia nodded her thanks. "You're a lifesaver." She smoothed her baggy slacks and loose blouse. After checking her severely tied-back hair, she turned to the nurse. "I look all right?"

"Fine." The woman smiled. "But I think I liked the sequins better."

Patricia grimaced as she headed back down the corridor.

In the elevator, she mumbled to herself.

"Rounds? Oh, I thought those were . . ." A pause. "Rounds? Of course. It's just that a patient had a crisis and I . . ." She took a deep breath as the elevator opened on the top floor.

The blue carpet, pale green walls, and soothing music always seemed, in some subliminal way, to make the walk down the long corridor much longer than it actually was. All the way, she concentrated on keeping her posture perfect, not looking to either side. She smiled softly at the woman behind the desk at the far end, who stared menacingly back in return.

"Good morning, Mrs. Lotte," Patricia said as she approached the rather masculine woman.

"Doctor." She picked up her phone and quickly dialed an intercom exchange. "Dr. Nellwyn, sir." A pause. "Of course, sir." She looked up at Patricia. "You may go in immediately."

Not good, Patricia thought. *Tabbart always keeps junior staff waiting.*

She walked through the door, closing it behind her.

D r. Klaus Manfred Tabbart, chief of staff of the Volker Institute, sat behind his highly polished, oversized desk, smiling pleasantly. The desk's surface was bare, not an inch of its mirrorlike surface covered by a loose sheet of paper or the slightest blemish or smear. It reflected the light back toward Tabbart, creating a halo effect.

Junior staff constantly debated whether the halo was an unintentional result, or the conscious attempt of the chief to make clear his godhood to subordinates. Either way, it was effective.

"Good morning, Dr. Nellwyn."

"Good morning, sir." She sat down in the indicated chair. It was soft-cushioned, causing anyone sitting in front of the desk to drop below Tabbart's head level, so that one had to look up to talk to him. "I'm sorry that I was unable to respond to your original . . ."

He waved it away. Not a good sign.

"Your absence was adequately explained," he began in his unusually high-pitched voice. "After all, patients must come first." He paused. "Do you not agree?"

"Of course, sir." She tried to think of something to say to ease the tension she felt emanating from across the desk. "The party was marvelous," she said timidly. "And your house is beautiful."

He nodded curtly. "Yes. The party." He paused a long time. "Are you happy here?"

"Yes, sir. Very happy."

"You would not prefer, perhaps, a more exciting practice? Perhaps in London, New York, or Los Angeles?"

"No, sir." It was worse than she thought. She swore to herself that if she got out of this okay, she would banish impulsiveness from her vocabulary, as well as that damned red dress.

"At times I wonder," he said softly. He swiveled in his chair so that he could look out the large bay window with his view of the grounds behind the main building. "By the by, you appeared most striking last night. What I believe you Americans call 'a real eye-catcher.' "

Banished and burned in a public square, sequin by bloody sequin.

He was waiting for her to say something.

"I had a, uh, some difficulties with my cleaners," she lied poorly.

Tabbart nodded. "I told several of the staff that is what must have happened. Something like that." He let out a short, high-pitched squeal which she had come to recognize as his laugh. "I told them you would not intentionally come into my home dressed as a common prostitute." He paused, turning to face her, definitely not smiling. "You would not deliberately embarrass yourself, your colleagues, this institution"—he paused again—"myself, in that manner."

"Of course not," she said as she felt herself growing more and more furious in the face of that unforgiving, mean-spirited gaze.

"Of course not. Dr. Nellwyn, let us be completely forthright with each other. Yes?"

"Of course," she said, louder than she'd intended.

"You are, madame, a brilliant, perhaps gifted practitioner. Your clinical record is beyond reproach. But it is in the other areas, beyond the clinic, where I feel that you are not Institute material."

"Really." Her voice was flat, angry, but with a submerged, building anger that was being held tightly under control.

For now, anyway.

"This silly affair last night, flaunting your, well, physicality. I will be blunt." He leaned forward, hands folded on the desk in front of him. "There were many present, myself included, who felt that your deportment reflected poorly upon yourself and the Institute that you represent."

"Really?" She seized on her anger at her own personal failings and turned them on Tabbart. As her father used to say, "If you're going to get shot, better be shot for a grizzly than a pig."

"Who exactly?"

"Your pardon?"

"Well," she said bitterly, "I seem to recall quite a few approv- ing reactions." She smiled. "Particularly from several men on senior staff."

Tabbart looked embarrassed. "Which I will be taking up with them later this day. But it is *you* we are discussing at this moment."

She interrupted him. "Yes. It is. You admit my work is more than adequate. Brilliant, gifted. I believe those were the words you used."

Tabbart seemed off balance. "Within these walls, yes. But . . ."

Patricia shook her head and leaned forward, resting her palms on the shiny desk. "That's what you pay me for. That work. If that isn't enough, that's too bad."

"Excuse, please?"

What the hell, she thought, *maybe a change is exactly what I need. God knows, nothing seems to be going right for me here.*

"If what I do," she said icily, "or how I do it ever impacts on my work here, I assure you, you'll have my letter of resignation immedi- ately. But until then, either accept my 'brilliant, gifted' work and what goes with it or fire me here and now. You misogynistic bastard!"

She leaned back in her seat, breathing heavily.

Tabbart gripped the edge of his desk so hard that his knuckles turned white and his wrists shook. His teeth were clenched, and a muscle was working convulsively in his right cheek.

"I have never been spoken to in such a fashion," he wheezed out.

Patricia looked at him, trying to decide if she'd prefer teaching at some midwestern med school, or maybe a mental health clinic in California. In scant seconds, she thought, she would be free to do either. Whatever, she knew she'd gone too far to back down now.

Tabbart seemed to pull himself together.

"Dr. Nellwyn," he said, taking deep breaths, "if it were left to me, you would not have to finish the day. But unlike yourself, *I* must subordinate my personal desires to the good of the Institute.

"You *are not* the sort of person we wish to have here, but the board of directors believes, rather naively in my opinion, that your gender has been discriminated against inappropriately. And so, you are here. There is nothing I can do about that."

He stood up, walking over to his window.

"There are also certain realities of a more material nature I must take into account." He paused for a long time. Finally, he turned back to her.

"I cannot conceive why, perhaps you are sleeping with someone influential, but your presence has been requested by Dr. Clemente on a special project he is overseeing. You may report to him immediately. Thank you for your time."

Patricia sat there, stunned.

Jack, good old Jack, had come through after all! She almost jumped from her seat before heading for the door.

"Dr. Nellwyn?"

She stopped, turning back to him.

"When you fail at this fool's task the Americans are paying for, rest assured, you will be dismissed from this institution. Without a word of protest from the board, I am sure."

Patricia smiled at him. "Is that all?" She was anxious to run down to Jack's office.

"One other thing," Tabbart said slowly. "If any of my words or my tone have caused you offense, my apologies."

She shook her head at the man's hypocrisy and hurried from the office.

Ten minutes later, she almost knocked Clemente over as she burst into his office.

"Jack! You beautiful, brilliant, terrific person," she said happily as she embraced him.

"You left out sexy," he said as he peeled her off of him.

She kissed him on both cheeks.

"Whatever you say!" She paused and looked up at him. "Thank you."

Jack held up his hands. "Not me."

Patricia looked puzzled. "Then who . . ." She followed his gaze across the room, unconsciously taking a step back when she saw Beck, sitting in a chair against a wall.

He stood up and walked over to them.

"What I was trying to say," Jack began, "is that it wasn't my decision."

She looked from Jack to Beck. "I don't understand."

Beck shrugged. "You seemed the right person for the job, Dr. Nellwyn."

She took a step toward him. "But last night? I thought I'd made an ass of myself. In fact, I've just been told as much."

Beck looked confused.

"Tabbart," Jack chimed in.

Beck nodded, then checked his watch. "Time for explanations later. Right now, we have a plane to catch."

In confused silence, she followed the two men out.

Ten hours later, on the Czech frontier in the small German town of Görlitz, they stood on the German side of the border, leaning on an ambulance. They blew on their hands to keep warm in the sudden fog.

Explanations had been brief, and the closer they had gotten to their destination, the more closemouthed Beck had become. For the last two hours, he hadn't said a word, just stood in front of the ambulance, staring across the border.

Patricia looked around.

When they arrived, they'd been met by a squad of heavily armed American soldiers. Beck had spoken to them briefly, and they had melted away into the shadows. But every few minutes, she thought she could hear a rustle or a sound as one of them moved to a better position.

"Is all this really necessary?" she asked Jack in a whisper. "I thought the wall came down a few years ago. You know, peaceful coexistence."

Jack nodded. "Between nations, yeah. With the people, it's sometimes not so peaceful." He stopped as the sound of a truck filled the air. A moment later, it could be seen pulling to a stop on the Czech side of the border.

A man in uniform got out and walked across the border.

Patricia flinched as she heard the unmistakable sound of automatic rifles being cocked around her.

Beck walked up to the man. "Alexander Beck."

"Major Valerii Vitenka." Vitenka handed Beck a thick folder.

They spoke in low tones for a couple of minutes, then Vitenka turned and waved to the truck. It started slowly across, pulling to a stop, five meters from the ambulance.

Beck walked to the back of the truck and beamed a flashlight inside. Nodding to Vitenka, he walked back to the ambulance.

Patricia watched, spellbound, as the back gate was dropped and a man inched forward from the truck's depths.

Chained hand and foot, chains running from his neck to his waist, he was helped down by two Russian soldiers, who immediately picked up their rifles, pointing them at the man.

The man looked around, then slowly shuffled toward the ambulance.

The men with the rifles, joined by two others from the truck's cab, also aiming at the man, seemed, to Patricia's trained eye, to be as tense as any men she'd ever seen.

By contrast, the man in the chains seemed loose and relaxed.

Vitenka watched the man shuffle past, then turned, heading back for the truck.

"Major Vitenka?" Beck called after him.

"Yes?"

"The keys, sir."

Vitenka seemed to hesitate, then reached into his pocket, lightly tossing a key ring to Beck's feet.

"I assume, General Beck, that you have men deployed undercover.

As I do." He paused, taking a deep breath. "If you unlock him before my men and I are well clear of this place, my snipers will cut him down." He turned, striding quickly back to the truck.

A moment later, it sped away.

Beck stood in silence next to the chained man. The others formed a half-circle around them; stood quietly, tensely.

Do it now, Beck thought. *It would be so easy.*

In fact, two U.S. Ranger snipers (covertly placed on the Czech side of the border) had already leveled their nearly invisible ultraviolet targeting dots on Newman's head and chest. Their spotters watched Beck's left hand for the tiniest movement that would be their go code.

Beck knew it was the right thing to do. Had argued to his superiors that it was the only thing to do. But they didn't or wouldn't understand and had overruled him. Newman must be kept alive.

But accidents happen, Beck thought. *A single shot in the night from the hostile side of the border.* A thing easily explained to Washington, to the Russians.

To Beck's God.

The true irony, Beck knew, was that it would end that way. There was no other possible conclusion to his nightmare. So why not end it here, on this cold, damp street? Stop the otherwise inescapable tragedy, save the inevitable victims. Through his death, spare Newman himself.

"So, Alex?" Newman looked deeply into Beck's soul.

Beck desperately wanted to look away. To avoid seeing the grotesquerie play itself out in front of him. But he couldn't look away from those intense questioning, accusing eyes.

He took a deep breath, then signaled.

Patricia watched in fascination as keys were matched to locks and Newman was set free.

Throughout, he never made a sound.

With the removal of the last chain and restraining strap, Newman slowly straightened. For five minutes, he soundlessly stretched cramped muscles. Then, as suddenly as he had started, he stopped and turned to Beck.

"Did he say *General?*" Newman said softly.

Beck nodded slightly. "For a couple of years now." Beck paused. "How are you, Brian?"

Newman shook his head sadly. "General. Well," he said as he turned away, "I'm sure your *men* earned the stars for you." He turned, spotting Jack and Patricia for the first time. "Who are they?"

Beck put his hand on Newman's shoulder. "They're here to help."

Newman looked down at the hand, then back at Beck.

"Help me . . . or you?"

A uniformed, armed security officer stood inside each of the two soundproof doors, augmenting the guards on the corridor side. On the floor of the small amphitheater, a small lectern stood, flanked by Beck and Patricia on one side, Jack Clemente and Dr. Tabbart on the other. Their expressions were uniformly blank.

The lecture hall, although the smallest at the Institute, was still two-thirds empty. The twenty orderlies, nurses, psychiatric social workers, and technicians slowly filled seats in the first three rows.

After three minutes of nervous buzz and rustling, the room grew quiet as Tabbart approached the podium.

"Good morning, colleagues." He spread his notes across the podium. He didn't need them, wouldn't be up there long enough to use them, but he always spread notes before speaking.

"You have each been selected for this"—he seemed to be looking for a word—"*appointment* on the basis of your record, qualifications, and accomplishments. You are all to be congratulated."

In the audience, some opened notebooks, others checked that their pens worked or kicked off their shoes. Few paid attention. They knew, from past experience, that this was just the warm-up. The main show would begin only after Tabbart left.

"We at the Volker Institute have a long honored tradition," Tabbart continued, "of being the first to blaze new frontiers in the ever-widening expanses of neuropsychiatric explorations. Today, we begin the journey anew."

Patricia, twice-bleached lab coat covering the ankle-length skirt and utilitarian blouse she'd particularly chosen for this morning, checked her notes, then sneaked a look at Beck. His jaw was tight, eyes staring straight ahead. Had she not known better, she'd have assumed he was the one about to undergo therapy.

"I am satisfied," Tabbart droned on, "that all of you will function in the highest traditions of the Institute. That all of you will give the difficult task ahead your best efforts. That all of you will do nothing to bring dishonor on those of us not privileged to be part of this noble effort."

He gathered his notes, bowed at Clemente and Beck, noticeably ignoring Patricia, then turned and walked briskly from the room.

Jack waited for the guard to close the door behind the chief of staff before walking over to the podium. He smiled out at the audience.

"Good morning."

They all came to attention, pens poised over pads.

He leaned casually against the lectern. "A couple of ground rules, to start. This project is classified at the highest levels. Since all of you here have worked under similar security before, I won't bother to go over each of the rules individually. You've all received copies of them. *Read them!* One thing more. All discussions of this project, even with other project personnel, must take place only within the project's confines itself. That is, within the walls of Unit A-249. Security insists on this."

He took a deep breath, looking over the group.

"Somebody once said, always open with a joke. Okay." He paused. "What do you get when you take a type A3 personality, thoroughly train him in the rather arcane arts of deep-penetration intelligence work, then subject him to over six years of solitary confinement in one of the harshest penal environments in the world?"

A long silence.

"No answers? No guesses?" Jack nodded slowly. "Precisely our problem. Our task here is threefold. First, answer the question I have just propounded. Second, find a way to undo whatever psychic damage his captivity did to him. Third, and this is the hard one, folks, return the subject to as close an approximation of normalcy as possible."

"Define normalcy," a voice from the audience called out as the others wrote furiously.

Jack thought about that for a moment.

"That's a valid question. Suppose you're standing in line for the movies on a cold day. Suddenly, a man cuts in front of you, getting the last available seat. You're forced to remain out in the cold for another two hours.

"A normal person would protest. A type A1 would protest, perhaps loud enough to call for the manager. Our subject, suffering from a decomposition of his personality, with occasional reversions to primitive behavior, would most likely attack and kill the interloper, and possibly the usher that allowed him in." He paused. "I'll settle for the type A1 response as normal in this case."

He turned and nodded at Patricia. She stood, took a deep breath as she walked to the podium, and began without pause.

"Our course of treatment is unclear at this point," she said in a strong voice, "but if we can rely on the record, four points are manifestly clear."

She opened a file.

"One: We must limit access to the subject, particularly during the early stages of treatment. Until we are convinced that his sudden mood changes and violent lapses are under control, only Dr. Clemente, myself, and one nurse and orderly per shift will be allowed in actual contact with him.

"Two: Due to the subject's very high intelligence, we must constantly question whether his demeanor and actions are true reflections of his actual emotional state or merely sophisticated masks, put into place to lull us into a false sense of security. You must never let your guard down around this man.

"Three: A preliminary diagnosis of decompensation lability syndrome has been arrived at. Since this is a relatively rare condition, I expect you all to read up on it. But let me give you this critical reminder."

Never good at public speaking, she picked a spot in the back of the room, directing her comments to a Chagall print.

"Although we have drastically reduced the stress that the subject is under, the erosion of his personality will continue as long as he remains under some form of close custody, no matter how lenient that custody is or is perceived. Go the extra mile, smile, laugh at his jokes if there are any. Give him maximum encouragement constantly. But be prepared for sudden rejection or violent reaction to the most trivial of things."

A hand was raised in the second row.

"Dr. Nellwyn," a nurse said quietly, "just how violent is the subject? How much risk *are* we in?"

Patricia looked over at Jack.

"We'll deal with that issue in due course," he said crisply.

Patricia slightly raised her eyebrows, then turned back to the audience.

"Fourth: Most important and apropos your question, never, under any circumstances, confront the patient over anything. Never paint him into a corner or limit his options." She took a deep breath. "Over and above his aberrant behavior reflexes and phased atavism, he has been trained"—she looked down at Beck—"to the finest edge, to respond to confrontation with overwhelming force and violence."

She paused, as if unsure where to go at that point. Finally, she turned to Beck.

"Before I conclude," she said softly, "it might well serve us to get the subject's history at this point."

She stepped aside as Beck took the podium.

"My name," he said in a steady voice, "is Brigadier General Alexander Beck, formerly SACSA to the Joint Chiefs."

"What?" several people in the audience said at once.

Beck smiled. "My apologies. The special assistant to the chief of staff for Counterinsurgency and Special Activities. Twelve years ago, I was tasked with creating a unit of special deep-penetration intelligence agents, capable of operating and surviving in a hostile urban or unpopulated environment without the need for support or instructions."

He leaned casually against the lectern.

"Simply put, take a man or woman, give them a task like, oh, severely curtail Soviet agricultural output in the Ukraine, or retard Chinese nuclear facility manufacture, then turn them loose. They would have the training, ability, and survivability to go out, do their jobs for a set period of time, then be extracted, say, six months later."

He smiled a private smile.

"It was the perfect concept. Completely self-sufficient, they would blend with the targeted communities, take whatever they needed to

live and carry out their missions from the targeted populace themselves. Low-maintenance, high-yield, covert, effective, human rifles.
Just point and shoot."

The audience was stilled.

"A study from the Horizon Institute in Santa Monica suggested
that, for the types of operations we were contemplating, we seek out
sociopathic personalities. It was felt that, given their lack of a traditional moral base, as well as their ability to carry out complex, high-
risk tasks without emotional judgments as to the relative rightness of
those tasks, they would make the perfect tools."

"Jesus," someone muttered.

Beck fixed him with a withering stare. "Unfortunately, sir, as it
turned out"—he paused a long time—"I wasn't."

As the project briefing continued, a briefing of another kind was
taking place inside Unit A-249.

On the edge of the grounds, the small, solitary building looked
from the outside like a large, typically German hunting lodge.

Surrounded by the Institute's vast lawn, less than a hundred meters
from the woods, there were precisely laid-out beds of color-coordinated
flowers, compacted dirt paths, and carefully controlled ivy vines creep-
ing up the sides of the building. The windows were tinted, preventing
anyone from looking in, and the doors were always locked.

Inside, the pastoral setting was quickly forgotten.

The ground floor, with its stark, hospital-white walls, utilitarian
carpet, and lack of decoration, always came as a shock to any of the
uninitiated upon first entering. Then, when passed through the
double, electronically controlled doors, the visitor would be further
surprised by the presence of a full nursing station. It was as if one were
on the intensive-care ward of any modern hospital.

With one exception.

There were no patient rooms anywhere in sight.

There was a fully manned, high-tech security room that featured
monitors revealing every inch of the surrounding grounds. There was a
fully stocked pharmacy including the newest, most experimental
drugs. There was a room, just off the nurse's station, that contained a
bank of monitors and sound equipment that eavesdropped on what

appeared to be patient rooms. But exactly where those rooms were, was unclear.

The second floor of the lodge/unit was the "decompression chamber."

Designed to be comfortable as well as functional, this floor contained a completely stocked kitchen, dining room, and two dormitory-like bedrooms, each capable of sleeping five.

Across from this living area were the office suites. Six offices grouped around two secretary's stations, they were linked to the Institute's main computers as well as the Internet. When fully staffed, there were no functions that could be done in the main building that could not be duplicated here.

There was also a second security office between the two suites.

But there was still no sign of patient rooms.

Deep below the building, at a depth of ten meters, about three stories down, surrounded by two-foot-thick reinforced-concrete walls, the patient rooms are found.

An elevator, its disguised doors behind the nurse's station on the ground floor, and in the security office on the second floor, ran noiselessly among the three floors. Controlled by only three keys, it led directly to an antechamber outside the patient's suite.

The chamber was small, three meters square, its only features a television monitor that displayed the interior of the suite and an intercom.

Then there was the door.

Steel-reinforced, barred, dead-bolted, and key-locked, it required two keys to open, as well as a switch being thrown in the upstairs security office.

The suite itself was comfortable. Five meters square with a two-and-a-half-meter ceiling, the main living area had a spacious feel to it. Very much like the suite in the five-star hotel it had been modeled after—with several notable exceptions.

All of the furniture was bolted to the floor with pneumatic torque wrenches. The paintings, silverized plastic mirrors, and the air duct grilles were similarly secured.

The books in the living room's bookcase were all paperbacks or softcovers, none weighing more than two pounds.

All clothes were stored in drawers that could not be removed from their bureaus.

Even the carpeting was specially secured and fire-resistant. Overkill, since there was no way to produce a flame anywhere in the suite.

Yet, despite it all, it was comfortable, even luxurious, by any standards. So much so that it had become the favorite trysting place for the junior staff during the many months of the year that the unit lay deserted and unused.

But thoughts of fervent lovers sneaking moments of passion in this underground, polished, and pampered dungeon were far from Konrad Edel's mind.

As head of the Institute's elaborate security force, and elder of his church, he was torn by the dichotomy of the job ahead.

He'd read the file, at least that part of it he'd been given, on Newman. And he agreed in principle with the decision to house him in this most maximum of maximum security units. The man's potential for mayhem was truly frightening. But he also felt that there was something very wrong with it.

A veteran of Germany's Grenzschützgruppe-9, he'd been on the front lines of his country's battle against terrorism and communism. He'd fought, been wounded, seen beloved comrades die. Most needlessly, in his opinion. He understood what the pressures and stresses of constant combat could do to a man. He'd seen many snap under a tenth of the pressure this Newman had been subjected to.

And yet, if the file was to be believed, Newman hadn't snapped. Far from it. He had done his job, completed every task assigned him, then, once in the hands of the bastard Russians, he had kept faith: revealed nothing, made their lives miserable, forced them to use inordinate resources to guard him, even escaped twice.

Edel thought about it constantly since Dr. Tabbart had given him this assignment.

If lives *were* taken by Newman in the process, and the bastard Russian files might well be lies to besmirch a genuine hero of the West, then, to Edel's mind, it was merely a soldier doing his duty. The fortunes of war.

And for those sacrifices, Newman was to be figuratively, almost literally, buried alive. Prodded and pushed by the headshrinkers who had never risked anything, who vilified men like Newman and Edel. Men who had stood on walls for countless generations, protecting those who would not lay it on the line and their right to not take the risks.

But Edel was, at heart, a product of the German military. He didn't know how not to follow orders. He turned to his men as they emerged from their tour of the unit, making a mental note to say a special prayer at this Wednesday's Bible study for Brian Newman.

"Come to attention!"

The former soldiers and cops that made up one of the highest-paid private security forces in Germany snapped to.

Edel slowly walked up and down the row of security men, adjusting a man's button here, ordering a haircut to another. Finally, he returned to the front of the formation.

"Gentlemen. We are expected to have all personnel and protocols in place as of 1400 today. The, uh, patient will be transferred at 1500. Condition-one security will be observed throughout the transfer.

"I have some *personal* orders for you, prior to those events."

He paused, his expression a mixture of severity and pathos.

"You will remain at least three meters from the patient as you have been instructed. You will remain constantly vigilant for any furtive movement from the patient as instructed. You will take whatever actions you deem appropriate to protect your life and the lives of others if the patient attempts to flee or attacks anyone. As instructed."

He held up a finger. When he spoke, his voice was choked with emotion.

"However, you *will* maintain and demonstrate respect for the man at all times. You *will* address him as 'sir.' You *will,* where there is no conflict with your orders, endeavor to make his confinement as"—he struggled for the word—"*livable* as possible. Always remember that he is a comrade in arms, whose glorious service must be exalted, even as we must confine him," he continued sadly, "for his own benefit."

He straightened.

"Remember the words of our beloved Savior. 'And should you not have compassion on your fellow servant as I have had on you.'

"Dismiss."

Looking across the lawn at the men assembled in front of the unit, Patricia hoped that they would remember that this was a hospital, not a prison camp. Although Edel had conceded that he wouldn't use guard dogs. Due primarily to the continuing German sensitivity to the image of armed, uniformed men shepherding vicious dogs.

Patricia turned back to the briefing as Dr. Clemente was finishing up.

"In essence," Jack was saying as he reviewed the medical chart he had just gone over, "we are talking about a man who has been alone since shortly after birth. Raised by a succession of foster families, he consistently received high grades despite being classified as a discipline problem.

"Graduating in the top eighth of his class, he turned down several academic scholarships, disappearing for two years until he enlisted in the army. Considered an exemplary recruit with extremely high leadership qualities, he was recommended for Officer Candidate School. Shortly thereafter, he was court-martialed for crippling a drill instructor who he believed was being unfair to him. Prior to trial, he was recruited for the deep-penetration project."

He paused and looked up from his notes.

"It is my personal opinion that the initial recruitment diagnosis was premature. However, the possibility cannot be discounted."

He picked up a single sheet of paper.

"The results of his Menninger/Coleman/Foresman Personality Inventory *are* strikingly similar to that of a sociopath."

He began to read from the paper.

"He manifests an inability to understand ethical values except on a verbal level. There exists a marked discrepancy between his intelligence and his conscience development. He is egocentrically impulsive. He has shown an inability to learn from previous mistakes, except"— he looked up—"and this exception is striking in and of itself—except by learning to exploit people and to escape punishment."

He returned to the report.

"He is hedonistic, living in the present without thought to past or future. He is charming, likable, with a disarming manner and a clear ability to win the liking and friendship of others. He is, beneath that facade, cynical, unsympathetic, ungrateful, and remorseless in his dealing with others. He has a quick ability to rationalize his behaviors, often cloaking them in favorable lights such as patriotic duty. And, needless to say, he has a most vivid imagination."

He took a long drink of water, gathering his thoughts, before continuing.

"But I must remind you, in closing, that his mere act of enlisting in the military, of joining the deep-penetration program, seems, at least superficially, to fly in the face of that diagnosis."

He closed the file and looked out across them.

"Therefore, assume *nothing* when dealing with him. Observe, report, theorize. Take no chances, but ignore no possible area of inquiry. Always remember that whether or not the subject is sociopathic, he is unquestionably deeply disturbed. The conditions of his incarceration would account for that at the very least."

He paused. "Questions?"

A young psychiatric social worker raised his hand. "Couldn't his enlistment, and then later volunteering, merely have been ways to escape presumed punishment? Certainly when he was facing a court-martial . . ."

Jack nodded. "Yes, but it must be remembered that after he was released on his first assignment, he had plenty of opportunities to escape. Yet he continually returned after completing those assignments admirably." He paused. "An act inconsistent with sociopathy."

An older nurse. "Any history of violence prior to his enlistment?"

Beck stood up. "Childhood fistfights. Teenage exploits with a car. At fifteen, an arrest for drunk and disorderly involving an altercation with an usher at a ball game. But nothing marked until the incident with the drill instructor."

A psychologist. "Any abnormalities in either his CAT scan or MRI?"

Jack shook his head. "His brain appears as normal as mine."

"That's *truly* frightening," an unidentified voice from the audience said amid light laughter.

A psychiatric resident. "What kind of drug regime are you anticipating?"

From her perch by the window, Patricia chimed in. "Hopefully, none. At least at the outset." She walked over to the lectern. "It'll be a helluva lot easier to diagnose and treat him if he's not half-zonked all the time." She paused. "If we have to, we'll tranq him on an incident-by-incident basis. Otherwise nothing." She sat down. "Besides, the Russians noted a distinct tolerance to most light and middle-level tranqs."

"According to their files," an elderly neurologist said under his breath.

"Speaking of which," a psychiatrist in the first row noted, "they are remarkably vague as to the details of what he was doing at the time of his arrest."

Beck looked over at her. "Your question?"

"It might be of help to know what exactly his assignment was and how well he accomplished it."

Beck hesitated, clearly pondering some deep conflict.

"It was strategic in nature," he said after a time.

"Can you be more specific?" the woman pressed.

"I can, but at this time I won't. Suffice it to say that his mission involved slowing the Soviet industrial base to create shortages of durable and factory-produced goods. Said shortages hopefully leading to civic unrest and pressure on the communist infrastructure."

"How does one man do that?" someone else asked.

"Hypothetically?" Beck's gaze was fixed, firm, resolute.

"Okay."

"In theory, a sufficient disruption in the power grid of a highly industrialized province, such as Abkhaz, where most heavy industry's spare parts were manufactured, would create an industrial chain reaction leading to the desired effect."

He paused.

"With the power grid off-line for a sufficiently long period of time, the supply of spare parts across the Soviet Union would, in theory, dwindle to the point of causing a near-complete industrial shutdown."

Throughout, his voice remained calm, almost professorial.

The entire audience stopped and looked up at Beck. There was something in the man's manner that suggested that his hypothetical example had far more substance than indicated.

"Abkhaz," an M.D. said in a far-off way. He pulled himself back from his thoughts to the problems at hand. "Whatever. Concerning the Russian notation about drug tolerances . . ." His voice trailed off as he seemed momentarily distracted. "Abkhaz." His voice was soft and distant. "Wasn't that where that Russian reactor blew up?"

A nervous buzz went through the room.

"Yeah," someone said. "A feeder reactor. It spread radiation over half of Eastern and Central Europe. Not to mention Central Asia. Killed a few thousand people."

"When was that?" someone else asked.

Beck's expression never changed. "It was a graphite, not a feeder

reactor. Responsible for ninety-three percent of the power requirements of Abkhaz." A long pause. "And it was approximately six and a
half years ago."

The room was immediately silenced. All eyes bore in on Beck,
whose firm jaw was set and unrevealing.

"Getting back to the earlier question," he said despite the stares,
"Mr. Newman fully accomplished his mission, in all respects, prior to
being taken into custody."

The silence persisted until a very Germanic neurologist held up his
hand. "General Beck, sir?"

"Yes?"

"No disrespect intended, sir, but there have been certain questions
raised about the information we have been provided with."

Beck locked eyes with the doctor, who appeared to be in his seven-
ties. "And?"

The doctor continued, in an almost gentle voice. "As I say, General,
I mean no disrespect. But you are the only one in this room who knows
the subject, who has known him for a period of time. Now we all"—he
stopped and looked around the room—"at least those of us who have
had the misfortune to deal with the former Soviet establishment in the
past, we know that often they have fabricated information against an
individual suspected of espionage. You, sir, have reviewed the file, and
you, sir, know the man."

He paused, as if trying to figure out how best to phrase his next
question.

"I have no wish to compromise NATO security in any way, sir,
but . . ."

Beck half nodded at him. "Go ahead."

The doctor nodded. "Thank you. The file indicates several escape
attempts from the penal colony, as well as a series of attacks on the
guards therein. As well as a string of fatalities of Soviet Military and
Civilian Authority personnel. Even more troubling, an apparent unprovoked attack on a civilian family, resulting in their deaths." He
paused. "General, can you shed any light on the veracity or prevarica-
tion of these accounts?"

This time, even Clemente and Patricia turned and stared at Beck.

He was quiet for a long time, sipping from a glass of water, head
down, deep in thought.

"Dr.—" he began with his head down.

"Kapf," the old man said pleasantly.

"Dr. Kapf, the Uniform Code of Military Conduct says that a soldier's first duty, upon being captured, is to attempt to escape. Failing that, he is to force the enemy to commit unusual amounts of men and matériel to maintain him in custody."

He continued looking down as he spoke.

"While I cannot vouchsafe the contents of the files that were turned over to us, I *can* make certain safe assumptions. Mr. Newman was trained to, and by nature was inclined to, do everything in his power to harass his captors. He was among the best we ever trained." A short pause. When he spoke again, it was as if he was talking to himself. "His personal resources and instinctive ingenuity are nothing short of frightening."

He raised his voice to a normal level, looking up at the doctor.

"Did he attempt to escape on at least two occasions? It seems reasonable. Did he inflict the maximum harm possible to his captors in those attempts? I would have. Was there a series of attacks on his guards during his captivity? Probably."

A sadness seemed to float slowly down his face, a furrow of his forehead, a look in his eyes, a firming of the lips.

"Did he, during one of those escape attempts, attack and kill an innocent family of four?" He paused, the sadness seeming to grow within him. "I just don't know."

He turned and started for the door. Something made him stop, halfway there, and turn around to face the somber audience.

"But he is capable of it."

Beck left the hall without looking back. He moved quickly through the corridors, turning left, then right, moving randomly through the sprawling complex, not caring about where he was or where he'd end up, just knowing that he had to get out of there.

After five minutes, he found himself at a door that led out to the rear lawn.

There was work to do, he reminded himself. People that had to be briefed, procedures to be planned. Systems to inspect.

Then there were the countless things that were piling up from his command back in the States. The things he'd guaranteed the chairman of the Joint Chiefs wouldn't suffer by his absence.

But they all had to wait.

The priority of the moment was air.

He stumbled through the door, onto the lawn.

About fifty meters from the main building, he stopped and loosened his tie, unbuttoning the collar with the same hand. Five deep, cleansing breaths later, leaning against a tree, he had pulled it all back together.

For the moment, at least.

The claustrophobia attacks were starting to come more often, less predictably.

No, that was a lie. They were as predictable as a Swiss watch or a Yosemite geyser.

And they were getting worse.

He was fifty-three years old. A one-star general with no chance at another one.

That was another lie. More exactly, a rationalization for the attacks.

He *would* get another promotion, and probably another one after that. Hell, the Corporation always rewarded success, and God knew how successful he had been.

But the attacks would continue.

Fifteen people—nine men, six women—recruited, trained, deployed.

Fifteen people sent as biological guided missiles against enemies real and perceived.

Fifteen people, twelve years ago. Six remaining today.

Four had died in the line, sacrificing themselves to God and country. At least he hoped they saw it that way.

But the other five, they were the ones he saw in his sleep, that pressed him in his waking hours. That stood so close to him, they cut off his air, forced him into wide-open spaces.

Tony and Joab, suicides after killing their wives and children, had been the first to collapse from whatever internal thing drove them.

Monica had gone ballistic when a man cut her off in traffic. After crashing through three cars to get to him, she'd slammed into his car five times before eluding the police.

But Beck found her. Just as he'd found Chris, who'd been systematically blowing up the billboards that obstructed his apartment's view of the mountains. And Colleen, who had found God, then shot to death the televangelist who'd betrayed her devotion and stolen her money.

He could see them all. Feel their hands in his, smell the fragrances of the women, the sweat of the men. See the look in their eyes as he blew their brains out.

And in that moment, the faces of the other six, Newman included, the ones still in the field, still practicing their pestilential skills in almost every corner of the world, would come to him.

And he knew he had to help them. Somehow find a way to let them live their lives under control, as normal individuals. Find the peace that their years of service had so completely earned them.

He *had* to help them find that peace!

Or, out of his love for them, for what they might have been without him, for what they were because of him, out of his personal guilt and rage, he must kill them.

Because, in the end, he believed that was a more humane act than leaving them to crash and burn—as they inevitably must.

With Newman, he believed he finally had his chance.

He turned, looking at the upper floors of the main building.

Alexander Beck was a soldier and he'd killed many times; personally, in Vietnam and the Persian Gulf, as well as by agent.

650 dead in the explosion and subsequent fire along the trans-Siberian oil pipeline.

1,100 dead after the collapse of missile shelter tunnel construction in Iraq.

1,632 dead after the destruction of a hydroelectric dam in Hunan, China.

Over 3,000 dead, perhaps 100,000 injured, untold thousands suffering long-term effects after the destruction of the graphite reactor at Abkhaz.

All of them dead, not by his hand, true, but by his order sure enough.

Stalin had once said the death of one man is a tragedy. The death of thousands, merely a statistic. Beck thought that was about right.

He would lose no sleep, have no panic attacks over the deaths he had ordered in the name of democracy. But each of those six, he knew he would carry the looks in their eyes at the moment he would have to shoot them, for the rest of his life.

He only prayed, if it came to that, that his would be a short life.

He buttoned his collar, fixed his tie, and headed back into the main building, trying to ignore the unblinking eyes that he felt sure stared down at him from the fifth floor.

Ten minutes later, cold water having been thrown on his face, hair neatly combed, Beck stepped out of an elevator on the fifth floor.

Showing his ID at each of the four checkpoints, he made his way to the holding area.

The guards outside the room snapped to attention at his approach. Beck nodded as he walked past them to the security monitor. He bent down and studied the scene.

Newman was sitting on a bed, casually flipping through a magazine.

Dressed in jeans and a T-shirt, he looked healthier than at the exchange, three days earlier. He'd already put on five pounds, lost the limp he had manifested after being unchained, and appeared to be adapting well.

But Beck knew him too well just to accept appearances. He pressed the intercom.

"Brian, it's Alex. Can I come in?"

Newman looked up from his newspaper. "Can I stop you?"

"Yes. With a word."

"Come ahead." He turned a page in the magazine.

Beck hesitated. "Will you guarantee my safety?"

A spasmodic smile played across the prisoner's lips. "Come ahead and find out."

Beck walked over to the door, signaling the guards as he came. They pulled their side arms, thumbed back the hammers, and watched as Beck unbolted the door. He stepped through and one of the guards slammed it shut behind him.

Newman still didn't look up. "Well," he said flatly, "I'll give you that. You haven't lost your balls."

Beck stood absolutely still. "I want to talk to you."

For the first time, Newman looked up. "Really? I'm honored."

"May I sit down?"

Newman shrugged. "It's your padded cell." He returned to his reading as Beck sat on a bed across from Newman.

"How're you feeling?"

Newman shook his head and clucked his tongue. "Wrong approach. Try again."

"Do you need anything?" Small droplets of sweat appeared on Beck's temples.

Newman shook his head. "Isn't that what *I'm* supposed to ask *you?*"

He paused, putting the magazine aside and looking fully at Beck for the first time. "What are we playing here, General?"

Beck smiled. "I just wanted to look in on you. Make sure an old friend was being well looked after."

Newman silently studied the older man for long minutes. Finally, satisfied at some psychic calculation, he nodded. "So that's it."

"What?"

Newman smiled. A warm, sincere smile. "Exactly how many of us are left, General?"

"You used to call me Alex."

"I remember, General. How many?"

Beck shrugged. "That's classified."

Newman nodded. "Ten? Five?" He paused. *"Good God,* if you'll forgive my taking your name in vain, don't tell me I'm the last?"

Beck looked around the small, padded room. "No," he said softly. "You're not the last."

The answer seemed to satisfy Newman. He returned to his magazine. "Got a lot to catch up on. I must say, I approve of the direction skirt lengths are going."

They sat together in total silence for the next half hour. Newman reading, Beck watching him read.

"We tried to get you out," Beck said softly.

Newman nodded in mock seriousness. "I'm sure you did."

"These things take time."

"Six years, seven months, twelve days, to be exact. 57,972 hours to be more exact. Just under three and a half *million* minutes. I know, I counted each one of them." He looked up. "Not exact enough? I can give you the seconds if you like." He paused. "No? Whatever. You like exactness as I recall, although it *has* been a long time." He returned to his magazine.

"We never stopped trying."

"I'm sorry," Newman said in a businesslike voice, "we're fresh out."

Beck looked puzzled. "Excuse me?"

Newman's voice dropped low and serious. "Odd words, coming from you." A pause and the business voice returned. "As I said, we're fresh out. Try again next week."

Newman stood and walked to the double-paned, iron-mesh-covered window.

Beck stood up, his face a torrent of confusion. "What are you talking about?"

Newman continued staring out the window. When he spoke, his voice was barely discernible.

"Absolution."

Beck stared at the man's back for a full minute before turning and pounding on the door. He heard the bolt thrown, but hesitated pushing it open.

"You're being transferred to more comfortable quarters this afternoon," Beck said in a defeated voice. "Please don't hurt anyone."

"Alex?" Newman turned to face Beck.

"Yes?" Beck turned toward him as the door opened.

Newman took a step forward, causing the guards to take closer aim. "For you. This once."

Beck nodded and walked out of the cell. The door was slammed behind him.

He spent the rest of the day, and well into the evening, sitting in the middle of the lawn, staring at the trees and trying to breathe.

It was late, a little before midnight. The unit was quiet as Patricia sat in an upstairs office, working on her notes. Mozart played in the background, her feet were up on the desk, as she tried to concentrate on the critical record keeping she must do.

But it was hard.

It had been the most exciting day Patricia had spent in years. For the first time, she had come face-to-face with the embodiment of the reasons she'd gotten into psychiatry. She had seen him, looked into his eyes, without the hindrance of guards or television monitors or restraints.

And, she thought, she had begun to understand.

She forced herself back to the paperwork titled "History and Setting."

"The patient was transferred," she read, "from the main building at approximately 1510 hours, the third day after his arrival, to Unit A-249. He exhibited no aggressive behavior at that time. His attitude was cooperative and helpful. Restraints were deemed unnecessary by Dr. Clemente."

Actually, despite the presence of the armed guards, it had all been very routine.

Newman was ready when they arrived at the holding area. In fact, he seemed anxious to get to what he called "my home away from home." He'd been rational, even-tempered, cooperative, even made a series of jokes about the absurdity of the scene (three doctors, six armed guards, a couple of orderlies with restraints).

"If this is how you transfer one of your voluntary, friendly patients," he'd laughed, "you got to call me when you move one of your really disturbed types. That, I don't want to miss!"

The scene had continued to border on the absurd as they marched down the corridor. It was compounded when, for avowed reasons of security, it was decided to walk down the several flights of stairs instead of taking the elevator. On the parade continued, winding its way down the stairs like a many-headed snake.

Newman had actually laughed.

"Don't nobody trip," he'd called out. "We'll all be crushed by the pile and *I'll* get the blame!"

She returned to her reading.

"Upon arrival at the unit, the patient asked to remain outside for 'a few minutes,' since he was aware that his quarters would be below-ground. How the patient obtained this information is currently under investigation."

And of great concern, she thought, *to several people.* Needlessly, she believed. Once he was locked away in the unit, what he knew about it and how he knew it were immaterial.

She turned the page.

"The stoppage of transfer lasted six minutes," she continued reading, "spent primarily looking at the sky, the woods, appreciating the landscaping in sight. Then the patient indicated he was prepared to enter the unit."

It had been an oddly nerve-wracking six minutes.

They were on the edge of the path that led into the unit when Newman had abruptly stopped, almost causing the guards behind him to collide. So quickly did they jump back to their previously safe distance that the guards in front, not realizing that anything had happened, just kept going. As a result, for almost thirty seconds, Newman stood almost alone.

Tension swept through the escorts.

The guards quickly recovered, raising their guns to shoulder level.

In the tension and confusion of those few seconds, Security Chief Edel had stepped in, instantly calming everyone.

"Is there a problem, sir?" he'd asked Newman as he moved close to the reputedly dangerous man.

Face-to-face close.

Patricia could still see the pleasantly surprised expression on the former prisoner's face. This was probably the closest that anyone had stood next to him in years.

"Before I scurry down my hole like a good little guinea pig," Newman had said, "I'd like to take a last look around for a few minutes. Breathe some unrecirculated air, smell the flowers. You know."

Edel looked at Clemente, and seeing no objection, he nodded.

"Of course, sir."

Newman stood there, turning slow circles, taking in all the beautiful landscaping of the Institute.

"Perhaps," Edel had said quietly, "it will not be long before they allow you regular visits to the gardens. Then, perhaps, your full release."

Newman had just looked at the man.

"I doubt it," he finally said.

"Still, I will pray for that, sir," Edel had said as they started into the unit.

Patricia pulled herself away from the memories and once again continued reading the report.

"Upon arrival at this quarters, he was given a full tour and a briefing as to the procedures. The only question he asked had to do with the lavatory facilities. He asked for, and was granted, limited privacy. An agreement, in which the lavatory camera would be shut down with sound remaining active, was quickly arrived at."

Stupid, she thought as she turned a page. *There should never have been a camera in there in the first place.*

"The patient read or watched television sporadically throughout that first afternoon. He ate dinner at 1900. Read until 2200, then retired for the evening."

She made a note to try and find out what he had watched and read.

"Monitors noted that he slept evenly and comfortably through the night.

"The patient arose at 0530 the next day, performing a series of calisthenic exercises. He showered, shaved, returning all soap and shaving equipment at the prearranged time and without incident.

"He permitted a medical examination at 0700, prior to his eating breakfast."

Physically, Newman was getting stronger every day. His weight was still below normal but climbing steadily. His strength and reflexes had improved to the point where they were classified as normal. Even his skin color was improving, despite the artificial lighting.

Another note, reminding herself to see that Newman received at least two hours of sunlight a week, beginning as soon as reasonable.

"Dr. Nellwyn arrived at the unit at 0615," the last page of the report read, "and observed the aforementioned prior to entering the patient's quarters at 0830."

She watched him, all right. Looking for any signs, no matter how small, of a deep neurosis. Overwashing of his hands, a need to be particularly neat or sloppy, the slightest tic or variable that might give her a direction to go.

But there was nothing.

"The interview," the report continued, "was conducted in the patient's quarters' living room area.

"The following is a complete transcript of that first interview, presented without comment."

And it was signed "Dr. Jonathon Clemente, Director, Behavioral Research."

She turned the page.

The transcript ran over sixty pages. Every word, every sound, had been recorded and carefully reduced to this paper record. Tomorrow, it would be circulated among the project's staff for comment.

Tonight, however, it was her chance to match her personal feelings about what had happened with the dry written record. Taking a sip of club soda and grape juice, she began to read.

"Dr. Nellwyn entered at 0832 . . ."

Standing outside the door, waiting for the guards to position themselves, she was filled with the same tremulous emotions she'd felt the first time she'd made love. She wet her lips, checked her hair, interesting parallels to that night, and signaled for the door to open.

She stepped inside as she felt the door closing behind her.

Newman was standing as instructed, facing away from the door at the entrance to the bedroom. When he heard the bolts thrown, he turned to face her. His expression was, well, wary.

"Good morning," Patricia said in her best therapist's voice.

"Is it? I wouldn't know down here in my burrow."

Taking a deep breath, she walked over to him, extending her hand.

"I don't think we ever officially met. My name is Patricia Nellwyn. I've been asked to help you through all this."

Carefully, clearly aware that his every move was being monitored, he reached out and shook her hand.

Patricia wasn't sure why, but she felt relieved by the warm, dry grasp.

Newman walked past her, settling in an overstuffed chair. "Help me through all what?"

Patricia settled herself on the couch. "Well, there's going to be a period of readjustment for you, after all you've been through. We just want to ease that transition."

"I see." His voice was noncommittal.

"How do you feel?"

For the first time since she'd first seen him on a foggy night near the Czech frontier, he smiled.

"Doctor, if we're going to—" He paused. "You *are* a doctor, aren't you?"

"Yes."

"What kind?"

She smiled, hopefully in a nonthreatening way. "I'm a psychiatrist."

Newman seemed to be amused by her answer.

"Beck must keep you busy." He leaned back in the chair. "If we're going to get along at all, Doctor, then I'm afraid you're going to have to expand your horizons beyond Basic Clinical Interviews 101."

"In what way?" she asked, noting the arrogant tone. It wasn't forced or put on, but it wasn't natural either.

"Don't waste my time with useless pleasantries," he said in the same semiarrogant, annoyed fashion. "Let's just do what we have to do, and do it as quickly and efficiently as we can."

The second reference to speed and efficiency. A clear reference, she believed, to his subconscious fear that she might discover some of his secrets.

She felt encouraged. "Don't you like being pleasant?"

He yawned as if he was being bored to death. In fact, Patricia believed, he was as anxious to pump her for information as she was him.

"Doctor, please."

"Sorry," she said conversationally. A brief pause. "Do you know why you're here?"

He closed his eyes. "Any number of reasons."

"Such as?"

"Offhand? The gamut from your patently absurd declaration of transitional counseling, to incarceration pending execution."

He said the word so flatly. As if he didn't care whether he lived or died.

"You think someone wants to kill you?"

"I said it was a possibility." He stretched his legs out in front of him, the image of a man relaxing after a long day.

"Why would anyone want to kill you?"

"Why does anyone kill?" he said in a near whisper.

"I haven't had any experience at it. Maybe you could enlighten me."

He opened his eyes, inclining his head to look over at her, without sitting up. "In my position as an expert?"

His voice had changed again. Become narrow, low, threatening.

Patricia worked to keep the effect of this new, somehow deadly voice out of her own. "Are you an expert?"

"I'm, let's see." He sat up, seeming to think the question over. "I'm a practitioner. Let's leave it at that."

"So?"

Newman smiled as he looked at her. A smile that showed all his teeth. Charming and unnerving at the same time.

"The casual practitioner, such as yourself, would cite any number of justifications. But that's just delusional self-effacement."

She made a show of writing the phrase down. "Delusional self-effacement. That's a new one on me."

He suddenly seemed bored again. He leaned back, closing his eyes again. "You ought to keep up on the literature."

"What does it mean?" she said in a who-cares voice.

Two could play this game. She understood that what was going on was a battle for control of their therapeutic relationship. If she tried too hard, begged him for answers, she would quickly find herself in a position of weakness.

And that, she reminded herself, she could never afford.

Not around Newman.

It worked.

Newman sat up again, and now he was starting to use his hands when he talked. He was being lured out of his primary defenses.

"You kill," he said in a professorial voice, "but you justify it as necessary at the moment of the act. Even though it secretly makes you feel good, you offer explanations such as 'I would have liked to avoid it, but . . .' "

She cut him off. "That's the second time you included me. Do you think I'm a killer?"

"We're all killers, Doctor."

He stood up and began moving around the room. Not agitated, but as if motion helped him talk. "You ever swat a fly, step on a bug, drown your piano teacher?" he said as he flipped through a book.

"I took accordion," Patricia said lightly.

He put down the book with a look of genuine distaste on his face. "Figures."

"So," she said, smiling at him, "the killing of a fly is equivalent to the killing of a man?"

He suddenly froze, showing her yet another face. "Or a woman."

His expression was purely predatory. Purely primal. He looked her over in a clearly sexual way.

Then, instantly, the face was gone. Replaced by the bored, smiling mask.

But she had seen it!

"How so?"

He shrugged. "A fly lives, breathes, procreates, has consciousness, has purpose. Your rolled-up newspaper takes all that away with considerably more pain and mess than a lamp cord wrapped around the throat."

"So," she said while making a note, "you hold all life on an equal footing. All equally dear."

"All equally fragile at any rate."

He collapsed back into the chair, seemingly exhausted. "You ought to use a little lotion on that," he said casually.

Patricia was looking at her notes. "Excuse me?"

"That dry spot on the inside of your left breast," he said simply. "Where you're not wearing your usual more restrictive, discount house bra." He smiled. It was a genuinely charming but also leering act. "And thank you."

Patricia straightened suddenly, her hand failing to appear casual as she checked her buttons.

"I'm glad you approve," she said in truth, as well as in an attempt to conceal just how flustered she really was.

"So," she forced out a moment later, "why would anyone want to kill you?"

He held up his hands and clapped slowly.

"Very good." He sat up grinning. "Very good, Doctor. I was afraid you'd forgotten your question."

"Do you have an answer?"

"Well, hypothetically of course."

"Of course."

He rubbed his mouth with his right index finger as he thought it over.

"They would give one of three possible justifications, I imagine." He paused. "But they would all be lies, you understand."

"Go on."

"First, they might say that I committed capital crimes back in the States, prior to my last assignment. They might say that these crimes weren't discovered until after I was beyond their jurisdiction and reach. They would then contend that the proper punishment, therefore, is death."

"But wouldn't that require some form of a trial prior to your execution?" She sounded genuinely interested.

Newman was clearly enjoying himself. He sat forward on the edge of the chair, eyes wide open, nodding as she talked.

"Maybe. Then again, maybe that's why I'm here. For some form of 'accident' to happen to save the cost and embarrassment of a trial."

"Go on."

"Second possibility. They claim that I'm a danger to the community and should be killed for the public good."

"And . . ." Patricia said softly. He was on a roll and she didn't want to say or do anything to slow him down.

"Third possibility," he said eagerly. "They might execute me as part of a secret deal with the Russians."

"You just lost me," she said with honest curiosity. "If the Russians wanted you dead, surely they would've just killed you in your prison cell?"

He shook his head. "It would've been politically insensitive for them to kill me, and the Russians are very sensitive to that kind of politics." He held up a finger in triumph. "But for my own people to do it on their behalf, that's possible. That's the kind of dialectic they appreciate."

He leaned back in the chair, keeping his eyes on hers. His every muscle, every look said "Aren't I smart? Smarter than anyone you've ever known. Smarter than you."

She ignored him.

"But none of those would be the real reasons," she said flatly.

"No." The arrogance dropped away. "Nothing so dramatic."

"Which brings us back to my original question."

"I forgot it," he said, reassuming the half-asleep pose.

"What would the real reason be? Why would they want to kill you?"

"Oh," he said, *"that question."*

He seemed to be waiting for her to say something, do something. But she just sat there, patiently looking at him.

Waiting.

Newman sighed deeply. "They would want me killed for the same reason you kill the fly." He paused. "It makes you feel good to be rid of an annoyance."

"And you think this is what's going to happen?" she asked softly.

He sat up so suddenly that she jumped.

He smiled at his second small triumph over her.

"Not really. Why would they want to kill me? They're the good guys, right?" His voice was happy, filled with false hopes and submerged anxieties.

He paused as he watched Patricia quickly recover herself. "But it is an interesting speculation. Don't you think?"

"So why are you here?" she asked, covering her nervousness by making a note.

Newman folded his hands in front of him. He appeared to be deep in thought. When he spoke, his voice was somehow disconnected from his body. As if speaking somehow intruded on the thought process.

"It would be pure speculation on my part," he said after a while. "I wouldn't want to take up your time."

"We have plenty of time," she said gently, sensing they were near some kind of admission.

"Can I have your word on that?" He paused. "Just kidding." His voice and humor were strained.

"If you can't think of an answer, we can move on," she gently prodded.

He stood up, quickly moving back toward the bedroom, picking up a magazine as he went.

"Excellent!" he said in a sarcastic tone. "Challenge the patient! Superior clinical technique, Doctor. My congratulations!"

She ignored the tone. "Why do you think you're here?"

He stopped in the bedroom doorway. "I suspect that something's gone very wrong with the program," he said with a tinge of sadness and something else. Worry or self-concern maybe.

"And I'm here," he said slowly, "for you to find out what and try to fix it."

"Interesting."

"Wait till you see my card tricks," he said as he walked into the bedroom.

Exhausted, Patricia closed the file.

There was so much going on in Newman, so many contradictory, mutually exclusive patterns. She would laser in on one, think she was getting close to the thread that might lead to an answer. Then up would jump some other complex, or neurosis, or unidentifiable thing that would shoot that theory to hell.

She slipped her feet back into her shoes and stood up.

She had hoped that a clinical rereading of the transcript would enable her to seize that thread, to ignore all others, and follow it to the root cause. But here she was, less than a third through the transcript, and more lost than ever.

As she tucked her blouse back in her skirt, uncomfortably conscious of the expensive designer bra she was wearing, she thought about the two conclusions that she was sure of.

Newman was an intelligent game player, skilled, with at least some psychoanalytic knowledge. Conventional approaches wouldn't work on him. She would have to come up with something new. Let Jack Clemente pound against the reinforced front door of that formidable fortress Newman had constructed. She would somehow slip around the back and try to climb in a window.

Second, and most important of all: Newman was a highly dangerous man.

Not unstable, not an unpredictable neurotic, not even unbalanced. Hell, the man seemed to maintain his equilibrium no matter what angle you approached him from. Like a cat.

No, he was dangerous in the most dangerous of ways.

He was a man who had simply decided, either through rational consideration or irrational leaps of illogic, that the rules of society simply didn't apply to him.

Thus liberated from accepted concepts of right and wrong, he was capable of anything.

As she rode the elevator down, a new, even more disturbing concept echoed through her brain.

If, as theorized, Newman had merely decided, after considering all the alternatives, that he would play by his own rules and not society's; if he was capable of living his life in a completely remorseless, hedonistic existence, was he really mentally ill?

Or was he something new, some sort of new man, that so terrified society that it demanded he be burned at the stake?

As she walked to her car, her mind awash with these and other unnerving thoughts, she forced her mind away from the logical next question.

What if Newman isn't the only *new man* out there?

Arriving home, she put in videocassettes of Disney cartoons to banish the thought from her mind, at least enough to let her sleep. But late that night, unbidden, the question returned.

The morning's sessions were also very much on the mind of the man who appeared to be sleeping in the subterranean patient quarters of Unit A-249.

Newman lay in the bed, dressed in sweatpants and a T-shirt, eyes closed, his breathing deep and regular. The room was silent, except for the periodic barely heard whir of the bedroom camera's lens as it pushed in for a closer look. It observed him roll over, fully loose and relaxed, in a deep, cleansing sleep.

Exactly as he intended.

For two hours now, he had lain there, eyes closed, gradually slowing his breathing. He'd started in a near-fetal position, gradually allowing his body to unkink itself. A tiny bit of drool slowly stained the pillow cover, as he adjusted his breathing to the deep autonomic breaths associated with deep sleep.

It was difficult, painstaking work, but he'd had six and a half years to perfect the technique.

He left one bare foot sticking out the side of the blanket, occasionally twitching to some dream stimuli. He allowed his hair to fall in front of his face, his shoulder to lie at an awkward position, then added just the slightest flutter to his eyelids.

He heard the camera whine as it pulled back to a normal, wide shot of the room, the unseen watcher having been convinced that Newman was dead to the world.

Only now, after two hours of carefully establishing his "night cover," did he allow his mind to turn back to the problem at hand.

Escape!

The hours spent in the holding area had been instructive.

From his upper-floor window, he'd been able to see most of the rear area of the Institute, including the building he was now housed in. He'd watched the casual patrols of the staff security, seen which lights came on when and how much was actually illuminated by them. But he had not been able to answer the most important question.

How deep were the woods to the rear of the Institute and were they fenced off or not?

But his actual transfer had answered other questions.

The compacted earth paths that connected the buildings were strictly portal-to-portal, they didn't go through the gardens or woods.

The lawn, seemingly so flat and manicured, was actually neither. Close up, it was immaculate, tight, closely cropped, in relatively level, hard soil. But as you moved farther from the main building, its surface became slightly more uneven, the soil looser and softer. When they'd stopped "to smell the roses," he'd actually felt his foot sink slightly in the soft grass.

Then there were the distances involved.

The first were long but the most exact, having been carefully paced off by Newman whenever they'd moved him.

61 meters for the width of the unit.

250 meters from the main door of the unit to the rear door of the main building.

90 meters for the width of the main building.

Now came the estimates.

He pulled his foot back under the covers, adjusted his head on the pillow away from the drooled-on spot. All with the spasmodic, retarded action of a person still in a deep sleep.

Upon pulling into the front gate of the Institute, they'd averaged about five miles per hour for the forty-two seconds it took them to arrive at the main entrance.

93.75 meters. Better figure 95.

By estimating the length of the main building as approximately 325 meters, noting that the unit seemed approximately aligned with the center of it, and that it extended approximately halfway to the east fence . . .

His lips moved slightly as he did the calculations. The orderly on duty noted it.

"Subject appears to be talking in his sleep although contents remain too indistinct for ambient microphones to record."

312 meters to the east fence from the unit. Better figure 315.

The process was repeated for the west fence.

187 meters, figure 190.

The distance from the back of the unit to the woods was trickier. The ground more uneven, and he'd never gotten a direct-line view. But, it seemed to Newman, it was just over twice the length of the unit itself.

122 meters. 125 to play safe.

And there was still the question of how deep the woods were and what lay beyond them.

But enough had been accomplished for the time being. He now knew exactly how long it would take him to reach any given point on the grounds from the main door of the unit.

In optimum conditions, running at 6.1 meters per second (approximately the speed of a slow college sprinter) . . . Again his lips moved and the technician in the observation room made the same notation as earlier.

To the main gate: one minute, nine seconds.

To the east fence: fifty-two seconds.

To the west fence: thirty-one seconds.

To the woods: twenty-one seconds.

Satisfied, he rolled over (physically and mentally) to a new position and new problem.

How to get to the main door of the unit?

A straight force approach was out. Too many guards, too many locked doors, too many cameras. Not to mention the problem of the elevator.

No, he would have to get them to allow him out of the unit. At that moment, lower their vigilance, lull them to sleep, and buy five minutes of free, unencumbered time.

But how to do that?

The answer was as obvious as the whining of the lens as it pushed in and pulled back.

They would have to want to do it.

He began to evaluate those members of the project's staff that he'd been able to observe close up.

Clemente was a traditional shrink, his techniques tried-and-true. He was cautious, experienced, conservative.

He was consigned to a back burner.

Nellwyn. Now, she was interesting.

Far less confident than she pretended, she also was the sharpest of the bunch by far. He'd dominated their interview earlier, but she'd allowed him to dominate. And that was intriguing.

He suspected she was probably a good shrink, but underappreciated. She tended toward the unconventional, seemed a little excitable, but intelligent, sharp, and perceptive.

But in her eyes, Newman could see that she also, with all her heart and soul, wanted not only to be right but to display her rightness. And there was one more thing besides.

Dr. Patricia Nellwyn, beneath her cool professional detachment and nice party manners, believed herself to be a chrysalis—an ugly caterpillar on the verge of becoming a beautiful butterfly; yet somehow unable to ever pull it off completely or for any length of time. So she spread her multicolored wings only in her mind.

But if she were to see *someone else* see her as a butterfly . . .

Front burner for her.

The security chief, Edel, was essentially basic. Probably career soldier or police. He seemed tough, honest, brave, and, unfortunately for
him, compassionate.

Front burner, but toward the rear. Newman would have to remind
himself to reread the Bible. That's where the key to Edel was.

Finally, for the hundredth time since his release, he turned his
attention to the one person he thought he could most easily manipu-
late into inadvertently helping.

Alexander Beck.

Beck's guilt was obvious and unhidden. The man seemed like a
porcelain doll that had been dropped one too many times. Riddled
with hairline, barely visible cracks, he was held together by force of
will, discipline, and routine. His need, his button waiting to be
pushed, was for a complete, soulful forgiveness.

He was a child begging for Mommy or Daddy to kiss it and make it
all better; who would do almost anything to achieve that moment of
peace and contentment.

But Beck was also an unknown.

Beck knew almost everything Newman knew, had taught him
much of it in the first place. And while his conscience and morality
wouldn't allow him the freedom of action that Newman had, if Beck
calculated that the gain was greater than the cost, he could be just as
effective.

But Beck had to do the mental gymnastics.

There was no question, Newman thought as he allowed sleep
to slowly rise up from within him, Beck was the weak link. Find a
way to turn the key in Beck, and the door to the unit would fly
open.

After Beck, there was Nellwyn. Then, possibly, Edel.

Three doors, closed, locked, but all vulnerable to the same human
key.

Then he was asleep.

It was almost three o'clock in the morning.

———

Outside, it was cold and misty. The security guards on patrol pulled their collars up as they walked, heads down, along their assigned route. At each checkpoint, they stopped, pulled out their radios, and gave the appropriate sign.

Along the east fence, midway between the main gate and the woods, they repeated the procedure.

"Patrol Seven, at point Echo Three."

"Patrol Seven, roger," the reply came through the light static. "Show 0256, confirm."

"0256, roger. Proceeding to point Echo Four."

They continued on, talking about an upcoming soccer match.

Never once did they notice the malevolent shadow that moved up to take their place.

The shade seemed to settle there for a moment, as if waiting for the two men to move farther along before deciding which direction to proceed. After five minutes, it slid soundlessly across the lawn to the west.

At a point very near the main building, it settled into the ground again. It waited there, a barely visible something, watching as a nurse and two orderlies walked down the path to the parking lot. Three minutes later, it was on the move again.

Across the back of the main building, stopping at the west fence. Moving north toward the woods, the fence at its right, Unit A-249 on its left, it came to a noiseless stop.

It stayed there, no movement, sound, or other indication that it existed. Merely the slightly darker darkness of itself against the total dark of the grounds in that isolated spot.

Twenty minutes later, with the sound of the two guards approaching from the woods area, it moved.

Suddenly and silently, it glided directly toward the unit, coming to a stop just outside the periphery of the surveillance cameras.

There it remained, frozen, immobile, detached from its surroundings, yet a part of them. A desolate, menacing nothing, with a clear view of the main entrance to the unit, the lawn between the unit and the main building, the lawn between the unit and the woods, and the lawn between the unit and the east fence.

And its mass stood between the unit and the west fence.

It remained through the night, as it would for many nights to come. It stood its black post without complaint or relief or explanation until twenty minutes before sunrise, when it roused itself and moved stealthily into the woods.

Five-thirty in the morning.

Patricia's alarm jangled loudly. She merely reached over, switching it off.

She'd been up for the better part of an hour. Reading.

No matter how many cartoons she watched, how much elevator music she assaulted herself with, thoughts of Newman could not be pushed completely from her consciousness. So she had returned to the transcript.

"Subject returned to the living area," she read, "after remaining in the bedroom for eleven minutes, apparently reading."

Patricia knew that this was a test. Newman expected to be left behind, to be abandoned as he felt he had been in Russia. So, to avoid that pain, he would do the abandoning, be the first to leave.

And if she was right, Patricia thought, she must remain there however long it took for him to return.

"Still here?" he asked affably as he returned his magazine to the table.

"Yup."

Newman turned on the music system. He tuned to a channel of soft rock, keeping the volume down low.

"I suppose you have a reason."

She nodded. "I want to help."

He raised his eyebrows. "Why?"

This was the one question she hadn't prepared herself for. Luckily, she didn't have to answer.

"I mean," Newman said as he collapsed back into the chair, "I know you must be getting a ton of money from Uncle." He paused. "How much am I worth, by the way?" He sounded genuinely interested.

"They don't tell us peasants things like that," she said with a smile. "But it must be quite a bit, don't you think?"

"Why?" Now he seemed to be off balance.

Patricia continued conversationally. "Well, not to sound egomaniacal, but our Institute doesn't come cheap. Add in the number of people that have been assigned just to your care and it stands to reason that somebody must care about you one heck of a lot."

"Not me, the program," he said after due consideration.

"Would they really go to all this length," she said with a smile, "give themselves this much exposure, if all they cared about was the program?"

"You don't know them."

"So educate me."

A long pause developed between them. So long that Patricia began to believe she had gone too far.

"Do you know anything about sharks, Doctor? Great white sharks?" His voice was so quiet, so subdued and out of character, that she had to strain to hear it.

"Not much."

He nodded. *"Carcharodon carcharias* is their scientific designation. They're solitary creatures. No one knows how long they live, or how they live, for that matter. All they do is swim, eat, and procreate."

She nodded, suppressing her exultation at getting Newman to open up about his feelings toward himself. Clearly the great white shark, the most feared terror of the oceans, was an analogy for himself.

"Go on."

His expression was far away. "Put an injured fish in the water, pour a tenth of a liter of blood in a choppy sea, and the great white will sense it from as far away as a hundred miles. They'll navigate flawlessly, around or through any obstacle, to get to it.

"When it arrives on the scene, despite its size, power, and obvious advantage, it waits. Circling until it's sure that its prey can't put up a fight, can't resist. Only then does it strike. Usually from behind."

What better metaphor than that for what Newman had become, Patricia thought. *The predator who, despite overwhelming superiority, still waits for its eventual victim to become defenseless.*

She fought the desire to make copious notes at this psychic unveiling.

"Yes?"

Newman nodded. "Now, fifteen million years ago, there was an ancestor of the great white. They call it *Carcharodon megalodon.* It was as much as ten times larger than the ones we know today. They found the fossilized tooth of one once. It was bigger than your hand."

Unconsciously, Patricia looked down at her hand.

Newman either didn't notice or ignored her.

"If it were still around today, and there is speculation about whether or not it is, it could swallow a small boat whole. Nothing could stand in its way." He paused, chuckling bitterly. "Let alone a little wounded fish."

She nodded gravely. "And you feel that through your personality and training," she said in an academic voice, "you have become this *megalodon,* this unstoppable leviathan. Of course, as always happens to the monster from the deep, you expect that those who created you now fear you and must kill you." She paused. "I understand."

Newman stood up and wearily shook his head. "I'm afraid not, Doctor." He took a deep breath and headed for the bathroom with heavy legs. "The *megalodon,* what I was describing, are the people I work for. The government. Yours and mine." He paused again. "Me? I'm just a wounded fish."

PART TWO

The Hunting Dogs

The theater let out into the brisk, Moscow fall night.

As was a century-old tradition, the audience lingered on the marble steps, clustered around the Corinthian columns, criticizing the performance they'd just seen. And, as tradition demanded, whether the performance was good or bad (tonight's had been particularly good), they found some flaw in it.

"Can you believe the colors they chose for the woman's dress?" one man said with disdain.

"The neckline," an older woman cawed, "you could almost fully see her breasts!"

"If she had any worth looking at," a man added smugly.

Vitenka shook his head as he worked his way across the portico.

Whether the revolution came or went, he thought, Muscovites remained the same.

He approached a group of his friends, the men in uniform, the women in expensive—for Russia—dresses.

"I wonder if the playwright really knows anything about life in Catherine's court," one of the young men was saying.

"Weren't the gowns delicious?" one of the women added.

Vitenka laughed.

"Certainly the women in them were."

One of the women playfully hit him in the shoulder.

"You were supposed to be watching the play, not the little . . ."

"Watch your language, my angel," Vitenka interrupted.

". . . *actresses* in it!"

They all laughed.

Vitenka turned, looking over the slowly departing crowd. As the conversation began to drift away from the play and onto which discotheques to visit, he suddenly froze.

"Excuse me, I'll be right back."

His friends barely noticed him leave.

He walked across the portico and down a few steps to a man standing by himself, sipping from a cup of steaming cider.

"Colonel Ruinov?"

The man looked up from his cup. "Ah," he said after a few moments, "Medverov's errand boy. Let me see." He paused. "Major Vitenka, wasn't it?"

"It still is," Vitenka said as they shook hands. "It has been too long a time, sir."

Ruinov looked the man over. "Not so long."

"Three months, sir."

Ruinov nodded. "How are you, Major? Still scurrying about for Medverov?"

"Essentially."

A difficult silence settled between the men.

"Sir," Vitenka finally said, "if you recall, when last we met it was under somewhat, uh, difficult circumstances."

"An interesting phrase, Major."

Vitenka took a deep breath. "We *both* had our orders, sir. And we carried them out as best we could."

Ruinov took a long drink, holding his face over the steaming cup for an extra moment or two. "I'm sure that will be comforting to Dnebronski's widow and three children."

Vitenka moved a step closer. "Was it ever proven that Newman actually did it?" The tone of his voice was compelling enough to force Ruinov to look up into the man's eyes.

"To me," he said in a low voice. "It was proven to me. To my satisfaction."

Vitenka nodded slowly, not exactly sure why. "I informed the general of the incident, but he insisted that we follow through on the release." He paused. "But I took all possible precautions."

Ruinov laughed bitterly. "With that man, that is an impossibility." He lit a cigarette as he tossed the remnants of his cider in a nearby can.

"What we did, Major, you, me, Medverov, was to release a plague into the world. And I assure you, when the time of judgment comes"—he drew a lungful of smoke from the cigarette and held it for long moments before exhaling the bluish cloud—"and it will come, I assure you—on that day, before God, we will be called to task for that action." He took deep drags on his cigarette.

As Vitenka stared into Ruinov's darkly circled eyes, his expression of tired cynicism, a question which had plagued him since he'd turned Newman over to the Americans suddenly found its voice.

"Colonel?"

Ruinov looked up at the earnest young man. "What is it now?"

Vitenka looked around, checking to see that no one was within earshot.

"Sir, I am also afraid of that final judgment." He looked at the older man. "I did my duty, to my general, to my country. But if that act were to cause what you believe, what I . . ." His voice trailed off and it took a moment for him to pull himself back from the nightmare that often invaded his nights. "Then I know it will be, at least in part, my fault."

Ruinov seemed to be studying him intently. "Your point, Major?"

"Sir," Vitenka began slowly, "as a soldier, as a man, I must ask." He took a deep breath. "Has he . . ."

"I can guarantee you, Major," Ruinov said in a low voice, "that since his release, Newman has caused no harm."

"You can guarantee?"

Ruinov nodded. "Since his release, he has been kept under the strictest of security at a sanitarium near Munich, Germany. And for the last three months, he has been kept in an escape-proof, underground cell." He paused. "He has harmed no one. In fact, his doctors believe he is well on his way to recovery."

"You know this?" Vitenka asked with a strain of incredulity in his voice.

"I do."

"Verified?"

Ruinov nodded slightly. "I have caused certain, shall we say, checks to be put in place. Old comrades from Afghanistan—now in control of certain networks in the West—have, well, indulged an old man." He chuckled bitterly. "My information, however, is authoritative."

One of Vitenka's friends waved for him to join them. He held up a patient hand.

"And he is near a cure. Thank God," Vitenka mumbled in relief.

Ruinov shook his head. "The man cannot be cured, Major. Evil is not a disease!"

"Nevertheless, sir . . ."

Ruinov interrupted him. "Good evening, Major." He crushed out his cigarette, then quickly started down the steps.

And in his heart, prepared for his inevitable damnation.

In the heart of Bavaria, standing on the roof of the main building of the Institute, another man contemplated eternity. He looked up at the same stars as Ruinov, equally concerned about the sins of this world passing on to the next.

But unlike the Russian colonel, Jack Clemente was thinking less about Newman and more about himself.

"I thought I'd find you up here," Patricia said as she came through the stairway door. She took several deep breaths. "Why can't you like communing in the garden like everybody else? Save me the trip up those damned stairs."

He ignored her, just continued staring at the stars.

"Jack?" she asked cautiously. "You okay?"

He turned, smiling at her. "In what sense?"

Patricia visibly relaxed. "Don't start." She walked over to him. "Meeting's in ten minutes."

Jack nodded. "I know."

Patricia looked up at the brilliant display of stars.

"My God."

Jack nodded. "Exactly what I was thinking," he said as he perched on the railing. A fit of coughing came over him, doubling the frail man over.

Patricia started to rush over to him, but he held up a hand to stop her.

For two full minutes, he hacked and coughed, each jolt shaking his body like a rag doll. Finally, it passed. He stood up, wiping a dribble of blood from his mouth.

"Could you . . . ," he croaked out, gesturing at a thermos.

Patricia quickly poured him a glass of what appeared to be apple juice. She started to hand it to him, but, noticing how badly his hands were shaking, she held it up to his lips.

He took a sip, then reached into his pocket, pulling out a small gold metal pillbox. He fumbled with the top, opening it and pulling out one of the large pills inside. He popped it in his mouth as Patricia again held the cup to his lips.

After a moment, he waved it away, smiling weakly at her.

"Thank you."

Patricia desperately wished she had within her the bedside manners or natural tact that all her colleagues seemed to possess in abundance.

"What are you taking?" was all she could think to say.

"Dilaudid."

"For how long?" she said in a hushed voice. Dilaudid was one of the most powerful painkillers available. Doctors prescribed it primarily in untreatable cancer cases.

"About a month, maybe six weeks," Jack said, his voice gradually regaining its former strength.

"I don't know what to say," she stammered out. "I'm sorry."

Jack smiled. "Truly one of the most eloquent and mercifully succinct statements I've heard lately." He paused, straightening himself. "And one of the few whose sentiments I believe. Thank you."

"Are you up to this meeting?"

He nodded. "I'm not exactly at death's door. Not yet, at least." He took the cup from her and drank. Noticing the pained expression on Patricia's face, he reached out and took her hand.

"You came up here for a reason?"

She nodded, tight-lipped.

"Go ahead," Jack urged. "I promise not to die on you. Not right now, at any rate."

A lot of people, perhaps most, would have been shocked at his joke.

Patricia just laughed. It was a strained laugh, but genuine, from the heart.

"I wanted to talk with you before we went down."

He leaned back on the railing. "So, talk."

She hesitated, drew strength from his supportive smile, then jumped in.

"Why do you think Tabbart's called this meeting?"

"Other than to hear himself talk, you tell me."

Patricia started to pace.

"I see two possibilities," she began.

"You're beginning to sound like Newman."

She paused, turning back to him. "When I figure out whether that's a compliment or a put-down, I'll respond with a biting reply." She thought for a moment. "First possibility, as head of the Institute, he wants an in-depth progress report on how far we've come and how far we still have to go."

"Logical, reasonable, and the avowed purpose for the show."

"But I don't believe it," she said, resuming her pacing.

"I agree with you."

"Which leaves us," she said slowly, "with the second possibility." She stopped, turning back to him. "He has something up his sleeve."

Jack walked over to the thermos, pouring himself another glass of juice.

"Undoubtedly. And I think I have a pretty good idea what it is."

Patricia walked over, taking a drink out of the thermos.

"So give?"

"You're an analyst," he chided, "a trained observer. Examine the behavior, the circumstances, the setting. Take into account your profile of the man, your knowledge of the project. Then answer your own question."

All sympathy was gone from her face, replaced by a deeply annoyed look. "I don't need lessons on clinical technique or office politics, ten minutes before the meeting!"

Jack raised his eyebrows. "Don't you? Patty, there are a heck of a lot of Tabbarts out there. You'd better learn how to deal with them sooner rather than later." He rubbed his forehead as he fought off a spasm of gut-wrenching pain. "Think! Why now? Why today? Why nine o'clock at night?"

Patricia was so taken up with concentrating that she didn't notice Jack slip another pill into his mouth.

"Today," she mumbled. "Tonight." She paused, head down, walking slowly back and forth. Suddenly, she stopped and stood bolt upright. "Damn!"

Jack nodded. "I think your clouds are beginning to clear."

"When does Beck get back?" She answered her own question. "Tomorrow, right? He gets back tomorrow with the review board from Washington." She paused. "Tabbart's decided to take over the presentation!"

"Exactly. He's going to play his little corporal show of 'I'm in charge, I know it all,' and then either kill or extend the project. Depending on what he hears tonight."

"He'll kill it," Patricia said sadly. "You know that."

The sickly man straightened, picked up the thermos, and walked over to her, putting his arm around her shoulders.

"Unless we, meaning you, can convince him otherwise."

"Me?" She looked shocked. "He hates me. Barely listens to anything I have to say, even when it's what he wants to hear!"

Jack began leading her toward the stairs. "Then make him listen."

"How?"

He smiled a crooked smile. "Think of him as a patient. A man who is convinced that he's perfectly sane, despite all evidence to the contrary. As his analyst, you must convince him of his psychosis."

"You're getting at something," she said suspiciously.

"Am I?" he said as he opened the door for her.

"Well," she said as she helped him down the stairs, "he is damned close to being a paranoid narcissist."

As they paused for breath at a landing, Jack patted her on the shoulder.

"And what is the most effective way of communicating with a paranoid narcissist?"

Patricia thought for a moment.

"Analogy?"

The old man shook his head and smiled. "Actually, I would've gone with flattery first."

Patricia shrugged. "I can't, I won't, flatter that man!"

Another shrug and a smile. "Then," Jack said as he started down the stairs again, "I suggest you go with your first instinct."

"For example?" she asked as she caught up with him.

"Tell him about the pigeon."

Fifteen minutes later, they sat around the conference table, along with the other main players in the project.

Tabbart sat at the table's head, useless files spread out before him, a pad, pristinely empty, sitting beneath a capped pen.

"Dr. Clemente, sir, if you would like to begin?"

Clemente nodded, took a sip of water, then began in a soft, professorial voice.

"We have just completed our twelfth week of observation and preliminary treatment of our subject. All requested neurological and brain imaging studies have been completed." He turned to the old German neurologist from the preliminary briefing. "Dr. Kapf?"

Kapf flipped through a file, then closed it before he said a word.

"We have conducted a full X-ray series, as well as a full imaging scan using high-resolution MRI, CT, and CAT technologies. To date, our findings are nonstriking. He has no mass lesions, no tumors, no temporal displacement. His brain appears to be of average size with no distinct malformations.

"There is a small lacunar bruise near the occipital cortex, of, in our opinion, childhood origin. However, due to its size, location, and other factors, it has been discounted as a possible factor in the alleged exhibited behavior recorded in the Soviet files."

Tabbart waited to be sure that the man had finished. "Then, Dr. Kapf, it is your best medical judgment that there is no physiological cause for the violent episodes?"

Kapf shook his head.

"Not in the constructs of the brain, no." He paused. "Not for any of the *alleged* incidents."

Tabbart ignored Kapf's use of *alleged*. Kapf was an old man, unwilling, in Tabbart's opinion, to let go of old tribal rivalries. He carefully uncapped his pen, made a detailed note, then recapped it, placing it exactly on the pad where it had been.

He nodded at Clemente to continue.

"We have also nearly concluded all of our blood and fluid work." He turned to a man across the table from him. "Dr. Goethering."

Goethering read from his file.

"Blood work is normal in all respects, with the exception of a declining anemia which, in our opinion, was due to malnutrition while in the Russians' hands. The condition seems to be correcting itself. In all other respects, we can find no contributory factors to account for any aberrant behaviors."

He closed the file and looked down.

"No contributory factors," Tabbart said as he wrote.

Clemente waited for Tabbart to look up, then added, "We've run every psych test we can think of on him. Most of them twice. Some three times." He selected his next words carefully. "The results were undramatic."

Tabbart immediately looked up.

"Undramatic? Indeed." Everyone at the table could see that he smelled blood. "Would you be so kind as to define your terms, Dr. Clemente?"

Clemente took a deep breath.

"His IQ tests out at 185, well above genius. He types out as A3, stress vulnerable, impatient, prone to frustration outbursts, resentments, extremes of emotion. He grades out a 7 of a possible 10 on the Kiernan Violence Index. A rating compatible with the A3 typing.

"There are no obvious signs of neurosis, psychosis, manias, or dementias. He's not delusional, at least not in the traditional sense. He appears rational, literate, cooperative in a grudging way."

Tabbart meticulously uncapped his pen and began to write. He read it back when he finished:

"The subject, after twelve weeks of full testing, is certified as being well within acceptable parameters of sanity. His behavior, although emotional, is not reflective of any neuropsychiatric condition."

"That's not what I said," Clemente interrupted in an angry tone.

Tabbart looked at him quizzically. "No? In what way am I misspeaking?" He looked around the table. "Has he experienced any violent outbursts?"

"No."

"Any reversions to primitive behavior?"

"No."

"Has he exhibited any personality decay, any decompensation or marked lability, mood swings, anything of that type?"

"No."

"Has he required any medications or restraints?"

"No."

The room grew very quiet.

Tabbart nodded, recapped the pen, looking pleasantly at Clemente. "Then please, enlighten us."

Clemente wiped his face with a clean handkerchief.

"I've had forty-eight clinical sessions with him. Approximately four a week. The tests might not show anything, but I can assure you, there's something there."

"How?"

He gestured as he tried to explain. "The man is arrogant to the point of absurdity. He seems to have acquired a background in the psychoanalytic technique and revels in allowing only glimpses of the real person beneath the arrogant facade."

Tabbart shook his head. "Are you sure it is a facade? In my rather substantial experience with intelligence types, I find that their arrogance is more often real than not."

He leaned back in his chair, folded his hands and began to lecture.

"It is essential to what they do, that they believe they are capable of accomplishing anything, no matter the obstacle. The arrogance, the aviator's scarf wrapped once around the throat and blowing in the wind behind him, is more often an actual component of their inner personality. Most definitely not a facade to hide a latent condition." He smiled a satisfied smile. "It is typical, not aberrant."

Clemente slowly shook his head. "Not this time." His voice was rock-solid.

Tabbart sighed deeply as he began to write and read again.

"Subject displays unusual personality traits, most likely due to his unusual profession type."

"I disagree," Clemente said again, this time with the slightest trace of anger.

Tabbart capped his pen, locking eyes with Clemente as he did.

"Dr. Clemente, precisely what conditions or maladies did you"—he twisted the next word on his tongue—"glimpse beneath the so-called facade?"

Clemente took a deep breath. He looked down at the table for a very long time.

"Well," Tabbart pushed, "does it or do they have a name?"

Clemente exhaled deeply. "Not by any conventional definition—"

"The supervising therapist cannot name any specific condition or malady that—" Tabbart's interruption was interrupted in kind by Patricia.

"At least let him finish before you twist his words!"

Tabbart stared daggers at her. "Forgive me," he said in an imperious tone. He turned to Clemente. "You may finish, Doctor."

Clemente looked like he had missed the exchange entirely. He was staring out a window, watching the leaves on a nearby tree blow in the night breeze.

"Jack," Patricia said softly.

He turned back to Tabbart. "By any conventional definition, as I said, there is no name. I've never even seen a description of this kind of symptomology in the texts."

Tabbart beamed. "Ah . . ."

"But," Clemente said sharply, "the symptoms and the condition do exist. I'm sure of that."

The chief of staff looked down at his notes. "I have heard nothing to alter my impressions as stated so far. Therefore . . ."

"Sir," Patricia said, venom dripping from her politeness.

The chief looked at her, pique on his face. "I believe I've heard enough, Dr. Nellwyn."

Patricia forced up a thin smile. "But you haven't heard my report yet, sir."

"Nor do I intend to. Dr. Clemente speaks for the Behavioral Unit and for the project. I have what I need."

Patricia nodded, an exaggerated nod.

"I quite understand, sir." She let a momentary look of triumph flash across the chief's face. "I'll just submit my report to the review board separately."

"You will what?" Tabbart's face grew instantly red.

"As the primary therapist on the grant, I have that right." She paused. "If you're too busy, I'll just present it to the board myself."

Everyone at the table tried to get out of the line of sight between Tabbart and Patricia. A vein started throbbing in his forehead.

"You may begin, Doctor," Tabbart said slowly with as much control as the furious man could muster.

"Are you sure?" Patricia smiled as she spoke in her sweetest voice.

"Don't milk it," Jack whispered to her.

She opened a file and arranged the papers in front of her.

"In the past three months, I have had sixty-one conversational sessions with Mr. Newman. They ranged from a short twenty minutes to a marathon three and a half hours. While I also have been unable to identify and quantify any reasonable, conventional, or common condition, I fully agree with Dr. Clemente that something is there."

"And of course, you have no evidence of this?" Tabbart's voice was snide and biting.

"On the contrary," she said lightly, "I have the pigeon."

Tabbart's eyes opened about as wide as they could. "What pigeon?"

"Actually," she said as she moved a page from one pile to another, "one pigeon and one cat."

It had happened at the end of the second month of Newman's new captivity.

The therapy sessions were getting nowhere. The tests were coming back inconclusive or negative. Even the round-the-clock observation of Newman revealed nothing.

He appeared to be what he was represented to be. An intelligent saboteur who was suffering only from the expected stresses growing out of his imprisonment by the Russians.

And yet . . .

There was something more involved here. Some unknown *thing,* always lurking just beneath the surface, laughing at their inability to find or name it.

So a plan had been developed. A plan, risky though it might be, that would administer a sudden, psychic shock to Newman. Hopefully, within his reactions to that shock, they would, at the very least, gain a momentary peek at his hidden self.

After days of discussion, it was decided that Patricia would lead the experiment.

As usual, the door to his quarters was opened at 8:30 and Patricia stepped through.

"Good morning," she said as he started to turn around.

He froze halfway.

The door, always instantly closed behind her, remained open.

"What are we playing here?" he said cautiously.

"I thought we'd have today's session outside," she'd said pleasantly and, she hoped, casually.

She didn't think one human being could be so still.

He stood there, not moving, not blinking, seeming not even to breathe. Only his eyes moved, slowly going back and forth between her and the open door.

"Guards?" he asked softly.

She shrugged. "This trip, yes. In the future, we'll see."

"How many? What are their orders?" He slowly turned to face her fully.

"I'm no expert," she said lightly, "but I think it's pretty much like when we brought you down here. If you follow the rules, they'll keep their distance and allow us our session in confidence."

His breathing seemed shallow, his muscles were contracted. Everything about the man screamed tension.

And preparedness.

"Not that I don't trust you, Doctor, but trust has never exactly worked to my advantage." He licked his lips quickly. "Give it to me by the numbers, if you please."

Inside, Patricia was rejoicing! This was a Newman they'd never seen before. A man that probably most approximated the man who had been in Russia. His physicality, his tone, were new. She prayed that the video was working.

"Okay," she said in as casual a voice as she could muster, "here's how it works. There are two guards outside the door with their guns drawn. We will walk together across the antechamber into the elevator. We will ride to the ground floor together."

"Alone?"

She smiled again. "Why not? Do I have some reason to be afraid of you?"

It was almost a full minute before he answered.

"I haven't decided yet" was his soft, flat-toned response. "Please continue."

She ignored the trace of tension she felt building within her.

"On the ground floor, there will be two more guards also with guns drawn. The corridor between the elevator and the main door will be empty and we are to proceed directly down it to the main entrance of the unit."

Newman seemed to relax, slightly.

"Go on."

Patricia shrugged. "There's not much to go on with. We go out the door onto the grounds and have our session." She turned to leave. "Shall we . . ."

"You left out the rules outside, Doctor." He sounded suspicious.

She turned back to him. "Common sense. There'll be guards and surveillance on us throughout." She hoped he noticed she was including herself. "We can go anywhere we like, so long as we stay within fifty meters of the building." She paused. "That's it."

Newman's mind was racing. Access to the grounds was something he'd been working toward, planning for, praying for! But something wasn't right here.

He'd expected a full briefing on rules and conditions before they allowed him out, even for a short period. And that, a day or two before. This was innately wrong.

It briefly crossed his mind that this was a setup, an opportunity for them to shoot him down "trying to escape."

But he had to get to the outside.

It took less than thirty seconds to make his decision.

He nodded at Patricia.

"After you, Doctor."

Newman followed her out of his quarters, noting that each of the guards was well out of reach, rock-steady hands pointing their Glock semiautomatic handguns at his head and torso respectively. They were calm, cool, obviously well trained.

As the elevator traveled upward, he reconfirmed his earlier timing of it.

"New dress?"

Patricia smiled easily. "For the occasion."

A spasmodic smile flashed across Newman's face as they stepped out of the elevator.

The ground floor was as empty as had been promised. Just two guards, stationed in a stagger down the corridor. Professional, well thought out. Whoever had arranged it worked it out so that even if Newman took out the nearest one, the other would have more than enough time to cut him down.

They walked slowly to the open door.

Newman could see the guards spread out in a loose semicircle about sixty meters in front of the building, their Glocks and Schmeissers held casually at their sides.

He hesitated stepping through.

"It's all right," Patricia urged.

Newman ignored her, concentrating instead on the approaching security chief.

"Good morning," Edel said pleasantly. "It seems our prayers have been answered."

Newman nodded. "Depending."

Patricia nervously watched the two men size each other up.

"There are no tricks here, sir," Edel said in a sincere voice. "If you make no furtive actions, do not attempt to escape or cause harm, my men will keep their distance and not intrude."

"Otherwise . . ."

Edel shrugged. "If, by some unexpected stroke of luck, you were able to get past the perimeter, my men on the roof would cut you down before you got twenty meters." His voice was matter-of-fact.

Newman looked at the ceiling above him, picturing the snipers that Edel had expertly placed. His opinion of the German security chief grew by the minute.

He smiled at Edel. "I praise thee, for thou art fearful and wonderful. Wonderful are thy works. Thou knowest me right well."

Edel grinned as he nodded. "You have been reading your Bible."

"Psalms," Newman said lightly, "139:14." He smiled. "It helps pass the time. Thank you."

"It was my pleasure." He started to turn away, then stopped, turning back to Newman. "Perhaps we could discuss your readings sometime?"

"I'd like that."

Edel nodded, half bowed to Patricia, then left to join his men.

Slowly, Newman stepped out into the sun, gratefully accepting the offered sunglasses from Patricia.

For ten minutes, they walked around the building. Newman seemed calm and relaxed, breathing the clean, fresh air deeply. Quietly taking it all in.

Patricia was becoming exhilarated. Newman seemed authentically relaxed and loose for the first time. Cautious, tentative early steps soon became full comfortable strides. At one point, he even crouched down under a tree on the west side of the building. She hoped he wasn't being overwhelmed by the experience.

He wasn't.

All of his defenses were going full out, set off by what he observed under this tree.

He compared the grass, the color, its uprightness to the grass around it. He looked for and found the locations of the nearest sprinkler heads and estimated how the water from them would fall on this area.

After two minutes, his suspicion was confirmed.

Many times in the recent past, perhaps nightly, after the sprinklers shut off at midnight and before the morning dew, someone had crouched on this spot. Crouched and remained for a period of hours. Probably concealed by a night camouflage cloak or boulder net, judging by the marks on the ground.

And that someone had not wanted to be detected by Edel's security force.

A new piece to the slowly evolving puzzle that Newman was mentally assembling.

He stood up and stretched.

Patricia relaxed as she saw a content expression on his face.

"Shall we begin?"

He nodded. "As long as we can keep walking. I need the exercise." *And a closer look around the rest of the perimeter,* he thought.

"We were talking about anger."

"Were we?"

She smiled. "We were." A pause. "How do you feel about that?"

Newman laughed. "Anger? Or talking about anger?" When she didn't answer, he went on. "A waste of time, really."

"Why?"

"Well," he said slowly, "define anger."

"How would you define it?" she responded quickly.

Newman stopped, turning to face her. "Forget the perfect clinical response, for once." He was smiling his charming smile. "Just answer the question."

"Okay." She thought for a moment. "A strong passion or emotion of displeasure, and usually, antagonism, excited by a sense of injury or insult." She paused. "How'd I do?"

He clapped lightly. "Brava. Except you left out a couple of things."

"Such as?"

"Anger is an active emotion. Unlike its opposite sentiment, calm, which is passive by definition." He crouched down to examine the grass. "Anger saps energy, raises blood pressure, cuts down the flow of oxygen to the brain, increases the heart rate, contracts the major muscle groups. Generally debilitates the body in a painfully short time."

Patricia nodded as he stood and moved on.

"But what about its serving as a release?" she asked. "Anger unexpressed can be even more harmful." She studied his manner carefully as he seemed to think about it.

"I disagree."

"Really?"

He smiled and laughed lightly. "It's not the suppression of the anger that's harmful, it's the fact that the root cause remains unchained when, most often, anger is checked at the door."

"You lost me," she said honestly.

He sat down on the grass, a spot where he could see through a parting in the trees in the woods. She sat down beside him.

"By your own definition," he began as he appeared to be looking at her, "anger is a response to a sense of injury or insult, right?"

"Go on."

"Well," he said while trying to see through the opening in the woods, "more often than not, when we give our anger voice, through its fury or hurt or pain, it begins to resolve the problem."

She nodded. "A necessary thing, yes?"

"Agreed. But why allow all that pain and anguish and physiological chaos?" He noticed a cat about to pounce on a pigeon.

Patricia followed his gaze.

He continued speaking as the cat jumped, hitting the pigeon in the wing. The injured bird managed to make it to a low branch of a nearby tree.

"Why allow all that shit to bubble up inside you, when you can avoid it by just addressing the problem up front?" He looked over at Edel and pointed at the pigeon. "Okay if I check that out?"

Edel nodded and redeployed his men, keeping the bulk of them between Newman and the woods.

Newman and Patricia, closely watched by the guards, moved toward the injured bird in the tree.

"If you address a problem through anger," Newman went on, "your judgment is impaired. You tend to do more or less than you really need to do." He stopped ten feet from the tree.

"Don't move," he said softly.

Patricia watched in fascination as Newman moved slowly, almost gracefully forward and reached up toward the injured bird. Everything about him was calm, cool, relaxed, unthreatening. The bird seemed to sense this and didn't resist as he gently lifted it off the branch.

He gently stroked the pigeon's feathers.

"Wing's broken," he said in a soft, soothing voice. He turned to Patricia. "When something is in pain, and no one gives a shit about it, that offends me, insults and injures me." He shrugged. "But I don't get angry, I deal with it."

Patricia watched as Newman grabbed the bird by its head, gave it a quick twist, snapping its neck more quickly than she could fathom. He dropped the instantly dead bird to the ground.

The guards flinched.

Edel nodded.

Patricia stood transfixed.

Newman started back toward the unit. A moment later, Patricia followed.

He continued speaking as if nothing had happened.

"No anger, no rage," he said coolly. "Just observation: I saw the bird attacked but not killed. Analysis: I saw that it was in pain and could not recover from its wounds. And finally, action: I put it out of its pain."

The cat walked up to them, rubbing against Newman's legs.

He looked down at it and smiled.

"I felt no more anger at that bird than he did," he said, nodding at the cat. "Of course . . ." He suddenly raised his foot and smashed it down on the cat's head, crushing its skull. Its body lay twitching on the grass for several moments before it became still.

Newman looked over at an ashen-faced Patricia.

"Of course," he said casually, "cats *really* piss me off!"

The conference room was stunned into silence. No one moved, talked, dared to break the silence which had followed the recounting of Newman's first trip outside the unit.

Tabbart was the first to recover.

"Well," he said slowly, "well."

Patricia tilted her head curiously. "If you'd like, we have the security video of the incident." She paused, reveling in Tabbart's evident discomfort. "I could arrange for you to view it."

Tabbart pretended to be making some notes. Unfortunately, he forgot to uncap his pen.

"No, uh, the reports will be, uh, sufficient." He suddenly realized his mistake and virtually tore the cap off. "Please continue."

Patricia smiled sweetly. "Of course, sir. After the incident, Newman calmly walked back to the unit. He was returned to his quarters without incident."

She turned to Clemente.

He bit his lower lip. "We did immediate and prolonged follow-up testing, as well as increased observation. We couldn't discover any change at all in his condition or demeanor from before the incident."

He opened a file. "In fact, his blood pressure, pulse, respiration, all his vitals actually lowered somewhat in the hours afterward."

Tabbart continued looking down at his nonexistent notes. "And we *have* excluded the possibility that the incident with the cat was an accident, have we?"

Patricia nodded. "As I said, sir, I'd be happy for you to look at the video and reach your own conclusion."

Clemente kicked her under the table.

"No, no. That won't be necessary," Tabbart said quickly. "What are your explanations for this rather *unusual* event?"

"We have arrived at four possible explanations," Jack said before Patricia could answer. He turned to the older neurologist. "Dr. Kapf?"

The old man was very still as he spoke.

"Examine the sequence of events." He paused. "A discussion of anger, its roots and outlets. The subject begins to lecture the therapist on anger avoidance, then, as if to illustrate a point, he puts the injured bird out of its evident misery. He doesn't appear to be angry about the unprovoked attack by the cat on the bird. Rather, he acts directly, ending the bird's suffering."

"And the cat?" Tabbart asked.

"The logical extension of his argument," the old man continued. "A second demonstration. Rather than express anger at the cat, he avenges the bird by killing the object he perceives as the proximal cause of the bird's death."

He took a sip of water.

"He sees himself as without anger or guilt. *He* is not the cause of either death. He is, instead, removed from both acts. When, in fact, his anger is actually directed at the cat for what he perceives as the cowardly attack, and the bird for allowing itself to be attacked."

"Dumb," Patricia said beneath her breath.

Clemente jumped in, trying to cover her obvious feelings of disdain.

"Dr. Kapf's opinion has not met with universal acceptance," he said. He turned to a youngish psychologist near the other end of the table. "Dr. Mont?"

The young man straightened his notes, then read from them without looking up.

"It is my belief, upon reviewing the tapes and transcripts, that the subject was attempting to express his contempt for the medical establishment, a group dedicated to healing, by causing these two deaths. First, he allows the cat to attack the pigeon so that he has a pretext for the acts. Then he callously kills the two animals in an overt attempt to shock us."

He closed his file, looking over at Tabbart.

"Next," Tabbart said, ignoring the crestfallen young man.

Jack smiled sympathetically at the young man.

"My personal view is, in effect, a combination of the first two espoused theories with one minor change."

A coughing fit interrupted him momentarily.

"I believe his action in killing the pigeon was genuine. Most of us agree on that. The cat, on the other hand, may well have become, to him, the symbol of *all of us* who are imprisoning and studying him. In therapy, he has referred to the government as a predator out of control. Much as the cat.

"Newman saw the imminent attack, but failed to act. For reasons as yet undetermined. His inaction caused the injury to the bird that compelled him to end its suffering. Then his unresolved, unacknowledged rage at us, at the government, at society in general which he views as universally hostile, boiled over. But his intellect recognized the threat to him if he reacted against us directly. So he selects the cat as our effigy."

He paused.

"Even the manner of the act, trodding it underfoot, not dirtying his hands so to speak, is evidence of his contempt for *all* authority." Another pause. "Now, imagine that mentality loose in society . . ." He allowed his voice to trail off.

Tabbart was making copious notes now. "Yet you still refuse to classify the subject as sociopathic?"

"It's as close as anything else but, no, he's not a sociopath. All of *his* actions, all of his thought processes, show that he has a keen awareness of future consequences, and more important, that he has been able to distinguish between those acts he can and those he cannot get away with. If he's a sociopath, he's demonstrated more self-control in those areas than I would imagine possible."

"Rubbish," Patricia said quietly.

Tabbart looked up. "Excuse me, Dr. Nellwyn?"

"I said rubbish."

"Might I assume, then, that yours is the fourth hypothesis?"

She nodded.

Tabbart looked at Clemente, then back to Patricia.

"You disagree with your superior?"

She took a deep breath. "With all due respect to Dr. Clemente, I do."

Tabbart, having gone into the meeting sure that he could get rid of this odious project easily, was in a tailspin. The opinions of men like Clemente and Kapf could not be ignored, young Mont's ridiculous ramblings notwithstanding. And the last thing he needed was some completely out-of-orbit hypothesis from this wild-eyed girl.

And yet, he was able to recognize that her relationship with Newman had been closer than any of the others'. Also, beneath the hubris of the efficient, Germanic administrator beat the heart of a psychiatric researcher who was beginning to become deeply intrigued by Brian Newman.

And disturbed.

"Go ahead, Dr. Nellwyn. But"—he gestured for effect—"please be brief."

Patricia looked at the faces in the room, all either skeptical or openly hostile. Including Clemente's. She took a deep breath, then began.

"I agree with Dr. Clemente," she said softly, "Newman is not a sociopath. A socio demonstrates an inadequately developed conscience, he feels no guilt for actions that harm others, but he does feel it for those actions that cause harm to himself. I think we can agree on at least that much."

She looked around the table. Even Tabbart nodded agreement.

"But," she continued, "as far as I can determine, Newman has never expressed any guilt at anything he's ever done. None."

She tossed a copy of Newman's background file into the center of the long table.

"Read it! From early childhood on, he decides to do a thing, and he does it, regardless of potential consequences. And there are definitely no indications of the man ever reacting out of rage at any time."

The skeptical looks were turning into overtly contemptuous ones.

"To the point, please, Doctor," Tabbart said as he checked his watch.

She ignored the tone in his voice. She pulled the file back to her, opened it, and began to read at random.

"His foster parents report that he seldom cries after the age of three. At the age of seven, he breaks a finger and calmly walks to his foster mother and tells her. At the age of eleven, he falls off his bicycle, causing a gash that requires thirteen stitches. He not only doesn't cry, but the E.R. physician notes that Newman clinically watches himself being stitched up, asking questions along the way."

"So he has a high pain threshold," Tabbart interrupted. "That doesn't mean—"

"At fifteen," she continued, interrupting the chief of staff, "he is found by a teacher, tampering with a stoplight. His explanation is that the Walk sign doesn't last long enough for him to safely cross the street. The teacher explains that his tampering could result in a horrible accident. He shrugs, saying only 'But at least I'll be able to get across.' And, unlike a sociopath, he never objects in any way to his punishment, which in this case was quite severe."

She paused.

"He simply did what he wanted to, when he wanted to, understanding and accepting the consequences of the act both to society and to himself."

Tabbart tried again. "I don't see . . ."

"Newman," Patricia continued, "I believe, is completely and wholly without a conscience. Based on the lack of any damage or malformations to his brain that we've been able to discover, my guess is that he was born that way. Unable to feel guilt, remorse, shame, fault, any of those things that are conscience-centered. Emotionally free to do anything he wants to do without ever feeling the slightest concern about it. Either for the consequences to others or himself."

Tabbart—the scientist—was intrigued, barely. "Cerebro-chemical imbalances have been ruled out, Dr. Nellwyn. Or hadn't you noticed?" He shook his head. "And for the type of condition you hypothesize, radical behavior changes leading to pseudo-sociopathy, one would expect to see a marked imbalance in the cerebrospinal fluid levels or pressures, no? Or at least some basic malformation of the choroid plexuses in one of the lateral ventricles of the brain."

Patricia nodded as a strange smile began to spread on her otherwise intense face.

"Not if the synapses are functioning in a wholly new way. Evolving into a state where they have no need for a neurotransmitter such as acetylcholine or . . ."

"Evolving?"

Patricia looked the little man right in the eye.

"Evolving," she said in a steady voice. "In my opinion—"

"The question at hand, Doctor," Tabbart interrupted, "involved the pigeon and the cat."

Patricia remained unfazed by the change in the chief's tone.

"Exactly my point. With apologies to Dr. Clemente, Dr. Kapf, and Dr. Mont, I don't think Newman had any deep-seated resentments or ulterior motivations. I think he killed the pigeon in a bald-faced attempt to curry favor with us, perhaps to gain some advantage by gaining our respect. Demonstrate his kindness in eliminating the animal's suffering."

"What about the cat?" Clemente interrupted for the first time.

She turned to face her friend and colleague. "Newman gave us the answer. He told us that day."

"You mean . . ."

She nodded. "Cats really piss him off. His exact words. And being a man without a conscience, he acted to remove the source of his irritation."

The table exploded in urgent voices.

Tabbart tapped the table for order but was ignored. Finally, Clemente got the others' attention.

"If you're right, why has he allowed us to keep him a virtual prisoner for three months without incident? Why not wildly strike out at us as he allegedly did to the Russians? Surely, we piss him off more than cats?"

All eyes turned to Patricia.

She thought for a long time before answering. Not about the answer, but about whether or not they would believe it.

She began very slowly.

"We agree he's not a sociopath, one of the traits of which is a failure to learn from past mistakes." Hearing no objections, she went on. "His IQ is well above genius. Higher in fact than anyone's at this table. He has no conscience, but he does have an almost infinite ability to learn.

"Note the escape attempts in Russia, each more successful than the previous. Stopped only by placing him in maximum isolation and threatening him with deadly force whenever they opened the door." She paused for effect. "Just as we've done here."

She gathered her papers and closed her file.

"He knew he could kill the cat without consequence to his inevitable plans. So, since he wanted to, he did."

"And what, pray tell," Tabbart said sarcastically, "are his inevitable plans?"

Patricia took a deep breath. "I think that's clear." She looked around the table for support that wasn't there. "He's learned from his past mistakes, and he's learning more every day. From us, about us. And one day, he will try to escape again. And when he does, he will do whatever he has to, without the slightest thought or compunction, in order to make the attempt successful."

The table was quiet, but she knew that wouldn't last long. Her only question was who would voice the obvious thought.

Tabbart cleared his throat.

"Dr. Nellwyn, do you believe that the subject is some kind of *Übermensch?* Some form of miraculously endowed deviant who can only be stopped by a silver bullet or stake through his heart?"

"No." Her voice was soft but firm. "He's no deviant."

"Then, please, enlighten us? What is he, in your expert opinion?"

It was now or never.

"It is indisputable," she began slowly, "that man is in a constant state of evolution. It is a given by many branches of anthropological science that our little fingers and little toes are getting smaller with every generation. It is equally accepted that they'll disappear within a thousand years or so."

"Do we really need—"

Clemente interrupted Tabbart. "Go on," he said in an intense voice.

"So why not our brains as well? Perhaps evolving in a slower, less obvious, but more complex way. Why can't they be evolving as well?"

She paused, waiting for the inevitable interruption.

It didn't come.

"Man has always been defined by the size and functions of his brain. From *Australopithecus robustus* with a brain 450 to 700 cubic centimeters in volume, to *Homo erectus* with its brain of 700 to 1,100cc. Finally, to modern man, *Homo sapiens,* literally 'Wise Man,' due to his brain of between 1,100 and 1,500cc."

"But," Kapf interrupted, "Newman's brain is well within that range—1,435cc, I believe."

Patricia shrugged. "We've all seen the work of Dan Dennett at the Center for Cognitive Studies at Tufts University; read Jared Diamond's *Three Chimpanzees.*" She paused, and when she spoke again, it was in a soft, slightly unsure tone. "All I'm doing is carrying their work to the next logical conclusion."

"My God," Tabbart said in genuine alarm. "You're not suggesting—"

Patricia cut him off. "What if the current evolution is neurological? Taking place *within* our brains? Not an expansion of the tissues, but a reworking of its very essence!"

Kapf stared at her. "Do you realize what you are saying?" His voice was quiet and shaky. "Man has remained essentially unchanged for well over 300,000 years."

She nodded slowly, ignoring the looks from around the table.

"*Australopithecus robustus* lived for 200,000 years before the first *Homo erectus* showed up. *Erectus* was unchallenged for another 200,000. Then *Homo sapiens* arrived on the scene. We've had longer runs than either of them. We're due." She paused. "Overdue, actually."

Shouts of disbelief, anger, and confusion mixed with the sound of Tabbart hammering on the table for order. Only Clemente, Kapf, and Patricia remained quiet, looking into each other's eyes deeply.

The noise subsided.

"Dr. Nellwyn," Tabbart spit out, "I strongly advise you not to express those absurd, imbecilic, unscientific . . ." He seemed to want to find yet another word to beat her down with. Failing that, he shook his head.

"This meeting is over. I will meet individually with those of you I need, prior to tomorrow's review." He stood up. "Dr. Nellwyn?"

She looked over at him.

"Dr. Nellwyn, if you mention any of these completely crazed notions of yours outside of this room, I will personally see to it that you are not only severed from this institution, but will never work in the mental health field again." He followed the group toward the door. "I recommend that you immediately reenter therapy and examine exactly what your motivations are. For that reason, you are hereby granted an immediate, indefinite leave of absence." He stood in the doorway. "A new man indeed!" He stormed out.

Patricia had closed her eyes as the anger, insult, and humiliation had been heaped on her by her departing colleagues. When she opened them again, the room was empty, except for Jack Clemente and Dr. Kapf.

"You really believe that, don't you?" Clemente said.

She nodded sadly. "Yes."

"Why? It's me—Jack. Just tell me simply and without ego. Why?"

She looked into his eyes and glimpsed—something. Disappointment in her, maybe.

"We're in the business," she said with a cry in her voice, "of defining the indefinable. Explaining the mysteries and perplexities of thoughts, emotions, actions, in an accepted way. Using an accepted vocabulary." She turned to him, reaching out, taking his hand in hers. "*You* said Newman's something we've never seen before. Something that defies any conventional explanation."

"A previously undiagnosed mental disorder."

"Why?" She stood up and began pacing. "Even Freud said sometimes a cigar is just a cigar! Why ignore an obvious possibility just because it comes from left field? Sometimes a cigar is just a cigar and sometimes something new is something new!"

Jack looked at her, stood, shaking his head sadly.

"I don't know," he said so softly she had to strain to hear him. He coughed briefly and seemed to slump. "I have to think about it." He turned and slowly walked from the room.

"Dr. Nellwyn?"

She whirled around, having forgotten that Kapf was still in the room.

"What do you want now?" she asked in a defeated voice. *Hell,* she thought, *if Jack won't believe me . . .*

"Dr. Nellwyn," the old man said in a reasonable voice, "I do not believe your theory is correct."

"Great," she spat out.

"However"—he walked over, putting his hand on her shoulder—"I may be wrong."

"What?"

"The sun does not circle a flat earth. Today's scientific fact is often tomorrow's unbelievably preposterous history." He patted her on the shoulder. "Man is an evolving creature. One day, the next age will begin. We will turn around to see an unfamiliar face or form and we will shrink back from it in abject fear. As we did today."

He gathered his files and started for the door. Halfway there, he stopped, turning back to her.

"It is my hope—no, it is my *prayer*—that this unfamiliar face or form will not be our Mr. Newman. A future of *Homo sapiens* confronted with *Homo crudelis* is a dark future indeed." He laughed. "At least for those of us *Homo sapiens. Gute Nacht*, Madame Doctor."

Patricia watched his retreating form, completely taken up by his imagery, her mind racing to comprehend the basic truth of the old man's words. And struggling to comprehend that one, most basic truth that he had voiced.

Homo sapiens against *Homo crudelis.*

Wise Man in an inevitably losing struggle against his predestined replacement.

Homo crudelis. Coldhearted Man. Free of all the restraints on behavior that we take for granted today. A hunter-killer with the intellect of modern man. Capable of anything and everything.

Kapf is right, she thought as she walked out of the conference room. *There is only one possible outcome.*

Ⅰn the unit, Edel was also preparing for the next day's review.

"So," he said to his senior supervisors, "where does all this planning leave us? Eh?"

One of his lieutenants sipped some coffee.

"The review board is scheduled to arrive at 0800," the man began. "That means the earliest they would want to see him, if Dr. Clemente's information is correct, would be 1030 to 1100."

Another man chimed in. "When he believes they are within a half hour of the time, Dr. Clemente will signal us at the nurse's station. We will then commence the movement."

Edel nodded. "I will personally escort the patient in the elevator."

He paused as he wiped his eyes. "I want two men in the antechamber, three by the nurse's station for emergency, and five on the office floor."

They all nodded.

"Relax, Konrad," the first lieutenant said. "We've taken care of everything. Relax. Get some sleep."

Edel looked at the men and smiled. *"Ja."*

He stood, stretched, and headed for the elevator. Once inside, he hesitated before pushing the button. He should go home, he was bone-tired. The increased security since the trip outside had been a strain on Edel and his staff. Now, with this dog and pony show tomorrow . . .

He made up his mind. Home and sleep would have to wait. He pressed the button for the subbasement.

He waved the guards back to their seats as he walked over to the monitor. He saw Newman sitting on the couch, watching a movie. He picked up a microphone.

"Mr. Newman, it is Konrad Edel, sir."

Newman looked up at the camera. "How are you, Herr Edel?"

"I am very well, sir. I was wondering, since you are still up, would you like to talk for a time?"

Newman smiled. "That would be nice."

A few minutes later, the door was closed and locked behind the security chief.

He walked over and shook Newman's hand.

"I apologize for not coming by lately. Things have been most busy."

Newman laughed lightly. "And I apologize if I've caused you any extra work."

Edel waived it away. "It is not you, it is the bureaucrats and doctors."

"They *can* be difficult."

"Indeed."

A silence settled over them for a moment.

"So, how do things go with you?" Edel asked. "Are you wanting for anything?"

They sat down next to each other on the couch. The picture of two old friends having a pleasant visit.

"They see to it that things go very much the same with me," Newman said. "And thanks to your kindness, I lack for nothing that matters." He gestured at a Bible that sat on the coffee table.

"It was nothing." Edel picked up the Bible, turning to the place marked by the thin red ribbon. "Isaiah?"

Newman recited the quotation easily.

"Comfort, comfort my people, says your God. Speak tenderly to Jerusalem and cry to her that her warfare is ended, that her iniquity is pardoned, that she has received from the Lord's hand double for all her sins."

Edel nodded gravely. "You despair of your government's wrath?"

"I do."

Edel turned a few pages. "You mustn't," he said as he searched for the passage. "You must put yourself in God's loving hands and count on his kindness, forgiveness, and everlasting love."

Newman seemed to be listening intently.

"I understand that, intellectually," he began in a hesitant voice, "but there is so much to forgive." A long pause during which his breathing quickened. "Perhaps even more than for God's taste," he said as he looked down.

Edel put his arm around the seemingly desolate man as he continued to turn pages.

"Have faith, Brian." He suddenly brightened, handing the Bible to Newman. "From verse sixteen."

Newman scanned down the page, then began to read.

"Turn thou to me, and be gracious to me; for I am lonely and afflicted. Relieve the troubles of my heart, and bring me out of my distresses. Consider my affliction and my trouble, and forgive all my sins."

A tear hung on the corner of his eye as he finished.

"Thank you," he said in a choked voice.

For the next forty-five minutes they read the Bible, exchanged their interpretations, and prayed together. Finally, Edel stood to leave.

"Take heart, Brian," the security chief said as Newman wiped his eyes. "The Lord is watching over you and the Lord *will* protect you."

"Amen," Newman said, and as the door opened, quickly calculated his options.

The door is open, only Edel and the two guards beyond . . . fifteen seconds tops.

Get Edel's elevator key, open the doors, push the button, doors close, elevator rises to the desired floor . . . forty-five seconds.

Three to five guards, confused, still reacting to my initial move. With luck, and a favorable break or two . . . thirty seconds.

One minute, thirty seconds from the quarters door to the front door of the unit. One minute, thirty seconds and six to eight armed individuals. Not counting night nurses or orderlies that might be foolish enough to interfere.

Probability of success . . . fifty-fifty.

Newman took a step toward Edel. "Good night, my friend."

Edel turned and smiled, unaware of how close he had come to testing the existence of Heaven.

"Good night, Brian. I will continue praying for your release."

And the door was closed and locked moments after he left.

Newman turned and walked into the bathroom. He pointed at the toilet, waiting for the camera and microphones to be turned off. When he was sure, he put the lid down and stepped onto it. Humming to himself, he continued his work of the last three months, fingers reaching, probing, pulling around the circulation fan immediately above.

For no longer than two minutes at a time, three or four times a day, he would work slowly, carefully. Because where there was a fan, reasonably, there was an air duct. Maybe *the* air duct, the one that supplied the full quarters.

And where there was a duct, there was a possibility of freedom.

When he felt sufficient time had elapsed, he quickly returned things to how they'd been, flushed the toilet, washed his hands, and walked back out to the living room.

The psychiatric social worker on duty upstairs pushed the camera in closer as Newman sat down on the couch and opened the Bible. He turned up the gain on the ambient microphones to hear what Newman seemed to be reciting.

"Consider how many are my foes, and with what violent hatred they hate me," he recited.

"Oh guard my life, and deliver me."

It was well after one when Newman finally retired for the night. The unit went on "late observation" status while a maintenance crew began its nightly regime of cleaning and polishing. Things settled into their usual, quiet, overnight rhythms.

On the three-block stretch of the Sigersonstrasse on the edge of Munich, known locally as the Devil's Playground, the exact opposite was happening.

It was noise, neon, cars, and bodies. The garish lights gave everything a reddish blue tinge. The hard-driving rock music, eight different songs blaring from twenty or so speakers at the same time, assaulted the passing bodies as well as their ears.

And the smell of sex was everywhere.

The cars moved slowly through the narrow streets, forced by the congestion and the gawking to a crawl. Their radios and exhaust fumes added their bits to the cacophony and the madness.

It would all continue until just before dawn.

There were three types of visitors to the Devil's Playground, and each had their unofficially assigned parts of the night.

The tourists, eager to see the decadence, the excitement, the wickedness, usually arrived just after eight. Almost always staying in their cars, they would drive up and down the Playground, pointing and leering, living vicariously off the sights, sounds, and imagined debauchery of the place. But they were mostly gone by midnight.

Then the users arrived.

The first taxis would begin arriving between midnight and 1:00 A.M. Their passengers would be dropped off either at the edges of the Playground or at the doors to the "private clubs." They would stay for a few minutes or hours, always returning to the waiting cabs, ready to whisk them away to the clean world. Secretly reliving their night of sinfulness over and over, until they would again return.

But it was after three in the morning, in those few hours before sunlight, that the "important clientele" would arrive.

The stretch silver or black limousines patiently waited their turns to pull up to the back doors of the private clubs. The passengers, wealthy and powerful men, sought twisted, evil pleasures, for which they would pay handsomely.

It was largely to these last visitors of the night that the Devil's Playground was dedicated. Anything they wanted, anything they could imagine, legalities and the church be damned, was provided. If they paid the price, of course.

And they always did.

The man stood across the street from the start of the Playground, smoking a cigarette that was more butt than anything else. He looked out at the chaos, the bedlam, felt the sounds, and sniffed the gentle scent of coitus floating around, mingling with the acrid fumes.

He took a deep drag of his cigarette, the glowing end drawing back to his fingers, burning them, adding the smell of charred flesh to the others of the night.

But he didn't move.

He took another drag and the butt extinguished itself against his fingers. He casually threw the remnants away, then pulled out and lit another. Raising his collar against the fall mist, and possible identification, he crossed the street.

Most of the tourists were gone. The street, still backed up but thinning quickly, was adjusting, pausing, waiting for the next wave to begin. The girls, still relatively fresh and energized, called out to him in German as he passed.

"Hey, baby!"

"I got what you want, big man!"

"Anything, sweetie, for you!"

"I got health certificates. We have good time, little boy!"

He ignored them all: the girls in the short skirts that didn't cover the spread legs; the see-through or open blouses; the touches and gropes which were all part of the journey down Sigerson.

He crossed the street in the middle, ignoring the young, preteen boys in their skintight jeans and mesh tank tops. The older boys in their leathers, the he/shes, the transvestites, the pathetically aged twenty-year-olds lingering in the hotel doorways.

The clubs started on the next block.

The music wasn't quite as loud there. The whores on the street seemed cleaner and less aggressive. Instead, doormen urged him in to see "the best show in the city," or "the show that goes so far I cannot even tell you about it!" or "We request you inform the management if you have a heart condition! Our show is considered dangerous to any that do!"

The man walked past them all, not even giving them a sideways glance. He crossed to the final block of the Playground.

Here, the sidewalks were almost deserted. The doormen, dressed in full livery, nodded or doffed their caps as he passed. It was cleaner, quieter, and somehow more foreboding.

He stopped at number 37, climbed the five steps as the doorman wordlessly opened the door for him.

The lobby was elegantly and richly furnished. Fine parquet flooring was covered by a thick Isfahan carpet in deep black and gold. Damask covered the walls, also in a gold and black pattern. The deep red French Provincial couch with its mahogany borders fit perfectly with the mahogany counter at the far end.

He walked up to the conservatively dressed, older man behind the counter.

"I am Ghislain. How may I help you, please?" the counterman said in German.

The man handed across a membership card.

Ghislain pulled out a laptop computer and punched in the code. A moment later, he nodded as he handed back the card.

Now he spoke in English.

"You are most welcome here, sir. May I take your coat?"

The man handed across his topcoat and scarf.

Ghislain disappeared into a back room with them, returning a minute later with a pale blue card.

"May I take your order, sir?"

The man reached out, took the card, and began to run his finger down it. He stopped, pointing out several of the items listed. He handed back the card.

Ghislain nodded and smiled a professional smile.

"Very discerning, sir. In the lyceum, sir?"

"Not tonight," the man said softly.

"Perhaps, then, the salons?"

The man nodded.

Ghislain placed the card in a canister, which he dropped into a tube. He pressed a button, causing a door to the left of the counter to open noiselessly.

As the man started for the door, Ghislain called after him.

"It is nice to have you with us again, sir. It has been too long."

The man closed the door behind him.

Upstairs, above the club, the supervisor pulled the tube from the pneumatic conveyance. She opened it, pulling out the pale blue card. She turned to the other women sitting in the room.

"Blonde, thirty-five to forty, professional type, middle-class, arrogant, shy, proper, English-speaking." She looked over the women. "Isa. Salon 24."

A short blond woman wearing only bikini panties and a demi-bra stood up, then walked over to a clothes rack and a bureau. The supervisor handed her the blue card as the girl took off her lingerie, replacing them with black lacy versions of the same.

She read the card, then selected a conservative, ankle-length skirt and utilitarian sports blouse. She pulled her hair straight back, tying it with a piece of red yarn. The supervisor handed her a small cameo to put over the top button of her blouse as she headed out the door.

Two minutes later, standing outside the door to salon 24, she took a deep breath, then knocked.

"Come in," a deep voice said.

She smiled simply.

"Hello, you asked to see me." Her voice was friendly but business-like.

"I"—the man kept his back to her—"I think I need some help, Doctor."

Isa walked over to a desk and pulled out a pad and pen. She walked over and sat down on a divan.

"Tell me all about it," she said professionally.

The man leaned on a dresser, still with his back to her.

"I get these feelings, urges." His voice was growing hoarse. "Sometimes I think I'm going to explode if I don't . . ."

Isa smiled and patted the divan beside her.

"Why don't you come and sit down beside me? We will talk about it."

The man slowly turned, walking over to her. He hesitated, but she smiled encouragingly. He sat down.

Isa quickly evaluated the man. He was strong, very fit, but certainly over fifty, with dark circles under his eyes. She decided how far she would go with him, then continued.

"How may I help you?" she said as she pretended to take notes.

"I feel things," the man said softly, "hear things. Things that make me want to do . . . things."

Isa felt him move closer to her, his leg brushing against hers. She moved a little bit away.

"What kind of things is it that these feelings make you want to do?"

"Ugly things," he said as he pressed up against her again. "Horribly ugly things. Things I know I can get away with that others can't." He put his hand on her leg, slowly rubbing it while he began to pull up her skirt.

Isa squirmed uncomfortably.

"Please, sir. This is not appropriate behavior."

He reached up and began fondling her breast.

She tried to pull away from him, but he forced her back, powerful callused hands pinning her to the divan as he continued.

"I can do anything!" he muttered hoarsely. "Anything! The rules don't apply to me!" He tore open her blouse.

She tried to push him off her, but received the back of his hand for her troubles.

"You little bitch!"

He pulled her from the divan and threw her to the thickly carpeted floor. Pulling her skirt up to her waist, he roughly groped her between her legs while savagely biting at her breasts. He suddenly straightened, his expression animalistic, and tore her clothes off, quickly reducing them to rags.

Isa, her face a picture of fear, measured the man, hoping she wouldn't have to give the emergency signal to the bodyguard outside the door.

"Please stop," she begged. "Don't! Why me?" She allowed tears to fill her eyes while she continued to measure the man's responses.

He straightened up again.

"Shut up, bitch! Why not you? I can do anything, have anything! You can't stop me! No one can!" He bent down again, roughly grabbing her legs and lifting them around his shoulders.

"You will do whatever I tell you to do, won't you?" His voice was thick with violence as he entered her.

"I will do whatever you want," Isa groaned out.

As his eyes glazed over, as he gasped for breath, he spoke again. This time in a vicious whisper.

"Then . . . call me . . . Newman."

"Now remember," Clemente said to the young man as they rode down in the elevator, "he'll try and test you early. There's bound to be some shock, anger, whatever, at Dr. Nellwyn's replacement. Address that first."

Dr. Mont nodded eagerly. "I have taken over patients before. I know what to expect."

Clemente shook his head. "That's exactly my point. This is not a usual patient. Don't expect. Don't anticipate. Just stay relaxed and open to anything." The doors of the elevator opened on the antechamber. "Just use today as a feeling-out session. Take it easy."

"As you say, Doctor," Mont said happily.

Mont *was* happy. This was his moment! His chance to show the senior staff at the Institute just how good he really was, that he deserved advancement and reward.

And on a deeper level, Mont saw this as an opportunity to prove his theory of the case. After all, these senior people were so out of touch with today's realities that they wouldn't recognize establishment resentment if it bit them on their spreading asses. Mont had, after all, already selected the title of the paper he would write after it was all over. As he stood to the side, waiting for the door to be opened, he whispered it to himself: "The proof of the fallacy of governmental brainwashing to improve the performance of the military."

"Did you say something, Mont?" Clemente asked. "Are you ready?"

"Uh, no, sir. Yes, sir," he stammered out.

Clemente walked over and held the younger man by the shoulder.

"Remember, we'll be monitoring everything. If anything happens, we'll be right in. If you think you're in trouble, just say the code word, and we'll be there."

Mont nodded with an amused expression on his face. This was just one more overreaction by the fogies.

"Yes, sir," he said.

Clemente looked doubtful. "Say it."

"What?"

"The code word. Say it. Use it in a phrase like you would around him. In some way that he wouldn't notice."

Mont was becoming bored with all this melodrama, but Clemente was head of the department.

"I would say something like, 'I was wondering if you ever had a chemical dependency problem.' How's that?"

"Fine." Clemente clapped him on the back as he moved off, behind the guards. "You'll be fine."

But somehow he didn't sound convinced.

Clemente walked out of the antechamber, through a narrow corridor, over to the control room, where Dr. Kapf was observing Newman through the monitor.

"You talked to him?" Kapf asked without looking up.

"He'll do fine."

Kapf looked up doubtfully. "He is a young man in a hurry. A most dangerous animal under any circumstances, let alone . . ." He nodded at Newman in the monitor.

Newman, as usual, stood with his back to the door, at the entrance to his bedroom. When he heard the door close and lock, he turned around, smiling. The smile quickly vanished.

"Who are you?" His voice was flat, atonal, his expression equally unrevealing.

Mont smiled and held out his hand. "My name is Dr. Pierre Mont. I will be taking over for Dr. Nellwyn for a time."

Newman didn't move. "Why?"

Mont lowered his hand but expanded the smile. "I believe she is experiencing something of a family situation."

Newman remained immobile. "Why?"

Mont was pleased. Newman's reactions were textbook expected. So, he responded with the textbook solution.

"I am sure she will return as soon as she can. In the meantime, she thought I might be able to substitute for her as it were."

"As it were," Newman parroted.

In the control room, Clemente was talking to himself. "Easy, play it easy."

"He should be less vague," Kapf said as they both stared at the two men in the patient's quarters.

Mont gestured at the chair. "May I sit down?"

Newman studied the young man.

No white lab coat, but a pale blue shirt with a white collar, and paisley tie. His hair was longish but stylishly cut. He had shaved less than an hour before coming in. And Newman could smell the man's smugness.

Harmless yuppie larva, Newman tagged him. But that didn't answer the more pressing question.

Why had they substituted him for Nellwyn and what did it mean for his plans?

Newman nodded, taking a seat on the far end of the couch as Mont settled himself in the chair.

"This is a most comfortable chair," Mont said pleasantly. "Do you like it?"

"Do you?"

Mont smiled. "Very much." He understood that there would be a few minutes of awkwardness. "Is there anything you would like to know about me? I thought we might use today's session to get to know each other."

"There is."

Mont nodded sincerely. "You may ask me anything, Mr. Newman."

"How much do you weigh?"

Mont was genuinely thrown, but he quickly recovered. "A most interesting question. Might I ask why you asked it?"

Newman shrugged and leaned back on the couch. "You said I could ask you anything."

Mont laughed a practiced, casual laugh. "I did indeed." He laughed. "I weigh approximately seventy-five kilos."

Newman thought about it.

"A hundred sixty-five pounds," he said quietly.

"More or less. And yourself?" Mont could feel the edges of a dialogue beginning.

"More" was Newman's atonal reply. He stared up at the ceiling. "What's your IQ?"

Standard attempt to take control of the conversation, Mont thought.

"I'm sure I don't know," he parried. "What's yours?"

"More."

In the control room, Kapf turned to Clemente. "If he challenges him now, it could mean disaster."

"He won't," Clemente said without conviction. "He'll just ignore it. He wouldn't give up his leverage."

Mont decided to take a different tack.

"If I were to concede to you your physical and intellectual superiority over myself, might we move on to another area?"

It seemed to work. Newman looked down and over at him. He smiled a genuine smile.

"Why not?" he said in a friendly, if still cautious, voice.

"Very good." Mont reached up and loosened his tie. "I hate these things," he said casually. He looked up at the camera conspiratorially. "But the senior staff around here, they insist."

"Really?"

Mont nodded. "They have a very strict dress code. It's a damned inconvenience. They control how we dress, how we act, even when we're not at the Institute or on Institute business."

Newman leaned forward slightly. "That doesn't seem right."

"No?" Mont could feel that they were close, very close, to establishing a deep rapport.

"I mean," Newman continued, "you're an individual, right? You have a right to express yourself in any way you see fit, right?"

"Right," Mont said, suppressing the urge to point up at the camera and yell "I told you so."

Newman slid down the couch until he was within a foot of the young doctor.

"On the other hand," Newman said softly, "you do represent them. To patients, to the public, you should exude an image of confidence, professionalism, trust." He paused. "Don't you think the people who sign your paycheck have the right to that?"

It wasn't the answer Mont had expected, but it was an answer. He carefully chose his next words.

"So, you believe in authority figures?"

Newman smiled. "May I confide in you, Pierre?" He leaned forward. "You don't mind if I call you Pierre, do you?"

"Not at all," said the excited young man.

Newman nodded and continued in a conversational tone.

"Pierre." He put his arm around him. "You asked me why I wanted to know your weight. Well, I'll tell you." He hesitated. "You see"—he edged closer—"I wanted to know exactly how hard it was going to be to throw your lifeless body at the guards as they come rushing in, a minute or so from now." He smiled a pleasant smile.

"What?" Mont didn't, couldn't, react fast enough.

Newman quickly dug his thumb deeply into the young man's neck as he raised his open, stiffened palm in front of the man's face. He carefully kept Mont's body between himself and the camera.

In the control room, they raised the gain on the microphones to try and hear what Newman seemed to be whispering to Mont.

"If you move," Newman said quietly and without any rancor, "you'll die. I promise it will be painless but I'm afraid it will be permanent. If you believe me, close both your eyes for one second."

Mont, in more pain than he imagined one thumb could cause, squinted both eyes closed, then reopened them. He stared at the rock-solid, unmoving palm that threatened to break his nose and drive the bone fragments into his brain.

"Good," Newman said in almost an amused tone. "Now, I'm sure they gave you some code word or phrase, in case you got in trouble?" His tone sounded genuinely curious.

Both eyes squeezed closed again.

"Now I want you to whisper it to me, very softly."

In the control booth, Clemente and Kapf bent low over the monitor.

"What is going on?" Kapf said to no one in particular.

At that moment, Newman leaned back a bit and smiled up at the camera.

"Chemical" was all he said.

Three minutes later, the emergency security entry team stood poised in front of the closed locked door to Newman's quarters.

After checking the arrangements, Edel returned to the control room.

"Where is he now?" he asked.

"Still on the couch," one of his men replied.

Edel nodded, walking over to Clemente and Kapf, who were huddled together.

"Gentlemen," Edel began slowly, "we need to make some most immediate decisions."

Clemente looked up at him. "What do you suggest?"

Edel took a deep breath. "We prepared for this situation. Planned and drilled. If it is your desire, my men will end this standoff in short order."

Kapf was studying the man carefully. "But that wouldn't be your first choice." He said it as a statement.

"No," the security chief replied. "It would not."

"Go ahead," Clemente urged.

"He has killed no one. Taken no defensive actions whatever. He has merely immobilized Dr. Mont and, in effect, asked to talk." He paused. "I believe we should."

Kapf nodded. "We agree. He could easily have killed Mont at any time. But, the problem remains, he will not respond to any of our calls over the speaker."

Edel shook his head and chuckled. "Nor, sir, would I in his position."

Clemente checked his watch. "Chief Edel, I agree with you that this may all be less than it appears. God knows I've wanted to kill Mont on more than one occasion. The man can be insufferable." His anger at Mont's amateurish approach was palpable.

"But," he continued, "I'm capable of controlling that impulse. Can we say the same for Mr. Newman?"

"If Newman wanted the doctor dead," Edel said flatly, "the doctor would now be dead." He paused. "He is a soldier, not the type who takes hostages for gain."

"What do you call Mont, then?"

Edel studied the monitor. "An attention-getter."

Kapf interrupted them. "Gentlemen, forgive me, but if this goes on much longer, I'm afraid our options will be taken away. There is time for analysis later." He looked at the unmoving figures on the monitor. "Now, we must act, in some way." He checked the monitor. "If we do not, this could all end up nothing but a waste, a tragedy."

Edel's expression became firm. "We must not allow that to happen."

Kapf smiled. "You are going in there, no?"

"Yes."

Clemente shook his head. "If anyone goes, it should be me or Kapf. We're the ones trained to deal with this kind of personality."

Kapf looked at Clemente quizzically. "There may never have been this type of personality before. Who can say who is trained to deal with it?"

Two minutes later, the door opened just enough for one man to enter, and was quickly slammed behind him.

Newman kept Mont between himself and the door.

"Who is that?"

"It is me, Brian. Konrad Edel."

"Welcome."

Edel remained just inside the door. He could see Mont tremble, could smell his fear. From Newman, however, there was nothing but a casual politeness.

"We have a difficulty here, Brian."

"Actually," Newman said, "it's this asshole who has the difficulty."

"Can you tell me what the problem is? Perhaps, together, we can resolve it." He stepped another two paces into the room.

"Well," Newman said pleasantly, "you were in the groups, GSG-9, right?"

"Yes."

"And when you were on assignment, and suddenly they changed your control officer on you, without any logical explanation, what would you have thought?"

"That I was being betrayed. Perhaps set up to be killed."

"Right the first time."

Newman stood up, dragging Mont to his feet at the same time. "Now, this morning I get up, have breakfast and all, then this jerk shows up with some specious explanations about his taking over for Nellwyn, who supposedly has some kind of nebulous personal problems." He paused. "Now I ask you, what would you do?" His voice was almost amused.

Edel thought it over. "Most likely what you have done."

Newman briefly bowed his head to the security chief. "So, here we are," he said.

Edel looked up at the camera. "Dr. Clemente?"

"Yes." Clemente's voice echoed through the very still room.

"Would you please tell Mr. Newman the true reason behind Dr. Nellwyn's replacement?" There was a long silence. "Dr. Clemente?"

"Yes."

This time, Edel sounded angry. "Do not take the time to fabricate another story. He will see through it as well." He looked over at Newman. "This man is owed the truth."

"She," the hesitant voice began after a moment, "she has expressed an opinion which has engendered some controversy."

Newman looked at Edel skeptically. "You see what I mean? I'm supposed to trust my survival to these people?"

Edel was nodding without realizing it. "The truth, Dr. Clemente!"

Kapf's voice came over the speaker. "This is Otto Kapf."

"Nice to talk to you, Dr. Kapf," Newman said pleasantly as he dug his thumb deeper into Mont's neck.

"Dr. Nellwyn advanced an opinion on your case that was met with resistance. As a result, Dr. Tabbart has removed her from your case."

"Oh." Newman released Mont, who collapsed to the floor. Then he looked up at the camera. "Now, was that so difficult?"

Edel walked over and helped the young man up. He half carried him to the door, which was quickly opened. Mont was pulled out of the room and the door relocked.

Edel turned back to Newman, who had sat down on the couch, turning on the television.

He sat down next to him.

"Is Dr. Nellwyn really so important to you?" Edel said sociably.

"Not really."

"I didn't think so." He paused. "So why all this theater?"

Newman seemed interested in the program. "Would you believe me if I said it was about fair play and mutual respect?"

"No," the security chief chuckled. "I would not."

Newman turned to him and smiled. "I knew there was a reason I liked you." He turned back to the program.

"So?"

"So," Newman said as he flipped through the channels, "what do you think it was about?"

"Control."

Newman slowly turned to him. "Damn straight."

Edel stood up, patting Newman on the shoulder. "Don't do it again, okay?"

Newman watched as he walked to the door. "No surprises from them, none from me."

The door opened, but Edel hesitated. "This afternoon, when you are brought up to the conference room, you will behave?"

Newman laughed a deep hearty laugh. "You really think they'll do that now?"

Edel nodded. "I think they are as embarrassed by Dr. Mont's behavior as I am by yours."

Newman hesitated, then stood up, walking over to the open door. The guards took careful aim at his chest and head.

"I'm sorry if I let you down," he said in a sad voice.

"If thou, O Lord, shouldst mark iniquities, Lord, who could stand?" Edel recited.

Newman finished the quotation. "But there is forgiveness with thee, that thou mayest be feared." He smiled naturally, with charm. "Psalm 130, verses three and four." He paused. "No trouble with the move. You have my word on that."

Edel smiled, clapped him on the shoulder, and walked through the door. "Try and get some rest."

The door was slammed and locked.

Two hours later, Beck, accompanied by five civilians, was met at the front entrance of the Institute by Tabbart and Clemente.

While Tabbart glad-handed the review board, Clemente took Beck aside.

Clemente looked down as they shook hands. "Have you hurt yourself, General?"

Beck held up the hand that had Band-Aids on two fingertips. "An accident," he said. "Minor burn unscrewing a light."

Clemente nodded without paying attention. "I see," he said vaguely. "Do we have the time to talk?"

One glance at Clemente's concerned expression and Beck nodded. "I'll make time."

As they walked toward the unit, Clemente brought Beck up to date about the late night conference, the scene that morning with Newman and Mont, everything.

When he finished, just outside the unit, Clemente stopped. "The question now, General, is where do we go from here?"

Beck seemed distracted. "Excuse me?"

"I was saying," Clemente began again, "the problem is what to do now. Have we damaged our relationship with Mr. Newman beyond repair? If not, how do we go about treating a man who has demonstrated so much animosity toward us? Not to mention the risk factor."

Beck suddenly seemed to hear him. "I thought we went through all that before we started?"

"And the staff was suitably warned." Clemente paused, looking around to make sure they weren't overheard. "But that was all in the abstract. We now are faced with reality. Between the incident with the cat and now Dr. Mont, well . . ."

"You're afraid you won't be able to get the staff to work with him?"

Clemente shrugged. "They'll do their jobs, I suppose. But there will always be an air about them. A vibration of fear that I'm sure Newman will pick up on." He paused. "It may be too much to overcome. Not to mention his distrust of us."

Beck looked at the older man. "What are you saying?"

Clemente took a deep breath. "Perhaps it would be better for all concerned if Newman were transferred to another facility." He laughed bitterly. "I'm sure you'll get no argument from Tabbart."

"Screw Tabbart," Beck spit out. "I'm thinking about Newman."

"So am I," Clemente responded. "It's for his good I'm suggesting the change."

Beck shook his head. "I don't think you understand, Doctor. Transfer is not an option."

"But if we can't—"

"Doctor, I've spent the last two weeks in Washington trying to explain what we're doing here to five bureaucrats who don't give a damn." He started pacing. "As far as they're concerned, Newman is just an expensive piece of sophisticated equipment. He's broken down, so they sent him to experts to repair." He turned to face Clemente. "If you say you can't do the job, they'll cut their losses and junk him like a used blender."

"Junk him?" Clemente looked confused.

"They'll smile, thank you for 'the marvelous humanitarian efforts' you've made, then arrange for a special ambulance and escort to pick him up. To transfer to another facility, you understand."

Clemente stepped closer. "And?"

Beck exhaled deeply. "And somewhere between here and nowhere, Brian Newman will cease to be. Disposed of efficiently, quietly, permanently."

An uneasy silence settled between them.

"I'm not sure what to say," Clemente said as another coughing fit overtook him.

Beck turned away. "Is there any chance of helping Newman?" he said quietly, not at all sure what he wanted the answer to be.

Clemente wiped his forehead, then stepped beside Beck. Together, they watched birds feeding off the lawn by the woods.

"We can't even name the disease, let alone begin to treat it," Clemente said in a still voice.

"If it is a disease."

"Patricia's theory is beyond the fantastic."

"But would her treatments in any way interfere with your approach?" Beck's voice was firming up, strengthening.

"I'm not even sure what her treatment would be! I mean, how do you treat the next generation of man, assuming for the moment that she's right?"

"Let's get her back in here and find out."

"Tabbart will never go for it."

Beck turned, looked across the large lawn at Tabbart and the approaching review board, then started off toward them.

"Just get her back now." He paused as he straightened his jacket. "Let me worry about Tabbart."

Clemente watched him go, tilted his head as if to align his vision to a world knocked off its axis, then went inside to make the call.

Ninety minutes later, Patricia arrived at the unit.

The board was seated behind a conference table on the second floor of the unit. Clemente sat at a small table to their right, Tabbart at another to their left. A third table was empty, directly in front of them.

"Dr. Clemente," one of the board members said icily, "you were with General Beck."

"Yes, sir."

"Well, where is he? We've been waiting . . ."

Beck came through the door, followed closely by Patricia.

"Gentlemen," Beck said, "if you'll bear with us just another few minutes."

"A very few," the board member said.

Tabbart jumped up as soon as he saw Patricia and rushed across the room.

"I warned you! You are under . . ."

"Why don't we take this outside?" Beck said as he gently moved them both toward the door.

They crossed the corridor, going into one of the offices.

As soon as the door was closed, Tabbart turned his full wrath on Patricia.

"This is the height of impertinence! After this, you won't even be able to show your face in a clinic, let alone any decent hospital! You are under full suspension pending dismissal as of now!" He was so angry, his voice came out in a series of high-pitched squeaks.

"Jerk," was all Patricia had to say.

Beck stepped between them. "Dr. Nellwyn, would you be so kind as to wait in the hall? Thank you very much."

Shaking her head, she slowly walked from the room.

Beck turned his attention to Tabbart. "Won't you sit down, Doctor?"

"I will not!" the little man bellowed. "You may not be familiar with what has transpired here of late, sir, but rest assured, I am. That woman has no business anywhere around this facility! And I will not allow her in front of that board!" He paused, momentarily running out of breath. "Why she is even here is beyond any—"

"I asked her to come."

"You?"

"Sit down, Doctor. Please."

"I will not! General Beck, this is my hospital, and I will assign or oust staff as I see fit!" He was trying to control his anger. "Now, you haven't been here for a fortnight, so I will let it go this time. You have no way of knowing what nonsense that girl has been spewing out. But in future, please bear in mind that you are here with my sanction, and it can be withdrawn at any time." He turned to leave.

"Doctor." Beck reached out, clamping his hand down hard on the little man's shoulder. "We're not done here."

Tabbart whirled around. "How dare you! I'll . . ." He was never able to finish his sentence as Beck spun him around, throwing him into a chair along the far wall.

"Shut the hell up, Tabbart!" Beck raged.

Tabbart stared up at the angry big man. His eyes shot out daggers, his mouth twisted in fury, he clenched and unclenched his fists, but he didn't say a word.

"Now listen to me, you little Nazi bastard! I'm sick and tired of all the bullshit I've been getting lately. From Washington, from Clemente, from Newman, now from you." He walked over to within inches of Tabbart. Towering over him.

"You're a professional. You know all about people who resort to violence for crisis resolution." He laughed bitterly. "Hell, that's what we're here about, right?" No answer. "Right?"

Tabbart nodded. "As you say," he said between clenched teeth.

"Right. And you know all about what happens when people like that, people like me, like our friend downstairs, can't find an appropriate outlet for their violent tendencies, right?"

"Yes."

Beck leaned over, picking up Tabbart by his jacket lapels. "If you don't get the hell out of the way of the people trying to help my"—he hesitated—"to help Newman"—he pulled the little man's face close to his—"there's going to be an accident." His voice was chilling.

Tabbart stared into the cold eyes, felt the hot breath in his face, and knew the truth.

Yet something in his personality wouldn't let him admit it.

"You would never get away with it," he heard himself say.

Beck shrugged, dragging Tabbart over to the window. With his foot, he bunched some of the throw rug together into a slight ridge.

"You were angry," Beck said quietly. "Carrying on like everyone knows you do. You stormed over to the window, tripped, and fell through it. Breaking your neck on the pavement below."

"You're crazier than Newman," Tabbart said softly as he saw the look in Beck's eyes.

"That remains to be seen," Beck said quietly. "Much as your decision. Think it over carefully."

Tabbart nodded slowly. "Dr. Nellwyn is reinstated," he said in a defeated voice.

Beck put him down, smoothing out his jacket.

"Thank you, Doctor. Very gracious of you." He reached into his own jacket, pulling out an envelope. He handed it to Tabbart. "A check from the DoD to your Institute. It should cover any inconvenience you think you've suffered."

Tabbart pocketed it without looking at it.

Beck shrugged and started out of the office.

"General Beck?"

"Yes?"

Tabbart labored to reacquire some of his lost dignity. "Newman will be your death. And it will be well deserved."

"Most likely," Beck said, and rejoined the review board across the hall.

Tabbart stood in the office for a long time. His mind raced over all the things he could and should do to Beck: Tell his government of the threats. Tell the local police and have him arrested. Confront him in front of the review board itself.

But, he told himself, he must consider the good of the Institute first. Always the Institute. The money from the Americans would allow it to continue much of its very good, very important work. That was the important thing. The Institute must go on, even if good men like himself had to sublimate themselves to its goals and suffer insult and injury from cretins like Beck.

He straightened his clothes, turned, and walked out of the room. But he could not avoid looking at the menacing ridge in the rug by the window.

———

In the subbasement, Newman turned around after he heard the door close and lock.

"Welcome back," he said to Patricia as she walked in and sat down on the couch. "Family problems all cleared up?" He smiled and came forward.

"You're sounding very satisfied with yourself," she said as she opened her pad.

"Shouldn't I?" He settled on the chair. "I mean, you *are* back. Aren't you?"

"So the whole show, that was for my benefit?"

"If you like."

She shook her head. "I don't."

Newman shrugged. "Whatever."

"Would you like to hear my theory about this morning?"

Newman leaned forward. "Absolutely. I hear your theories are all the rage." He was clearly enjoying himself.

She ignored him. "I think you got scared."

"Really?"

"Really. I think you had this nice comfortable thing going. Everything in its place, everything in its time. Then, suddenly, someone dared to do something different. And they had the unmitigated gall not to consult you." She paused. "How am I doing?"

Newman looked bored. "I'm sorry," he said in a distracted voice, "did you say something?" He leaned back in the chair.

"They changed things up on you," she continued in the same mocking voice. "And you couldn't handle it. You got scared and threw a tantrum like a two-year-old."

"Is that the official line? The sociopath, unable to adjust to change, acted out his resentments." He shook his head. "You can do better than that."

"That's not what I said, and you know it."

"Do I?"

"Um-hm. You got scared." She made a note. "Oh, not like I would or Jack Clemente would, but it was a form of being scared anyway."

"Scared of what?" he said as he yawned.

She hesitated.

"Scared of losing your chance to escape from here. Scared of being trapped, unable to do whatever it is that you plan to do."

"And what, exactly, is that? What is it that I am so diabolically planning?"

She was silent for a long time.

"I'm not sure yet. But whatever it is, you're going to try and use me to accomplish it. So, when Dr. Mont replaced me, you got scared and acted out."

Newman laughed. "I wouldn't call *that* scared, Doctor."

"What would you call it?"

He thought about it for a moment.

"Unnerved, perhaps. Or maybe unsettled." He paused. "Yes. Let's call it unsettled. I'll concede unsettled to you."

"Thank you so much." She paused. "So what made you feel so— unsettled?"

"Pretty much as you said," he began. "In my line of work, change, particularly unexpected change, is never a good thing." He paused. "Particularly since my scheming runs so deep," he said in a mock-serious voice.

"So you took it out on Dr. Mont. Very logical." Her voice dripped with sarcasm.

Newman stood up and began to pace. "The man is a jerk."

"That's a good reason," she chided.

"He comes in here, spouting some bull about how I must hate establishment figures, trying to prove some ridiculous, half-assed theory. Hell, I *am* the establishment."

"Really?" she said quietly.

"You don't think so?"

She shrugged. "Being a tool of the establishment is not the same as being the establishment."

Newman stopped, turning to look her straight in the eye. "Just what was that theory that got you in so much trouble?"

"How are you the establishment?" she pressed.

"Now who's unsettled?" he teased.

They stared at each other for long moments. In the control booth, Edel and Kapf watched uneasily.

"You don't believe a word I'm saying," Newman finally said in a flat voice.

"How are you the establishment?" She stared back at him, unflinchingly.

"Did they give you a code word for emergencies, like they did Dr. Denton?"

Patricia smiled. "They don't care that much about me," she said in a relaxed tone. "How are you the establishment?"

"Didn't they tell you not to corner me? Not to antagonize or upset me?"

"I'm not good at following instructions. The last bicycle I put together turned into a piece of modern art."

He moved very close to her. His eyes narrowed, his voice dropped low and menacing. "I could kill you. Right now. There would be nothing they could do."

She seemed to be thinking about it.

"You could try," she said, looking up at him calmly. "But then who would you have these scintillating conversations with—Dr. Mont?" She returned to her pad. "How are you the establishment?"

Newman stood there for a moment, then visibly relaxed. He walked over and collapsed into the chair. "The establishment is composed of three elements, right?"

"If you say so."

Newman arched his eyebrows at her response, as if it surprised him. "I do."

He seemed to be thinking as he talked.

"At the lowest level, you have the masses. The losers, the people Nietzsche called 'the failed and the lost.' People who live their lives through a constant series of failures. Never attaining even a glimpse of whatever their goals might be.

"At the next level are the users. People who take the failed and the lost and use them for fodder. They own factories, cities, countries sometimes. And, due to their skill at manipulating the lowest level, they rise to this middle point. They have attained some of their goals, realized some of their dreams. But they never quite get it all. Like an Oreo without the filling."

Patricia made some notes.

"But I thought Nietzsche didn't believe in a middle class?"

Newman looked at her scornfully. "Nietzsche was talking theory. I'm talking reality."

"My apologies," she said with a smile. "And the highest level of the establishment is?"

"What was your theory about me?"

"I wouldn't want to be accused of distracting you. You don't seem to handle that well." She flipped back some pages in her notebook. "We have the failed and the lost on the bottom, the users in the middle, and . . ."

"The masters," he said, returning to his professorial voice. "They have it all. Either from birth or through hard work coupled with an admirable lack of ethics. They own or control everything. They don't strive for a dream; they are the dream. They decided how things are going to be, and they're never wrong."

"They're omnipotent?"

Newman nodded. "If you own everything, control everything, you make the rules. And the one who makes the rules is never wrong."

"So," she said conversationally, "where do you fall in this rather impressive hierarchy?"

"What was your theory about me?"

"It would only bore you. It seems to me that this establishment you've described would be constantly at odds. The bottom level fighting the users. The users chafing at the dictums from the masters."

Newman nodded. "Take a look around lately? The establishment is more than fraying at the seams."

"But you still haven't told me where you fit in this grand scheme of things."

"And you haven't told me what your theory about me is."

Patricia put down her pad and looked him in the eyes. "I'll show you mine if . . ."

"I show you mine. Deal." He leaned forward and began gesturing with his hands.

"You have three massively disparate structures. Each with significantly different, often conflicting goals. Each pulling against the other two, threatening to topple the whole edifice. Right?"

"Okay."

"So, the only thing that keeps it all together, the one common band, the thread, the glue as it were . . ."

"As it were," she parroted back to him.

He gave her an irritated look.

"The thing that holds them all together is their hate. A commonly expressed, mutually held, deep, all-abiding hatred for the same thing." He paused, taking a sip of water.

"And that one unifying force," he continued after a moment, "is the deviant. The night rider. The thing that goes bump in the night."

"Very poetic," Patricia said with a chuckle.

He ignored her.

"All levels of the establishment despise the deviant equally. His independence, his ability to put himself above the rules, because he knows that he *is* above their stupid rules."

"So," she said, "you consider yourself a deviant."

Newman held up a restraining hand.

"The *establishment* considers me a deviant." He paused. "I prefer the night rider analogy, personally."

"I thought you might." Patricia smiled. "You were saying they all hate the deviant?"

He nodded. "The lowest level because they don't have the guts to do what he does. The users because the deviant represents the most direct threat to their piece of the pie."

"And the masters?" Patricia asked.

"They know they can't control him. Not fully. They can punish, execute, condemn all they want, but they can never completely control him. And control is what the masters are all about."

He smiled at her triumphantly.

"By having the deviant around, they all have the opportunity to vent their anger against a common foe and not each other." He laughed. "Hell, without me, the establishment would crumble from its own weight."

Patricia started laughing. "You just made all that up, didn't you?"

Newman looked disappointed. "Did I?" He paused. "Your turn, Doctor. What is this theory you have about me?"

She walked over to the door and signaled for it to be opened.

"I'm not going to tell you," she said as the door opened.

"But you promised."

"I lied."

Newman paused, a blankness coming over his face. Then, slowly, a broad grin spread and he started laughing loud, genuine, belly laughs.

"Brava, Doctor!" He was applauding. "Brava! Game and set!"

She turned back to him just before stepping through the door. "Not match?"

He shook his head slowly as the laughter started to subside. "No," he said with a smile. "Not quite yet."

"I don't dream."

"Really?"

"No."

"Never?"

"Well . . . sometimes I remember."

Kapf leaned back in his chair. "What's it like?"

Newman shrugged. "Remembering is remembering," he said in a faraway voice.

"Does it happen often?"

"What?"

"The remembering."

Newman turned and looked at the old man. "You're one of those that attach great importance to dreams."

Kapf nodded. "I am."

"I told you, I don't dream."

"I asked about your remembering."

"It happens."

Kapf looked at him with piercing eyes. "When does it happen?"

Newman seemed distant, as if his mind was busy with another problem far away from his subterranean prison.

Kapf had noticed the mood descend shortly after Newman's session with Patricia. An hour later, he walked into the quarters to try and take advantage of it.

"After I first wake up in the morning."

"Really?"

"I wake up and sometimes they come." His voice drifted off again.

"What do you remember?"

Newman's eyes glazed over, his body drooped. "Pain."

"What do you remember?"

"I remember school."

"And school is pain?"

"No."

"But school is related to the pain." It was a statement, not a question.

"Yes."

Newman fidgeted, then stood and walked over to the stereo. He began to fiddle with the knobs.

"How is school related to pain?" Kapf said gently.

Newman crouched, checking the station on the radio dial.

"How is school related to pain?"

"School," he said without turning around, "is where I first noticed it."

"The pain?"

He shook his head. "The difference."

Kapf nodded slightly. "Being different in school can be most painful."

Newman stood staring at the bookshelf as if it was a window through which he could see. "They wanted to party, to smoke, to drink, to screw."

"Your classmates?"

"They didn't care about anything, didn't know anything. They grew their hair long, wore wild clothes, flaunted any authority they could find, did everything they could to rebel against—hell! I doubt they even had any idea what it was they were rebelling against!"

Newman paused.

"But God, they did it all so effortlessly."

"And you?"

"Nothing was effortless."

"Go on."

Newman turned back to Kapf. "You think you can get inside me." He smiled a tired smile. "Maybe this once." He chuckled. "We'll call it an experiment, right?"

"Nothing was effortless for you," Kapf repeated.

"I was clumsy, awkward, hopelessly naive, never good in crowds." His voice trailed off as the faraway expression returned.

"By the time I was ten I'd read and understood the works of Keats, Shelley, and Byron, had read the original text of Stoker's *Dracula* and Benét's 'Nightmare at Noon.' Even looked at the stars, and understood what they were, where they were, and what they meant." His voice trailed off. "But I couldn't look a girl in the eye."

"An eclectic knowledge," Kapf said in a friendly fashion.

"Not really." Newman shook his head. "Just a hopeless, but incompetent, romantic."

He smiled spasmodically.

"I can remember standing in the yard, looking up at the Canes Venacti, the Hunting Dogs." He looked over at Kapf.

The old man nodded. "I have seen the constellation."

Newman smiled warmly. "I love dogs," he said softly. "I used to turn to the Hunting Dogs on fall nights, when they would be the most visible, and talk to them. I'd tell them my problems, wait for their advice."

Kapf seemed pleased. "And did you take their advice?"

Newman looked at him sadly. "Do I hear the voices of dogs telling me what to do?" He chuckled. "Doctor, please."

"My apologies. You were shy around girls."

Newman stared at Kapf, into Kapf, for about a minute, then continued.

"The foster families I grew up in were never terribly good at showing emotions. Not positively anyway. So I was painfully shy." He paused again. "This the kind of stuff you want to hear? I wouldn't want to disappoint you."

"You were shy," Kapf said slowly. "You were not confident. And nothing was effortless."

"I realized early on that I didn't see things the way they all did. It was like I was given more vision than any of them. They didn't see, they didn't care. Didn't understand why I did."

"What did you care about?"

"Nothing."

"What did you see that they could not?"

"Nothing."

"You were different?"

Newman raised his eyebrows. "Was I?"

"How?"

Newman hesitated before answering.

"I wore my hair very short. Wore conservative, solid-colored clothes, walked with my head down. Sat by myself, kept to myself."

"Why?"

"I didn't want anyone to notice."

"Notice what?"

"That I was different."

Kapf thought for a moment, then nodded. "And if they saw that cosmetic difference?" he said.

Newman smiled. "Then they wouldn't look for the other." He sat down on the couch. "But it didn't matter anyway, after a while I just stopped going to school."

"Where did you go?"

Newman laughed. A deep, hearty laugh. "Would you believe the library?"

"I would. But weren't you ever caught?"

"Rarely."

"Why not? Your foster parents surely . . ."

"Were good people, but they both worked. And they relied on me to go. Trust, I believe you call it." He paused. "I used to be an accomplished liar, Doctor. Remarkably so."

"No longer?"

"No need."

"Why?"

"My feelings exactly."

An uncomfortable silence settled between them.

"But the school authorities," Kapf ventured, "didn't they ever contact your foster parents?"

Again, the spasmodic smile.

"Occasionally. Once or twice a semester. After I'd been gone for five or six weeks."

"No more?"

"I said, I was different." He stood and began to pace. "I saw things, understood things, that no one else seemed to."

"What did you understand?"

This time the smile seemed almost reluctant. Almost painful.

"That to understand a bureaucracy is to control it."

Newman paused, as if he expected Kapf to understand it all. When it was clear this wasn't happening, he shook his head and continued.

"I did a series of experiments, attending some classes, skipping others. Keeping elaborate charts on when I got caught, how, after how long. Simple, really."

"And you were how old?"

"Oh, I don't know. Ten, eleven maybe."

Kapf was silent for a very long time.

"And the pain?"

"What pain?"

"In your memories at the moment of waking?"

Newman looked genuinely confused. "Why, Doctor, whatever are you talking about?"

The loudspeaker cut off any further discussion.

"Dr. Kapf?" an unseen voice called.

"Yes?" He sounded irritated.

"You are wanted at the conference, sir."

Reluctantly, Kapf nodded.

Newman walked him halfway to the door. "I hope I wasn't too boring," he said.

Kapf shook his head, a sad expression spreading across his ancient face.

"Mr. Newman," he said slowly, as if against his own will, "I wonder if you are truly as complex as you would have us believe."

Newman shrugged. "Complex is a relative term. The wheel would be considered complex in a society without wheels. Routine in one with."

They heard the locks being thrown.

"And in our society, Mr. Newman, among the people here, which are you?"

Newman's face lost all expression. His eyes seemed to drain of color as a stillness settled over him. As the door was opening, he turned, starting back for the bedroom.

"Watch and learn, Doctor," he said as he went. "Watch and learn."

U pstairs, the conference with the review board had been going on for two hours by the time Kapf joined it.

The review board paid professional attention to every word. And despite their comical code names (Mr. Red, White, Blue, Green, and Ms. Gray), they at least appeared to understand what was being said.

Step by step, with meticulous Germanic precision, Tabbart took the board through every test and every result that had been obtained. He carefully avoided expressing any opinion or looking at Beck. His presentation was clear, thorough, unbiased.

An hour and a half after Kapf arrived, Tabbart wrapped up.

"This concludes the strictly medical portion of our studies," he said as he looked the board over. "If you have any questions?"

"Dr. Tabbart," the man known only as Mr. Red asked, "have all possibilities of a mass lesion or cerebral injury been eliminated?"

"Conclusively, sir."

Mr. Green spoke next. "Any chance of a randomly occurring phenomenon such as an intermittently thrown embolus accounting for the behavior changes?"

"None, sir."

"Can you diagnose any injuries or trauma sustained by Newman during his captivity?" Mr. Blue's voice was terse.

"Only those accounted for in the files turned over to us. It would appear they are most forthright."

"All right," Mr. White said, making a note, "let's move on."

"Very well," Ms. Gray said, checking her agenda. "Dr. Clemente is next with an overview of the psychiatric aspects." She looked over at Clemente, who was in a whispered conversation with Patricia and Kapf. "Dr. Clemente?"

He nodded at Patricia and Kapf, both upset, then turned to the review board.

"You have my report. There is very little to add to it except, perhaps, to reinforce several key points.

"At no time since he was placed in our custody and control has Mr. Newman demonstrated atavistic tendencies or decompensation lability syndrome. Quite the opposite, in fact. He has been mostly cooperative, demonstrated a willingness, however reluctant, to abide within our rules, and has asserted his personality in vivid acts. All of this in direct contraindication of DLS."

"How do you explain the discrepancy from the original diagnosis?" White asked.

Clemente thought for a moment.

"Either it was wholly wrong, or the stress that caused the decompensation in the first place has been sufficiently reduced. Rather like lowering the flame under a pot of boiling water."

"But," Red pushed, "he is still in close custody. Still unable to do as he pleases."

Clemente nodded. "But he understands this as a temporary condition. That, while he might not consider us friends, we are certainly not the enemy."

"Proceed," Red said, making a note.

"Despite the lack of direct evidence of DLS, despite no direct atavistic, primitive behavioral outbreaks . . ."

"What about the cat?" This from Gray.

"That seems pretty primitive behavior to me," Red said sharply.

Clemente bit his lower lip. "The cat. Yes." He paused, gathering his thoughts. "I do not believe that this one incident was in and of itself a determinant in any way."

"Except to the cat," Blue said under his breath.

"If, and I stress that word," Ms. Gray said firmly, "DLS and phased atavism are not the diagnosis, what is?"

"We cannot say," Clemente said slowly, "with complete confidence, at this time."

"Is he psychotic?"

"It's hard to say. He might be."

"Is he schizophrenic?" Red asked.

"I don't believe so."

"Is he paranoid?" Green said with a skeptical look.

"Perhaps. Within certain definitions. He is certainly cautious."

"Is he sociopathic?" Red tried.

"It seems unlikely but remains a possibility."

Ms. Gray shook her head. "You cannot say with confidence. He might be. You don't believe so. Perhaps. It seems unlikely." She paused. "Doctor, what *do* you know?"

At that moment, Clemente was overtaken by a coughing fit.

Kapf poured him some water. The coughing continued, worsening by the second. The color drained from the man's face, as his handkerchief was stained a thin crimson.

Kapf helped Clemente to his feet and, along with Patricia, walked him to the door. Two of the junior staffers took him at that point, leading him out, toward a waiting nurse.

But before he would leave, Clemente turned to Kapf. "Take over, please, Otto."

Kapf nodded as the dying man was taken away.

He and Patricia returned to their table. He checked his notes, glanced at Clemente's, then faced the board.

The board had politely found other things to look at until Kapf returned.

"Lady and gentlemen, our apologies, but Dr. Clemente has not been well for some time. Perhaps I can answer your questions?"

Mr. Red nodded. "That would be refreshing."

Kapf checked some notes he had made. "I believe you can best be helped to understand Mr. Newman's condition by exclusion." He paused. "He has not demonstrated regressive behavior, inappropriate moods, delusions, or hallucinations. He has shown no loss of contact with reality or any disintegration of his core personality.

"While the incident with the cat suggests a lack of impulse control, when that event is taken in perspective, it is clear that he has demonstrated great impulse control. The cat would then be more appropriately placed in a category of chosen behavior for a specific effect. Not an impulsive act."

The board was making copious notes.

Kapf took a sip of coffee, carefully studied their faces, then continued.

"As we have eliminated basic psychosis, we must also eliminate schizophrenia. Again, because he simply does not display the appropriate symptomology.

"As for paranoia, he evinces no delusions of grandeur or persecution beyond that which, in my opinion, any individual who has done what he has, and has been treated as he has, would naturally display.

"Is he a sociopath? Only by the strictest definition. He displays no conscience, his intelligence is high, but, and this is critical, he *does* display a marked moral sensibility!" He started to gesture as he talked.

"They may not be your morals, or mine, or those of any of our acquaintances, but he does possess them."

Mr. Blue looked up. "So where does that leave us?"

Kapf shrugged. "With either a new, hereto-undefined psychiatric or medical ailment involving both the conscience centers and the behavior centers of the brain or . . ."

"Yes?"

He paused, then made his decision.

"Or a new man."

To Patricia's shock, the board sat there placidly making notes.

Kapf looked at them closely, then merely nodded his head slightly. "But then," he said quietly, "I believe you already considered that possibility."

Patricia leaned over to him and whispered, "Otto, what do you think . . ."

Kapf never took his eyes off the board. "Look at them," he said to Patricia in a conversational voice. "They must have suspected all along. They merely looked to us to confirm or deny their suspicions." He paused as the shocked psychiatrists behind him looked over at the review board. "Gentlemen?"

"Proceed, Doctor," Ms. Gray said quietly.

Kapf leaned back in his chair. "Dr. Nellwyn will continue with the presentation at this time."

As she began, Kapf observed the board's tacit confession of the truth, then looked at Patricia, eyes aglow with the prospect of acceptance, advancement, and a major paper that would shake the psychiatric and anthropological worlds to their foundations.

Then he thought of Newman, a man incredibly racked with an unknown mental disease that threatened to tear him apart; or the first of a new breed of coldhearted men that would have to battle for their very survival against the species that they must inevitably replace.

And it occurred to him, at that moment, in that room of experts, healers, professionals, and specialists, that he was the only one thinking of Newman.

He tried to concentrate on Patricia's presentation, but a wave of sadness engulfed him, making concentration nearly impossible.

Three hours later, he realized that they all had stopped talking.

"Excuse me?"

Mr. Blue smiled at Kapf. "I was just saying, Dr. Kapf, that we seem to have reached an impasse."

"In what sense?"

"Dr. Nellwyn's thesis would seem to be open to two differing inter-pretations. The new man postulate; and the new disease conjecture."

"They are not mutually exclusive," Kapf quickly pointed out.

"No?"

He shook his head. "The one is a logical extension of the other." The board members looked confused. "A wheel in a society without wheels might well be considered aberrant. But in a more evolved, advanced world, the wheel would be considered routine. Time will diagnose Mr. Newman's disease or evolution."

White shook his head. "An interesting conundrum, Doctor. But I'm afraid this review board does not have the luxury of time." He turned to his colleagues. "Perhaps we should hear from the subject now?"

They all nodded.

"I'll have him brought up," Patricia said as she reached for a phone.

"One moment, please," Kapf interrupted.

Patricia froze, receiver in midair.

"Is it essential for you to hear from Mr. Newman?" Kapf asked with a hint of tension in his voice.

"I think it only fair," Ms. Gray said.

"What's wrong?" Patricia appeared confused.

Kapf stroked his beard as his mind raced. Something from his ses-sion with Newman had set off alarm bells and they were clanging deafeningly now.

Watch and learn.

"Perhaps it would be more advisable, if this is absolutely necessary, for you to go down to his quarters, instead."

"Why?"

Kapf paused. "There is the security aspect to consider for one," he said in a subdued voice. "Then, there is the question of how a change in environment might affect his long-term treatment."

Neither was the real reason. He didn't know the real reason, but deep in his soul, he knew moving Newman would be a mistake.

"Security Chief Edel?" Gray asked as she searched the room for him.

Edel stood by his seat in the back of the room. "Madame?"

"Can you address Dr. Kapf's first concerns?"

Edel thought it over.

"Since we were informed of your visit, we have had plans in place to bring Mr. Newman to this room. I will escort him personally and he will be under the guard of five of my best men.

"If it would be more to your desires," he added, thinking as he talked, "I can have him shackled during the move and your visit." He paused. "But I do not believe that will be necessary."

"I agree," Patricia added.

"Dr. Nellwyn."

Patricia stood up and began pacing.

"At this point in our analysis of the man, reshackling him as the Russians did would, in my opinion, cause him to revert to the previous defensive behaviors he apparently exhibited while in Russian custody."

Mr. Red made a note. "And Dr. Kapf's other concerns? About a sudden change in his environment?"

Patricia smiled confidently. "Negligible," she said firmly. "He might be a little reticent, a little defensive at first, but he adapts quickly." She perched on her table. "I've had close to a hundred sessions with the man. We've established a very special rapport, so I'll be able to spot any changes in him, any danger signals, long before anything might happen."

Red turned to Kapf. "Doctor?"

Watch and learn.

Kapf sipped his long-cold coffee.

"He may do nothing. He may be charming and cooperative. He may be militant, aggressive, and combative. Or he may yet find a new face to display to you. Regardless, I believe the maximum steps should be taken to guard against any eventuality."

Patricia was staring at him angrily. Then she turned to the review board.

"Bring him up in chains and I guarantee you he'll be uncooperative." She paused. "Let me talk with him, and I'm sure there'll be no problems." She smiled, a somehow private act. "He'll listen to me."

The board talked among themselves for a moment.

"Talk to him, Dr. Nellwyn," Mr. Blue said after a time. "And if you believe he's stable, bring him up."

Forty-five minutes later, as the red-orange rays of the setting sun flooded the room through its one bay window, Newman was escorted in by Patricia, Edel, and five security men.

As Newman settled himself behind a table directly in front of the review board, Patricia took Kapf aside.

"He's fine," she said in a whisper. "Cooperative, polite, in a good phase right now."

"And you are sure of that?"

She smiled supportively. "He recognizes that there's no gain in causing a disruption. There's the security here, in the corridor, and he's almost as far above the ground-floor door as he was below it." She patted Kapf on the back, like a grandchild might her senile old grandfather.

"He sees that his only possibility of gain is by being helpful. And we both know, he always recognizes and exploits any chance of gain. Not to mention to perform." She returned to her seat.

Kapf stood there, watching Newman settle himself.

"Perhaps," Kapf muttered to himself.

"General Beck?" Ms. Gray looked at the tired man in the corner. "Would you begin?"

Reluctantly, Beck stood and walked to a place in front of the room. Newman watched him, smiling politely.

"Brian," Beck began in a quiet voice, "this is a review panel from the States. They're here to see how you're doing. I think you know some of them."

Newman looked from Beck to the board and back again.

"In visions of the dark night, I have dreamed of joy departed; but a waking dream of life and light hath left me brokenhearted."

The board members looked at each other.

"Brian," Beck tried again, "will you answer their questions?"

"Ah, what is not a dream by day to him whose eyes are cast on things around him, with a ray turned back upon the past?"

Beck rubbed his forehead as the board members stared.

"Mr. Newman?" Patricia walked around to the front of the room. "Brian? I thought you wanted to cooperate?"

"I lied."

She smiled. "Afraid they'll figure you out?"

Newman laughed lightly. "Not likely."

"So?"

"Okay."

Patricia nodded at Beck. "Go ahead."

Beck stood up again. "Brian, do you remember your last mission?"

"That holy dream, that holy dream, while all the world were chiding, hath cheered me as a lovely beam a lonely spirit guiding." He turned to Patricia. "I said I'd answer *their* questions."

Beck collapsed into a chair.

Patricia looked at the board and shrugged.

"Mr. Newman?" Ms. Gray asked.

Newman sat bolt upright in his chair. "Ma'am!"

"How are you feeling?"

"Ma'am! Very well, ma'am!"

Gray smiled. "And are you willing to answer our questions?"

"Ma'am! Yes, ma'am!"

She nodded to Mr. White.

"Your military bearing is appreciated, Mr. Newman, but why don't we keep this a casual conversation? Okay?"

"If you prefer, sir."

"Do you remember your last mission?"

"Yes, sir." Newman was concentrating on whoever asked the questions.

"And would you recount it to us?"

Newman looked around the room. "I'd prefer not to, sir."

"Why?"

"Sir, with due respect, you don't tell a stranger you use whips and chains in the bedroom; and you don't talk about your missions in front of them either."

White seemed pleased by the answer. "If we were to meet in an executive session, would you be willing to?"

"Absolutely, sir!"

White nodded to Mr. Green.

"During your captivity, did you ever compromise any operations or personnel of the department?"

"No, sir."

"Did you ever have occasion to observe any other American personnel create such a compromise?"

Newman thought for a moment.

"Sir, I was kept isolated from other Americans throughout my ordeal. I regret I cannot furnish you with any information in that area."

Green nodded and Red began.

"Newman, you know me."

"Yes, sir, I do."

"Let's cut out all the bullshit and playacting, okay?"

"Yes, sir."

Red put down his pen, leaning forward to look Newman in the eye. "Did you kill any Russian personnel in that damned camp?"

Newman didn't answer.

"C'mon," Red pressed, "I thought we were stopping all the game playing?"

Newman smiled a cold, angry smile. "I'm sorry, sir. I was just remembering what you said the last time we met."

"What was that?"

"I believe you said that anyone who would answer a question like that must be crazy. So I'm trying to figure out exactly how to answer you." He paused. "I wouldn't want to be seen as crazy, would I?"

Patricia walked over to him. "Are you okay? Do you want to go?"

Newman ignored her and concentrated on Blue, who was consulting his notes.

"Mr. Newman," Blue said gently, "do you consider yourself crazy?"

"No, sir."

"Depressed or psychotic?"

"I'm a little depressed, sir," he said with a sigh. "It isn't easy being this close to being home and still locked up and all."

"Why do you think you are still locked up?"

"I'm sure you know that far better than I, sir."

Ms. Gray turned to the board. "Before we continue, I'd like the sense of the board. Is the subject in condition to be debriefed?"

Slowly, one by one, they nodded.

Patricia patted Newman on the back for encouragement.

Kapf noted the spasmodic smile that played across Newman's lips for the briefest instant, immediately replaced by a blank, open look.

For the next forty-five minutes they discussed Newman's background, his history up to the final mission, a mass of little things that helped the board get a clearer picture of the man. Finally, they reached the central issue of the session.

All junior staffers, with the exception of Patricia, were cleared from the room. Over Kapf's objections, three of the five security men were cleared out. Tape recorders were shut off, pencils put down, and the serious business began.

"I would like to remind you, Dr. Nellwyn, Dr. Kapf, Chief Edel, General Beck," Ms. Gray began slowly, "and you two security men, that what you are about to hear is classified on the highest level. Revealing this information, or even the existence of this information, is a violation of German and American law and is punishable as such."

They all nodded.

"Very well." She turned to her right. "Mr. Red."

"Newman, let's talk about Abkhaz one five."

Newman took on a serious expression. "Yes, sir."

For the next three hours, without a break, they laboriously went over every aspect of Newman's last mission. Every day, hour, and detail reported, scrutinized, disassembled, and examined.

It took its toll on everyone.

The board made notes and guzzled coffee.

Patricia, always hovering near Newman, finally sat down just behind him, propping her head on her hands.

Edel and his two security men constantly shifted their weight from one foot to another, trying to keep focused and alert.

Kapf, already exhausted by the tension of the day, found himself drifting off several times.

Even Newman seemed not to be exempt from the tedium. He stretched his legs out in front of him, seemed a little drowsy, but continued to answer the ever-coming questions.

"Was it your intention to . . . ?"

"Yes."

"Did you consider . . . ?"

"In general terms."

"What was your state of mind when . . ."

"I didn't really think about it."

Finally, just before 7:00 P.M., Ms. Gray signaled for the last round of questioning to begin.

"Mr. Green."

"Thank you," he said, suppressing a yawn. "Only two questions." He turned to Newman. "Our satellite intel was not as specific as we would've liked. Were you able to get any kind of actual damage assessment?"

Newman seemed deep in thought.

"All I know is that I overheard a colonel from the Soviet Nuclear Commission saying that they would have to contain the remainder of the reactor in some kind of outer shell of lead and concrete. That it would have to remain off-line, as would its progeny reactors."

"Any estimate as to the costs they were incurring as a result of the action?"

"No, sir," Newman droned as he yawned. "None."

Gray turned to her right. "Mr. Red."

"Only one question. Is it your impression that the Haygood Network was still intact after your arrest?"

"Yes, sir."

"Mr. Blue," Gray said as she wiped at her eyes.

"Thank you. My questions concern what you discovered of the construction of the reactor's inner service module."

Red looked at him, shook his head, and poured himself another cup of coffee.

Newman stretched long and hard.

"This may take a while." He paused, closing his eyes while he thought.

Patricia bent her head back and forth from shoulder to shoulder to try and stay awake.

"It was a two-stage process," Newman began. "Initially, there was a chromium hatch that appeared set in a composite wall that was perpendicular to the southern, bilateral retaining wall."

Edel stood, took a position by the door, and signaled that it was all right for his men to sit down.

"The chromium hatch was set into the composite wall with nine, apparently steel rivets. Each group of nine was set in a triangular . . ."

It was only by checking the security videotape, slowing it down to an almost frame-by-frame viewing, that anyone was able to reconstruct what happened next.

In a quick spasmodic kick, Newman lifted the small table in front of him, sending it flying on top of the board table. It caught Mr. Blue and Mr. White in the upper bodies, knocking them backward, sending the other board members flying.

In almost the same movement, Newman rocked forward, quickly coming to his feet. His right hand sent his chair flying backward, past a stunned Patricia and into the lap of the nearest guard.

And Newman was already on the move.

On a straight line toward the window, Newman smashed his forearm and elbow into Beck's forehead without slowing down. As Beck fell backward, Newman grabbed his chair, swinging it in a short, vicious arc, launching it at the window. As it shattered in a rainfall of glass splinters, Newman dropped to his knees—barely in time to avoid the first and only shot that Konrad Edel would get off.

Newman rolled back to his feet and dived, arms outstretched, through the gaping hole in the window.

By the time Edel got to the window, less than ten seconds had elapsed.

He thrust his smoking semiautomatic through the hole that Newman had dived through and desperately searched for a target, but it was too late.

Newman was nowhere in sight.

Edel and the eventual pursuers were the furthest thing from Newman's mind as he sprinted into the woods. He was functioning purely on conditioned instinct, following a plan he had rehearsed a hundred times in his head over the last three months, and had been modifying throughout the debriefing session. He knew the distances, he knew the obstacles; now he just had to execute.

He made the edge of the woods two seconds quicker than he had estimated. The ground was soft and moist and he knew that he would be easy to track. He instantly altered his course to a rock-strewn path that ran parallel to the edge of the woods, about a hundred meters in.

Suddenly, two armed security men appeared in his path, their MP-5K assault rifles pointing at his head.

Newman never hesitated.

"Don't shoot! Don't—" he yelled as he launched himself at them.

The men hesitated for one fateful second.

Newman's shoulder caught the first man in the midsection like a linebacker tackle. As they tumbled to the ground, Newman grabbed the man, raising the guard's hands (still holding the deadly weapon), and forced his finger down on the trigger.

The second guard died instantly as ten 9mm rounds tore through his body in the three-second burst.

Newman rolled lightly to his feet, pointing the smoking gun at the head of the prone first guard.

"Run away," he said in a guttural voice.

The guard hesitated, then scrambled to his feet, fleeing in the opposite direction, never seeing Newman toss the rifle aside as he took off again. The sounds of a gunfight would only serve to bring the security forces right to him. And he had no desire to kill them.

As he sprinted, his eyes took in everything. He knew he had, at best, thirty more seconds before he would have to give up, abandon the woods, and try for the east fence.

Then, miraculously, he found what he was looking for.

Alarm sirens sounded throughout the compound.

Edel recovered first in the commotion. He immediately punched the panic button in the conference room, then dashed for the door, shouting as he went.

In less than two minutes, he had ten men outside the unit, fanning out toward the woods at a dead run, guns at the ready.

But he knew that Newman had disappeared into the woods at least a minute and a half before they even reached the grounds.

Another ten men were dispatched to the west fence area, and five more to the front gate of the Institute.

By the time five minutes had elapsed, Edel's men had been reinforced by twenty-five standby guards, who were split between the east fence and the woods.

As he watched the heavily armed men disappear into the foliage, he prayed that Newman wouldn't kill too many of them before the night was over.

Forty-five minutes into the search, he wearily returned to the upstairs offices of the unit.

Members of the review board had either left or were being treated for minor injuries in the Institute's main building.

Patricia, Kapf, Tabbart, Beck (looking ninety), and a white-faced, erratically breathing Clemente were sitting in the deserted conference room, silently waiting.

They all looked up hopefully as Edel walked in.

Edel slowly shook his head. "We have completed our first pass through the woods and are beginning a second. We have searched all open areas of the property and are now beginning a room-by-room, floor-by-floor search of the main building and all outbuildings." He collapsed into a chair. "However, since the discovery of Security Officer Brunelle's body, there has been no sign." He exhaled deeply. "I am not hopeful."

Kapf took a deep breath. "We must notify the authorities," he said in a steady voice.

"Of what?" Tabbart asked angrily. "Technically the man was a voluntary commitment. And we must not allow it to be known that the Institute was housing a violent, extraordinarily dangerous individual and then allowed him to escape." He paused, taking a stiff drink from his glass of schnapps. "I was opposed to taking on this case from the beginning. I said so! I made it clear! I . . ." He seemed to withdraw into himself.

"Is he really dangerous?" Patricia ventured. "I mean he's got what he wanted now, right? Maybe we're overreacting." But her tone showed that even she didn't believe it.

"I thought you were supposed to be able to spot any danger signs, you stupid little . . ."

Patricia whirled on Beck. "*You* trained him! Hell, you probably *created* him! Why didn't you see this coming?"

Beck jumped to his feet. "I didn't create him!" he screamed. "I used him, gave him technique, direction, but goddammit, I did not create him!"

Clemente weakly raised his hand. "Please. Done is done." His voice was weak and hoarse from the almost constant coughing. "The chief is right. We cannot tell the police who Newman is." He took a sip of water. "But we must tell them that a possibly dangerous patient has, well, left, without our approval. We can ask them to keep a lookout, but not approach him, merely notify us if they see him."

They all seemed to agree.

"I will see to that," Edel said as he went to a phone.

"And," Clemente said between coughs, "we must take steps to find him."

Beck was rubbing the large welt on his forehead. He had refused treatment. "I've already called NATO Security Command in Augsburg," he said wearily. "They're fifty-three kilometers northeast of here. That's about thirty-five minutes away." He paused and reapplied an ice pack to his head. "They'll have two covert search teams here within the hour."

Clemente nodded as a violent coughing fit overcame him.

Kapf, who had been silent since the incident, stood and gestured for the nurse, standing just outside, to come in. Together, they lifted Clemente into a wheelchair. She wheeled him out. Kapf followed.

"Otto?"

He turned back to face Patricia.

She was pale, trembling slightly.

"Newman won't hurt anyone unless he's cornered. I'm sure of it." Her voice was beseeching him. "I know the man!"

Kapf nodded sadly. "So you have said." He turned and followed the nurse into the elevator.

Eight hours after the escape, after the woods, the buildings, everything had been searched five times each, the Institute began to return to normal.

It was a little after four in the morning, the guards had resumed their regular patrol, the special covert search teams had fanned out across the countryside, and the unit had been closed down. Everybody was sworn to secrecy and sent home.

In the woods, along the rock-strewn path, a night bird stirred. A sound very high up in one of the still heavily foliated trees caused it to stop, look up, then quickly wing away.

Newman dropped soundlessly to the ground.

He remained crouched for five minutes, listening, watching, smelling.

His eyes narrowed, his nostrils flared, his fingers bent and tensed more like an animal's than a man's.

Finally satisfied, he slowly stood up and started down the path, back toward the unit.

He stood on the edge of the woods, looking at the dangerously wide-open lawn in front of him. He looked up at the gradually clearing sky, seemed to be searching for a moment, then smiled.

Taking his bearing from the rising constellation Canes Venacti, the Hunting Dogs, he casually stepped out and began walking across the great lawn toward the main building.

"Keep an eye out, guys," he said softly as he walked.

As he approached the unit, some instinct caused him to stop short. He stood there, at the ready, as an indistinct darkness rose up out of the ground in front of him.

A man, in his thirties and powerfully built, tossed aside his boulder camouflage tarpaulin and turned to face Newman.

In his left hand he lightly cradled a Randall assault knife with brass knuckles.

Newman nodded at him. "I don't know you."

"Since your time, I expect," the man said evenly. "Let's do it."

"We don't have to," Newman said as he took a step toward the man. "I have nothing against you."

The man took a hesitant step toward Newman. "I have my orders."

The man lunged forward, a snakelike strike at Newman's throat.

Newman dropped straight down, shooting his right leg forward as he fell. Catching the tip of his foot behind the upright man's ankle, he pulled. The man fell backward.

Newman rolled to his right, bringing his left arm in a short, tight whirl toward the man's head. Less than a second later, the man lay dying, his larynx and windpipe crushed, unable to make a sound or move as his lungs filled with blood.

Newman stood up, looked around, then brushed off his clothes.

"Pity" was all he said as he stepped around the drowning man and disappeared into the night.

PART THREE

Vigils

The coffee shop was half empty.

Waitresses perched on the back tables, gossiping, the cook stood in the doorway to the kitchen trading barbs with the maître d', who sat in the entrance to the bar. The entire place seemed to be winding itself down, or up perhaps, as it recovered from the late afternoon traffic and braced for the dinner trade that would begin in an hour or so.

Two men sat alone in a corner booth, as they had almost every Wednesday at this time for the last nine years. They would sip their coffee, talk softly, then overtip and leave separately.

Years ago, the men had been grist for wild speculations, but now, well, what were two old fags who were regulars and tipped well.

"I'm growing anxious," the taller of the two said quietly. "It's been almost a month and yet I still get nothing but words from you. I don't come here for words!"

The smaller man shrugged. "Do you think I enjoy this? I want to give you more, I do!" He paused. "I just can't right now. Please try to understand." His voice was sad, almost begging for understanding.

The tall man slowly nodded, then reached out, taking the smaller man's hands in his. He patted them gently. "I'm sorry," he said with the hint of a smile. "I'm just getting crotchety in my old age."

"I shouldn't have snapped at you," the smaller man said. "Do you forgive me?"

"Of course." He sounded sincere. "So, what can I tell our friends about the investigation?"

Tabbart, the smaller man, handed an envelope under the table to the tall man. "These are the latest report summaries."

The tall man pocketed the envelope without looking in it. "It seems awfully thin."

Tabbart shrugged. "Their investigation is likewise thin."

"Our friends are anxious for more than this," the tall man said in a disappointed tone.

"Why?" Tabbart seemed genuinely confused. "Why is Moscow in such a state over one psychotic American agent at large in Germany?"

"You know," the tall man said with a smile, "the last time I was in Moscow, I went over to Yeltsin's house and asked him that very question." He adopted a self-important, comedic tone. " 'Boris,' I said, 'why do you care anything about this crazy American?' Do you know what he said to me?"

"What?" Tabbart chuckled.

Instantly, the tall man's face took on a serious, somehow dangerous expression. "He said, 'Stop asking stupid questions and get me some fucking answers!' " For a moment, his expression froze, a picture of rage and fury. Then it was gone, replaced by the gentle expression that had been there before. "What do you think of that, my good doctor?"

Tabbart froze. When he finally spoke, his voice was seasoned with anxiety. "I have heard some small things."

"Tell me."

"It seems," Tabbart began, then stopped as a young streetwalker came in and sat down three tables away. After she was served, he continued, but in a noticeably lower voice.

"It seems that they are about to expand the search abroad, and reduce it locally."

"Why?" The tall man's gaze was demanding.

"Directives from Washington and NATO Command, Brussels. They are dissatisfied with the results to date and are becoming convinced that Newman must have moved on."

"And what is the opinion of the Search Commander?"

Tabbart looked over at the streetwalker as she sipped her coffee. She noticed and smiled at him.

"Shameless," he said softly, never taking his eyes off her. "Her skirt is so short you can almost see her—"

"I don't care what you can almost see!" the tall man demanded as he noisily put his cup down. "She has nothing you would recognize anyway!" He paused as a near-trembling Tabbart turned back to him.

"You have no right to speak to me in such a fashion," he said in his distressed squeak. "No right! For twenty years, more, I have been faithful to you, to our cause."

The tall man sighed deeply before beginning again. "Manfred, old friend," he said soothingly, "forgive me." He began stroking Tabbart's clenched hands. They slowly opened up like flower petals, rapidly wrapping themselves around the tall man's big hand. "Manfred, the times have changed and not for the better, I'm afraid."

He seemed torn on the edges of a dilemma. Then, with a sharp nod of his head, he continued.

"If I do not satisfy their needs, they will find someone else who will." He looked down at the table, lowering his voice as well, to what he hoped was an appropriate mixture of sadness and surrender. "Perhaps that would be for the better. I am old."

"No!" Tabbart's voice was insistent. He reached out and raised the tall man's head with his hand under the man's chin. "You are not old!"

The tall man smiled bitterly. "I have never before failed them in any task." He paused as he looked deeply into Tabbart's eyes. "Or raised my voice to you, my Maddalenna. Perhaps I have failed you as well."

Tabbart smiled as he cried.

He raised the tall man's hand to his lips and kissed it softly.

"No," Tabbart said with deep feeling. "You have not, could not, ever fail me." He patted the hand. "There must be some other things we can tell them!"

"Like what?" the tall man said in a sad, distant voice.

Tabbart was deep in thought as he continued to cling to the big man's hand. "Personnel changes, perhaps?"

"Personnel changes?" The tall man sounded unconvinced.

"They identified the second man that Newman killed on the grounds."

"So?"

"He was one of Beck's automatons. General Dreck put him there as a contingency in case of Newman's escape."

"Go on," the tall man said quietly, still looking down mournfully. But his eyes were sharp, clear, and ablaze with triumph.

Tabbart leaned closer to the tall man. "Since the abominable failures of General Dreck Beck, they have discussed splitting command of the search between him and the unit commander of the covert search team."

The tall man shrugged. "And?" he said, sounding very unmoved.

Again, Tabbart reached out and lifted the tall man's face. "Beck would still be the overall commander, but the unit commander would make all the operational decisions." He looked into the apparently nonunderstanding eyes. "If they go through with it, then it effectively castrates Beck. Not that he doesn't deserve it," he added angrily.

The tall man started to seem interested. "But do we know anything about this other man? The man who would be taking over?"

Tabbart smiled. "I will personally put his personnel file into your hands, my passion."

The tall man hesitated, then leaned forward and kissed Tabbart on the cheek.

The streetwalker stood up, shook her head as she noticed the two old men, then walked out of the coffee shop.

Once clear of the shop's windows, she hurried down the street to a phone box. She opened her tiny purse, taking out a photocopy of a small pencil sketch. She nodded as she deposited the coins and dialed the number.

"Hallo?"

She looked around to make sure she was alone.

"Ingrid Sprenger."

The male voice on the other end hesitated before answering. Then, with sudden recognition, his voice came firmly through the receiver.

"*Ja, Ingrid?*"

"I have found the one you are seeking."

———

On the outskirts of Munich, some thirty miles away, another search was about to be the subject of discussion.

The converted barn had long tables lining the two long sides. Each was covered with maps, loose papers, bound reports, all interspersed with telephones and radios. The far end was a stage of sorts, with a huge movie screen, a large white board, and a narrow table.

But dominating the room, high above the movie screen, was a large blowup of Brian Newman. He seemed to look down on the crowded barn, his expression somewhere between bemusement and sadness.

The thirty-two people in the room finished arranging their chairs in the center, facing the stage, just as the main players stepped onto it.

Captain John Kilgore, the first man out, was young, no more than thirty. He wore blue jeans, a tight turtleneck that didn't hide the fact that he was in perfect condition, and, somewhat jarringly, combat boots.

He walked in and sat down facing the men. His eyes were clear, his posture perfect, his expression set.

Next came Beck.

He looked twenty years older than his fifty-two years. Deep black circles virtually surrounded his eyes. His skin was the color of day-old ground beef, and he had a tic under his left ear. His clothes looked slept in, he appeared not to have shaved in a week, as he dropped heavily into his chair.

The last man out was Dr. Kapf.

Looking as indecipherable as usual, he took his seat next to Beck, immediately opening up the folder in front of him. He read it for a moment, then closed it, looking calmly out at the audience.

Kilgore leaned over, whispered something to Beck, who nodded. Then Kilgore stood up.

"Good evening, people," he began in a strong, deep voice. "This is day thirty-three of Probe 95–0707. As of 1600 today, the suspect is still at large. Still considered possibly armed and definitely dangerous."

He turned a page in the folder in front of him.

"The reported sighting in Mannsbruck was fully investigated by the 342nd Military Police Detachment out of Wiesbaden Air Base. The individual reported in the sighting was satisfactorily identified as a

German national and was released, with apologies, after six hours of close detention."

He signaled to the back of the room, and a photograph of the German came up on the screen.

Kilgore shook his head.

"Now, this is exactly what we've been talking about, guys." His tone was casual. "There's a superficial resemblance, sure. But check out the eyes, the spacing between them, their relation to the bridge of the nose, their alignment at the edges of the mouth." He laughed. "This guy ain't even close!"

He nodded, and the projector was shut off.

"Remember, concentrate on the things that are the hardest to change. Our Probe is an experienced operative. He'll change his appearance as much as possible, but there's nothing he can easily do about the eyes, the nose, the mouth." He paused. "Burn them into your minds."

He checked his notes and then turned to Beck. "General, is there anything you'd care to add?"

Beck just silently shook his head.

"All right then, let's get to it." Kilgore looked around the room. "Ground staff?"

A young man stood up in the first row. "We have men on the ground as far north as Leipzig, as far west as Stuttgart. We're currently covering twenty-one cities within that triangle on a rotating basis. But, to be absolutely honest, if any of our guys spot him, it'll be the purest of luck." He sat down with a sad expression on his face.

"Air?"

Another man stood up, this time in the back of the room. "We have every small air park covered round the clock. No aircraft have been reported missing since those three that we accounted for this morning. By the way, the local narco squad sent us an official thank-you for identing those drug runners."

"Glad to see we're finding someone," Kilgore laughed. "Liaison?"

An older man hung up a telephone and turned to face the stage. "We're still getting good cooperation from the German authorities, thanks to intervention from the German Interior Ministry. They're getting a little pissed off at us, but they're still circulating the photographs and keeping an eye out. But frankly, I don't think they're trying as hard as they were."

"Are we?" Kilgore chided. He turned to Kapf. "Psy Ops?"

Kapf shrugged. "I have nothing new to add at this time. Except my belief that Mr. Newman is still somewhere in the vicinity. Possibly very close."

Kilgore looked down at him as if he were about to ask a question. Thinking better of it, he turned back to the men.

"Immigration."

A woman looked up from her phone. "Hold on," she said quietly into it. "All U.S. points of entry are on full alert status with likenesses, full descriptions, and computer-altered photographs of the Probe showing him as he might appear in any number of disguises. So far, no bites. German border guards report nothing as well." She turned back to her phone.

"Strike commander?" Kilgore looked through the room. "Strike commander?"

A man came hurrying in. "Sorry, John."

"Go ahead."

"We've still got four teams on full standby to move anywhere in the country within three hours. You find him, we'll take him down." He paused as he sat down. "Just try and find us real targets next time."

Kilgore nodded. "How is the gentleman from Mannsbruck?"

"Threatening to sue all of us, both governments, and anyone else he can think of."

Kilgore smiled. "Okay, everybody see your lawyers on your own time."

They all laughed lightly.

Kilgore let it go on for a moment before continuing.

"Let's grim up." He paused as they settled down. "It's been thirty-three days, guys! Thirty-three days!" He sounded legitimately angry. "Granted this guy is a pro, fully trained in SERE, probably almost to an instinctive level; and he makes his living avoiding guys like us, but come on! We make our living catching guys like him! Get off your asses and find this guy"—he paused to let the anger drain out of him—"before I turn you all in for a pack of elderly blood hounds. Dismiss."

They all quickly returned to work.

Kapf and Beck followed Kilgore off the stage to his small private office.

"I am always surprised," Kapf said as he settled into an easy chair, "at your informality, Captain."

Kilgore shrugged. "They're under enough pressure just trying to do their jobs, without me screaming about uniform buttons, haircuts, and proper military etiquette." He sat down on a small couch opposite Kapf.

"We're wasting time," Beck said as he slowly shook his head.

The younger officer looked over at him. "Sir?"

"I'm going out," he slurred as he turned and started out of the room. "We're not going to find him here!"

Kilgore stared at the spot Beck had stood on for a long time. "I'm starting to worry about him," he said without looking away.

Kapf nodded solemnly. "He is under more stress than I have ever observed in any individual. Most of it self-inflicted, in my opinion."

Kilgore turned to face the psychiatrist. "Speaking of your opinions . . ."

Kapf smiled. "You still don't believe that Mr. Newman is close at hand?"

"No."

"Why not?"

"Because *I* wouldn't be." His tone was anything but that of "Captain Friendly" of a few moments before.

"I've had a lot of the same training he's had. I know all the rules." Kilgore began to tick them off on his fingers. "Don't run in a straight line. Don't stay in one place more than six hours. Don't travel during the day. Don't look anybody in the eye, but don't look away either." He moved forward, onto the edge of the couch. "But all the rules presuppose movement."

"And I assure you, Captain, that Mr. Newman knows them as well. Further, he knows that you know them. As you pointed out to your men, he is an expert in SERE—survival, evasion, resistance, and escape. Has most likely improved it from an art to a science."

He paused, deep in thought, then continued.

"His rules may now be considerably different than yours. He will assume that you, as a creature of the military, as an issue of proper procedure and discipline, will do as you have done. Begin your search in the middle, slowly spiraling your way outward. He would consider the safest place to be within your perimeter, not fleeing from it. Witness his remaining on the Institute's grounds until the search had moved on." He smiled briefly, as if in admiration, then instantly banished the expression.

"Then he's trapped," Kilgore said softly.

Kapf smiled a sad, nearly defeated smile. "Far from it. He merely finds a place where he can hide without any major difficulties and waits for your search to pass him by. He knows eventually you'll move on, then he'll be free to go wherever he pleases."

Kilgore raised his eyebrows. "He's that calculating?"

"And far more so," Kapf said.

Kilgore stood up and walked behind the desk. "So what am I supposed to do?"

"What are your orders?"

The young soldier picked up a sheet of paper and handed it to Kapf. "Continue to expand the search," he recited, "until we reach all four borders. Then disband the core operation and leave it to Intelligence to come up with a lead."

"As expected," Kapf said as he read. "As Newman would expect."

"So what would you advise?"

Kapf handed back the orders. "Ignore that rubbish. Concentrate your efforts within the distance that Mr. Newman could have gotten by sunrise on the day he escaped from the Institute."

Kilgore checked a wall chart that held all the vital statistics of Probe 95–0707.

"He killed the general's man sometime between two and four." He checked some papers on the desk. "Sunrise was at 0732."

"Three and a half to five and a half hours," Kapf said. "There were no reports of any stolen vehicles?"

"None."

Now Kilgore was doing the math.

"Figure an average foot speed of six kilometers per hour, we're talking a maximum perimeter of . . . thirty-three kilometers."

"*That* should be your search area, Captain." Kapf stood to leave. "He will most likely be within that tract."

Kilgore appeared honestly torn between his orders and Kapf's advice. After a long moment of silence, he sadly shook his head.

"Command's already talking about changing our assignment. They're convinced that he's already left the country." He paused. "And they're worried about their budgets. This is costing a ton of bucks."

Kapf stopped at the door. "So, what will you do?"

"What I know. I'll follow my orders and keep expanding the search. But," he said as Kapf started to protest, "I'll also increase local coverage by twenty-five percent."

Kapf nodded as he left. "I'm overdue at the Institute."

"I'll walk you out, Doctor."

The two men walked silently through the search headquarters, stopping at the far door.

"It's the best I can do, Doctor. Believe me. I know them. They won't accept any greater commitment of forces."

"It will not be enough, Captain."

"You're sure?"

"Yes."

"How?"

Kapf turned back to the earnest young officer, then pointed up at the huge photograph of Newman that seemed to be watching them. "Because I know him."

At the Volker Institute, things had long ago returned to normal.

Most of the staff, never having been aware of Newman's presence in the first place, simply went on, uninterrupted with their usual routine. Those that had been assigned to the unit had been briefed, sworn to secrecy, and returned to their jobs.

With two exceptions.

Jack Clemente lay in a top-floor, VIP suite, racked with pain, slowly being eaten away by the malignancy within him. He hadn't been out of bed since the day of Newman's escape.

And Patricia, although apparently healthy and back at work, was sick at heart. Tormented by unanswerable questions, laden with guilt, she'd show up for work each morning, see her patient load for the day, give her lectures, then retreat into her office allegedly to work on a paper about her experiences with Newman.

Actually, to brood and despair.

She'd gone over it all so many times. Analyzed every facet of it. Viewed every minute of video available, read the transcripts. Yet still, a month after the fact, she couldn't find her mistake.

Maybe, she was beginning to think, *there was no mistake.*

As she watched the sun setting through her office window, she turned on her tape recorder and began to dictate.

"Notes on subsection three." She paused as she watched a shadow move across the unit off in the distance. She shut the recorder off and put it down as she allowed her mind to free-associate.

Immediately after the escape, things had been utter chaos. There'd really been no time for postmortems or second-guessing. There'd just been a flat-out dash to find and subdue the missing man.

Guards had been everywhere. Briefings for the special military people, for Department of Defense brass, debriefings of the people that had been there when he'd made his break, had tumbled one upon the other. And at no time, in no way, did anyone even mention the prospect of what might happen if they couldn't catch him.

But that had been a month ago.

And since then, nothing had happened.

Patricia began absently playing with a rubber band as her mind continued its slow-motion replay.

After two weeks and no sign of Newman, the pace eased. Regular duties began to intrude themselves into everyone's schedule, the demands of the searchers on the staff lessened, and finally they were confronted with returning to normal.

That's when Tabbart had called the meeting.

Patricia had arrived at the chief's office with her resignation neatly typed up. She knew that her end at the Institute was now inevitable. Tabbart was going to need a scapegoat and who better than the woman who, in his twisted little mind, was responsible?

And how it is, a voice deep inside reminded her.

She had expected this to be a pro forma meeting where Tabbart would ask for, and she would tender, her resignation. Hell, since she'd been the one that had argued against Newman being in restraints, Tabbart had more than enough ammunition to do her in.

But it was more complicated than that, she told herself. Newman had had some button pushed by the panel, something that triggered this unpredictable behavior. That was the only possible explanation for it all. But of course, Tabbart would find a way to twist that all around.

She had expected it to be a short, ugly, depressing meeting.

She was shown into Tabbart's office, receiving the first of what would be several surprises that day.

Rather than its usual sterile emptiness, the room was packed with people.

Jack Clemente, in a wheelchair and on oxygen, sat to the left of Tabbart. Otto Kapf and Pierre Mont lounged on the sofa, while General Beck sat by the bay window, staring out across the lawn.

Dr. Tabbart sat behind his large, shiny desk, sipping tea from a glass. He nodded formally at Patricia as she entered and sat down in front of him.

Clemente looked terrible. The ravages of the cancer had been compounded by the stress of Newman's escape. She tried to make eye contact with him, smiled in his direction, but he just looked down, waiting for Tabbart to begin.

"Very well," the chief of staff finally said, "I have been informed by the military that, other than an occasional consultation, they are done with us. Therefore, I believe it is time for us to assess for ourselves exactly what has happened, why, where responsibility lies, and what remedial actions need to be taken."

He'd looked right at her during that last part.

"After long discussions with Dr. Clemente, I have reached the following preliminary conclusions. I would like all your opinions on them so that I might best formulate a report to the board of directors."

Patricia braced herself for the worst.

Tabbart began to read from a typed list.

"One: From his arrival into our care, until he was brought up to appear before the review board, the subject was always in the complete custody and control of the personnel at Unit A-249." He paused. "Is there any dissent or discussion to that point?"

Clemente briefly removed his oxygen mask. Looking directly at Patricia, he spoke in a wheezy, weak voice. "None at all." He held her eye contact for a long time.

Patricia got the message and nodded ever so slightly.

Tabbart had looked back down at his sheet.

"Two: Throughout his custody and care, no unanticipated difficulties of a behavioral nature were observed or reported that in any way threatened either unit personnel or the possible unplanned release of the subject." Another pause. "Dissent or discussion?"

He was looking right at Mont.

"The man almost killed me," Mont muttered under his breath.

Tabbart shook his head. "The word in question here, Dr. Mont, is 'unanticipated.' Your occurrence with the subject was well anticipated. You cornered him, metaphorically speaking, and he reacted in a completely anticipated, semihostile manner."

Patricia was beginning to understand.

"His semihostile manner almost semikilled me, metaphorically speaking!" Mont said angrily.

"But it was not unanticipated, I think you'll agree," Tabbart said patiently.

"Of course not, Dr. Tabbart," Patricia ventured.

The little man turned to her and smiled. "Thank you, Dr. Nellwyn."

He returned to his paper. "Three: The DoD review board was advised that it would be unsafe for the subject to be removed from his quarters and brought up to meet with them. It was suggested by senior staff that they go down to meet with the subject or that he be brought up to them shackled and restrained. They rejected these recommendations fully. Dissent or discussion?"

It was to be a full-scale cover-up.

Patricia began to smile.

"Four," Tabbart read on. "In the face of the unwise demands of the DoD review board, all steps were taken to ensure the maximum safety and security of all involved. These included, but were not limited to, a full session between Dr. Nellwyn and the subject. Her advice was that the subject appeared cooperative, but that she would remain alert to any warning signs of change." He looked up at Patricia. "Dissent or discussion?"

"None at all," she said in a pleasant voice.

Tabbart droned on for the next twenty minutes with the official version of the chain of events that led to Newman's eventual escape.

The Institute was blameless. The review board had been unwise, reckless in their dealings with Newman. The review board shouldered full responsibility; the Institute, full credit for keeping it from happening before.

When he finished, he quickly went around the room. Kapf and

Clemente immediately agreed with Tabbart's report. Beck nodded silently. Mont grunted his unwilling assent. Then Tabbart turned back to Patricia.

"Dr. Nellwyn, I will be blunt. We have not always seen eye-to-eye on this and other matters, but I propose we set our differences aside for the sake of the Institute."

She fingered the letter of resignation in her pocket.

"For the sake of a long, prosperous future together?" she asked in a voice tinged slightly with nerves.

Clemente flinched at the tone in her voice, but she never took her eyes off Tabbart, who sat stock-still for a full minute before nodding.

"Agreed," Tabbart said quietly.

"Agreed," she responded.

Since then, she had returned to work, at least that work that Tabbart would allow her.

They had reached an unspoken agreement in return for her support of Tabbart's cover-up. She would remain at the Institute, would probably be promoted to senior staff eventually, but Tabbart would see to it that she would never again receive important patients or assignments.

But, for the moment at least, it was tolerable.

She could work on her paper about Newman. The Institute would support her research into the possibilities of human evolution, however grudgingly. And, after a time, she would move on. Probably to a think tank or university back in the States.

But despite this victory of attrition, Patricia knew that she would always consider herself a failure until and unless she finally put the question of Brian Newman to rest.

She picked up the recorder and began again.

"If the basis for this paper is sound, if the subject is an example of man's inevitable evolutinary development, if the subject suspected this, then perhaps he feared that the panel would, out of fear or malevolence, seek to exterminate him. This action, from the perspective of the subject, would be seen as the logical extension of their fears of what he might do, and what he might mean to their sense of genetic security."

She stopped and played it back. As she listened, she pictured the outrage, the controversy, that would explode when she published this paper. She would be instantly deified and demonized.

But neither prospect gave her any personal satisfaction. Not any-more.

The only thing that mattered was Newman. The truths, the answers that lay within him, were the Holy Grail of everything Patricia believed in. She felt within her an unquenchable desire to know, beyond any doubts or conjecture, where mankind was going. Who and what he was going to become in the millennia ahead.

And Newman was the Rosetta stone to unscrambling that puzzle.

But he was gone.

Sighing deeply, she decided to stop by Jack Clemente's room before leaving for the day. She felt a responsibility to be there for him now as he had been for her.

She hated sick room scenes. Always ended up depressed after them. But she owed Jack.

Even dying, being slowly consumed from within, he had forced Tabbart to keep her on staff. To allow her another possible shot at Newman.

She forced up a smile as she knocked on the door.

His wife was sitting next to his bed, silently knitting, while the television murmured in the background. Clemente seemed to be sleep-ing—fitfully, but sleeping nonetheless.

Jenny looked up as Patricia walked in. The old woman smiled.

"How are you, darling?" Jenny's voice was a perky whisper. She warmly embraced Patricia.

For a moment, Patricia wondered if Jenny truly realized just how sick her husband was. But of course she knew. After all her years of devotion to Jack, she wasn't going to let him down now by playing the grieving widow anywhere he could see it.

Patricia kissed her on the cheek. "How are you?"

Jenny shrugged. "He had a tough afternoon, but he's much better now, I think." She looked over at the only man she had ever loved. "I think he looks better, don't you?"

Patricia didn't.

"Absolutely," she said, trying to sound sincere. Already, she was dying to leap for the door and run away. But her sense of duty over-came her anxiety. "I don't want to wake him." She took a half-step toward the bed, then turned back to Jenny. "Can I do anything for you?"

"What about me?" Clemente said from the bed.

Jenny smiled broadly, walked over, and kissed him on the cheek.

"Well," she said brightly, "look who's awake!"

"Dr. Nellwyn," Clemente said in a mock-professional wheeze, "would you kindly order my wife to go home. Get something to eat, some rest."

Patricia walked over and kissed him on the other cheek.

"You see," Clemente said, smiling at his wife, "you're worried how I look, and young, sexy women can't keep their lips off me. Go!"

Jenny nodded, picked up her purse, then kissed her husband again.

"Just a little bite in the cafeteria, sweetheart."

Patricia put her arm around her. "I'll stay until you get back."

Jenny nodded, turned, and started for the door. She opened it, stopped, and turned back.

"I love you," she said in a voice laden with tears.

"Go!" Clemente demanded.

Jenny turned and hurried away before he could see the tears begin to run.

Patricia pulled a chair alongside the bed. "So, old man, how they treatin' you?" Her expression said nothing's wrong, just two old friends passing the time of day.

Clemente managed a shrug. "I'm dying." He said it simply. "One of the more natural processes of life." He coughed, causing him to put the oxygen mask on for two minutes. Finally, he took it off. "I just wish it wouldn't take so damn long!"

Patricia didn't know what to say or do.

Clemente, sensing it, just smiled. "So, how are things in internal exile?"

"Quiet."

"I can imagine." He paused and took her hand. "How's the paper coming?"

"You really want to know about this? I mean . . ." She looked around at all the apparatus that labored to keep him alive.

"Your bedside manner, as always, is impeccable."

Patricia looked embarrassed.

"We can talk about my carcinoma if you'd prefer," Clemente said casually. "I have some rather nice Polaroids taken during last week's operation."

Patricia laughed and held up her hands in surrender. "I'll pass." An awkward pause. "The paper, right. Well, it's coming. Slowly, but it's coming."

"What's the problem?"

"I keep running into walls."

"Go on."

She stood up and began to pace. "Kapf's dichotomy," she said. "If Newman is mentally diseased, we can only know for sure with the passage of time. Simultaneously, if he's not sick, if he *is* the next evolutionary stage of man, we can only know for sure with the passage of time."

"And?"

"Without Newman, or being unable to conduct further tests and studies on a higher level than anything we've ever run before, we can neither prove nor disprove either theory."

Clemente was silent for a moment. "And how do you feel about that?"

Patricia spun to face him. "Don't you try to analyze me, Jack Clemente. Bedridden or not, I'll pop you one."

Clemente inclined his head to one side, thinking it over. "What's the matter? Clinical Patty just have a nerve hit?"

"You're not dying," she said as she sat down, "you're just using that as an excuse to be a pain in the ass!"

"True," he said in a weaker voice. "But you never answered my question. How do you feel about not having Newman around to prove your theory?" His voice might have been weak, but his eyes demanded an answer.

"Truth?"

"Sure."

She leaned close to him and whispered. "Relieved."

"Ahh."

She looked surprised. "What's that supposed to mean?"

"I was wondering if you'd ever admit that you're worried you might be wrong."

She shook her head. "That's not it," she said as the door opened behind her. "I'm scared to death that I might be right."

She turned to see who had come in, but there was no one. Only the door silently swinging closed.

She shrugged and changed the subject to Institute gossip until Jenny returned an hour later.

Five floors below Clemente's room, the Institute's chapel sat off to one side of the main lobby. Always dimly lit, the nondenominational place for prayer and meditation was open around the clock throughout the week.

But in truth, it was seldom used by anyone other than the occasional day visitor.

Tonight, though, one man kneeled behind a front pew, hands clasped together, head bowed, leaning against them.

Konrad Edel, as was his practice these last few weeks, had stopped to say a prayer on his way out of the building.

"We humble ourselves before you, O Lord," he mumbled. "Yours is the greatness and the good. Yours is the power and the glory. Yours is the hope and the redemption and the inspiration."

He squeezed his eyes tighter as he felt the spirit well up within him.

"My God, as thou has before, watch over your humble servant. My way is your way. In your steps, I seek to stride. Grant me the wisdom and the strength to bear my burdens silently; the humility to place the needs of others above my own; the sure and certain faith in the perfection of your plan for us in your universe."

The chapel door opened behind him, but he didn't let it disturb the sense of grace that he always felt as he neared the end of his prayers.

"My Lord, grant rest and comfort to Jack Clemente, who suffers the terrible pains of cancer. Grant peace of mind to Alexander Beck, who stands on the precipice of that most terrible place you put within us all.

"And my Lord God, bestow upon your lost lamb, Brian Newman, your gentle kindness and tender mercies. Bring down upon him the calm, serenity, and peace that he so desperately seeks. Grant to him the self-control and the wisdom to do the right thing in this, his moment of greatest trial.

"In the name of your son, I do beseech you. Amen."

Edel paused, then pulled himself to his feet. As he turned, starting back up the aisle, he noticed a man kneeling, deep in prayer in one of the shadowy corners of the chapel. He looked away, not wishing to intrude.

"Amen," Newman said as he raised his head to look at the door as it slowly swung shut behind the security chief.

Ghislain walked up the rickety stairs to the attic. His level of dread and foreboding increased with every step as he approached the room reserved for the "special patrons" of his private club.

The room had a dark history and the occupants often had to pay a high price to have their "messes" cleaned up after they left. Telltale stains would be removed from carpets, or the carpeting itself would be replaced. The source of the stains would either be handsomely paid off or deposited from some dark bank into the icy green waters of the Isar River.

Green, Ghislain often thought, for the color of the money that would be paid on each occasion that a predawn visit ended with the quiet splash of a rolled-up carpet weighted down with the remains of an unfortunate who would never be missed.

But the man who would soon come to the room was different from any that had come before.

The usual patrons of the room were powerful men, wealthy heads of multinational corporations or high political officials. Controlling men—with a need to be completely out of control, if only for a night, an hour, a moment.

And for the right price they were guaranteed their men, women, children, animals, with no rules, no laws, no judgments, either moral or legal, to hinder their enjoyment of the experience.

But the man who would soon come to the room had no such need to be out of control. A man who balanced on the thinnest of edges between control and chaos and never, ever, toppled one way or the other.

Just over two weeks earlier, it had begun.

It had been almost noon, the middle of the night to the sex club proprietor. Ghislain was asleep in the master suite of his expensive, heavily secured home outside Munich. The children were in school, his wife somewhere downstairs puttering around.

Suddenly, to this day he had no clear idea why, he awoke, certain that something was very wrong.

He sat bolt upright in his bed and looked around. His wife, Frieda, was standing by the foot of the bed, staring at him with a strange expression.

"Friedie, was ist los?"

She didn't move, didn't speak, just stood there, eyes wide open, darting to her left.

Ghislain slowly turned to his right.

A man with a pleasant expression on his pale face stood there, pointing a sawed-off shotgun at Frieda's head.

"If you move," the man said in a relaxed voice, "your children will come home to discover pieces of you both sticking to the wall." He spoke in schoolboy German with an American accent.

Ghislain remained stock-still.

"I have money," he began slowly, "in the safe, maybe thirty thousand marks. Also my wife's jewelry. Take it all. We will not fight." He worked hard to keep his voice rock-steady.

"Thank you, I will," the man said evenly, "if it comes to that. But I'd much rather add to your safe than lighten it." He paused. "I have a business proposition for you."

"I do not discuss business with guns pointed at my wife!" Ghislain had been surprised to hear himself say.

"You will today" had been the man's soft reply.

"Why?"

The man had shrugged. "Because I'm the one pointing the gun."

The ease, the casualness, of the way the man spoke caused the hairs on the back of Ghislain's neck to stand up.

For the next fifteen minutes, the man spoke in detail about what he wanted and what he was willing to do for it. At some point, the man, sensing that Ghislain's fear had been replaced by intrigue, lowered the shotgun.

After twenty-five minutes, Ghislain ordered his wife to make coffee and say nothing to anyone.

After forty-five minutes, the bargain had been struck.

The man wanted a full set of identity papers of the highest quality. The kind that would withstand the closest visual scrutiny. He wanted three men located. Not picked up, not killed (which would have been cheaper), just found. Most of all, he wanted a place where, as he put it, "I can conduct my business" with the men he was seeking.

And he offered the most extraordinary thing in return! Payment of a kind that the very audacity of the offer made it almost irresistible.

Ghislain had made the deal instantly. In fact, he'd had no choice. For he knew that the pleasant-faced man would kill both him and his wife without a thought if he was refused.

Besides, Ghislain had thought at the time, once the man was out of the house, he could always be given over to the police.

Or others of Ghislain's acquaintance.

But deep down, he felt that the man was no lunatic or boastful hood trying to impress. And he knew, without a word being said, what the cost would be if he ever crossed up the smiling, pleasant man.

As for the man's method of introducing himself, well, that one simple act of getting past three armed security guards and through an elaborate alarm system, all in a heavily patrolled, gated community in the middle of the day, was as eloquent a letter of introduction as Ghislain could imagine.

That had all been seventeen days ago and things had gone even better than the smiling man had promised.

Each of the five clubs in the Playground that were real competition for Ghislain had suffered major "accidents," forcing them to close down.

The Erotica had burned to the ground.

The Pleasure Spa had suffered from natural gas explosions.

Bacchus' Playground had experienced a wave of unexplained mechanical failures that injured twelve.

Limousine patrons of two other clubs had been photographed by an unknown source who had released some of the photos to the newspapers. The clubs had quickly been abandoned by their customers, then their owners.

And most of the five clubs' patrons, especially the late night limousine trade which would go nowhere near the slightest possibility of notoriety, had ended up at Ghislain's.

His business increased fivefold. He'd had to put on more girls, bartenders, was even thinking of expanding into the building next door to deal with the increased traffic.

But now it was time for the Devil to collect his due.

Ghislain stopped at the attic landing, straightened his tie, smoothed back his hair, and unlocked the door.

The room was furnished as an expensive, sophisticated master suite. A Victorian four-poster bed was the centerpiece of plush carpets, mahogany antique furniture, and lush wallpaper. Designer lamps brightly lit the room, reflecting off the finest gilt mirrors in Germany. A dressing room and full bath suite stood off to one side.

Ghislain saw all of this in a second, was satisfied that all was as it should be, then walked across the thick carpet. He pulled aside the heavy velvet curtains, pulled up the shade behind it, exposing the heavily barred windows.

Searching in his pocket, he came up with a large, old-fashioned stick key, with which he unlocked the window, then the barred grate that protected the outside.

Briefly, almost expectantly, he looked down into the alley below, but could see nothing.

It didn't comfort him.

He hurriedly closed the window, lowered the shade, and returned the heavy curtains to their original position. He left the light on, the door unlocked, as he quickly climbed down the three flights of stairs to the street. He let himself out a side exit of the club.

Moving around the back of the building, into the alley, he stopped at a point directly beneath the attic room. He looked around but could only see garbage cans, locked doors, and the occasional scurrying rat.

He checked his watch. It was five minutes to one in the morning.

"It is Ghislain," he said softly. "I am here."

There was no answer.

"Apollyon, it is Ghislain. I have news."

Again, no answer.

A moment later, movement in one of the doorways caught his attention. He watched, stunned, as the smiling man he had come to know as Apollyon slowly emerged from the shadows.

"Glad to hear it" was all Newman said. He gestured to the club owner, who reluctantly walked over.

In the dim light of the alley, Ghislain noticed that Newman had put on about ten pounds in the three weeks he'd known him. His skin was darker, with a healthy tan replacing the pallor. He was also well on his way to growing a beard and mustache.

"The third man," Ghislain began, handing over the pencil sketch of Tabbart. "A girl in the Reisch District spotted him."

Newman looked at the sketch. "Good."

"I caused inquiries to be made," Ghislain said too quickly as the dark, the alley, and the presence of this man who reeked of lethality combined to reinforce every fear, real or imagined, the brothel owner had ever had. "Once every week to ten days, your man arrives at a café for a rendezvous with another man. They stay, talk for about an hour, then leave separately. I have no information on the other man except that he is supposed to be a dealer in Russian icons. I am causing further inquiries to be made." He self-consciously wiped his sweaty palms on his pants.

Newman nodded. "Of course."

Suddenly, he changed into what Ghislain recognized, with some relief, as his friendly mode.

"How's business?"

The older man grinned. "Never better. We are, how do you Americans say, standing room only, almost every night." He paused. "Our program of public relations has been even more successful than you had said it would be." He laughed lightly.

Newman smiled. "We aim to please," he said casually. "I come from an old established firm and we appreciate a satisfied customer. Besides"—his voice started to drift away as it sometimes did—"it feels good to work again."

He looked off into the distance as if completely caught up in a memory.

Suddenly, he realized that Ghislain was staring at him.

"Your wife and children," he said with a half-smile, "how're they doing?"

Not for a moment did Ghislain feel soothed by the relaxed expression on the smiling face. The simple, polite question sent chills through him.

"Fine," he said quickly, returning to the business at hand. "I also have good news of your papers."

"Glad to hear it." Newman sensed the man's nerves. "If there's no problem, you've got nothing to worry about. Relax."

Ghislain took a small piece of paper out of his pocket.

"As requested, your name will be Charon Apollyon, a naturalized Greek American citizen from New York City." He paused. "Are you sure you wish to use such a unique name? It could cause unwanted attention."

"Just the opposite," Newman said as he read over Ghislain's shoulder. "The more bizarre the name, the less attention the immigration people pay. You want to get stopped, use Joe Smith."

Ghislain shrugged. "As you say." He reached into his jacket and handed across a sealed envelope. "These are the credit cards, club membership cards, and other New York state and civic papers you requested."

"The others?" Newman asked as he opened the envelope and sorted through it.

"Driver's license and Social Security card in two days. The passport maybe then, maybe a day later."

They both looked up as Ghislain's cellular phone began to ring.

He answered it quickly.

"*Ja.*" A long pause. "*Ein Moment.*" He turned to Newman. "The first man, he has arrived."

Newman nodded, then walked toward the club. "Delay him."

Ghislain spoke hurriedly into the phone, then switched it off.

"Everything is as you requested," he said uneasily in Newman's direction.

"Good."

A long silence enveloped the alley. Finally, Newman walked back, smiling at Ghislain.

"I'll need the remaining ID in two days. No longer."

"Of course."

"I'll call you with the place and time later this evening."

Something was changing in the man. He seemed slightly upset, slightly tense. Almost like an athlete in the moments before a championship match.

"Shall I have him brought up?"

Newman looked around the alley, checking out the club's exterior wall, the metal lacework fire escape. Finally, he nodded.

"Fine."

Ghislain switched on his cellular.

"Imagine the coincidence," he said as he dialed. "The first man you sought, already being a member of my club."

Newman walked over to the base of the fire escape, moving a garbage can over as he did. He estimated the distance from the top of the can to the base of the suspended ladder, then nodded to himself.

Suddenly, he seemed to remember that Ghislain was still there.

"From such coincidences," he said with a private smile, "the Erotica's ashes blow away and your club thrives."

Newman watched the nervous club owner hurry away, casting anxious looks over his shoulder. When he'd gone, Newman looked up the length of the fire escape, ending at the attic room's window.

In his head, he did the calculations.

Two minutes for Beck to go through the formalities of making his selection for the evening.

Five minutes more for him to be escorted up the three flights of stairs.

Another three minutes for the girl to arrive.

Ghislain had briefed Newman on the general's proclivities, and Newman himself had talked to two of the girls that had serviced Beck in the past.

Four more minutes for the charade to play itself out to the point that Newman wanted.

Fourteen minutes in total.

He looked at his watch: 1:03 A.M. He melted back into the doorway to continue his wait and his think.

He knew that he was being incredibly stupid for pursuing this private agenda. It entailed massive risks, depleted his resources, which, after the club hits, now stood around 30,400 marks (about $23,000, most of which he would need for his eventual escape), and exposed him needlessly to the possibility of arrest or death.

In the long run, it would accomplish nothing, not even serve a need for vengeance that he didn't feel anyway.

But he'd known that he had to do it almost from the first moments of his freedom.

Sitting quietly in the upper branches of the heavily leafed tree, he'd watched the search for him grow. First Edel's security men, then, about an hour later, the better trained, highly disciplined military teams.

Twice in the first three hours, he heard them come to a stop just below his tree. The leaves were too thick for them to see him or for him to see them for that matter, but he had heard them, though he'd largely ignored their presence, feeling safe and secure in his hidden perch.

He'd allowed his mind to wander, to analyze and muse over the various courses his life could take from that moment forward.

He knew that eventually the searchers would move on and that he would be free. But free to do what?

Initially, he thought of heading south into Austria, from there maybe Yugoslavia, a small, chaotic Adriatic port, and a slow boat home to the States, where he could disappear into one of the giant melting pots that he could move in comfortably.

He thought of heading east to Spain, losing himself in the olive groves and peaceful quiet of Catalonia.

In fact, when he'd dropped from the tree, he hadn't made up his mind which way to go.

Beck's man changed that.

The implications of that one futile act, that pointless message sent by Beck, raised so many questions in Newman's mind that it instantly altered all of his planning and thoughts.

And the message was unquestionably clear.

If Newman could not be contained, he must be killed.

But it didn't make sense.

Agents had gone rogue before, many of them far more important than he was. Killing was always the last option, only after all other options had been tried and exhausted in an attempt to recover the missing man or woman.

But Beck had gone to the stick first.

Why?

Newman posed no threat to any ongoing intelligence operations. Beck and the government knew that he could never be made to compromise any intelligence networks still in place. And he bore them no serious animosities.

Well, not enough to have him killed over.

But Beck had tried anyway. And Beck never did anything without higher sanction, which begged the question.

Why?

He remembered looking back at the corpse of the victim Beck had set in his path and wondering. What was it that he possessed that made him such a threat? What was the reason behind his bizarre incarceration and now the death hunt?

The thought had continued rattling around inside him as he left the grounds.

He'd casually walked away from the institute, hitchhiking a ride from a friendly Belgian trucker as far as Freising, about forty kilometers north of Munich. The man had even loaned Newman forty marks, about thirty dollars American.

He'd spent those first few days hiding in a drainage pipe just outside the city.

At night, he would walk or hitch his way into the small farming town to get the lay of the land. But his mind never wandered far from the question that plagued him throughout his daylight hours of semi-sleep, deep in the damp, cool mildew of the pipe.

Why?

By his third day, he'd decided, knowing that it was the wrong thing to do, that he had to find the answer before he left.

He quickly used up the forty marks on food and basic clothing, so he put his search aside and concentrated on taking care of the most immediate business.

If he was going to stay, he'd need more money and a more permanent, safer place to live.

On nights four through six, a series of late night burglaries was reported in the Freising business district. The small German businessman's propensity for keeping locked boxes with large amounts of cash in them fit well with his plans and, after his fifth illegal entry, he took his 1,815 marks (just under $1,400) and headed for the town closest to the institute.

He rented a small dilapidated grocery store in a run-down, poor section for 900 marks. No questions were asked by the absentee land-lord. The landlord owned the entire block of stores and they had been mostly vacant ever since the recession hit after the wall came down. The entire transaction had been accomplished through the mail and over the phone.

The location was perfect. The neighborhood was quiet and mostly deserted. The few stores that were open functioned merely as fronts for the Turkish drug dealers and anarchists who rented them.

Newman liked that. These were people who would ask no questions and were not likely to help out when, inevitably, the searchers came around.

He had no illusions about the searchers. Right now, he was behind them, but before they abandoned the hunt, they would recheck every trail once more. They would begin by canvassing and recanvassing all hotels, lodges, hostels, but would eventually get around to the storefronts.

The trick would be in the timing.

The grocery quickly became his base of operations, fully stocked with two weeks of dried food, a first-aid kit, clothes, and basic weapons (both purchased and stolen). The walls were filled with carefully marked maps, as well as intricately designed charts.

By night, he surveilled the Institute, often taking the inordinate risk of actually walking in the front door and breaking into offices, reading the files within.

By day, he would fill out his charts, staring at them on the walls for hours, trying to find the pattern, the secret message that would lead him where he had to go.

Still, he'd been unable to find his answer.

But he was close.

Hastily photocopied memoranda, read at his leisure back at the grocery, sketched out that there was "a theory of unusual definition" about him. And it appeared that this theory, although clearly contro-versial, was driving the government's actions.

He watched Patricia, in her office, on rounds, driving to and from work. He'd thought of her theory, the one that had gotten her tempo-rarily replaced, and he wondered if it was the same as the one men-tioned in the memos.

Once, he'd even stood in her bedroom, over her sleeping form, and thought about forcing the answer from her.

He knew that it would be easy to do, but that it would be an irrevocable step that could only energize his pursuers. And he'd been unwilling to do that.

Then.

So he had settled for a brief reading of the contents of her briefcase. Some outline for a paper on something she called *Homo crudelis.* Coldhearted Man. He quickly put it aside, finding the concept interesting mental masturbation, but not relating to his problem at hand.

Then, with a mischievous smile, he had an idea.

Patricia awakened to find a flower on the pillow beside her head. Fear was almost immediately replaced by exhilaration.

Three nights in the next five, a silent, invisible intruder had visited her. Each time leaving a flower.

Each time rifling her briefcase.

For the first time, she felt in complete control of the situation that she'd kept to herself. And she began to record her thoughts in a secret journal she kept locked in her files at the Institute.

"Newman is scared," she wrote, "alone, reaching out to the one person in the world he feels a bond with. A connection, probably sexual, has been established between subject and therapist. It is a fragile thing, but if properly nourished (the therapist's physical well-being borne in mind) it might eventually yield the clearest picture of the subject yet."

And she'd begun doing her part to ease the *nourishment.*

More detailed papers from her reports were kept in her briefcase for her seminightly visitor's education. She slept lighter, when she slept, wearing the more feminine, sexier—more revealing—night things she was sure Newman preferred. Thought about approaching him many times when she'd hear him prowling through the house. Or just opening her eyes when she felt his presence above her.

The next move belonged to Newman, she thought, believed. Hoped.

But the visits eventually dwindled, and she began to miss the flowers as she mourned the end of yet another of "Clinical Patty's" relationships.

For his part, Newman watched, read, concealed himself during the day, sought his answers by night.

Until that one night, just over two weeks after his escape, when by sheerest luck he had stumbled across Beck walking into the Devil's Playground.

Newman, whose cash was beginning to run low, had come to the red-light district in search of some easy victims who carried cash and were unlikely to report a robbery.

While sizing up a likely prospect, he was stunned to see the general, topcoat collar pulled up to help hide his identity, walk right past him. All thoughts of money disappeared as he immediately became a fanged shadow in the general's wake.

He watched as the general went into Ghislain's club.

He waited two hours until the general had come out again, looking pale and spent.

He'd spent the last of his money on bribes to find out about the club, about Ghislain, and for the bus ride out to Ghislain's suburban home.

And the plan had been put into effect.

He looked around the alley. It was still deserted. Checking his watch, he counted five minutes to go. He walked over, standing next to the garbage can under the ladder.

Ghislain had always been the big question, but Newman had come to realize that the man was completely without scruples or morality. Exactly the type Newman needed right now.

He knew that eventually the man would betray him. It was written across his face in bright green dollar signs. But that was acceptable. At least it would be an honest betrayal born of greed, not political expedience.

And even that betrayal would, in its way, contribute to Newman's overall plans.

He smiled as he climbed on top of the can.

It was 1:15.

Time to begin.

————

Beck liked the attic room, but he still felt uneasy about it.

Never having been there before, he'd walked through every inch of it, assuring himself that there were no hidden cameras or microphones. Finally satisfied, he sat down in an antique rocker to wait for the girl.

He was tired. God was he tired! He felt it in every sinew of his body and every fiber of his brain. He wasn't sleeping, had virtually stopped eating, was falling apart in most every way. But somehow he held at least the appearance of sanity together by sheer force of will.

It hadn't been easy.

Since Newman's escape, he'd been tortured by waking nightmares of a demonic Newman stalking an unsuspecting world, striking randomly. Beck would always be one step behind him, always coming upon the dismembered, decomposing corpses as they exhaled their last breaths.

And all of them would look into his soul with their dead eyes, silently accusing and damning him to Hell eternal.

So, he had returned to Ghislain's club.

The girl's soft knock on the door caused him to flinch. He pulled himself together, straightened his jacket, and took a deep breath.

"Come in."

She was young, not more than twenty. Her sweet open face, shiny blond hair, firm full body beneath the conservative clothes, were all that he had asked for and more.

"I am sorry to have kept you waiting," she said sweetly as she walked over, extending her hand. "How might I help you this evening?"

Beck slowly reached out, taking her hand in his. Squeezing it tightly.

"I'm not sure you can," he said in a voice hoarse from lust and pain combined into one, unnamed, black emotion.

"Please, sir," she said demurely. "You may tell me anything."

He pulled her close, grabbing her buttocks, forcing her against his face.

She squirmed uncomfortably. "Sir, please, this is not right!"

He began to pull at her. She struggled, suddenly losing her balance, toppling onto the floor. He fell on top of her as she began to fight.

"Bitch!" he said as he began to tear at her clothes. "You little tease!

You think you can analyze me! Can get inside my head!" He tore her blouse off and began to pull up her skirt. "Not bloody likely!" He tore at her exposed breasts.

At that moment, flushed with excitement, with rage, his skin beet red as he reached the climax of his assault on the seemingly defenseless girl, he felt a gentle, cool night breeze reach out and brush his cheek. It was so unexpected that it distracted him for a moment. But he quickly ignored it and returned to the girl.

"Call me . . . Newman," he growled. "Brian Newman."

"That could get a little confusing," a familiar voice said from the corner of the room.

Beck froze.

His eyes searched the room until he spotted Newman standing by the velvet curtains, a sad expression on his face.

The girl quietly gathered her clothes and left the room, closing the door behind her.

For a full minute, the two men just stared at each other, then Beck slowly came to a sitting position.

Newman walked deeper into the room, coming to a stop between Beck and the door. He saw Beck sneak a glance at his topcoat which lay across the foot of the bed. He smiled as he simultaneously recognized the bulge in the coat and the look in the general's eyes.

"You'll never make it," Newman said casually. "You know me. You know what I mean."

Beck bit his lower lip, seemed to give in to the inevitable, then launched himself toward the bed.

Newman's heel caught the general in the small of the back, driving him painfully to the floor inches short of the gun in his coat. Desperately, Beck reached for it again, only to have his spread fingers casually grabbed by the man behind him, then bent painfully back. As he was forced to a sitting position, Newman's knee slammed into the older man's face.

Beck collapsed in a broken pile of blood and irredeemable sins at Newman's feet. He turned back to Newman, his enemy/friend, student/creation, a look of soulful pain, terror, and relief in his rheumy eyes.

"Are you done?" Newman's voice was calm, sad, almost patronizing.

Beck was quiet for a long time. "Are you going to kill me?"

Newman shrugged while he studied the man on the floor. "Interesting little scene just now."

Beck wanted to look away. Wanted to disappear into the thick carpet and never be seen again. Instead, he just continued looking at Newman.

Newman took the .45 from Beck's coat, then casually sat down in an antique rocker by the door.

"You'll have to forgive me, my Freudian analysis skills aren't what they once were." He paused. "Is this wish fulfillment or a latent desire to be punished for your sins?"

No answer.

"Oh come on," he chided, "don't be a spoilsport. Which is it?" He sounded genuinely amused.

"What do you want?" Beck choked out.

"A great many things, I assure you. Care to be more specific?"

After a long silence, which Newman was clearly not going to break, Beck shook his head.

"You'll never get away."

"But I already have. Or didn't you notice? By the way, just for the record, what was his name?"

"Who?" Beck looked confused, then he suddenly understood. "Oh." A pause. "Leonard Pelikan. He had a wife and three children, in case you'd like that for the record also," the general spit out.

Newman seemed unimpressed.

"Hope he was insured." Newman shook his head slowly as he looked, unblinkingly, at his former commander. "What the hell happened to you in the last six and a half years?" His voice took on an edge of genuine concern laced with pity.

Beck looked down at the carpet.

"I got old."

"Bullshit."

"I got tired."

"Bullshit."

Beck looked up at him, his eyes beginning to water, just a little bit.

"I got used up."

"That, I believe."

"Can I get up?"

Newman nodded and gestured at the chair across from him. He smiled as Beck fixed his clothes, stood, then sat down in the chair.

"How'd it happen?" Newman asked, his tone sounding sincere.

Beck shrugged. "Too many years fighting other people's wars, I guess. Too many friends buried in unmarked graves in unreachable places. Too many shared memories of their pain. Too much blood, too many bodies. Too much, period."

"Touching," Newman said, suppressing a laugh. "I can just picture it. The sensitive colonel, forgive me, general, grieving over the loss of his men. Feeling their pain, living their horrors." He paused, his face taking on a grim look. "Funny, I don't remember seeing you in any of my cells."

"I tried to get you out," Beck said softly.

Newman ignored him. "I looked for you, you know? When they began, what was it they call it?" He thought for a moment. "Ah yes! The audit sessions! That's it!" He leaned forward.

"They would begin their audit sessions and I'd look for you. They'd attach their electrodes to my balls and I'd look for you. The needles with their God knows what spiking into my veins and I'd look for you. The heating elements tied to the bottoms of my feet and I'd look for you." He paused as if deep in memory. "The chandelier, and I would most definitely look for you."

His voice dropping low and dangerous. "God how I wanted to share all that with you!"

Beck was trembling slightly. "I don't understand," he said softly. "The chandelier?"

Newman's face brightened. "You mean you don't know? It wasn't in the reports or the files you got from our dear new friends the Russians?" He smiled, standing up in front of Beck. "Well, let me give you a full report."

"You don't have to," Beck said mournfully as a muscle in his cheek began twitching uncontrollably.

"But I do! I do! What kind of toy soldier would I be if I didn't?"

Newman looked around the room, finally spotting what he was looking for. He walked over to the curtains and ripped down a long length of curtain cord. He carried it back over to Beck, tying a slip-knot in each end as he did.

"It's an interesting little game that my interrogators liked to play whenever they thought my attention was lagging." He held the two ends in front of Beck.

"Stand up," he said pleasantly.

"Please don't," Beck said in a scared, almost childlike voice.

"Stand up."

Slowly, Beck stood.

Newman put his arm around the man's shoulders and led him to the center of the room.

"Now the first thing they did was throw the middle of the rope over a chandelier hook." Newman lightly tossed the cord over a bare hook in the ceiling that he had installed several days before. "Then they would tie one of the loops around my right wrist"—he did it as he talked—"and the other around my left ankle."

He tucked the gun in his belt as he held the loose end of the cord out to Beck.

"If you'd please, General." Newman stood on his right foot, raising his left leg behind him about two and a half feet off the floor.

Beck just stood there, precariously balancing on legs that seemed about to give way.

"C'mon, General! It's your big chance. I'll be completely at your mercy!" He smiled, but the grin was not at all comforting. "DO IT!" he commanded.

Beck slowly took the cord and, with shaking hands, pulled it around Newman's upraised left ankle.

"Good. Make it tight now." Newman seemed completely relaxed. "It takes a while to work, but I think you can understand the principle behind it. Eventually, my right leg gives out and I drop my left foot. This pulls my arm up sharply, threatening to rip it out of the socket."

His eyes were locked with Beck's.

"I'm at your mercy, General."

Beck didn't move.

"Just like I was with our new friends the Russians," Newman said coldly. "There's nothing I can do. I'm all yours. You can stand there and wait until my leg gives out, then you can watch me swing here for a while. Or you can call the hunters, have them come, wrap me up, and take me away."

Beck's trembling was sweeping through his body. He took a step toward the door, stopped. Took a step toward Newman and stopped. Sweat poured from his body, staining his shirt, dripping onto the carpet, stinging his eyes.

"C'mon, Alex! This is your big break! Make the call!" Newman paused. "Or maybe you'd rather take back your great big gun and kill me yourself."

Beck had been staring down at the floor. His head snapped up at the statement.

"What?"

"Go ahead," Newman said in a seductive whisper. "Do it. Blow my brains all over this nice blue carpet. Make pretty patterns with my guts all over the wall. C'mon, be a sport. Be a pal." He paused. "Be a hero!"

Beck's trembling suddenly stopped. He straightened, took several deep, labored breaths, then took a step toward Newman.

"Good," Newman coaxed. "Just a few more feet."

Beck started to reach out, tried to extend his arm down to the gun. He reached out with his other arm, with both arms, tried desperately to reach it.

Sweat poured off his fingers. His mouth opened and closed spasmodically. His breath came in short gulps, his eyes glazed over.

Newman shook his head as he watched the scene.

"It's okay, Alex," he said in a soothing tone. "It's okay, old man."

Beck's shoulders slumped. A moment later, he had removed the cord from around the younger man's ankle.

Newman never took his eyes off the destroyed man in front of him. He slowly loosened the loop around his wrist.

"You know, Alex, after tonight we'll never see each other again."

"I know."

"And there's something I want you to know, before we go any further."

"Yeah?" Beck looked as though he'd been awake for a century.

Newman put his hand on Beck's shoulder. "Yes." He paused. "I'm not your fault."

Both men were quiet for a long time. Finally, Beck broke the silence.

"Thank you," he said weakly.

Newman smiled a friendly smile.

Then he held out the cord to the general.

"Shall we begin?"

Beck looked at the cord, took it, and slowly put it around his wrist.

It was almost morning.

The deep blue of the night sky was slowly giving way to deep grays and could not much longer hold off the inevitable dawn.

No matter how much Beck wanted it to.

He sat in one of the rockers, gently massaging his aching leg and his broken ego. He wasn't really hurt, not in any meaningful, physical way. There were no broken bones, no obvious bruises. But there was a wound, and it cut completely through him to that secret place within us all where our *selves* are most protected.

And the pain was unnamable!

For almost five hours, it had gone on. Relentless. Implacable. Carefully planned techniques guaranteed to obtain the desired results. To ensure against lies. To anticipate and circumvent trained defenses and improvised trickery.

Newman had learned well from his Russian teachers.

Beck told Newman the little that he knew. Why not? The man had a right to know. And he would find out eventually anyway.

How couldn't he?

Already Beck was beginning to view Newman openly, in the way that he'd always thought of him secretly. As a force of nature. A human leviathan, capable of anything, anywhere, anytime. What Kapf had called the *Übermensch.*

The unstoppable superman of Nietzsche's dreams and other philosophers' nightmares.

It didn't take long before he told Newman of Patricia's theory, as much as he understood of it anyway. He told him Clemente's theory of his case. Hell, he'd even told him Mont's theory of Newman's antiestablishment neurosis.

But he'd left out Kapf.

Why? Even now, he had no clear idea.

But hang on to it he did, with the persistence of an oyster to a pearl—a pearl he would not let Newman see.

Newman had been considerate, at least as considerate as a torturer could be to his victim. He could have pressed harder, caused more, deeper, physical pain, but he'd intentionally held back from it.

It was as if even now, with all the barriers stripped away, with all the bullshit that had passed between them flushed into the dank sewer of their past lives, he couldn't bring himself to *really* torture Beck.

Too much had passed between them for that.

But he could ask his questions.

And he could demand his answers.

He'd asked about the searchers. Who was commanding them? What was he like? Where were they based? How many, where, when . . . But always he came back to the one, central theme.

Why?

And always, Beck's answer remained the same.

"Orders from higher authority."

Beck had expected that to enrage Newman, to drive him into an emotional and physical fury that would end the session there and then—maybe, mercifully, forever.

But his response had always been the same.

"From whom? On what authority? What do they know? Why?"

Then they would start again. The answers would pour out like thickening blood from a held-open wound. Slower, ever slower, but constantly and with no end in sight.

"Patricia—evolution. Clemente—disease. Mont—neurosis."

And Beck's mind raced.

Don't tell him Kapf! Never Kapf! Don't talk about Kapf! Hold it back!
Save something! Beat him at something! Gotta have a win. Just one win.
Gotta have something, anything . . . Oh God! My God! Where are you?
Over here! PLEASE! No. No. Mustn't call God! No! He might notice. Can't
let him see! Can't let him find out . . . OH HELL! SAVE ME!

Then it was over.

Newman helped him to bed, carefully tended his chafed and rope-burned wrist and ankle. Got him a cold, damp towel from the bathroom. Some cold water to soothe the dry throat.

"I'll have some ice sent up for that shoulder," Newman had said calmly. "Maybe they have some liniment or something."

He'd started for the door, then turned back.

"If you leave this room in less than three hours, you'll be dead. After that, I don't care what you do." He paused, seeming to study his former mentor. "You're an interesting man, General. An interesting man. It's a shame you don't have a clue about what's going on."

"I know," Beck muttered.

"What was that?"

"I know."

"Do you?"

Newman walked back, looking him over with a surgeon's stare.

The jaw set. The expression resolved. The eyes red with exhaustion and pain. Looking up at Newman, not with fear of dying or of more pain, but something else entirely. A deep soul-tearing fear, like a soothsayer seeing not his own death in his crystal ball, but the deaths of many, hundreds, thousands, millions.

Everyone.

The two men had stared at each other for over two minutes. Then Newman had slowly nodded.

"Good."

Again, Newman started for the door. "But whatever you do," he laughed, "do it under your own name, okay? The other is just too embarrassing." He turned, leaving the room, chuckling to himself.

Beck straightened in the chair. Slowly, he began unbuttoning his shirt. Then carefully removed his shoes and socks. Five minutes later, he stood naked in the room, his clothes folded neatly in proper G.I. fashion at the foot of the bed.

"I've lived one day too long," he muttered as he walked into the bathroom suite. A moment later, the shower could be heard running.

"One day too long."

On the other side of Munich, at Fürstenfeldbruck Air Station, a variation of the thought was being echoed.

Too long, Ruinov thought as he waited for his Ilushyin Airbus to stop its rollout. *He's been loose too long.*

The nonstop flight from St. Petersburg, through stormy weather, had left the former detention barracks commander moody and foul-tempered. Or perhaps it had been the dispatches that he'd received. Either way, he was determined that there was going to be hell to pay.

In the finest traditions of the Spetsnaz commandos, where he'd proudly served before being exiled as a prison guard, Ruinov kept his face a blank as he stood in the endless customs line. It was easy, considering his mind was elsewhere.

News of Newman's escape had sent shock waves through that small part of the Russian intelligence community that was familiar with his case.

Those who had tried to arrest him almost seven years before drank toasts of success to the men who would now have to try and catch him.

Those who had tried to interrogate him saw it as divine retribution to the Americans who had created him.

And those who had imprisoned him, people like Colonel Ruinov and the surviving guards of Detention Barracks 6210, said private prayers or kneeled in dark churches, praying that he would be caught before . . . Or they flew through storms to Munich.

Forty minutes later, Ruinov cleared customs. He looked for his contact in the reception lounge, then recognized the appropriate identification procedure and fell into step alongside the tall man who had met with Tabbart.

"Is everything ready?" Ruinov kept his voice down as they walked.

"As far as I could with the information on hand," the tall man responded.

They climbed into a Volkswagen van that was double-parked at the curb, a Munich tradition.

"Have there been any sightings?"

"No."

"Any leads?"

"None."

Ruinov allowed his mind to flash over every possibility.

"Do we know as certain that the Americans still believe that the man is in the country?"

The tall man pulled onto the autobahn and accelerated to 110 kph.

"There appears to be a dispute within the search team. The commander has asked for permission to redouble his efforts within seventy-five kilometers of the institute on the advice of one of the doctors attached to his team. Higher command believes that the man has already left the country."

Ruinov thought it over.

"What does our expert say?"

The tall man smiled. "We will find out over breakfast, Colonel. I promise you." He sensed Ruinov's growing unease. "Don't worry, sir. If he's still here, we'll find him for you."

Ruinov nodded and stared out the window.

The tall man drove on, occasionally sneaking glances at Ruinov.

"So," the driver said at length, "what has this bastard done to draw a full colonel of the Northern Security Command after his ass?"

Ruinov just kept staring out the window. "Nothing yet," he mumbled. "I hope."

An hour after sunrise, similar thoughts pervaded the mostly empty search headquarters.

As it slowly geared up for the day's activities, those few actually in the HQ moved around almost in a daze.

They had been working flat out for thirty-five days. Following every lead, searching out every possibility no matter how unlikely, never finding so much as a scent of their quarry. It was a thoroughly unprecedented situation for this elite urban search unit. And throughout,

Newman's enormous face looked down on them with what seemed like unhidden delight.

Tabbart wandered into the converted barn, nodding at some of the early morning staff. He smiled and accepted a cup of bad coffee. He made small talk about the weather. Finally, he made his way to the "overnight desk," the center of communications through which all reports and leads from the night before were channeled.

"Good morning, Sergeant," he said in his most professionally friendly voice. "How are you this fine morning?"

The tired man rubbed his eyes. "I wouldn't know. You're the doc."

Tabbart laughed, despite his personal revulsion for that particular word. "You look no worse than the other men," he said gently.

The sergeant smiled. "That bad?"

Tabbart shrugged. "Our problem child has been keeping you all very busy, has he not?"

"It's like he fell off the face of the planet," the sergeant said wearily. "I've never seen anything like it before." He shook his head. "It's damned frustrating!"

Tabbart motioned toward a chair beside the man. The sergeant pulled it out and Tabbart sat down next to him.

"You know, perhaps it would do you good to talk to someone about this. I have mentioned to Captain Kilgore that my staff remains available to provide whatever counseling you men may need."

The sergeant smiled. "Who has the time for that? Right now, we're sixteen hours on and eight off. That leaves just about enough time to eat and sleep." He paused. "Assuming we don't have to scramble after another false lead in the middle of the night."

"It sounds very stressful," Tabbart prompted.

The young man laughed. "And then some."

Tabbart looked around, then slid his chair closer to the man. "If you would like to talk . . ."

"I don't think so, sir," the sergeant responded. "No offense but security is job one around here."

Tabbart smiled like a patient parent. "Of course. As it should be," his gentle, guiding voice said. "But, you know, I possess top-secret-and-above clearance. Many of my senior staff do. A necessary by-product of the important work the Institute does for your government." He pulled out his plastic, embossed access card and showed it to him.

The sergeant examined it closely. "I didn't know that," he said, clearly impressed.

"So, if it would make you feel better to unburden yourself," he said, smiling a fatherly smile, "I would be only too pleased to listen."

The young man looked around the room at the growing numbers of staff that were filing in. He shook his head. "I don't know. If the other guys knew about it . . ."

Tabbart stood up and patted the young man on the back. "I completely understand," he said easily. "Your shift is over when? In fifteen minutes?"

The sergeant nodded.

Tabbart assumed a serious expression. "And if, when your shift is over, you decided to take a walk outside, and if on that walk, say by the field, we should happen to meet and walk together for a time, that would be completely innocent, would it not?"

"Yeah. It would."

"Two comrades taking a walk in the morning freshness, passing the time. It could be most"—he actually winked—"therapeutic, no?"

A brief nod was his answer as the sergeant returned to sorting some papers in front of him.

"It's getting a little busy now, Doctor. I have to get all this done before the end of my shift."

Tabbart halfbowed. "Of course. Forgive the interruption, please." He turned back toward the room. "I think I will take a little walk by the field just outside for a time." He wandered away, greeting and talking small talk to various staffers as they reported for the shift change.

The sergeant watched him go, shook his head, then returned to his work.

"The guy's not such an asshole after all," he muttered before taking a phone call.

Two hours later, in the small coffee shop in the Reisch District, Tabbart sat down at a booth across from the tall man and Ruinov.

"Maddalenna," the tall man said quietly, "I would like to introduce you to my partner from Moscow. Sergei Jov." He turned to Ruinov. "Sergei, it is my most inestimable pleasure to introduce to you our hardest and most faithful worker, Maddalenna."

Ruinov reached across the table and took Tabbart's hand.

"Doctor," he said softly but with deep respect, "it is indeed a profound honor to meet a man with the courage, fortitude, intelligence, and fidelity of yourself."

Tabbart beamed as they shook hands.

"You know," Ruinov continued, "I have admired your work for a long time and feel personally flattered that you would agree to see me on such short notice."

Tabbart waved the compliment away. "Please, Herr Jov, anything I can do to assist your noble, uh, company is my honor."

Ruinov nodded. The man was exactly as his file and the tall man's description had said. Self-involved, self-important, and obsequious.

"I do not mean to be rude," Ruinov pressed, leaning forward, "but I understand you can give us an update on the, shall we call it the situation?"

"Of course," Tabbart replied. "As an important official myself, I understand the demands upon you." He puffed himself up to his full, inadequate height.

"Thank you for understanding." Ruinov smiled, pushing down his inclination to slap the man in front of him.

"It is nothing. Now then, to business." He looked around the half-empty coffee shop carefully before he spoke again.

"I have obtained the latest updates from the search unit. Effective as of 0700 today."

Ruinov turned to the tall man. "He is everything I'd read of and more." Amazingly, he didn't get sick to his stomach as he said it.

"Please go on, Maddalenna," the tall man said.

Tabbart pulled out a small notepad and referred to it as he talked.

Ruinov cringed. For an agent to carry written notes was among the most forbidden things. But he needed this man more than he needed to discipline him.

At least for now.

"There have been three new developments since my last report." He paused. "You received that, or would you like me to recapitulate?"

"Please go on, Doctor. Your earlier reports were most thorough and enlightening."

Tabbart preened. "As you wish." He checked his notes. "First. The search unit has been ordered to demonstrate some concrete results within seventy-two hours or they are going to be returned to barracks."

"Indeed."

"Yes. Their frustration level has grown very high. I understand that this is the first time they have ever failed in subduing their prey. They are taking it most personally."

"Forgive me for interrupting, Doctor . . ."

"Not at all. I want you to feel free to have me elucidate any of the details that perplex you, Herr Jov. I am an expert after all."

"As I am well aware, Doctor." He paused. "Why, in your opinion, have they been unable to capture the man?"

Tabbart seemed to think it over carefully.

"The rigidity of their command structure is such that, in my expert opinion, they are unable to adapt to the ever-changing conditions of the chase. This has placed them in an impossible position when dealing with a psychopath who acts without reason or structure."

Ruinov nodded, appearing impressed, as he decided that there would be nothing to gain by asking Tabbart for opinions.

"Please go on with your report," he said with a smile.

"The second development is more bizarre yet. One of my senior staff, Otto Kapf, has foolishly convinced the commander of the search unit to pull men back from the outer search areas in order to concentrate on the villages and towns around the Institute. He has deluded himself that Newman—excuse me, the man—has formed some kind of salmonesqe attachment to the place and will be found not far from it."

The look on Tabbart's face was of complete disgust.

Ruinov thought it over. He'd read the file on Kapf and been impressed. The man had a reputation for conservatism, thoroughness, and intuitive insight. Any theory of his must be given careful consideration, despite what this fool postured.

"And the third development, if I'm not being premature, Doctor?"

"Ah. Yes. The third development." He smiled. "It would appear that the man with the titular charge of the search has gone missing."

"General Beck?"

"The very same."

"Go on, Doctor. You have my rapt attention," Ruinov said. He pictured the man whose file he'd so carefully studied on the flight from Russia. A man so much like himself—warriors no longer allowed in battle. Practiced killers whose only goal, desire, prayer, was the end of a human plague. The end of Brian Newman.

He tried to focus on what Tabbart was saying.

"The general was scheduled to brief Washington this morning at four o'clock by Autovon secured circuits. When he failed to arrive in time, Captain Kilgore, the unit's commander, was called in. He ordered the general brought in to headquarters, but the men he sent found the general's quarters unoccupied, his bed unslept in."

"Indeed," the tall man said, for the first time truly impressed by Tabbart's information.

"Yes," the doctor continued. "They have not yet informed Washington, but they have begun a search for him."

"Do they have any theories?" Ruinov pressed, his mind creating its own answers.

Tabbart shrugged. "If they have, they are keeping them to themselves at the moment. However, I will continue to probe." He paused. "I have, of course, my own theory on the matter." He seemed to be waiting to be asked.

"Please, Doctor. I would be most appreciative of any assistance you can give me." But Ruinov really didn't pay attention as the man talked.

Tabbart made a show of thinking.

"I have observed the general at close proximity for many months. And I have reached certain conclusions about him. He possesses an inferior personality construct, lacks personal discipline, often overreacts to even the most mild criticism." He paused. "It is my opinion that he has succumbed to the pressure of the situation and is off somewhere getting drunk. They will undoubtedly find him passed out in some gutter."

Ruinov was quiet for a long time after that. The tall man continued the doctor's debriefing, but Ruinov knew the man had nothing more of value to offer. So, he let his mind wander.

To Kapf, to Beck, and always, to Newman.

Half an hour away from the coffee shop, safely secured in his grocery, Newman spread out his early morning purchases.

A container of coffee, a bag of sausages wrapped in pastry, two newspapers, some tape, and thirty marker pens in assorted colors. He uncovered the coffee, took a bite of the sausages, and began to work.

Slowly, carefully, he took each page of the papers and taped them in double layers over the front windows. Several times in the twenty minutes that it took, he went outside to make sure that no one could see in. Finally satisfied, he laid out the markers on a small card table he'd purchased, and turned to the walls.

The work was hard, done mostly from memory and several books that he'd bought especially for the occasion. After half an hour, he tied a bandanna around his forehead to keep the sweat out of his eyes.

He worked in pencil first, carefully drawing the outlines, erasing, adjusting height for dimension. Erasing, changing the spatial axis, the form slowly becoming clear along the wall canvas. Then he turned to the pens.

Painstakingly selecting the right color for the right locus, he balanced shadings, played with perspective and contour, altered the original outlines to conform to his vision in progress. He experimented on darkening, lightening, putting color on color, all with an eye to the eventual finished product.

By midmorning, it had become clear that it would take him most of the day, perhaps even into the night. It would require at least one more trip to the stationery store for more markers. But he couldn't stop until it was done.

It was too important a part of his newly formed grand design.

Across town, breaking his long-standing tradition of never being seen in the Playground before 1500, Ghislain pulled his Mercedes into the garage of his club. After setting the alarm, closing and locking the garage, he walked out into the alley, then froze.

He didn't know why, there was no reason really, but being in the same spot where he'd last seen Apollyon gave him chills. He looked around, assuring himself that the alley was empty, carefully avoided looking up the fire escape, and let himself into the club by the side door.

First stop, his office.

Opening the credenza, he rewound the video from the hidden cameras in the stairway. He settled into his chair, watching the speeding images of his girls, their clients, racing up and down the stairs at breakneck pace, all carefully time-indexed.

He uncovered his Styrofoam cup of coffee and began to drink when suddenly a fleeting image caught his attention. He rewound the tape and played it back in slow motion.

Time Stamp: 0523. Apollyon walks jauntily down the stairs, completely unaware of his being photographed.

Ghislain shook his head. The man had been up there with the other man for over four hours! He pushed all thoughts of what mess might await him in the attic as he settled back to finish his coffee before beginning the cleanup.

Abruptly, he jumped forward, spilling his coffee on his lap and shirt.

Time Stamp: 0525. Apollyon, out of nowhere, leans into the secreted camera's sight, studies it carefully, then smiles and waves. A large palm covers the camera for thirty seconds, then it lifts, and all is clear again.

Cursing his clumsiness, trying desperately to regain his nerve and calm his heart, Ghislain changed into a running suit that he kept in the office. Then, ignoring the dull pain in his temples, he headed out, up the steps.

Halfway up the first flight, he paused to stare at a large circle that had been drawn around one of the mirrored side panels. It was precisely at the spot where the camera had been so cleverly concealed. On the top, bottom, and both sides were large arrows pointing in, toward the center.

Above it in German, French, and English was the word CAMERA!

Rubbing his forehead, he swallowed some downers and continued up the stairs.

At the attic door, he took a deep breath, tried the knob, and opened the door.

He had seen many things on the days after he had let the attic room. Bodies, body parts, blood, dead animals, all were part of the way things went, but something about this scene made him stop and mutter a silent prayer.

Hanging from the hook that Apollyon had installed, swinging at the end of a doubled-up curtain cord, was the first man that Apollyon had sought. The man whom he had lured to this room last night.

He was fully dressed, immaculately so. His hair was combed and gelled in place. He had shaved recently, smelled like he had bathed, and his shoes appeared to have been freshly cleaned.

His eyes were open, staring not ahead but straight up, as if he had been watching the rope at the moment of his death. His head was lolling over onto his left shoulder, his arms hung loosely at his side.

And shoved under his watchband was a folded piece of paper.

Ghislain carefully reached out and pulled it free. He unfolded it, reading the three words scrawled there.

"Duty. Honor. Country."

He shook his head and pocketed the paper.

Ordinarily, his next steps would be routine, but Apollyon had carefully instructed Ghislain on what he should do if he discovered the first man's lifeless body when he arrived in the morning.

Carefully, he straightened the stool that had been clearly kicked away by the suicide, lifted the dead man's weight onto his shoulder, and cut the cord.

He laid the body on the floor.

The noose was removed from his neck, his pockets were carefully searched for any other notes, then he was carefully and completely undressed.

Ghislain didn't like any of it, was repulsed by the tasks, but Apollyon had demanded that it be done this way.

And he was not prepared to cross Apollyon. Not yet, anyway.

He went to the closet, pulling out the package that he knew would be there, and dressed the corpse in the clothes Apollyon had provided. He was careful, as Apollyon had ordered, to change the man's underwear, which had become soiled by the hanging.

After a half hour, it was done.

He checked that he still had the sealed envelope that Apollyon had given him expressly for this contingency, and pulled out his cellular phone, dialing a number. It answered on the third ring.

"Ghislain . . . Yeah. Shut up and listen. I got a special, okay . . . Yeah. The attic . . . No . . . I said no! This one is not to go in the river! . . . I know but I'm willing to pay extra, okay? . . . Good. Now here is what you must do . . ."

T wo hours later, just after 1300, a U.S. government car pulled to a stop outside a small house owned by the Institute. Kilgore, the driver, got out, followed by Kapf. They looked around, then started up the path to the door.

"I don't buy it, Doctor," Kilgore was saying, continuing their conversation from the car. "The way you describe him, the things you say." He paused. "You make him out to be some kind of superman." He laughed as he knocked on the door. "I'll believe that when I see the red 'S' on his chest."

"I never called him a superman. I used Nietzsche's term, *Übermensch.*"

"Which means the same thing, right?"

"Not precisely. *Übermensch* means 'over man.' A refining, a sharpening, an improving of man. But still man. Yet capable of almost anything because of his constant evolutionary refinements."

Kilgore knocked again.

"Now you're talking semantics." There was still no answer so Kilgore pulled out a key and opened the door.

"Hello? General Beck? Sir? It's Kilgore! Hello?" He looked over at Kapf. "Still gone."

They walked in, closing the door behind them.

They wandered through the hallway into the living room. The house seemed orderly, clean, and completely empty.

"Listen," Kilgore said as they walked into the den, "I'm not denying the man is good. Hell! No one's been able to stay hidden from my men for this long before. He's talented, well trained, and based on his file, he's experienced." He looked at some papers on a coffee table. "But that's all."

Kapf shook his head as he walked into the kitchen. "He is more than that, Captain. Much more. His IQ is well above genius. He thinks in the abstract effortlessly, as his primary thought process; a thing you and I do only with conscious effort and work. That means that he has analyzed all the available options before he acts, continues to evaluate them as he acts, constantly improvising and adapting his plans as he goes."

Kilgore checked the fully stocked refrigerator.

"I'll grant you his intelligence. I'll also grant you he's the luckiest son of a bitch I've ever chased. But he doesn't have X-ray vision, can't fly, and, as far as I can tell, will die from a bullet in the brain just like anyone else."

They moved down the hall into the first bedroom. It was clean and undisturbed.

"Brian Newman is a man," Kapf conceded as they moved on. "Of that, there is no doubt. But"—he put his hand on Kilgore's shoulder—"he is not like you or me." He paused, trying to find a way to make his point to the career officer. "Did you ever hear of a countryman of yours named Theodore Bundy?"

"Of course."

"He killed perhaps as many as sixty-three women in an eight-year period without the police being able to even come close to him. He committed his crimes in total anonymity, left no clues to his identity, easily avoided a nationwide manhunt by your FBI, all while living quite openly."

Kilgore opened the door to the master bedroom.

"But they did catch him. I think he died in the electric chair."

They walked through the dressing area as they continued their debate.

"They caught him," Kapf said. "They executed him. But only after eight years and sixty-three deaths."

Kilgore stopped and turned back to the psychiatrist. "Are you saying that Newman is like Bundy?" His voice was deadly serious.

Kapf nodded as they opened the sliding curtain that separated the dressing area from the sleeping area.

"In a great many ways. With one important exception."

"And that is?"

Kapf walked into the sleeping area. "Bundy was insane. Newman is not."

He stopped, staring at the king-sized bed in front of him.

"Captain Kilgore?"

Kilgore looked up from the closet he'd been poking through. "Yes, Doctor . . ." He froze as he straightened up.

Lying on the bed, in full-dress uniform with every hair in place and button polished, his hands folded peacefully across his chest, was General Alexander Beck.

Both men stood there, stunned into silence by the scene. Then Kilgore reacted.

He quickly drew his .45, moving silently and swiftly through the rest of the master suite. Satisfied that they were alone, he headed out for the rest of the house. "Stay here," he said in an urgent whisper.

Kapf shook his head. "He is not here," he mumbled as Kilgore moved out of earshot.

With a deeply sad expression, Kapf walked over to the bed, checked Beck's pulse to confirm the obvious, then began a visual examination of the man. He noted the discoloration around the throat, tested how easily the head moved, and reached his opinion.

Kilgore returned five minutes later to find Kapf sitting on a nearby chair, reading a piece of paper.

"The place is empty and locked tight," Kilgore said as he put away his gun.

Kapf ignored him, so he looked at Beck. "Can you tell what happened to him?"

Kapf never looked up from his reading. "He was hanged. Whether voluntarily or not, I cannot say." He continued reading.

Kilgore shook his head and walked over to the doctor. "What's that?" he asked, gesturing at the paper.

Kapf continued reading, handing Kilgore an envelope. "It was beneath his hands."

It was addressed simply "To All My Friends Onshore."

"What's it say?" Kilgore reached out for the paper.

Kapf looked up, surprised by the outstretched hand in front of him.

"I will read it to you," he said simply. Then he began.

"Gentlemen (and ladies if there are any present): I commit to you the physical remains of Brigadier General Alexander Chamberlin Beck, Army of the United States. I rely on your humanity to see that he receives a proper military burial with honors. I assure you he is deserving of one, not only because of his exemplary record (up to a few years ago of course) but also because he fell in the line of duty. A soldier's noblest end.

"The specifics of his death are not important. I assume, of course, that I will be held responsible. There is both truth and untruth in that statement, but I accept it nonetheless. One thing about it you should know, as it is indicative of the man that he once was, is that of all your experts, your muddled psychiatrists, your shiny aluminum soldiers, your review bores, he is the one that first came upon me.

"Now, to my point.

"I bear no significant animosity toward any of the individuals charged with my detention and (such as it was) treatment. I accept your flaccid explanation that you were merely looking out for my best interests. Now that is no longer necessary. I wish only to close out a bit of unfinished business, then move on. Allow me this privilege of my birthright as an American, and all will be well. I will go on with my life and you will be allowed to go on with yours.

"If you do not allow me this simple thing . . .

"Sincerely, Brian Newman."

Kilgore reached out and took the offered letter, quickly skimming it.

"It seems I owe you an apology, Doctor. He *is* still around."

Kapf stood up and walked to a window, staring out at the street beyond in silence as Kilgore picked up the phone.

I t was just after 9:00 P.M. when Newman stood back, wiped the sweat from his eyes, and smiled.

The drawing was more primitive than he'd planned, coarser, more raw. But that wasn't necessarily a bad thing. Its vibrant colors, sharp images, and vivid depictions created exactly the effect he'd hoped for.

Touching it in several areas to make sure it was dry, he carefully hung a sheet from three nails above it, covering the mural completely. Then he sat down, looking at the off-white sheet, but actually picturing the reactions of the intended viewers when, at last, it was unveiled.

Will it have the desired effect? Does it go far enough, or too far? Years from now, when the students and professors argue over its meaning, will any of them truly divine its buried secret?

He stood, cleaned himself off, changed into a dark running suit, and left the grocery.

The gallery had been prepared.

It was time to deliver the invitations.

PART FOUR

The Grand Design

CHAPTER TWELVE

The late fall fog slowly wrapped itself around the buildings of the Volker Institute, plunging all into a gray-white haze.

Security was doubled at all the gates, passes were closely checked; flashlights illuminated the interiors of the few cars that drove up; patrols were increased to one every twenty minutes. Guards sat at television monitors, trying to pierce the white sheet that had descended. Others, dressed as orderlies, patrolled the interior of the main building and the few open outbuildings.

It had been ten hours since Beck's body had been discovered. Ten hours of hurried meetings, frantic phone calls, and frenzied expressions. The initial shock, followed by agitated dismay, had now given way to nervous looks and people traveling in groups across the grounds instead of on their own.

The final meeting had just broken up with no real agreement on any issue save one.

Brian Newman was, indeed, still in the area.

Konrad Edel paced on the roof of the Institute, damning the fog, constantly redeploying his men. And, desperately trying to figure out what had happened.

He'd been present at Beck's autopsy. Had felt a need, almost a responsibility, to be.

The findings were not surprising. Beck had died of a broken neck, most probably obtained by being hung with a doubled, narrow cord. His body also showed signs of light trauma to the legs, arms, and upper torso. The pathologist was unable to say "with any degree of certainty" whether the bruising was due to an accident or deliberate action.

But Edel knew.

Nor could the doctor say whether Beck had been hung by another or had committed suicide.

But Edel knew. He knew and he cursed himself for allowing it to get that far.

Newman had betrayed him, he thought on that cold, damp, isolated rooftop. Betrayed him, his trust, made a mockery of his faith and beliefs, using them to create the environment he needed for his escape.

And Beck was dead because of it.

Now, after a brief trip to his church to see that a prayer vigil would be started for the soul of Alex Beck, he stood on the roof and waited.

The search team's intelligence analysts were convinced that Newman would move on now that Beck was dead.

Patricia believed that Newman must have discovered the dead Beck, then laid him out so that he would retain his dignity. The final act of a close friend.

Kapf had remained mysteriously noncommittal.

But none of it mattered. Not really.

Edel knew that Newman would come. He didn't know why, didn't know when or how.

But that he would come, Edel was certain.

And he would be ready when they met again.

"Three Seven to Zero One."

Edel pulled the radio from its holster on the opposite hip from the gun.

"This is Zero One."

"This is Three Seven. We are completely fog-blind here. Visibility is zero. Over."

"This is Zero One. It is the same everywhere. And still coming in from the north. Over."

"This is Three Seven. I request permission to pull back to C.P. Over."

"This is Zero One. Negative." Edel paused, looking out at the fog-shrouded countryside surrounding the Institute.

"All grounds units, this is Zero One. Maintain positions. Repeat, maintain positions. Switch to L.P. status. I repeat, become listening posts."

The four men that made up Security Unit Three Seven stood around their improvised post along the east fence and shook their heads as they heard their chief's instructions.

"The old man's losing it," one said glumly.

"We're going to freeze our nuts off," another said as he began to stow the night-vision equipment from the damp.

The oldest of the four just kept staring out into the fog. "Quiet. We're a listening post now!"

The fourth man smiled as he pulled out a thermos of coffee. "It's going to be a long night." He began pouring steaming cups for each of the men. When he turned to the oldest one, he stopped, puzzled by the man's posture.

The man had taken a few steps out of the post, was standing stock-still, his head cocked to the side, eyes closed.

"Albert?" the man with the coffee said softly.

"Shh" was the older man's brief reply.

The other men noticed and put down their cups. Weapons were drawn and cocked. They silently moved into support positions around the older man.

"What is it, Albert?" the man with the coffee said as he put aside the thermos, picking up a compact MP-5K assault rifle.

Albert shook his head. "I thought . . . I don't know." He was quiet for long seconds. Suddenly, he cocked his head to one side. "Maybe fifty meters at twelve o'clock." He stared into the moving cloud that had dropped around them. Then, slowly, he shook his head. "Maybe I was wrong." He started to turn back to the post, then stopped, turning again to the men.

"But stay alert anyway."

In Clemente's upper-floor room, the tension was just as thick.

Patricia and Kapf sat alongside the bed sipping coffee. Clemente sat up in the bed, IVs running into both arms, an oxygen mask slurring his words. Jenny sat off to the side, not a part of the sober conversation, but unwilling to leave the room at this stage of her husband's illness.

Clemente's skin was a pale yellow-white, his eyes crusted, his hands trembling whenever he found the strength to move them. He breathed in wheezy hisses, barely participating in the conversation, but clearly following it closely.

Patricia shook her head slowly.

"I disagree," she said in an exhausted voice. "There's no evidence to suggest that."

"There is the note," Kapf said as he took a drink of coffee.

"The note. Well, at least there we agree. It is the key to all of this." She pulled her copy of the note out of her nearby briefcase. "You've read it. I think it speaks for itself."

"I agree," Kapf said calmly.

"But you're still not willing to concede that Newman isn't responsible for Beck's death."

Kapf looked at Clemente, who shrugged, while smiling weakly.

"He accepts responsibility for the action," Kapf said simply. He paused. "Why would you dispute him?"

"Read the man's words!" Patricia's voice was becoming harsh. She began to read aloud from the photocopy.

"I quote: 'I assume, of course, that I will be held responsible.' Unquote." She looked up at the two men. "What could be clearer?"

Blank looks from both of them.

She shook her head and began again.

"Here he is, alone, one of a kind, hunted merely because he is one of a kind. He comes across Beck shortly after the man kills himself. He knows that we're going to blame him. Why not? The Russians blamed him for everything bad that happened around him. In his mind, we're no different."

Clemente lifted his oxygen mask. "There's nothing to support that," he wheezed.

"There's everything to support it," Patricia shot back, ignoring the condition of the man in the bed. "Read the letter." She held it up in

front of them. "Newman refers to his 'detention,' to our 'flaccid explanation' for how we were treating him." She looked right at Kapf.
"Words, Doctor, very close to the ones you used several months ago
referring to the Russians."

"So," Kapf countered, "why not leave the scene intact? Certainly it
would be easier for us to determine the true cause of the general's
death if he were discovered still hanging from the rope. Mr. Newman
is more than bright enough to understand that, no?"

"And why," Clemente said softly, "take the risk of transporting the
general's body to his home and laying him out so carefully?"

Patricia shrugged. "He must have felt at least some form of guilt
over the man's death. Maybe it had to do with the years they'd spent
together before his imprisonment. A mutual respect, if you will, that
caused him to want to see the general's memory preserved in as noble a
fashion as possible."

"I thought your *Homo crudelis* was without emotions," Kapf said,
smiling. "How do you reconcile such intense grief reaction?"

She put down the letter and poured herself some coffee. "When we
get him back, give me a few sessions. I'll find out."

Kapf shook his head as he turned to Clemente. "The optimism of
youth."

Clemente nodded.

Patricia looked confused. "What do you mean?" She paused,
looking from one to the other. "The search teams have orders to
use nonlethal force when they find him," she said slowly. "Don't
they?"

Clemente's eyes took on a deeply sorrowful look. "Clinical Patty,"
he murmured. "You never did quite get it."

"Get what?" Her voice was low and cautious.

"That the patient does not exist in a vacuum for your personal
contemplation."

Kapf looked at Clemente, then turned back to Patricia. "A line
general of the American military is dead under, at the very least,
questionable circumstances. An American agent with known, demonstrated, violent tendencies, formerly under the command of this general, is missing and acknowledges at least a tacit involvement in the
general's death." He looked deeply into the young woman's eyes.
"What do you think the response of the Americans will be?"

"My God!"

Kapf nodded. "If Captain Kilgore has not received orders to shoot on sight by now, then it is only because of the inevitable delays of any large command structure. We have, perhaps, twelve hours, probably less, before such orders are received."

"They can't," Patricia said weakly. "Don't they realize what he is? What further study of him could mean?"

"They realize it," Kapf said quietly. "And that realization will be part of their reasoning."

For five long minutes, no one said a word. Eventually, Patricia looked up.

"You said that once before," she said as she looked questioningly at Kapf. "At the hearing. You said, what was it?" She thought back to the events of one month before. "You said that they always knew what he was, or something like that."

"I did," Kapf nodded.

"What did you mean?"

Kapf began to put his papers away in his briefcase. "Is there any purpose served from restirring the stew?"

"What did you mean?" Her voice was becoming insistent.

Clemente pulled the mask off. "Tell her, Otto." He looked over at Patricia. "She'll just pester it out of you anyway."

He smiled at her as he put his mask back on. Something about that weak, amused smile cut through all the garbage, straight to Patricia's soul.

"Maybe we ought to continue this elsewhere," she whispered to Kapf.

Clemente held up a hand. "I am not dead yet, Dr. Nellwyn!" he wheezed through the mask. "And I am still your department head and project supervisor!"

She smiled at him. "And still a pain in the ass," she said with a tear in her eye.

Clemente raised his eyebrows as he pulled the mask off again. "Thank you for noticing. Dr. Kapf, please continue."

Kapf sighed. "Very well." He stood and walked to the window, looking down on the blanket of fog that covered the grounds. He continued to stare out as he talked.

"The concept of using society's outcasts for dangerous, deniable missions is nothing new to the world. In the last century, prison labor was often used to build railroads through hostile lands in Asia. In this century, violent murderers have been offered clemency in exchange for political contract killings. It has been an accepted practice."

"Granted."

Patricia had never seen Kapf like this. So . . . inward.

"As those missions grew more dangerous and simultaneously more complex," Kapf continued, "it is a logical extension of the thought that mere convict recruits could never accomplish the needed goals."

"Which is why they suggested sociopaths," Patricia chimed in.

"Sociopaths. Yes." Kapf turned back to face her.

Clemente pulled down his oxygen mask, letting it rest on the uneven rise and fall of his chest. "It would never work," he said firmly. "Sociopaths are too 'me'-oriented. They could never be trusted not to sell out their secrets to the other side if they were offered a better deal. Or just out of spite."

He took a hit of the oxygen as Kapf continued the thought.

"They are too unstable, too unpredictable, with a loyalty only to themselves. They could never be truly relied on."

Patricia shook her head. "What are you saying, exactly?"

Clemente reached out and took the young woman's hand. "As much of a shock as this is going to be to you, you are not the only one who has theorized about the next generational evolution of man."

Kapf smiled. "I wrote my first paper on the subject before you were born. It was based on twenty or so works written before that."

Clemente nodded. "And Nietzsche beat us all by over a hundred years."

"Consider the theorists at the Horizon Institute. Sitting in their ivory tower, reading down the list of requirements submitted to them." Kapf turned back to the window. "The specifications demanded could never possibly be met by any existing personality type. But . . ."

Clemente took some oxygen and finished the thought.

"Theoretically, a person with the lack of emotional restraints of a sociopath; with a capability for violence like a phased atavist; with a high IQ—that person could fit the bill."

"To the Horizon Institute," Kapf said, "it would all have been an interesting mental exercise. An abstract man, if you will. Either a new man or a mutated current man. Either way, it didn't matter. There was only a one-twentieth of one percent chance that the man actually existed."

His face took on a dismayed look.

"But to a government with 265 million souls to choose from, it was merely a challenge."

Kapf took a calculator from his pocket and tossed it to the tray in front of Patricia.

"Do the mathematics if you like. In a population of 265 million people there would be a pool of well over 130,000 possible candidates." He laughed bitterly. "In the standing military alone, over 13,000 possible Newmans."

Clemente closed his eyes. "They know what Brian Newman is," he said quietly. "They know because they set out to find him. And because they know what he is, because he's no longer under their control, is developing a—a—"

Jenny came over and gently put the mask back on her husband. After checking his pulse and seeing that his breathing had settled into a normal sleep pattern, she returned to her chair and continued her reading.

Kapf kissed her on the cheek, waited for Patricia to hug her, then escorted his young colleague out into the hall.

"What was Jack trying to say?" Patricia asked Kapf.

Kapf pushed the button for the elevator. He took a deep breath.

"Because they know what Mr. Newman is or may be, because he is no longer under their control, and because he is developing self-awareness of what he may be . . ." The doors opened. He gestured for Patricia to proceed him, but she indicated she was going back to Clemente's room.

Kapf smiled sadly and stepped in.

"Because of that, they must destroy him."

The doors started to close, but Patricia suddenly held out her hand.

"We've got to stop them from killing him!" She looked around, then leaned forward. "You think he's some kind of mutated intelligence. I think he's the next evolutionary step. Fine. Either way we need to study him, to find out! Don't you agree?"

"My dear Dr. Nellwyn, it is a large world. Over four and a half billion people. Do the math. There are a possible one and a quarter million Brian Newmans out there."

He gently reached out and removed her hand from the door.

"And, I suspect, it will not be long before we begin to hear from each of them."

He rode down to his office floor, deeply concerned about Jack Clemente's health; about Patricia Nellwyn's naiveté; about his own steadily more jaundiced view of life. He ignored greetings from the few nurses and orderlies he encountered, shook his head at the security men so ineptly trying to appear as orderlies, and slowly made his way to his office. After unlocking the door, he flipped on the light and stepped in.

"Close the door, please, Doctor."

Kapf froze at the sound of Newman's voice coming from somewhere to his left.

"The door," Newman urged in a flat, toneless voice.

Kapf closed the door.

"Lock it, please."

Without turning around, the old man reached back and clicked the lock into place.

"Now, if you would walk to the window and casually close the curtains, I'd deeply appreciate it." Newman's voice came from somewhere near the floor.

Kapf complied. He walked over and pulled the curtains shut, careful to do only what he was told to do. Nothing more, nothing less.

"You can turn around now, Doctor."

Kapf turned toward the voice.

Newman sat on the floor in a corner of the room near the door. He smiled as he leisurely stood up and stretched. He gestured at the desk.

"Please, Dr. Kapf, sit down. Get comfortable." He groaned slightly as he stretched. "I'm getting too old to hide in corners." He smiled. "How are you?"

Kapf walked over and sat down. Carefully, he scrutinized the fugitive in front of him.

Newman was clean, seemed to have put on weight, was tanned, healthy-looking, and smiling. He acted as if he had just dropped by to visit. Perhaps gossip a bit. And Kapf hoped that this was exactly the reason he was here.

The alternative was too horrible to contemplate.

Newman seemed to be reading Kapf's mind.

"Relax," he laughed lightly, "I've got nothing against you." He paused, chuckling happily. "If I did, you'd never have seen me."

"Did General Beck?" Kapf gambled.

Newman sat down in an overstuffed chair in front of the desk.

"Did General Beck what?"

"See you before he"—a pause—"died."

Newman concentrated on adjusting himself in the chair. "Is Beck dead?"

Kapf nodded gravely.

"Pity."

Kapf carefully studied the man in front of him. "The authorities believe you killed him."

Newman just smiled and raised his eyebrows. *"Moi?"*

"Vous."

Newman seemed preoccupied with the chair. "What do you think?" he said in an offhand sort of way.

Reminding himself of exactly who was sitting across from him, Kapf thought that question over carefully. Newman was relaxed, unconcerned, even casual in his presentation. Yet all of that could just be still another mask hiding a sinister truth.

Or a cigar could just be a cigar.

"No," Kapf finally said. "I do not think you killed the general."

Newman half turned to him. "Really?"

There was something different about Newman, but as yet, Kapf couldn't identify it.

"I have read your note," Kapf said.

Newman smiled like a child on Christmas Day and his birthday combined. "Did you like it?" He turned fully to Kapf, an eager expression on his face. "I mean really like it?"

Kapf ignored the tone. "What does it mean?" he said in a clinical tone. "To all my friends onshore?"

"I worked very hard on that letter. Tried to make it clear, easy to read, yet still entertaining. How'd I do?"

"Do you feel adrift in the world, cut suddenly loose from the anchors you have always had?"

"And the spacing was important. An inch-and-a-half margin all around." Newman paused. "Neatness is very important in a business correspondence."

Kapf pulled out his pipe and began to fill it from the humidor on his desk.

"To all my friends onshore," he said thoughtfully. "It suggests a person away on a trip, perhaps a cruise."

"We were talking about the letter, not the envelope," Newman said as he picked up the humidor, beginning to examine the intricate carving on it.

"No," Kapf corrected, *"you* were talking about the letter." He took his time lighting the pipe. "To all my friends onshore. It is an interesting phrase." He looked up. "Are you planning on taking a long trip over water?" He smiled as he said it.

Newman made a buzzing sound. "One down, nine to go."

Kapf shrugged. "I like to eliminate the obvious."

"Good policy."

Incredibly, they were both silent for ten long minutes.

"You have the gift of stillness, Doctor. I admire that," Newman finally said.

"How are you?"

Newman leaned back in the chair. "Busy."

"I can imagine," Kapf said seriously. "You appear well."

Newman stood up and slowly turned around, like a child being inspected by his parent. "It's amazing what a little freedom of action can do for your mental and physical health," he said.

"You are eating well?"

"On a budget, but well enough."

"Getting sufficient exercise?"

"I walk a lot."

"And are you sleeping?"

"Five or six hours a day. Sometimes more."

"Is that really enough?"

"Seems to be. I wake up refreshed."

"You wake up refreshed." Kapf paused. "And you remember the pain."

Newman's eyes burned with an inner fire. "I missed you."

"Tell me about the pain."

"We never did finish that last session, did we?"

"Tell me about the pain." Kapf's eyes also burned.

Newman sat back. "What pain?"

Kapf leaned back and puffed on his pipe. "You were smarter, more aware of things than your schoolmates."

"Yes."

"You were awkward, clumsy with girls."

"Yes."

"You made elaborate plans to become a truant. To spend the days, weeks, months in a library."

"Yes."

"Tell me about the pain."

The smile slowly vanished from Newman's lips, replaced by a non-look, a complete lack of any expression at all. It was unnerving, but Kapf showed no sign of it.

"Tell me about the pain."

Newman barely nodded. "Do you speak Japanese?"

"No."

"Know anything about eighth-century Japanese society and customs?"

"No."

"Imagine waking up one morning, cozy and comfy in your bed. You get up, go to the john, take a shower, brush your teeth, dress, shave, comb your hair, then step outside to begin your day." Newman paused. "Got the picture?"

"Yes."

"Now you step through the door, and suddenly find yourself standing in eighth-century Japan. You wander through the unfamiliar streets, you know you have to get somewhere, but you can't remember where or find your way! Got it?"

"Yes."

Newman's voice remained flat, his face expressionless, but anger flowed off him as if it were a physical thing. Like the sweat of a boxer being thrown onto the crowd as he's nailed with a mammoth punch.

"Crowds quickly surround you. They're jabbering at you in this totally incomprehensible, guttural language, everyone speaking, yelling at once! You grab them by the shoulders, one at a time, shake them as you yell at the top of your voice, 'WHERE AM I? WHERE AM I SUPPOSED TO GO? WHAT AM I SUPPOSED TO DO?' Got it?"

Kapf nodded.

Newman leaned back, his body uncoiling, his anger waning.

"Now imagine," he said in a muffled voice, "that you are thirteen years old at the time." He paused. "That, Doctor, is pain."

Kapf had allowed his pipe to go out. He went through the process of relighting it as he tried to fathom the confusion, the pain, of the teenage Newman. Trapped in a world that only he could perceive, desperate to make contact with someone, anyone, that could tell him how to deal with these gifts or curses which he could only just begin to realize.

"Go on," he said after a time.

"There's not much more."

"Go on."

"You're a busy man. Maybe another time." Newman smiled and stood up.

But Kapf noticed that he didn't turn toward the door.

"The pain stopped, did it not?"

Newman nodded.

"You made it stop?"

"Yes."

"How?"

The smile changed into a near grimace. "I think you know."

"How did you stop the pain?"

Newman leaned forward, his hands coming to rest on the edge of the desk. "By realizing that the problem wasn't mine."

"Go on."

"By realizing that it was the others' responsibility to make contact with me. Not the other way 'round."

"To all my friends onshore," Kapf said in a firm voice.

Newman ignored him. "By realizing that through accident of birth, evolutionary prank, or capriciousness of God, there was nothing I couldn't do. By realizing that, when it came right down to it"—Newman's voice grew so soft that Kapf had to strain to hear it—"my difference, my talents, made me strong. Stronger than anyone or anything else."

"To all my friends onshore."

"In time, Doctor," Newman said as he walked to the door. "In time." He turned the lock, opening the door a crack to peek out. Satisfied, he opened it all the way.

"Why did you come back?" Kapf pressed him.

Newman stopped, slowly turning back to Kapf. "There was something I had to find out."

"And that was?"

Newman shook his head. "No matter. I know what I need to know."

He started to step into the corridor.

"To all my friends onshore," Kapf tried one last time.

But he was speaking to an empty doorway.

By midnight, the fog still hadn't lifted, in fact seemed markedly worse. The roads were closed, and travel out of the city was just not possible.

In anticipation, they had agreed to meet in the bar of the Nine Muses Hotel and Spa in Munich City Center. But despite that planning, one of the men was running over an hour late.

"How long do we have to wait, sir?" the youngish sergeant said as he shook his head. "We've got better things to do."

Kilgore smiled. "But we're not going to get any of it done in this soup," he said casually. "We'll wait another hour."

At that moment, a barmaid came up to their table, smiled alluringly at Kilgore, and handed him a note.

Kilgore tipped her, watching her walk all the way back to the bar before he opened it. "Might even have to spend the night," he muttered happily as he thumbed open the envelope.

He quickly read through the short note.

"We're on," he said as he left money on the table for the drinks. "Upstairs, 1458."

Five minutes later, the two soldiers stood outside suite 1458 and knocked on the door. The tall man opened it.

"Captain Kilgore?"

"And you are?" Kilgore said as he walked past him.

"Superfluous to your business." He put a restraining hand on the sergeant's chest. "As is he."

The sergeant looked at Kilgore, waiting for the silent signal that would turn him loose. But Kilgore just waited, then nodded. "It's okay," he said quietly. "Wait outside."

The sergeant nodded and followed the tall man out.

Kilgore walked into the sitting room of the luxury suite, admiring the crystal wine service that was laid out on the antique coffee table. The room was warm, comfortable, expensive in every sense of the word. It appeared empty.

He walked over to the coffee table, picking up the bottle of wine from the table.

"Nice," he said in genuine admiration as he read the label.

"I never developed a taste," a voice behind Kilgore said gruffly.

Kilgore didn't turn around. "You must get paid better than I do, Colonel. This stuff goes for around 850 marks a bottle."

Ruinov walked all the way into the room.

"It belongs to my colleague" was all the ramrod-straight Russian officer said.

They shook hands.

"It's your meeting," Kilgore said while pouring himself a glass of the fine wine.

Ruinov spoke forcefully, but with the discomfort of a man who had dedicated his life to combating men like the young American across from him.

"You are having difficulty locating Brian Newman."

"Am I?"

Ruinov nodded. "You are."

"And you care about that?"

"I do."

"Why? Why is Moscow worried about a man that is no longer their responsibility?"

Ruinov walked over to Kilgore. They sat down.

"Responsibility is the operative word here, Captain Kilgore. There are those who believe that Mr. Newman should never have been released in the first place. Not out of political retribution or international brinksmanship, but out of basic human responsibility."

Kilgore put down his glass. "Regardless, he was released. Now he's our responsibility, not yours."

Ruinov looked at the American soldier and shook his head. How could he get the man to understand, to recognize the problem? He decided to try another tactic.

"Putting aside the issue of responsibility for the moment," he began again, "can you honestly say that you need no assistance whatever?"

"Yes."

The two men stared at each other for a long moment.

"How can I prove to you that I have no ulterior motives?" Ruinov stared into the young, hard face, a face that was in so many ways a mirror of his own distant past. "My purpose is only to see that Newman is, well, neutralized. And to that end, I am prepared to share resources with you."

"Share?"

"I will put my networks at your disposal, with appropriate cutouts, of course. And you will share with me what actions you have taken, and what your future plans are."

Kilgore laughed. He had been ordered to meet with this Russian, had seen his file, but it still seemed ridiculous. The very idea that a semiretired Russian officer, a man with no direct intelligence ties, could lend any assistance to the army's most elite urban search team was absurd.

"Don't be angry if I seem rude, Colonel Ruinov, but this is just a waste of time. You don't have any resources that I don't have." He paused and chuckled. "Cold war's over, Colonel. You lost and have been downsizing ever since. Hell, that's one of the reasons you're free to be here, isn't it? They've closed down most of the old D.B.'s and you've been unassigned for the last two months."

Ruinov nodded. "Your intelligence is most thorough, Captain. Even if you have reached the wrong conclusions from it." His anger at the American's arrogance showed.

Kilgore put down his glass and stood up. "I've been ordered to meet with you. I've done that. If you have anything further to contribute in the future, you know how to reach me. But I see no purpose in taking anything beyond that point." He turned. "Good night, sir."

Ruinov watched him walk to the door. "You will never find him on your own, Captain."

Kilgore stopped, turning back to Ruinov. "No?"

Ruinov stood up slowly. "No." He walked over to Kilgore. "You will not. It is not a reflection on you or your men. But it is a fact."

"Really?" Kilgore was getting annoyed.

"Really."

The Russian seemed so sure, so arrogant, that Kilgore felt like smacking him. Discipline won out over desire.

"But with the help of our noble allies, with their superior techniques and rotting networks, you'll ride in and save the day. Is that it?" He paused, calming himself down. "I always knew you people were bellicose, but you, Colonel, are something special."

Ruinov ignored the man's tone. He'd probably react the same way if Kilgore had come to him in the same situation. But somehow he had to get through to Kilgore. To make him see the dangers. He decided to make one last attempt to speak to the man plain soldier.

"Captain Kilgore, I do not claim to be better than you. And you are quite right, our networks are decaying. I freely admit that you and your men are the best at what you do. But Newman is better."

He tried desperately to find the words.

"My only thought is, and I say this with all due respect, sir, that combined, perhaps, we can stop this man before a major tragedy transpires."

Kilgore studied him closely. There was something fearful about the man. But not fear for himself. It was more a fear of the unknown. Some unknown black devastation that the man couldn't put into words.

"Colonel." Kilgore paused, not sure what to say. "You have my number." He turned and walked uneasily toward the door.

"Have you ever met him, Captain?" Ruinov called after him.

"No." Kilgore had one hand on the doorknob.

"I have." He walked over to the American. "I spent almost seven years staring into the monster's eyes, seeing for myself the blackness of his soul."

He took a deep breath, straightened, and seemed to come back from the dark abyss he'd been descending into.

"And I have seen his victims."

Ruinov's eyes burned with an intensity that Kilgore had seen only once before. In another man—dedicated to the same cause, killed by that same demon.

"Make your point, Colonel," Kilgore said nervously.

Ruinov hesitated, seemingly unable to put his thoughts into words.

"Captain," he finally said, "I must advise you that you are making a tragic mistake. I beg you to reconsider."

Kilgore studied the man.

Beneath the below-average suit and the gruff, almost militant manner, Kilgore noticed, for the first time, a deep exhaustion. Both physical and spiritual, it lay just beneath the surface, threatening to consume the Russian.

"I'll give you five more minutes," Kilgore said.

Ruinov nodded and led him back to the couch.

"I want to tell you about Line Sergeant Dnebronski."

I t was almost sunrise when the fog finally began to lift.

Edel, after a long, stressful night, made his way down from the
Institute roof to begin the debriefing of the night shift. On his way to
the conference room, Albert from Security Unit Three Seven caught up
with him.

Edel shook his head as he looked at the exhausted man.

"You look terrible," he said with a smile.

"Look who's talking," Albert shot back. "You look over a hundred."

"I feel over a hundred."

The two men walked together into the security building off to one
side of the main building.

"How'd it go last night?"

Albert shrugged. "Damned fog."

Edel poured them each a cup of coffee.

Albert took a deep drink, then continued.

"Can't see shit. Every sound makes you jump." He shook his head.
"It happens again tonight, we got to do something."

"Kilgore is supposed to get us the motion detectors by 1300. We'll
try and have them in by sunset."

Edel noticed Kapf walking toward him and excused himself.

"I'm sorry I couldn't get back to you earlier, Doctor. It was a long,
hard night."

"Any casualties?"

Edel smiled weakly. "Only a few head colds. But then our visitor
didn't show last night." He seemed surprised by the expression on
Kapf's face. "What is it, Dr. Kapf?"

Kapf's expression was distant.

"Excuse me?" He looked at Edel's concerned expression.

"Is something wrong? Did something happen?"

Kapf's mind raced.

Fearing a confrontation between Newman and the security teams, which, in Kapf's mind, could only end with several deaths, he had delayed calling security after Newman had left.

After taking twenty minutes to fully record his impressions of the meeting with Newman, he'd tried to reach the security chief. He'd been told that Edel was out reviewing security procedures but could be reached by radio if it was urgent.

For reasons Kapf didn't quite want to face up to, he'd not insisted.

Then, this morning, when he'd finally called back and been told that Edel could be reached at the debriefing, he'd copied those notes and headed right down. Only to stop short again.

"Dr. Kapf?"

The old psychiatrist turned back to Edel with a sheepish smile. "I'm sorry."

"Is there something I can do for you?"

Kapf took a deep breath. "May I sit in on your debriefing?"

Edel shrugged at the continually strange requests of the head-shrinkers that he worked for. "Of course, Doctor. Take any chair. Excuse me." He walked to the front of the room shaking his head.

Taking the offered file from his secretary, he placed it on the podium and, while he waited for the men to settle down, he began to flip through it.

Copies of the shift reports; requests for equipment upgrades; pleas from nine of the eleven security teams for space heaters and hot food.

And a sealed envelope labeled merely, "Konrad."

He held the envelope up to his secretary. "What's this?"

She shrugged. "It was on your desk when I came on shift this morning."

Edel nodded and set it aside for later. He looked out at the security men. "If the festivities are quite over, gentlemen?"

They settled into their seats, but then Albert held up his hand. "Seven Four isn't here yet."

"Where are they?" Edel asked crossly.

Albert laughed. "They have to come all the way from the back of the woods. Maybe they got lost in the fog."

Everyone laughed except Edel.

"We'll give them five minutes." He turned back to the file and began to sort the papers. Finally, noticing the envelope, he picked it up and thumbed it open just as Seven Four walked in.

Edel shook his head as he took an exaggerated look at the clock.

"The fog," their team leader said weakly.

Edel gave them a withering stare. "Get some coffee and sit down. I want to get this thing started." He pulled the paper from the envelope and began to read. After a moment, his hand shaking, he folded the paper and put it back in the envelope.

"There will be a ten-minute delay in the debriefing," he said to a sea of shocked faces. He gestured for Kapf to join him as he hurried into a side room.

"He was here," Edel whispered to Kapf. He held out the note to Kapf, who slowly read down the single sheet of paper.

Dear Konrad:

Forgive me for not writing sooner, but you know how hectic moving can be. I am well and hope you are the same. From what little I can see for myself, you appear just fine.

You probably won't believe me, but my actions were in no way directed at you. I did what I felt I had to do, to protect myself and my future. I believe, when you are over the shock and feelings of disloyalty, you will agree that I only did what you would have done in the same situation.

I miss our talks, our discussion of Scriptures, our sharing of past misadventures. I miss your wise counsel. Need it more than ever now.

If you would be willing, if you can find it in your heart to grant forgiveness one last time to this perpetual sinner, I would like very much to meet with you one last time. To explain myself, to explain Beck, to seek one last moment of gladness before I begin what will undoubtedly be a long journey of personal exile with only one possible end.

If you agree, and I pray to whatever you would call the Supreme Being that you will, be at your office phone this afternoon at 5:30. I will call with the arrangements.

If you cannot forgive me, know that I understand and still

deeply appreciate all you tried to do to quiet the clanging in my mind. To stop the rage that threatened to consume my soul.

With trust that the wisdom of the Supreme Being, whatever that might be, will make whatever you decide the right decision, I remain your brother in arms . . . Brian Newman C.A.

Kapf looked up at Edel. "What are you going to do?"

Edel seemed deep in thought. "What he doesn't expect, I hope."

Kapf looked down at the note again. "The C.A., do you know what it means?"

Edel shook his head as he hurried back into the conference room. "Probably nothing," he said.

"That," Kapf said to himself, "I do not believe." He walked slowly into the room, muttering to himself as he went.

It was a midrange restaurant. Serving neither gourmet nor fast food, it catered to a middle-class clientele. A singer/pianist played popular American music badly while tuxedoed waiters and gowned barmaids moved freely among the too many tables.

Edel shook his head as he walked in the door. The place was not to his taste. He'd prefer a quiet supper club, or a nice, quiet coffee shop. This place was too cloying. Trying too hard to be sweet and lovable for its diners from the nearby American air base.

But then, Edel hadn't selected it.

It had all started hours ago, sitting at his desk, waiting for the phone to ring.

They had all been there. Kilgore, Kapf, Patricia, even Tabbart had put in an appearance. They sat silently, everything having been said in the marathon meetings throughout the day. The plans had been laid, arrangements checked, equipment brought over, then portioned out, personnel positioned.

Now there was only the waiting.

5:15 . . . 5:20 . . . 5:25 . . . 5:30.

Nothing.

5:31 . . . 5:32 . . . 5:33 . . . Long minutes seeming like hours. Then a knock on the door causing everyone to jump.

"What is it?" Edel almost yelled.

The shocked orderly took a step back. "Hey! Sorry, you know? But there's this guy on the pay phone in the lobby, saying he's got to talk to you." The young man was almost trampled as the occupants of the small office raced for the door.

Out of security headquarters, through a side door of the main building, into the large, ornate lobby. Edel spotted the pay phone with the receiver lying on top of it.

And a nurse starting to hang it up.

"Halt!" Edel had yelled.

The frightened nurse dropped the receiver as she was pushed roughly aside by Edel. Tabbart took her aside, whispering quickly, as Edel held the phone to his ear.

"Konrad Edel."

"Did you think to tap the pay phones, Konrad?" Newman's voice sounded amused.

"No." He stood out of the way as Kilgore took down the number, then raced to another phone.

"Well," Newman said consolingly, "that's going to make your life a little more complicated, isn't it?"

"I'm getting used to it."

"Are you?" Newman chuckled. "My apologies for that as well."

"I received your letter."

"And?" Newman sounded expectant.

Kilgore came up to him, stretching his hands apart, mouthing the words "need time."

"I would like to talk about it."

"I'm sure you would, but unfortunately I don't have the time."

Kilgore's eyes were begging for more time. Patricia was writing something on a pad.

"I need to know," Edel said after delaying as long as he dared, "that you will guarantee my safety."

"Will you guarantee mine?"

"Are you suddenly afraid of me?"

This time, Newman paused. "There's nothing sudden about it."

Patricia held up her pad to the sweating security chief.

Edel nodded, then read from it.

"I do not really think we have anything to talk about."

"Really."

Edel paraphrased the next note from Patricia.

"Perhaps it would be better for both of us if we ended our relationship here and now."

A brief silence.

"Very good," Newman said. "Tell Dr. Nellwyn that the patient refuses to be challenged into prolonged discussion. And give me your answer. I'm hanging up in thirty seconds."

Edel looked quickly around the group. Seeing no other options, he turned back to the phone.

"I agree to meet with you."

"I thought you might." Newman sounded satisfied. "The phone box at the northeast corner of Jalischbourg and Kleemstrasse, in thirty minutes."

The line went dead.

So it had gone throughout the night.

Edel would drive from phone box to phone box, each time being given terse instruction to the next call and a set time to get there.

But that was over five hours ago. Now he was in this annoying restaurant, having just received his instructions from a phone box outside.

He walked up to the maître d'.

"Yes, sir," the formally dressed man said as Edel approached. "May I assist you in some way?"

"Konrad Edel."

The man beamed, the result of a 150-mark tip received earlier that evening.

"Ah, yes, sir! Your companion is expecting you! Would you please come this way?"

He led Edel through the main dining room to a curtained booth in the back.

"May I take your coat, sir?"

Edel shook his head as he stared at the closed curtain.

"Very well, sir. Enjoy your meal." The man hurried away.

Edel took a deep breath, tried to calm his racing heart, then stepped through the curtain.

The table was set with an assortment of foods, ranging from sandwiches to elaborate dinners. A strange man sat at its head, quietly staring at Edel.

"Who are you?" Edel demanded.

Ghislain wiped his hand with a silken napkin, stood up, then held out his hand to the security chief.

"That's not really necessary, is it? I represent the man you seek."

Edel didn't move as he looked around the isolated booth. "What is this?"

Ghislain withdrew his hand. "Sir," he said in a tense voice, "you have your instructions. And I have mine. We are neither of us going anywhere for the moment. Not if we wish to avoid catastrophe."

"Where is he?" Edel asked in a steely tone.

Ghislain shook his head. "Please. If you would sit down, I'm sure you would be more comfortable. You're going to be here an hour or so."

They stood there, tensely staring at each other for nearly a minute. Then slowly, reluctantly, Edel sat down, joined by his host.

Ghislain smiled a strained smile. "I recommend the beef in oyster sauce, personally." When Edel didn't move, Ghislain shook his head. "If you leave before I instruct you, your meeting will never take place." He paused. "That would be bad for you, but immeasurably worse for me, I am quite sure. For both our sakes, I urge you to comply with your instructions."

Edel seemed to relax, a little bit.

"I'm sure it has been a long evening for you," Ghislain said. "Have something to eat, please. It has all been paid for."

For the next hour, Edel sat there silently. He picked at a salad, sipped from a beer. But he never took his eyes off Ghislain.

Finally, Edel heard the buzz of a cellular phone.

"Yes?" Ghislain handed it across to Edel.

"Hello."

"Enjoy the meal?"

"How long is this charade to go on?"

"You sound tired. Maybe we ought to forget the whole thing?"

Edel remained silent.

"Okay," Newman said, "next step. You will remove all of your clothes including underwear, shoes, and socks. Also all jewelry, watches, whatever. My associate will provide you with suitable attire and footwear."

Edel saw Ghislain lift a small duffel onto the table and begin unloading the clothes within.

"Your belongings will be returned to you by the afternoon post tomorrow. You have my word," Newman said in a somehow changed voice.

"When you've changed," Newman continued, "leave through the back of the restaurant, turn right, down the alley. That'll take you to Brenstrasse. Turn left and you'll be contacted at the first phone box."

The line went dead.

Ten minutes later, in workman's coveralls, work boots, and a wool cap, Edel approached the phone box. Ten seconds later, it rang.

"Yes?"

"Turn around, please," Ghislain's voice said. Then he hung up.

Confused, unsure of what was happening, Edel slowly turned around.

"Hello, Konrad," Newman said as he stepped out of a nearby doorway. "Care to take a walk?" He gestured down the street to Edel's right. "Ten feet in front of me, if you please."

They started off together, Newman trailing Edel by about three meters.

"Were all these theatrics really necessary?" Edel asked, without looking back.

"Please hold all questions till the end of the tour" was the amused response.

They walked for twenty minutes. At Newman's direction, they turned down alleys, crossed dark, badly lit streets, doubled back on themselves several times.

They moved into a Turkish neighborhood. The smells of Turkish coffee, hashish, and marijuana mixed in the still, night air. These, combined with the boarded-up buildings, told Edel exactly where they were.

Finally, they stopped in front of a small grocery. Newman tossed him a set of keys, and Edel unlocked the door. Newman locked it again as soon as they were inside.

For a few minutes, he stared through a tiny tear in the newspapers covering the windows before he put on the lights.

As the bare, almost empty store lit up, Newman smiled, spreading his arms, gesturing at the walls.

"Welcome," he said happily, "to *Chez l'ennemi!*"

"Are you my enemy?"

Newman shrugged. "I must be somebody's. I mean, look at all the fuss you people have gone to."

Edel looked around the deserted store, noticing for the first time the sheet-covered wall behind him.

He turned back to Newman. "What is this place?"

"A simple thing but mine own."

"So, we are to play word games, eh?" Edel managed a rough smile. "I apologize in advance for my lack of vocabulary."

Newman gestured at a pair of folding chairs nearby. They both walked over and sat down.

"No games," he said quietly. "Just some straight talk."

"That would be refreshing."

"So, how are you, Konrad?" Newman seemed distracted.

"Tired. And you?"

Newman nodded. "The same." He picked up a marker cap from the floor and started playing with it. "I've been thinking about our talks."

"Yes?"

"They were very important to me. Had a great deal of influence on my thoughts this last month or so."

Edel nodded sadly. "I could tell that by the way you left, the last time we saw each other."

Newman looked up and smiled. "You resent my escape?" He seemed genuinely interested in the answer.

"No," Edel said firmly. "I am certain you felt you were justified."

"Thank you," Newman said with mock graveness.

"What I resent," the security chief continued, "no—what I *regret* is that you lied to me. I had thought that we had reached a place together where that was no longer necessary."

Newman looked shocked. "When did I lie to you?"

"You promised not to try and escape."

"I never made any such promise!" A hurt expression quickly passed across his face. "I never lie about the important things!"

Edel shook his head. "You have a convenient memory, my friend."

"You tell me when I promised not to escape and I'll go back with you right now. Peacefully, no trouble."

"Very well." He paused. "It was immediately after that silly affair with Dr. Mont. Do you remember?"

"The man was an ass," Newman spat out.

"We talked about the review board. You didn't think they would see you after the incident."

"I remember that," Newman said, genuinely trying to remember the moment.

"I assured you that the meeting would take place." He paused. "That is when you made the promise."

Newman thought for a long moment. Then, oddly, he smiled. "I was getting worried," he said easily. "I thought I was in trouble just now."

"What do you mean?" Edel said with real interest.

"I did make you a promise," Newman said, leaning close to Edel. "But not how you remember it."

"Indeed?"

"If you will remember, I promised not to make any trouble during the transfer to the review board." He smiled at Edel. "I didn't say anything about the meeting itself."

Edel thought it over for a moment.

"My apologies," he finally said while he sneaked a glance at his watch. "You are quite right."

That seemed to please Newman.

"So maybe we can start over. What do you say?"

Ten more minutes, Edel thought, delay, agree, pause; wait.

Edel smiled and nodded. "Perhaps."

Newman gestured at Edel's clothes. "I apologize for the clothes, but I had to take precautions."

"I understand." He looked around, noticing two Bibles on a nearby table. "You've continued to study?"

Newman walked over to them.

"King James and Revised Standard. I'm also looking for one in the original Greek and Hebrew."

For one brief moment, Edel forgot why he was there and what was going to happen.

In just eight more minutes.

"Any passages in particular?"

Newman nodded, then handed one of the Bibles to Edel.

Edel opened it to one of the marked pages and read the underlined passage.

"And when they had brought them forth, they said, 'Flee for your life; do not look back or stop anywhere in the valley; flee to the hills, lest you be consumed.' "

Newman nodded solemnly. "Sound advice."

Edel looked up from the Bible. "But you haven't taken it."

"No."

"Why not?"

Newman took the Bible and opened it to another marker. Grim-faced, he handed it back to Edel.

As the security man read silently, Newman recited the passage from memory.

"I did not sit in the company of merrymakers, nor did I rejoice; I sat alone, because thy hand was upon me, for thou hadst filled me with indignation."

Edel looked up as Newman continued, a pained expression in his eyes, his fists clenching and unclenching.

"Why is my pain unceasing, my wound incurable, refusing to be healed? Wilt thou be to me like a deceitful brook, like waters that fail?"

Edel stood up, then walked over to the younger man. When he spoke, his voice was soft, caring, pastoral. Forgotten, for that one moment, was who the man in front of him was, what he had done. As well as what he could do.

And that less than three minutes remained.

"You blame God for your troubles?"

Newman turned away from him.

Edel persisted.

"You once said to me that you took responsibility for your actions. As a soldier must do." He paused. "God is your salvation, not your tormentor."

With his back to Edel, Newman smiled, but when he spoke, his voice seemed filled with pain.

"Which do you believe, that I'm a freak of nature or an evolutionary harbinger?"

Edel put his hand on Newman's shoulder. "I believe that you are a troubled child of God." He paused. "I believe that you have been shabbily used and abandoned. I believe that you are confused and need help. I believe that you will not begin to heal until you take the Lord into your heart."

Newman turned around. "I never said that I blamed God," he said coldly.

"No?"

"No. On the contrary, I thank him for those gifts."

Edel looked completely confused. "I—I—I don't understand. What gifts?" The man was completely off balance.

Newman walked deeper into the storefront. "My isolation, indignation; my pain, my wounds, even my eternal abandonment have been blessings, not curses."

"What are you saying?"

Newman smiled, walked over to the sheet on the wall, looked at Edel, then ripped the sheet down.

Edel turned, looked, then froze.

"Jesus Christ!" was all he could think to say.

Newman raised his eyebrows. "Not quite."

And there was one minute left.

O utside the grocery, the search team was almost fully deployed.

Following the miniature tracking beacon that Edel had swallowed before leaving the Institute, they'd stayed several miles behind him until his movements had stopped.

In the restaurant, an advance scout had moved up and established, with a covert listening device, that Edel wasn't meeting with Newman. They had waited it out, two scouts following Ghislain when he'd left five minutes after Edel.

But when the trackers had noted a series of sharp turns and backtracking by Edel, Kilgore had known that he must now be with Newman. They had begun to move in as soon as movement had stopped.

Edel had been fully in agreement with the plan of attack. They would wait fifteen minutes after he finally met with their target, then they would come in hard and fast.

As a former counterterrorist himself, Edel understood the necessities of what would be an overwhelming assault. SSV it was called in the commando community.

Surprise.

Speed.

Violence.

All of it would be required to secure this target.

Kilgore checked his watch. One minute to go.

"Big Dog Five, from Big Dog One. Report."

"Big Dog Five. We are secured in the establishment north of the target. Charges are in place on the common wall and we are ready to break through on command."

"Big Dog Nine, from Big Dog One. Report."

"Big Dog Nine. We are secured in the bakery to the south of target. Charges secured to the common wall. We're go."

"Big Dog Seven, from Big Dog One. Report."

"Big Dog Seven. It's a solid brick wall back here. No windows or obvious egress points. But we'll stand by."

"High Dog One and Two, from Big Dog One. Report."

"High Dog Two for One. We are in position and have clear, downward, thirty-degree angles on all front windows and doors. Light silhouettes on the paper. Not identifiable."

"Big Dog One, copy."

Kilgore checked his watch. It was time, but still he hesitated. He turned to the small crowd that was standing by his command van.

"This is going to be our best opportunity. If you have any alternatives, now's the time."

One by one, they shook their heads. Patricia, Kapf, Tabbart, none of them said a word. But their fears were written on their faces.

Ruinov, standing well back at Kilgore's request, slowly shook his head, then melted off into the shadows.

Kilgore nodded, then picked up the microphone.

"High Dog One, from Big Dog One. Give me one Flight Right each, in the north and south front windows. On my command."

"High Dog One. Copy, one Flight Right, north and south."

Patricia leaned over to Kapf. "What's a Flight Right?"

He never took his eyes off the door to the grocery. "An explosive tear gas projectile."

"Big Dog Five. Big Dog Nine. From Big Dog One. Go with entry and flash bangs on three count after Flight Rights."

"Big Dog Five, copy."

"Big Dog Nine, copy."

As she was leaning over to ask, Kapf mumbled her answer. "Concussion grenades that give out a momentarily blinding light."

Kilgore checked his watch. "I can't risk any more time. High Dog One, from Big Dog One."

"High Dog Two for One."

"Wait ten, then green light to fire."

"High Dog Two for One. Copy."

Ten seconds later, the small, unassuming grocery became a fire-breathing dragon.

Eight or nine booming roars echoed through the street as blinding flashes of orange and blue light leapt up inside the store. Smoke poured through the shattered windows and combined with falling glass from nearby buildings to make a surreal, hellish scene on the street.

Instantly, the heavily armed and gas-masked search teams moved in. Smashing through the door and remnants of the windows, they poured into the tiny store like ants on an animal carcass. Kilgore was with the second wave.

Ten minutes later, a soot-stained Kilgore walked slowly back to the psychiatrists, who had moved to the street in front of the blasted store.

"Nothing."

"What?" Tabbart's voice rose two octaves.

Kilgore shook his head. "Nothing. The place's empty." He took a deep slug of oxygen from his mask, then continued as his eyes teared up, mostly from the gas.

"They *were* there, but there's a freakin' big hole near the back of the place." He paused for more oxygen. "The son of a bitch dug right through the freakin' foundation into an old sewer line. Looks like it dates from the war. I got men down there now, but it's a goddamned maze."

"How soon before you catch up to him?" Tabbart asked hopefully.

Kilgore fixed him with an angry look. "Last time took thirty-five days."

As the psychiatrists fell into an urgent conversation among themselves, Kilgore took more oxygen, then wiped his eyes with a damp handkerchief.

"There's one more thing, guys."

They instantly looked up at him.

"There's something in there you need to see."

———

One kilometer away, deep in Wittelsbach Park, a sewer grate creaked and moaned under the constant pressure of four hands. Finally, it gave way with a noisy crack.

A pair of eyes cautiously appeared through the open grate. Almost indiscernibly, they made a 360-degree inspection of the green park, then, like some subterranean creature, ducked back down. A minute later, Edel, followed quickly by Newman, climbed out.

"Hey," Newman was saying as he straightened, "you didn't have to come."

Edel was bleeding slightly from the nose. "I wasn't given any choice."

The young former commando smiled at the old former commando.

"All I did was throw you in. If I hadn't, you'd be looking at a state funeral about now." He looked around. "Time to go." He took a few steps, then turned back to the beaten-up security chief. "Don't follow me, okay? I don't want to save your life, then end it in the same hour."

Edel looked up at his . . . comrade. "Don't run. Let me bring you in. I promise you will not be harmed."

Newman stopped, then turned around. "You mean like that little display back there? No thank you."

Edel walked over to him. "Listen to me, Brian . . ."

A shot rang out.

Newman threw himself to the ground and rolled to his side. In almost the same movement, he pulled the Tokarev TT-33 pistol that he'd had Ghislain get for him. Quickly, he fired four rounds at the spot he'd seen the muzzle flash.

When no fire was returned, he rolled to a kneeling position, then fired four more rounds into the dark. He dropped the clip and threw in another. As he did, a figure jumped up from behind a rock and raced off.

Newman fired five rounds at the running form, then slowly stood up.

"I know him," he said softly as he stared at the spot the man had run from. Then he turned back to Edel. "How the hell'd you figure out where to . . ." He stopped.

Edel was crouched on all fours near the spot he'd been standing. His head was down, and he was breathing heavily.

Newman walked over to him and knelt down. "Where?" he asked softly.

"A . . . not . . . good . . . place," Edel wheezed out.

Newman took a deep breath.

"Shit."

They had brought up large fans to ventilate the small storefront, but even now, after twenty minutes had passed, the smell of the CS gas still permeated the place. The three doctors held bandannas over their faces as they picked their way around the debris of the forced entry.

Evidence-gathering specialists were carefully picking through the wreckage. Sifting through every used Styrofoam cup, paper bag, or piece of clothing for any clue that might set them back on Newman's trail.

Technicians were busily setting up sodium vapor lights to brighten the dark span near the back where the explosives and projectiles had knocked out the lights.

The three entry teams stood by gaping holes in the north and south walls with their debriefers, carefully replaying their actions, assessing successes and failures for use the next time.

But the same thought went through everyone's mind.

Will there be a next time?

Kilgore led the doctors through the shattered scene toward the back of the store.

"It's here, on the back wall."

Patricia looked around as they walked. "Can we get copies of everything you find, Captain? It might help in figuring out his next move."

"I'll see to it," Kilgore said as he stopped short. "Here it is." He shined his flashlight along the wall.

The psychiatrists peered through the gloom, trying to make it out.

"It's some kind of mural," Patricia said as she slowly appreciated its size.

Tabbart nodded. "Ink, I believe."

Kilgore pointed the flashlight on the floor. Eight or nine marker pens of different colors lay against the wall. "We found about fifty of them scattered all over the place," he said.

Kapf walked within inches of the drawing.

"Captain," Kapf said as he squinted to make out the detail, "can we possibly get more light?"

Kilgore turned to a corporal who was walking by. "How long, Tony?"

"Another few seconds, boss."

Thirty seconds later, the sodium vapor lights sizzled to life, then threw the entire area into a painfully bright resolution.

"Remarkable," Patricia said in an excited voice.

"Extraordinary," Tabbart said in a hushed voice.

Kapf moved back a few feet to take in the entire mural at once. He stood there for a full minute, not saying a word, his only expression an unnoticed tear working its way down his grim face.

"Is it possible it predates Newman's occupancy?" Patricia asked.

Kapf shook his head. "Look at the faces."

The mural was set in a field.

A light purple sky with orange clouds serenely looked down on a green field. The background was dotted with hills covered in green bushes, and a series of what appeared to be dirt paths crisscrossed each other. The paths seemed heavily trodden, lying deeper than the grass on the hills.

In the middle of this pastoral scene were six people. Five men and a woman. They were running, naked, toward the hills. Their faces were twisted in agony, their naked bodies bleeding from angry welts all over their exposed skin.

And they bore an eerie but not exact resemblance to Alexander Beck, Manfred Tabbart, Jack Clemente, Otto Kapf, Konrad Edel, and Patricia Nellwyn.

They seemed to be running through piles of tortured, dismembered, decomposing bodies, almost knee-deep. And behind them, flying midway between the ground and the sky, was a swarm of . . . things.

They were insectlike, about half the size of the running figures. Their translucent wings seemed to beat heavily in the air as they pursued the runners through the field. Their bodies seemed to be covered by machined steel, contoured plates, seven or eight of them, held in place by metal bolts.

They had long, jointed, upwardly curving tails with painfully sharp red stingers at the end. Blood dripped from some; a dismembered human arm hung off another; a still-beating heart was impaled on yet another.

The insect things' heads, disproportionately large for their bodies, had long, apparently silky blond hair topped by golden five-pointed crowns. Their faces, some in profile, some partially hidden, others facing the spectators, were human, and all too familiar to the people in the storefront.

From the face of each of the insect things, Brian Newman looked out at them or down at the bodies and the running figures. His eyes were yellow-orange, his teeth exaggerated in length and sharpness, his expression purely feral, but it was Newman.

Off in the farthest corner of the mural, next to what appeared to be the mouth of a volcano, the point from which the insect things appeared to be swarming, stood another figure.

The three doctors, after standing in mute shock for ten minutes as they tried to take in the enormity of the mural, crowded around that corner of the picture. They examined it with a magnifying glass that Kilgore found on the floor, each in turn studying what turned out to be the silhouette of a man. Behind him, gaps in the smoke from the volcano appeared to form a series of numbers over his head: 2–27–9–1–11.

"This needs to be carefully preserved," Patricia whispered.

"I agree," Tabbart said in the contagious hushed tone.

Kapf stepped away from the mural, biting his lower lip, shaking his head, seeming to be deeply conflicted. He wandered through the debris, ignoring the mural which the others couldn't take their eyes off.

Finally, he stopped, kneeled down, then dusted off the book he'd pulled from under a chunk of wall. He sat down and began flipping through it.

"The resentment directed at who he perceives as his tormentors," Tabbart said clinically, "I understand. But what I find interesting is his subconscious manifestation of himself as a form of insect life. Perhaps subconsciously viewing himself in the light of a latent inferiority complex. Mosquito-swatting man, so to speak."

Patricia shook her head. "More like a metamorphosis. Caterpillar to pupa to chrysalis to evolved form." She pointed as she talked. "Newman's attempt to explain his evolutionary progression. From weak, defenseless *Homo sapiens* to *Homo crudelis.* Coldhearted, relentless man, forged in the bowels of the volcano, emerging to challenge the weaker evolutionary form for dominance on the planet."

Before Tabbart could interrupt, Kapf's voice cut through, causing them both to turn to him.

"And the fifth angel blew his trumpet," Kapf read in a strong voice, "and I saw a star fallen from heaven to earth, and he was given the key of the shaft of the bottomless pit; he opened the shaft of the bottomless pit, and from the shaft rose smoke like the smoke of a great furnace, and the sun and the air were darkened with the smoke from the shaft."

Patricia and Tabbart turned back to the mural, looking from the smoking eruption to the purplish sky.

Kapf continued.

"Then from the smoke came locusts on the earth, and they were given power like the scorpions of the earth; they were told not to harm the grass of the earth or any green growth or any tree, but only those of mankind who have not the seal of God upon their foreheads."

Kapf stood up, then walked over to the mural.

"It begins to become clear," he said softly. "The strange inscription on the envelope, the statements that others need adjust to him rather than the opposite. The initials after his signature." He paused. "This drawing."

He continued reading aloud.

"In appearance the locusts were like horses arrayed for battle; on their heads were what looked like crowns of gold; their faces were like human faces, their hair like women's hair, and their teeth like lions' teeth; they had scales like iron breastplates. . . . They have tails like scorpions, and stings."

He closed the book, finishing from memory.

"They have as king over them the angel of the bottomless pit; his name in Hebrew is Abaddon, and in Greek he is called Apollyon."

Tabbart was trembling as he looked from Kapf to the mural, but Patricia just looked confused.

"Spell it out for me," she said hesitantly.

Kapf laughed cynically. "It is all too apparent." He paused. "Brian Newman has gone quite insane."

"What?"

Kilgore, who had been speaking on a cell phone for the last few minutes, came up and joined the conversation.

"We've got the man who met with Edel. He's a porn house operator from the East Side." He looked at the frozen expressions on Patricia's and Kapf's faces. "Did I miss something?"

Kapf turned to him. "Please go on, Captain."

Nervously, Kilgore continued. "Well, the man's cooperating. He's given us Newman's alias, and the local cops think we'll get a lot more from him."

"Which is it, Captain? The last name, is it Abaddon or Apollyon?"

Kilgore was stunned. "Apollyon," he said quietly. "How did you . . ."

"So he is now Charon Apollyon." Kapf seemed to be in deep contemplation.

Kilgore looked down at the slip of paper in his hand. "How in hell did you know that?"

As Kapf answered the soldier, he kept his gaze locked on Patricia. "I was raised in a more rigid world than this," he said slowly. "My upbringing consisted of school and church. And, as with most of my countrymen, the chief of staff included," he said as he looked over at the trembling Tabbart, "the tale depicted in Mr. Newman's rather frightening representation is well known to me. It was used on a great many occasions, I'm afraid, to, as you Americans say, put the fear of God into me. I recognized it almost instantly, as I suspect Chief Edel must have." He paused. "Has he been located yet?"

"No." Kilgore was studying the mural.

Kapf sighed. "No." He paused. "The numbers appearing above the darkened figure merely confirmed my impression. They are from the archaic Lutheran Steganograph."

He handed the Bible to Kilgore.

"Two indicates the second or new testament. Twenty-seven, the book of Revelation. Nine, the ninth chapter. One, the first verse is the starting point; eleven, the eleventh verse is the end."

Kilgore looked it up, read the passage, then looked back at the mural. "Damned close," he said. "But the first name he's using?"

"To all my friends onshore." He smiled. "Do not forget the inscription on the envelope. Charon is the Greek figure of mythology who ferried the souls of the damned across the river Styx. When you confirmed that he had chosen the Greek form of the angel of the bottom-less pit, the rest was clear." He walked over to the mural. "Remember that he signed his note to Chief Edel with the letters 'C,' 'A,' after his name. Charon Apollyon. All perfectly clear."

"Not to me," Patricia said angrily. "Not at all!" She took several steps away before whirling back to face Kapf. "And who says that's he's gone insane!"

Kapf shook his head, then stepped away from the mural. He nodded at the gruesome depictions.

"Newman" was his sad-voiced answer.

At the edge of Wittelsbach Park, in a bus kiosk lit by a single bulb, Newman helped Edel lie down on the broad stone bench. Newman pulled off his shirt, balled it up, and placed it tenderly beneath the older man's head. Edel groaned as a spasm of pain shook his body.

"It is, I think," he said in a weak voice, "over with me."

Newman nodded. "I think you've lost part of a major abdominal vessel. Massive internal bleeding, probably severe damage to several organs."

Edel's face took on an amused look. "After all these years—" He coughed up some blood. Newman wiped the dying man's face. "After all these years, to be shot down by my own." He smiled weakly. "It is a supreme irony."

Newman looked down at him. "I don't know if it will make you feel any better, but it wasn't one of ours."

"No?"

Newman shook his head. "It was a Russian." His eyes went cold, violence pouring off him like an odor. "A Russian colonel named Ruinov."

That seemed, in some odd way, to please Edel.

"There is symmetry in that," the former cold warrior said softly. He looked up into Newman's eyes. "You will kill this Russian colonel?"

"Without a doubt." Newman's voice was gunmetal cold.

Edel nodded, causing another paroxysm of pain to roll through his body.

"It is not Christian of me," he said in a pained voice, "but, somehow, that makes me feel . . ." He struggled for the word. "Clean. Do you understand?"

"I do." Newman brushed the man's hair out of his eyes. "Is there anything I can do for you? Any arrangements you want made?" His voice was soft, but not comforting.

Edel shook his head. "I am alone except for my church." He paused. "But I would like to be buried in the churchyard. By the juniper, I think."

"I'll make sure they know," he said. "And if they don't, I'll move you there myself. You have my word."

Edel smiled as he coughed up more blood. "This is one of the important things, yes?"

"Yes."

The security chief seemed satisfied.

"There is just one other thing."

"Name it."

"They have all said a great many things about you." He tried to smile but the spasms were too much now. "The talkers, the doubters, the doctors. And I have seen the picture. Your picture."

He paused to let some of the pain pass. "I would like to know, please."

Newman smiled, then bent down and whispered in the dying man's ear. Slowly, a forced smile spread over the man's face. Newman straightened up.

"Ah," Edel said, "that is as it should be." He looked up at Newman with a deep longing in his eyes. "I do not believe in allowing men to suffer needlessly, do you?"

Newman shook his head, came to attention, then snapped a salute.

Edel straightened himself, closed his eyes, then began reciting.

"Our father, who art in heaven, hallowed be thy name. Thy kingdom come, thy will be done . . ."

Newman's right hand flashed out, smashing Edel across the bridge of his nose, sending bone fragments flying into his brain. He quivered for a moment, then lay quiet.

". . . on earth as it is in heaven," Newman finished as he turned and walked off into the night.

She had been going for over thirty hours without a break. Despite the late night cold, she'd sweated through her blouse and jacket hours ago. Her temples were throbbing from sleep deprivation, hunger, confusion, and anger.

Patricia threw her purse on her bed as she stripped off her clothes. Whatever the theories, disagreements, or worries, her priorities right now were a shower, a meal, then a couple of hours sleep. The rest she would take up later.

She grabbed her robe and walked into the bathroom.

As she walked through the door, a powerful hand reached out, grabbing her by the throat. She was actually picked up by that iron grip and brutally shoved against the wall of the bathroom.

She could barely breathe, barely think, as Newman put his face inches from hers.

His eyes were wide open and unblinking. Nostrils flared, taking deep even breaths, his expression was beyond fury. Later, she would remember thinking that if death had a face, this must surely be it.

"I have a message for you and your associates," Newman whispered in a guttural voice. "I'm making you responsible for delivering it. Nod for yes, die for no."

She felt his breath on her face as she nodded.

"Konrad Edel is dead. By my hand but not by my wish. He is to be buried in the yard of his church by the juniper. I'm making you responsible for it. Nod for yes, die for no."

She nodded quickly.

"I'm leaving soon. Any attempt to stop me will cause the greatest possible disaster you can conceive of." He paused. "There are reactors in places other than Abkhaz. You and your associates will not interfere with my leaving the country. I'm making you responsible for it. Nod for yes, die for no."

Again, a quick, terrified nod.

He pulled her off the wall and dragged her back into the bedroom. He threw her onto the bed. She frantically tried to crawl across it to reach the gun she kept in the night table.

He effortlessly grabbed her by the leg, dragging her back to him. Two minutes later, she was tied firmly and securely.

Despite the overwhelming terror that was welling up inside her, "Clinical Patty" felt something else—an exhilaration at this unclinical, raw, exposed contact with the demon/hero of her papers and dreams.

As Newman reached across her to grab a scarf from the far night table, his face passed within inches of hers, his right hand accidentally sliding across her bare breast.

She shivered in anticipation, then almost as an afterthought gasped out, "No! Please don't!"

Newman looked at her with an odd expression. Then he chuckled, looked around, picked up the robe, and tossed it on top of her.

"You never have quite got it, have you?" he said in an amused voice. Instantly, the amusement was replaced by the death mask.

"Last thing," he said as he bent low over her prone form. "After it's all over, after I've left the country and you all start to forget what really happened. When all you'll be thinking about are your precious theories and unanswered questions."

He paused and put his mouth against her trembling ear.

"Don't come after me. Ever," he whispered. "Leave me alone. Anyone comes looking for me . . . I'm making you responsible."

He gagged her, got off the bed, then walked over to the telephone. Calmly, he dialed a number, waiting for it to be answered.

"Hi," he said in an upbeat tone, "can I speak with John Kilgore, room 1296? Thanks loads."

He turned to Patricia, loosening the ropes on her ankles as he waited. He suddenly turned back to the phone.

"Captain Kilgore?"

"Who is this?"

"Charon Apollyon."

A long silence on the line.

"Yes?"

"I'm sorry we never got to meet personally," Newman said casually. "I think we might have been friends."

"We still can be," Kilgore said cautiously. "Why don't we meet somewhere and talk about it?"

"Okay."

"What? Uh, okay. Where would you like to . . ."

Newman raised his eyebrows as he smiled at Patricia.

"I'm at Patricia Nellwyn's. Why don't we get together here?" He paused. "You have forty minutes," he said as he hung up.

He smiled at Patricia, who looked terrified.

"Relax, Doc. I'm leaving, but someone's got to untie you." He turned and started out of the room.

Suddenly, he stopped, seemed to be thinking something over, then came back.

He looked down at her, then pulled the robe off, tossing it back into the bathroom.

Newman smiled down at her exposed, naked body, nodding in approval.

"When a bunch of guys come busting in here in twenty minutes or so, it should make for a humbling scene."

He headed for the door.

"You could use the humility."

Often called the Queen of the Danube, Vienna, Austria, lies on the Danube River, at a point where almost all European trade routes cross. It is a great port, trading center; a manufacturing city; and a city of immense history and drama.

It is one other thing as well: it is arguably the espionage capital of the world.

A recent study by the National Foreign Intelligence Advisory Board estimated that one out of every six spies in the world either works or is based in Vienna.

Being the only city in the world with embassies from every United Nations member, as well as over thirty legations from "liberation movements," a day hardly goes by without one intrigue or another.

The center of Vienna is called the Inner City. With wide boulevards built where the ancient city walls once stood, and the Ringstrasse with its scores of parks circling the many international and local government buildings, the Inner City invariably draws every visitor to Vienna, at least once during their trip, including those in and on the periphery of international espionage.

At the center of the Inner City, just southwest of Vienna's most famous building, the 450-foot-high Saint Stephen's Cathedral, lies the Rathaus.

A Gothic building in the center of a small park, its clock tower reaches over 320 feet in the air, and its walls contain the city library, the Historical Museum, and, off to one side, the world's most famous historical collection of weapons.

And among that collection, every Monday and Thursday morning from nine to noon, sits Abd al-Qadir Yaman ibn Musa Abu Khayyat, counterfeit document dealer to the world.

In his $2,000 Italian suits, $500 shoes, and expensive daily hairstyling, he sits in front of the exhibits of sixteenth-century firearms, quietly reading his London *Times.*

As the clock in the tower above him chimes for the twelfth time at noon, he stands, carefully folds his paper, places it in his calfskin briefcase, and leaves.

Along with whoever had been sent, from whatever intelligence service that day, to watch him.

He didn't mind the surveillance, not really. His clients, many of those same intelligence services that watched him so closely, knew better than to come themselves. In fact, it was said that Abd al-Qadir, as he was known to his intimates, alone supported the bulk of the thriving intermediary business in Vienna.

He was not surprised when a man quietly sat down next to him on that Monday morning.

He continued reading his paper. "We have some business acquaintance in common?"

"Armairco."

"Go on." Abd al-Qadir turned the page of his paper.

"Navinco."

The documents dealer nodded slightly. "And?"

"Florida Meridian Air."

Abd al-Qadir frowned as he continued to read. The names were good ones, organs of U.S. Intelligence that he had dealt with in the past. But none of them in the last five years.

"They strike a nostalgic tone," he said as he glanced at the man next to him.

He was in his forties, with longish hair, a clumpy beard, and large sunglasses beneath a battered felt fedora.

Not one of his regulars.

The man remained silent.

"Very well," Abd al-Qadir finally said. "You may place the order, but I will require a larger than normal advance."

"Agreed."

The man put a small slip of paper on the bench between them. Casually, Abd al-Qadir picked it up, unfolded it with one hand, then held it behind his paper.

"The travel documents are routine enough: 1,965 deutsche marks apiece. The birth certification and baptismal documents, say, 982 DM each." He paused. "The other two, they are going to be problematic."

The man didn't react.

Abd al-Qadir got a very strange feeling from that. There were always negotiations over the difficult documents.

"But," Abd al-Qadir said after a time, "I have my resources. I will have to charge a premium, however."

"Fine."

"6,550 DM. Each."

"And they'll stand up to a computer search?"

"Of course." He did the calculations in his head. "Three travel documents, the birth records, and the others." He paused. "20,959 DM. Or $15,000 American."

The man smiled for the first time. "I didn't know you gave discounts." He placed a small envelope on the bench. "Photos, the name, the histories, instructions on delivery. Also 10,000 marks. The remaining $7,366.41 in American currency on delivery."

Abd al-Qadir picked up the envelope. "Agreed."

"How long?"

"Ten days. No less. The special requests will take time to process."

The man thought for a moment, then stood up. "Ten days."

He walked away, casually examining the ancient broadswords, suits of armor, and shields as he went.

A pair of young lovers, obviously unable to take in anything other than each other, drifted out behind him. On the steps of the Rathaus, they stopped, the young woman posing against one of the ornate columns, as her husband or boyfriend took her picture.

With a close-up of the man who had met with Abd al-Qadir as the dominant feature of the photo.

———

"He's in Vienna!"

The sergeant came running into Kilgore's office.

"What?"

The young man held out the photograph taken in front of the Rathaus.

"Greek Intelligence spotted him making a deal with a paper dealer in Vienna."

Kilgore examined the photo with a magnifying glass.

"It could be him," he said carefully.

"It gets better," the sergeant virtually gushed. "Their people on the ground followed him for a while. They were able to recover a paper cup he used. Fingerprints are conclusive!" He handed the report to Kilgore.

It had been three weeks since the debacle at the grocery. Since the embarrassing raid at Dr. Nellwyn's house.

Since the discovery of Konrad Edel's body.

The porn dealer had been interrogated by the search team and German authorities. Other than the name Charon Apollyon, he'd yielded nothing of importance.

Everything in the grocery had been examined, dissected, and interpreted. Specialists in art interpretation had been brought in to examine the mural before it had been cut from the wall and removed to the Institute for further study.

Patricia had submitted to hypnosis, then every aspect of her confrontation with Newman had been deliberated and analyzed. Her house had been gone over three times for even the slightest amounts of trace evidence.

But no trace of Newman could be found.

There was one other issue that also remained floating in the air.

Would Newman follow through on his nuclear threat if he discovered that they were still actively pursuing him?

They'd taken every possible precaution to avoid discovering that answer.

Patricia had supervised the funeral for Edel, in his churchyard near a group of juniper bushes. They had all attended. The premier of the Federal Republic of Germany had made a speech about "men on walls"; the minister had talked of "final rewards"; and Dr. Tabbart had spoken of "efficiency and dignity."

Throughout, Kilgore had watched the rooftops, the windows across the street, the crowd of media and onlookers, hoping to find the face that he felt certain must be there somewhere.

They had made a great show of breaking down the headquarters in the barn; ostentatiously pulled their men and equipment out of the Institute.

They'd massively lowered their profile across the board, but they had far from abandoned the search.

In a highly secured hangar at Rheinsgarth Air Base, they continually processed all the leads they could come up with, now that they were in their covert mode. They met secretly with staff from the Institute, trying to put together a psychological profile of Newman aka Charon Apollyon.

And they had circulated a worldwide communiqué to all arms of American Intelligence.

Newman had become the number one priority among all other intelligence demands.

"Wanted—Dead or Alive."

But that had all been three weeks ago, and nothing since. Not until this young sergeant had come bursting in with the Viennese photograph.

Kilgore walked out to the analysis room, where five others were examining copies of the photograph and fingerprints.

"Well?"

A lieutenant looked up. "It's him. No question."

Kilgore still hesitated to act.

In the fifty-six days that Newman had been at large, he had yet to make even the slightest mistake. Even with them tracking him to the grocery. There, Dr. Kapf was convinced, Newman wanted his mural seen, would've led them to it if they hadn't found him.

No mistakes.

But Kapf had been cautionary when Kilgore had brought the point up.

"If," the elderly professor had said, "Newman's personality has become submerged into the psychosis of Apollyon, it is possible that he will begin to become slightly erratic. And an erratic man makes mistakes."

An erratic man makes mistakes.

One.

In fifty-six days.

He allows himself to be observed meeting with a known documents dealer in an environment about as far from secure as possible, in the most dangerous city in Europe.

It seemed all so remarkably convenient.

Yet, it also seemed possible.

Kilgore turned to his liaison officer. "Can we lean on the paper bug?"

"Negative," the man said. "He's on the protected list."

Kilgore looked over at his second-in-command. "Well?"

The man shrugged. "We were due for some luck." He paused. "But it *is* awfully lucky."

Kilgore took a few steps away as he thought it over. Finally, after about a minute, he turned around decisively.

"Bob," he said to his deputy, "take a forward logistics team and two scout units to Vienna. Set up a forward C.P. and begin the initial search. I want a full hazard assessment in thirty-six hours."

The man nodded and hurried out to another office.

Kilgore turned back to the liaison officer. "Make plans to move the whole team out on two hours notice. Make whatever preliminary contacts you have to in Austria." Kilgore continued on to his office door. "And somebody get me Dr. Kapf on the phone."

Sixty-four kilometers away, a little under an hour's drive, Tabbart pulled out of the Institute's driveway on his way home.

For the first time in days, Brian Newman was not on his mind, hadn't even come up during the long, trying day. That, to Tabbart, made it a very good day after all.

But there had been crises.

Jack Clemente had entered the final stages of his battle with the cancer. Tabbart felt sorry for him, but was more deeply concerned about who would replace him.

The board wanted to promote from within, meaning, he suspected, Patricia Nellwyn. He would never allow that to happen. His plan was to hire from abroad, but he was meeting strong resistance.

Also, the board of directors was considering expanding the Institute's facilities by clear-cutting almost half of the woods. Now, loud, obnoxious members of Germany's Greens Party were starting to show up, chaining themselves to trees and chanting for the news cameras.

At a facility that prided itself on its discretion and privacy, this could be a disaster.

Then there was the problem of insurance carriers.

Three major carriers, in fact, who had all decided to drop the Volker Institute from their accepted list due to the "exorbitant" charges. Tabbart spent three full hours in meetings on this problem alone.

It wasn't that the Institute really needed the business of those carriers, who made up less than 7 percent of the adjusted gross anyway. No, it was the principle of the thing.

The Volker Institute, the "People's" Institute, always prided itself on the number of community patients it accepted every year. It added to the image that Tabbart had worked so hard to craft in the last nine years. So, he would fight any attempt to force them to cut back there.

A day of crises, but none involving Brian Newman, so he smiled as he drove.

He slowed as he pulled up to the one-lane bridge that crossed a tributary of the Isar near his home. A car was in front of him, so he waited, as the law demanded, for it to cross first, as the bridge passage light flashed green for traffic from this direction.

But instead, it just sat.

He shook his head at the stupidity of most drivers, then honked his horn.

Still, no movement.

He honked again, then turned at a knocking on the glass of his driver's side window.

The man was standing so close that Tabbart could only make out his torso. He seemed to be looking over the top of the Mercedes touring car.

"Was ist los?" Tabbart asked.

A muffled response.

"Idiot," Tabbart murmured as he lowered the window.

The man started to bend down to him.

"*Was ist . . .*" He never finished the question as a rag soaked in chlorpromazine covered his face, instantly rendering him unconscious.

Thirty-five minutes later, he slowly came to.

"Good evening," a male voice said from nearby.

Tabbart's vision was still cloudy. His head was throbbing, and he was sick to his stomach.

"What is going on?" he demanded in German. "I am an important man! You had better release me immediately!"

He heard steps come toward him, then flinched as a cool, damp rag was applied to his face.

The male voice spoke again. "Blink it into your eyes. It'll help."

Tabbart did as he was told, then slowly opened his eyes as he felt it being removed.

"My God!"

Newman shook his head. "I wish you people would stop saying that."

"What—you—how?" Tabbart stuttered.

"I have some questions for you," Newman said flatly.

Tabbart began to pull himself together as the initial shock wore off. "I will tell you nothing! Now release me at once!"

"Who's the tall Russian you meet with at the Hofkeller in the Reisch District?"

The fear deepened, as did Tabbart's resolve not to say anything. He firmly clenched his jaw.

Newman pulled his chair closer to the bound man.

"Now, Manfred," he said in a casual, friendly voice, "we both know that you're going to tell me everything I want to know. Why not make it easy on yourself?"

He pulled a large hunting knife from a scabbard in his boot.

"The Hofkeller. In the Reisch District. A tall Russian man who deals in icons and antiques. Remember?"

Tabbart couldn't take his eyes off the blade of the knife as it reflected the light of the one bare lightbulb in the room.

"Please," he said weakly, his momentary strength evaporating as each flash of light shot off the highly polished blade. "Please! I know nothing!"

"You know anatomy." Newman's voice was still casual, but beginning to flatten out like a tape running down.

He reached out, quickly undoing Tabbart's trousers. He pulled them and the boxer shorts down to the man's ankles.

Tabbart struggled against his bonds, wanted to scream, to shout for help.

All he could manage was a weak whimper.

"It'll go like this," Newman continued. "None of the cuts will be lethal. All will be immediately treated and bandaged. I will then wait an hour or so for you to sufficiently recover, then repeat the process." He paused, bringing his face to within inches of Tabbart's.

"You're a doctor. You know how many things I can slice up." He dropped the blade of the knife until it touched Tabbart's exposed penis. "Or cut off, without causing death."

Tabbart tried to pull back, tried to make the chair topple over backward, but Newman reached out and grabbed the flaccid organ in his hand and gripped it tight.

"No!" Tabbart screamed.

Newman made a very light incision on the top of the taut member.

"The Hofkeller. In the Reisch District. A tall Russian man who deals in icons and antiques. Remember?"

I n the electronically secured conference room at the institute, Kapf shook his head as he hung up the phone.

"The chief must have stopped on the way home," he said. "I suggest we proceed without him."

"Okay," Kilgore said as he settled himself at the table. He looked over at Patricia, who quickly looked down at the file. He smiled. "Dr. Nellwyn, you want to start?"

She nodded tersely. "Right." She flipped through some pages in the file. "We have two things here really. First, why is he in Austria? Second, what are his intentions? Where is he going and how will he try to get there?"

"So," Kilgore said, "you're convinced all of this is genuine? Not some kind of trick?"

She nodded, still without looking at him. "Of course. Why shouldn't it be?" She paused. "He's on the run, we're only a couple of hours from the Austrian border here. It's the logical first move. And logic is the dominant force in this man."

"I disagree."

All eyes turned to Kapf.

"Dr. Kapf?" Kilgore said.

Kapf shook his head. "Logic is not what drives this man. Passion is."

"Don't be absurd, Otto," Patricia chuckled.

Kilgore held up a restraining hand. "Go ahead, Doctor."

"Do not misunderstand me. I do not mean passion as you know it." He smiled cynically. "Nothing about Newman, Apollyon if you prefer, is what conventional science would call normal. But, nevertheless, he is a man driven by passion."

"Which means?" Kilgore asked.

"Which means that Newman/Apollyon will not leave, at least not permanently, until he has completed the task that his passion undoubtedly demands."

"You don't believe the reports, then," Kilgore said glumly.

Kapf shrugged. "Whether he has been in Vienna, is still there, or not, it makes no difference." He paused. "He will be back. He will feel compelled to finish what others have started."

Patricia finally looked up, smiling patronizingly. "That is?" Her voice was laced with good-natured sarcasm.

"Avenging his friend." He said it flatly, like it was an established fact.

"Unbelievable," Patricia said as she suppressed a smile.

Kilgore noticed. "Dr. Nellwyn?"

This time, she returned Kilgore's gaze. "The last, first. Newman, not Newman/Apollyon, but Newman is incapable of forming *any* friendships. Let alone one of sufficient closeness and intimacy that the removal of it would drive him to a homicidal rage. Especially with the man who he must view as his chief incarcerator.

"In point of fact, he is completely incapable of any such rage. He is virtually emotionless, cold, removed, remote. Capable of aping genuine emotion when it serves him, but incapable of ever truly feeling it."

She consulted her notes.

"Passion? Never. Not in that man. Not ever." She took a deep breath before continuing. "He could have, should have, killed or raped me at the very least, when he had the opportunity. A passionate man would've."

Kilgore looked away as he remembered the feel of her bare skin against his hand when he had untied her legs that day.

"That I'm still here," she continued, "relatively unbruised, is testimony that the man is completely dispassionate."

Kapf shook his head. "He did not rape you, so he is dispassionate. If he had raped you, you would call him a sexual psychopath." He paused, looking seriously at Patricia. "What you are still not realizing, child, is that in either case, he would still be the same man. His purpose in visiting you was to deliver a message, nothing more. Everything else was or would have been, as you Americans are so fond of saying, simply window dressing."

Kilgore always felt uncomfortable when these shrinks began to get off on their weird tangents. "Can we get back to the issue at hand?"

Patricia glanced at him, then looked back at Kapf.

"Look," she said cajolingly, "at some point we're all going to have to sit down and accept that Brian Newman is the next wave. The next generation of man. Lane Fenton wrote about it thirty years ago. Living things change in special ways. And chief among these is the reality that whole races grow old, just as individuals do."

Kapf shook his head. "Professor Lane Fenton's theories have never been generally accepted by the scientific community."

Patricia shrugged. "They have been by me." She turned to Kilgore. "We've had three hundred thousand years, it's time we concede the inevitable and try to live alongside it as long as we can."

She stood up, then began to pace.

"Dr. Kapf, and believe me when I say how much I admire him, is just not capable of understanding this man."

Kapf seemed amused. "Indeed? May I ask why?"

"I think you should." She turned to Kilgore. "At the grocery, he said it himself. Dr. Kapf grew up in war and postwar Germany. The product of one of the most disciplined, conservative societies in the world's history. His age, socialization, cultural nexus, all force him into conventional answers to unconventional questions."

"Fascinating," Kapf said quietly, a touch of sadness in his voice.

Patricia continued, talking directly to Kilgore.

"Dr. Kapf had referred to *Homo crudelis.* Coldhearted Man. Let's get that straight before we go any further." She turned to Kapf. "That's almost right on.

"Newman is not hampered by the petty moralities, conventions, or mores that we are. He is completely free to do what he wants, when he wants, how he wants. If somebody should try to stop him—" She shrugged. "It wouldn't matter any more to him than the pigeon or the cat."

She paused.

"That's all we are to him, or all we should be!" She was beginning to speak in an excited, speeded-up voice.

"*Erectus* couldn't stand up for long to *sapiens,* because he didn't have the brainpower. We won't be able to stand up to the Newmans because we remain crippled by these stupid, superfluous, inbred handicaps we so haughtily call emotions and morality."

Kapf looked at her without blinking. "So *crudelis* becomes the dominant creature, as *Homo sapiens* slowly but surely dies out?"

She walked over to him, leaning her hands on the table, her every sinew begging for Kapf to understand.

"Not *crudelis.* Not Coldhearted Man." She paused. *"Homo superbus."*

"Superior man?" Kapf asked softly.

Patricia nodded. *"Homo superbus.* Stapleton saw it coming almost seventy years ago. Think of it!" She seemed to drift off for a moment. When she spoke, her voice was dreamlike.

"All the things we've screwed up, all the things we couldn't do because we considered them 'wrong' or 'immoral.' Population control leading to feeding the hungry. Scientific advances at a breakneck pace. No more wars, no more hatred, no more discrimination."

Kapf sadly nodded. "I have heard this all before," he said, looking directly at her, "as you have pointed out."

Patricia looked blank.

"You are in illustrious company, Dr. Nellwyn," he said as he stood up, sweeping his papers into his briefcase.

She nodded. "Stapleton, Nietzsche, Kirkegaard."

Kapf opened the door, then turned back to her, disappointment and something akin to anger in his eyes.

"Eichmann," he said, "Mengele, Speer, Himmler, and of course, Hitler." He paused. "Quite illustrious company."

Patricia froze, a stunned expression slowly spreading across her face.

Kapf turned to Kilgore. "You have my opinion, Captain," he said quietly. "Please excuse me." He closed the door behind him.

Patricia stood there, staring at the closed door.

"He doesn't understand," she muttered so softly that Kilgore could barely make it out. "He doesn't understand."

Kilgore's mind was swimming. He'd come for help in deciding how best to track a fugitive, then found himself knee-deep in a philosophy debate. He sighed deeply.

"Dr. Nellwyn?"

She slowly turned to him.

"Dr. Nellwyn, if I can cut through the third-year philosophy class . . ."

She walked over and began gathering her things.

"Where," he said in an exasperated voice, "where do I find Newman?"

She picked up her things, heading for the door.

"I'm going to Vienna." She headed out into the corridor. "He just doesn't understand," she muttered as she went.

Kilgore stood up, took a deep breath, and gathered his papers.

He was a strong man, an honest, hardworking, moral man, and he didn't think of himself as weak because of that.

But he did think of himself as alone.

Almost at the very moment that Kilgore sat down with the psychiatrists to discuss what to do about Newman, Ruinov was holding a similar consultation in his hotel suite.

The tall man had delivered intercepted copies of the Greek Intelligence and, together, they sat down and pored over it.

"I know Abd al-Qadir," the tall man said, "he won't talk. Even if we were allowed to question him."

"The quality of his work, is it that good?" Ruinov asked.

The tall man nodded. "If Newman receives whatever documents he has ordered, he will most certainly vanish completely from sight."

Ruinov sighed. "What do we have available in Vienna?"

"Black, brown, and purple networks, as well as a cut-down Spetsnaz commando unit at our U.N. mission. I have taken the liberty of putting them on alert."

"Good," Ruinov said. He paused. "Captain Kilgore has been less than forthcoming since the foolishness at the grocery. What do we know of his intentions?"

The tall man shrugged. "I've been trying to reach Maddalenna, with no success as yet."

"I want to talk to him before we leave."

"Yes, sir," the tall man said as he poured himself another glass of wine.

Then there was a knock at the door.

Ruinov looked at him. "The fool isn't stupid enough to contact us here, is he?"

The tall man nodded reluctantly. He stood up and walked to the door.

"Who?" he asked through the closed door.

"Maddalenna," came the high-pitched reply.

The tall man angrily shook his head. "He apparently *is* that stupid." He unlocked and opened the door.

Ruinov heard a muffled popping sound, turning in time to see the tall man crumble to the floor, as the door closed.

"Colonel." Newman pointed the Tokarev at Ruinov's eyes and walked deeper into the room.

Ruinov didn't move, didn't breathe, didn't make the slightest sound. He just stared at the man behind the gun and thought of all the things he would never do.

"It's been a long time," Newman said as he sat down opposite Ruinov. He lowered the gun to his lap.

"Not long enough, I think."

Newman laughed, but there was no humor in it.

"You're developing a sense of irony late in life," he said as he examined the wine bottle. He curled his lip distastefully. "Vinegar."

Ruinov fought against trembling. "Shall I beg for my life?"

Newman shrugged. "It wouldn't help." He sniffed at the tall man's wineglass, then put it down, shaking his head.

"I will give you a choice, though." He looked Ruinov in the eyes. "You can die painlessly or not."

Ruinov took a deep breath. "What do you want?"

"How did you find me?"

Ruinov licked his lips nervously. "I knew you would not leave yourself without a way out." He gestured at the tall man who lay dead on the floor. "He knew of the old, fascist tunnel system. It was part of his assignment to know such things. I ordered men to all of the most isolated exits." He paused. "That I was at the one you emerged from was sheer luck."

"Bad luck."

"So it would appear."

Newman's eyes narrowed as his voice dropped low and cold. "Why'd you kill Konrad Edel?"

"The security man?"

Newman didn't react, just raised the Tokarev to eye level. "Why?"

"An unfortunate accident. I was aiming at you."

Newman studied the man closely for a long time.

"All right," he said softly.

He pulled the trigger once, watching as Ruinov was thrown out of his chair by the heavy impact of the Tokarev slug into his brain. He was dead before he hit the floor.

Painlessly.

Ten minutes after midnight, the Institute having settled down to its normal late night rhythms, Kapf, assisted by an orderly, carried several cardboard boxes into his office. He piled them in a corner as the orderly unloaded rolls of tape and string from his pockets.

"Call me if you need anything else, Doctor."

Kapf waved the young man away as he began to sort through his files, putting some in a box, leaving others in the drawers. A few minutes into the job, he looked up as Patricia walked in.

"Can I help you, Dr. Nellwyn?" His voice was calm, relaxed, decided.

"Jack Clemente's dead."

Kapf nodded silently.

"It seems he just stopped breathing when no one was around," she said matter-of-factly.

Kapf steadied himself on his desk. "There *is* a merciful force in the universe."

She shivered. "God, it's cold in here tonight."

"The heating is not working properly, again."

She looked at the boxes. "What's going on?"

He resumed packing. "I am leaving this place."

Patricia hesitated, then took a step forward. "Why? Was it my . . ."

"Jack Clemente was right, your arrogance is indeed a marvel to behold." He paused, forcing up a bitter smile. "I am not, would not, leave because of a disagreement in diagnosis."

She seemed to want to say something, but couldn't quite figure out how. "Things got a little out of control back at the meeting. We all said things we didn't really mean."

Kapf began loading his desk articles into a box. "Indeed? I meant everything I said." He looked her in the eye. "And I believe you did as well."

Patricia looked at him, then sat down on the couch. "So, you think I'm a Nazi."

"I think you are arrogant and naive. A most dangerous combination."

A silence settled between them.

Finally, Patricia looked up and tried a smile. "So, why are you leaving?"

Kapf turned to the books stacked on his windowsill. "There is nothing here for me anymore. As you have pointed out, I am old. Perhaps, I sometimes think, the oldest human being on this planet. It may well be time for, what did you call it, the next wave? It may well be time for the next wave to take their place at the table."

He looked out the window at a lightly falling snow.

"I am merely opening up a seat."

"Look," Patricia said, standing and taking a step toward him, "I've got no tact. I'm abrupt, impolite, and sometimes don't have the sense God gave a turnip, but that doesn't mean you have to leave." She paused. "Come with me to Vienna. When we recapture Newman, we can find out, together, what he is and where man is going!" Her eyes were alive with the excitement of the hunt.

Kapf shook his head. "Captain Kilgore has received orders to assassinate Newman when he is found," he said flatly.

"I know," she said softly. "Help me fight them."

"No."

"Why not?" she said in an anxious voice.

He didn't answer for a very long time. He seemed to be studying something on the lawn beneath his window.

"Why not?" she tried again.

Kapf suddenly turned and started out of the office in a hurry. "Because I agree with them."

He rushed downstairs, leaving the Institute's main building through a back door. Ignoring the falling snow and growing cold, he walked straight across the lawn toward Unit A-249.

Where it had all begun.

He stopped under the tree where Beck's man had been killed.

"It is dangerous for you to be here," he said quietly to a figure in the shadows.

Newman shrugged. "The world is a dangerous place." He slowly walked over to Kapf. "I just wanted to say good-bye. We won't see each other again."

"I know."

Newman noticed that the old man was shivering in his shirtsleeves. He took off his jacket and put it around Kapf's shoulders.

"You should take better care of yourself," he said to the elderly man. "You ain't as young as springtime anymore."

Kapf stared into the younger man's eyes. "So I have been told." He paused. "Where will you go?"

"Home, I guess."

"Where is that?"

"That's to find out."

"What will you do?"

Newman smiled, with a sparkle in his eyes. "Don't *you* know?"

Kapf remained silent.

"Consider. Speculate. Study," Newman finally said.

Kapf nodded. "In search of yourself," he said in a strong voice.

"No," Newman said softly. "In search of others like me"—he paused—"like you."

Kapf straightened. "Me?"

"Lie to others, if you like. But not to me . . . brother."

Kapf studied the firmness of the jaw, the confident light in the eyes, then nodded slowly. "You know." It was a statement, not a question.

"I didn't know, then I knew."

"How?"

"I just did."

Kapf turned his back on Newman. "Very well," he said in a hushed, emotion-choked voice. "I told them you were insane," he said at last.

"Then you understood my portrait."

"I understood."

Newman walked around in front of Kapf. "I won't spend the rest of my life on display for charlatans and mountebanks like the good Dr. Nellwyn."

"She means well."

Newman ignored him.

"And I will not spend the rest of my life in hiding. I had to make sure that they wouldn't try and take me alive."

"Kilgore has his orders to shoot on sight," Kapf said softly.

"Of course." Newman said. "Brian Newman has gone 'round the bend. Convinced himself he's some avenging angel from Hell's depths out to destroy mankind." His voice was tinged with amusement. "The DoD just can't allow that kind of behavior from one of its assets." He laughed lightly.

Kapf looked at him sadly. "I looked into that portrait, then looked into myself. Then I knew. The only way they would ever stop looking is if they had killed you themselves." He paused. "It is what I would have done."

Newman smiled. "Family ties."

Kapf looked at Newman with a deep pain coming from somewhere inside of his very being.

"What are we?" he asked.

"Don't you know?" Newman said gently.

Kapf barely shook his head. "For the majority of my seventy-eight years, I have asked that question. I have fought the temptations, the desires, the hatred, the frustration. I imposed my own personal discipline, then accepted the disciplines of my country and my profession. I have lived the life of an ascetic, being always vigilant to never allow a lapse, a vagrant moment when what is within me might become loosed." He paused. "But I have found no answers."

"What was it Nellwyn said? That we were the next evolutionary stage of man?" He laughed easily. "I think you called it *Homo crudelis?*"

Kapf nodded sadly.

"Very poetic of you," the young man said lightly.

He smiled warmly and put his arm around the old man.

"We're not the next step. Not even close to it."

"No?"

"No." Newman turned Kapf to face him. "Maybe a half-step, maybe even less than that, but I'm fairly certain that we're still *Homo sapiens.*" He laughed again.

"A friend asked me what I was, not too very long ago." Newman seemed to drift off for a moment.

"What did you say?"

Newman looked back at Kapf. *"Homo sapiens saevus."*

Kapf smiled for the first time. "The Savage Wise Man. A half-step indeed."

Newman looked around, noticed that people, in groups of two or three, seemed to be randomly walking on the lawn. Out for a night's walk in the snow perhaps, but moving toward them nonetheless.

Slowly encircling them.

"The question is," he said as he began to stretch his legs and upper arms, "a half-step in what direction? Evolution or de-evolution? Forward or back?"

Kapf noticed the people for the first time.

"You have thought this through?"

Newman nodded. "As man evolves, he's slowly losing his little toe and little finger," he said absently as he watched the slowly approaching, still-indistinct people, over Kapf's shoulder. "If he de-evolves, they'll grow longer." He paused. "I guess that that's how we'll know which way we're going."

Kapf looked at him, a tear trickling down his cheek.

"And which do you think it is?" he asked, trying to ignore what was about to happen.

"I'll let you know, brother," Newman said as he took a step away from Kapf. He looked out at the fifteen or twenty people in a semicircle around him.

"Farewell."

He sprinted off to his left.

Instantly, floodlights came on, illuminating every inch of the back lawn in an unrelenting brilliance.

Shouts were raised back and forth as the American search team spread out, not firing, but steadily closing the circle around their quarry.

"Watch him! Watch him!"

"He's heading for the woods! Close it off! Close it off!"

"Watch him! Don't expose yourself! Take it slow!"

Newman zigzagged across the lawn, changing direction randomly, but keeping the same general course. He ran at his top speed, bent over, low to the ground, his head down.

"Watch the fence! Goddammit! He's heading for the fence!"

Five black-uniformed men fell to fully prone firing position between Newman and the east fence.

Effortlessly, he shifted direction one more time.

"Where's he going? Dammit, cut him off!"

His mind was clear, precise, functioning, analyzing, seeing everything and playing out each possible permutation.

One hundred meters! he thought. *Ninety meters!*

The first shots lashed out at him from behind.

He instantly dropped to his knees, rolled once, then came up running again.

A Humvee came rolling onto the lawn to his right. He could hear the snap of its .50-caliber belt-fed machine gun being cocked above the noise of the pursuing soldiers.

Fifty meters!

The heavy *kachunk-kachunk-kachunk* of the .50-caliber rose above the din, as large divets were dug up from the lawn in front of him from the great man-killer slugs of the heavy automatic weapon.

I guess they don't want me going in there, he had time to think.

Thirty meters more!

Another burst from the .50 caught him in the right calf, knocking him over.

They'll stop, he thought. *Stop, look to see, pause.*

The firing stopped.

Wait, Newman thought. *A little longer . . . now!*

He jumped to his feet and, with a final burst of speed, threw himself through the heating plant's open doorway, just ahead of a new burst from the .50.

"Hold it!"

Newman could hear Kilgore's voice coming from the direction of the Humvee.

"Second squad! Around the back! Nobody fire! You hear me? Nobody fire! We've got natural gas lines and stored petrol in there! Hold your fire, dammit!"

Newman forced himself to his feet, ignoring his heavily bleeding leg. His mind was clear, the pain was tolerable, he was calm, collected, exactly where he wanted to be.

He pulled himself toward the center of the heating plant, to the great pipe that carried the superheated air from the powerful natural gas furnaces below him to the main building.

"Brian Newman!" Kilgore called through a bullhorn. "Brian Newman! Come out with your hands above your head and you will not be harmed."

Newman found the box that he'd left by the pipe hours before. He opened the lid and began to throw switches.

"Charon Apollyon! This is Captain John Kilgore of the United States Army. Come out with your hands above your head and you will not be harmed!"

Kilgore turned to a sergeant standing beside him, behind the Humvee.

"Entry teams to access points."

The sergeant nodded and spoke softly into his headset.

"Charon Apollyon!" Kilgore said into the speaker's microphone. "If you come out now, we can work all this . . ."

He was cut off by two small roars, followed by a low rumble. Then, as if the earth itself was vomiting forth hellfire and brimstone, a fireball broke loose from the small building. It carried with it an explosion that knocked out all the glass in the Institute's main building.

The concussion knocked most of the commandos instantly unconscious.

Up it rose, an almost perfect sphere of fire and fury expanding ever
upward and outward. Red-orange, its heat exploding the gas tanks of
cars parked over two hundred meters away, it rose, unsparingly, into
the midnight sky, spreading its smoke and toxic fumes across most of
northern Munich.

Newman's portrait had come alive.

Twelve were dead.

Sixty-five injured.

Four were missing.

A crater more than thirty feet in diameter remained the only marker of where the heating plant had stood.

The people of Munich had been told that an unexploded bomb from the war had gone off near an underground gas line. NATO was praised for responding so quickly to this peacetime emergency.

After a few hours of desultory interest, even the tabloid press had gone home.

For three days, the military firemen and rescue workers had gone through the rubble, fighting the constant flare-ups of the gas lines, clearing debris from the back of the main building, much of which had sheared off cleanly, like opening a doll's house.

Five of Kilgore's men had been killed in the explosion, many more suffered broken bones, hearing loss, or burns. Kilgore himself, partially shielded from the blast by the Humvee, had sustained a crushed right leg and a dislocated shoulder when a secondary explosion had rolled the utility vehicle on top of him and his sergeant.

But he was on the scene, each morning since, nevertheless. Supervising the last act of his search for Brian Newman.

The Institute lay virtually empty, a battered, abandoned monument. Its VIP patients had fled, its community patients were gone, the Munich building inspectors had declared the west wing uninhabitable and dangerous.

But Tabbart could be seen wandering its corridors, looking into its empty rooms, straightening crooked pictures. A forlorn figure who now spoke only in monosyllables when he spoke at all.

But every morning, starting with first light, a special team of NATO military rescue and forensic experts probed through the crater and surrounding wreckage.

Patricia and Kapf stood by the crater on the fourth morning, watching in dumbstruck shock.

"Why?" was about all Patricia had been able to say in the last three days. "Why?"

Kapf couldn't remember the last time he slept.

After being knocked to the ground in the explosion, he had hurried to the scene, helping where he could to keep the wounded alive until the emergency services of Munich could arrive.

He'd performed surgery for the first time in thirty-five years, saved many lives, but he still felt drained and empty. As if something newly given to him had been snatched away in that moment of flame, frenzy, and destruction.

He forced that emotion, made himself wallow in it, because to comtemplate the alternative, to repeat the thought that had, since the explosion, kept forcing itself to his attention, was too dangerous to consider.

Patricia tapped him on the shoulder and pointed at some activity in the tent that had been set up for the forensic people. They slowly walked over.

She noticed Kilgore, sitting in a wheelchair, nodding grimly as he made notes on a clipboard. They approached him quietly.

"Captain?" she said when he finished writing. "What's going on?"

He looked up at them with a dour expression.

"It's over," he said flatly.

"What?"

"It's over. They found Newman. Or what's left of him anyway."

"They're sure?" Patricia sounded torn between relief and disbelief.

Kilgore nodded. "They're sure. We got prints, blood typing, and preliminary DNA results." He gestured at an examining table in front of him.

Kapf moved in behind the technicians and pathologists who were bent over the table.

"Man," one of them joked, "that must have hurt!"

"Ouch!" another said.

"Shut up and start preserving them!" the lead pathologist said as he gently lifted the torn-out little finger with a pair of forceps. Lying next to it was a torn-out little toe.

Kapf turned and walked away.

His car had been heavily damaged in the explosion, so he walked around to the front of the main building where NATO soldiers were performing taxi duty for the remaining VIPs. He got into the back of one of the olive-green staff cars.

"25 Rambertstrasse."

The driver nodded and pulled out.

For the first time since that night, Kapf realized that he was still wearing Newman's jacket. Without knowing why, he looked in the pockets. All he found was a card envelope.

He held it up to his blurred eyes.

"Mon Frère" was all it said.

He opened the envelope and read the single sheet of paper contained within. He recognized it as part of a poem by an American poet, he couldn't remember which one.

> Thy soul shall find itself alone
> 'Mid dark thoughts of the gray tombstone—
> Not one, of all the crowd, to pry
> Into thine hour of secrecy.
> Be silent in that solitude
> Which is not loneliness, for then
> The spirits of the dead who stood
> In life before thee are again
> In death around thee, and their will
> Shall overshadow thee:
> Be still.

Kapf smiled, folded the note, put it back in his pocket, and easily fell asleep in the back of the car.

The Gemini Man would not have been possible without the generous assistance, support, and belief of many people. Too many to thank individually. So, I'll take this opportunity to thank a special few; and through them, the rest.

Among the many are: Dr. Caroll Lane Fenton; Professors James C. Coleman and Jared Diamond of UCLA; Dr. Roy F. Baumeister of Case Western Reserve University; and Professor Daniel C. Dennett for his work as Director of the Center for Cognitive Studies at Tufts University.

Also: Dr. Karl A. Menninger; Dr. C. S. Bluemel; Special Agent John Douglas, FBI, retired; Dr. Phyllis Greenacre; and particularly Dr. Walter Bromberg.

Less technically, and more personally, this novel wouldn't have been possible if not for the kindness, support, friendship, and unwavering belief of a select few.

Particularly: all the staff at Carraz, Glendale; "Reverend" Bill Johnson; Tom Couch; Mary Lattig; and Juris Jurjevics. Also: the entire Aguila family (Alex, Suzanne, Adrian, Ama, Antoinette and her banana nut loafs). Norm Allen, a fellow artist of steadfast faith. The

Glendale Galleria Kiwanians for their early, enthusiastic belief. And my constant musical companion on this journey—Meat Loaf!

A special thanks to Brandon Saltz—early and consistent enthusiast and champion of *The Gemini Man*—as well as the other good people and consummate professionals at Doubleday.

And especially, for knocking away all that obscured the view; understanding and preserving my original vision, while allowing me to "just worry about the writing": my heartfelt thanks to Shawn Coyne— editor of any writer's dreams! It's been a blast, let's do it again!

Finally, my last, most important acknowledgment.

To my agent, guru, friend . . . Robert Thixton, and all the other tremendously dedicated, supportive people at Pinder Lane Productions/Garon-Brooke Associates—especially Roger Hayes, without whom only my computer would've been able to read this book—my deepest thanks and gratitude. With people like you behind me, no matter whatever else happens, I've already won!

Success!
RICHARD B. STEINBERG
Somewhere in America
Spring 1998

ABOUT THE AUTHOR

RICHARD STEINBERG worked his way through college by age twenty. He founded his own high-risk international security firm at twenty-four. After recovering from a gunshot wound incurred in the line of duty, he now lectures on issues including counterterrorism, international security matters, and the history of assassinations in America.